A Sweet Mess

A Sweet Mess

A Sweet Mess

JAYCI LEE

ST. MARTIN'S GRIFFIN
NEW YORK

First published in the United States by St. Martin's Griffin, an imprint of St. Martin's Publishing Group

A SWEET MESS. Copyright © 2020 by Judith J. Yi. All rights reserved. Printed in the United States of America. For information, address St. Martin's Publishing Group, 120 Broadway, New York, NY 10271.

www.stmartins.com

Designed by Devan Norman

Library of Congress Cataloging-in-Publication Data

Names: Lee, Jayci, author.
Title: A sweet mess / Jayci Lee.
Description: First edition. | New York : St. Martin's Griffin, 2020. |
Identifiers: LCCN 2020001336 | ISBN 9781250621108 (trade paperback) |
    ISBN 9781250621115 (ebook)
Subjects: GSAFD: Love stories.
Classification: LCC PS3612.E2239 S94 2020 | DDC 813/.6—dc23
LC record available at https://lccn.loc.gov/2020001336

Our books may be purchased in bulk for promotional, educational, or business use. Please contact your local bookseller or the Macmillan Corporate and Premium Sales Department at 1-800-221-7945, extension 5442, or by email at MacmillanSpecialMarkets@macmillan.com.

First Edition: 2020

D   10 9   8   7   6   5   4   3

To my remarkable boys,
you amaze and complete me in each and
every way, each and every day.
I love you with all my heart. Always.

—Mom

A Sweet Mess

A Sweet
Mess

1

"What do you mean you gave away the Frankencake?"

Aubrey kept her voice low and calm while she roared and stomped like a *T. rex* in her head. Her high school part-timer had already locked herself in the bathroom/locker room. There was no point freaking her out any further.

"I served it to someone," Lily whispered with a tremor in her voice. "It's gone."

She breathed through her nose, ten seconds in and fifteen seconds out. Aubrey had been in the kitchen checking on a batch of gelato when Lily sold the wrong cake. If not for the worst timing in the world, she could've stopped the switcheroo.

The birthday girl's chocolate Bundt cake looked exactly like the bakery's special of the week. On the outside. The surprise lay inside—gummy worms, cream cheese, and peanut butter. The six-year-old's logic was if you mix something tasty with something else tasty, it would be twice as tasty. In this case, thrice as tasty. An unfortunate and erroneous hypothesis.

Her pint-size customer wailed with renewed grief beyond the kitchen doors. With a sinking sigh, she left Lily in the safety of her hiding place and pushed through the swinging doors to the shop front.

"Please don't cry, Andy." Aubrey wished she could conjure up a rainbow, a unicorn, or a rainbow unicorn that trailed cotton candy from its mane. Anything to cheer her up. "I'm so sorry."

"B-b-but . . . that was *my* . . . cake."

This was the biggest crisis Comfort Zone had ever faced. Customers came first and foremost for her, and she'd never made a customer cry before. The business was overextended to move to a larger, more visible location, and Aubrey was running low on time, energy, and patience. She had her life and work balanced so perilously that one false move could knock her world down. But she wouldn't let an unfortunate mistake shake her. Despite the less-than-ideal timing, Aubrey Choi, owner and baker of Comfort Zone, had to woman up and take charge.

"I'll have a new cake delivered to your house in three hours, tops. Will that work?" she asked Andy's mom.

"Oh, totally," she said with an easy smile. "Her birthday party won't start for another hour, and we're not serving the cake till the end."

Thank you, Aubrey mouthed to her, then knelt beside Andy. "I pinkie promise that your cake will be perfect and right on time. I won't take my eyes off it until it's safely in your hands."

"O . . . o . . . kay." Her voice wobbled, but she pinched her lips tightly until her tears receded. *What a trooper.* "Pinkie promise."

"Good girl." She ruffled the kiddo's hair and waved goodbye. "See you soon."

Once the door swung closed behind the mother and her hiccupping child, Aubrey faced her waiting customers. "Sorry for the wait, guys. Reinforcement is on the way. We'll throw in some cashew brittles with your orders. Thanks for being so patient."

She ran into the kitchen and wrapped her apron around her waist, cinching it with a quick flat knot. "Lily, stop hiding in there. I need you to man the front."

"Is it safe?" Her part-timer peeked out from the bathroom. "I'm so sorry. I don't even remember who I gave the cake to."

"Don't worry about it, hon," Aubrey said, pushing aside her frustration. The sad, worried expression on Lily's normally deadpan face made her heart heavy. "But you'd better hurry before the customers form an angry mob. They're raising tiny forks and brandishing birthday candles. Go."

Lily rolled her eyes with lightning teenage reflexes—forgetting she was "so sorry"—and marched through the swinging kitchen doors. *That's more like it.* With Lily back to her sardonic self, it was time for Aubrey to make Andy happy. Exhaling the tension from her shoulders, she got to work.

Comfort Zone was a tiny bakery hidden away in Weldon, a quiet California town on the outer edges of the Sierra Nevada. It saw a fair share of adventurers passing through, but Weldon was rarely the final destination, and the town still belonged to its tightly knit locals. It was these locals who filled the mismatched chairs and smiled through the pictures clustered across the bakery walls. It was for them, her extended family, Aubrey kneaded her dough and mixed her batters in unholy hours of the morning. Nothing made her happier than seeing a customer's face light up with delight after taking a bite of her goodies.

But with the highs come the lows. That afternoon Aubrey learned that nothing deflated her more than a customer's face crumpling with disappointment. Intent on wiping away Andy's tears, she baked Frankencake II with special care. It felt odd to be acutely aware of cracking a single egg, something she usually did by the dozens with the speed and precision of a machine. Even the flour felt softer when she gave it her undivided attention. She loved baking, but baking a one-and-only cake for a special customer was decadent.

The chocolate cake batter moved like silk and glistened when it caught the light. She thinned and smoothed the peanut butter and cream cheese filling, but the gummy worms were on their own. There was no improving them. She crinkled her nose in distaste, but her preferences didn't matter for this one. It was all about Andy.

By the time Aubrey drizzled the glaze on the cake, she had seventeen minutes left on the clock. She poked her head through the kitchen doors. "Lily, I need to deliver this cake right this second before my pinkie shrivels off."

"Yeah." Her employee raised an eyebrow at her but kindly left the *you are* so *weird* unsaid. "Sure."

Aubrey tripped on her sprint to the car, but she righted herself before the cake splattered on the road. Breathing deeply through her nose, she knit the last bits of her patience together and forced herself to stay calm. After securing the cake box on the floor of the passenger seat, she slid into her fifteen-year-old Jeep and sped out of her parking spot.

She couldn't breathe properly until she pulled into Andy's driveway with one-and-a-half minutes to spare. Her deodorant had failed under pressure, leaving stains the size of dinner plates under her arms, and her shirt clung to her clammy chest and back. Aubrey lifted the cake box with excruciating care as if it held newly hatched chicks—delicate and precious. Her body wanted to run, but her brain forced her to walk toward the house. A wise call, since her head might blow up in a mushroom cloud if she tripped and ruined the cake.

The front door swung open before her knuckles made contact, giving Aubrey a split second to hike the cake over her head before the birthday girl launched herself at her.

"Oh, thank you. Thank you. Thank you." Andy gave her a

giant grin, her two missing teeth doubling her cute factor. The smile and the little arms circling her midriff warmed Aubrey from head to toe. "You're the best cake lady in the world."

This. She had the best job in the world.

"I would never break a pinkie promise," she replied, her voice husky with emotion.

"Thank you so much, Aubrey." Andy's mom lifted the cake box out of Aubrey's hands and detached her daughter from her waist.

"My pleasure. Sorry again about the mix-up."

Aubrey jogged back to her Jeep without pausing to savor the moment. She had to get back to the bakery for closing. The adrenaline drained from her, leaving her limp and tired, and she wasn't looking forward to the scrubbing and mopping waiting for her.

When she pulled up to the shop, she saw the SORRY WE MISSED YOU sign displayed on the door. It was perfectly askew, just the way she liked it, and the lights inside were dimmed to a soft glow. With confused wonder, she heaved her leaden body out of the Jeep and shuffled to the shop.

"Wow. Awesome adulting," Aubrey said as gratitude squeezed her heart in a bear hug. Lily was halfway finished with the cleanup, showing more initiative than she ever had. Sniffing back silly tears, Aubrey grabbed a bottle of organic surface cleaner and a dish towel. "I really appreciate your help. The adrenaline wore off, and I'm running on empty. Thank you."

"It's . . ." Her teenage scowl slipped, and she suddenly looked so young and sweet. "You're welcome."

They cleaned in quiet harmony and closed up shop only half an hour late. Lily zoomed in and out of the locker room, securing her earbuds and pulling her hoodie over her head. She was halfway to the door when she waved good-bye without bothering to turn around. Aubrey smiled. Lily could pretend otherwise, but she liked her dorky boss.

Aubrey stuffed her arms into a black windbreaker and slung her purse across her torso. She reached for the doorknob but hesitated. The day didn't end in complete disaster, but the disappearance of the original Frankencake niggled at the back of her mind. And her body still twitched from the ups and downs of the day. If she wanted some decent REM cycles, she had to decompress before heading home.

Aubrey took a wary sniff of her shirt. "Ugh. Ew."

She couldn't walk into a public establishment like this. People would probably see noxious, green fumes wafting from her top and reach for their clothespins. Twisting her neck far away from her stinky self, Aubrey hurried to the locker room and disposed of the offending shirt, wrapping it tightly in a plastic bag. Wetting some paper towels, she wiped away the evidence of her stress and tugged her arms through a spare shirt she kept for emergencies. It had a picture of Cookie Monster hugging a jar of cookies with the caption MY PRECIOUS below him.

It wasn't a fancy work-to-evening transformation, but she was weeknight-presentable. With anticipation in her steps, Aubrey set out on foot to her favorite pub, Weldon Brewery. The three-block walk there should skim off more of her anxiety.

The brewery stood on the edge of downtown, and it was fast becoming Sierra Nevada's worst-kept secret. They'd swept top-beer awards across the country for five consecutive years, and craft beer aficionados pilgrimaged to the brewery and packed the place to the brim. The head brewer, Tara Park, happened to be Aubrey's best friend. *Lucky me.*

The air was nippy for an early-summer evening, so she stuffed her hands inside her jean pockets but didn't pick up her pace. The setting sun drenched the cozy town in a blanket of deep coral and whispers of violet—a scene from a storybook come to life. A dreamy smile broke through Aubrey's restlessness. Weldon was *home*. Even after four years, it was hard to believe Comfort Zone stood nestled among the brightly colored mom-and-pop stores lining the tidy streets.

When she pushed through the sturdy wooden doors of the brewery, the high ceiling, repurposed wood beams, and floor-to-ceiling windows welcomed her with their warm, rustic charm. It was a weeknight, so it wasn't too crowded, but it was busy enough to hum with conversation and laughter.

"Give me the good stuff, woman." Aubrey settled onto a barstool and pounded her fist on the bar for effect. "Ow."

"Wuss. You're an embarrassment to badass, bar-pounding women everywhere. Here." Tara plunked down a pint of blond ale and narrowed her eyes as Aubrey gulped down a third of it. "Damn, girl. I'll take back calling you a wuss; slow down. I don't want to drag your drunk ass home tonight."

"Some friend you are."

"I give you free beer and a shoulder to lean on. You wouldn't find a better friend even if you scoured the earth for one."

Tara was right. Life wouldn't be complete without her. Aubrey lifted her mug in agreement and took a daintier gulp.

"Rough day in sugar land?"

"You could say that. Remember Andy's special-order cake?" Tara made a gag face. *Okay. She remembers.* "Lily gave her cake to the wrong customer, so I baked another one and delivered it to Andy's house. In the middle of afternoon rush. But you know what the scariest part is?"

"Andy made you stay and eat a slice of Frankencake?"

"No, it's even worse. Lily has no idea who she sold the monstrosity to. It has to be some poor out-of-towner who desperately needed a chocolate Bundt cake. Tragically, they got the

Frankencake instead and probably ended up choking on a peanut butter–covered gummy worm."

"Yeah, that sounds very likely. Murder by Bizarro cake."
Her friend's tone was dry, but her eyes softened with a smile.
"You did everything you could. Now relax and enjoy my scin-
tillating company."

"Scintillating? Last week, it was electrifying." Despite her
grumbling, Aubrey did as directed, breathing deeply through
her nose and drawing her shoulders away from her ears. Her
next gulp of beer tasted even better, and all the day's stress
melted away.

"So which one's your pride and joy?" A deep, delicious voice
spoke from behind her.

A thrill rushed through Aubrey, and goose bumps spread
down her arms. *Maybe I shouldn't have chugged all that beer on
an empty stomach.*

"Spank Me," Tara said, checking out the customer under
her lashes.

"I usually reserve that kind of fun for the third date." The
flirtatious response came much too easily, but his voice made it
sound sophisticated and enticing.

Tara snorted and mouthed *holy crap* to Aubrey behind her
hand. If her friend's reaction was any indication, the dude must
be up in the clouds on the hotness scale. Curiosity won, and
Aubrey swiveled around on the stool to explain that Spank Me
was the brewery's überhoppy, gold-medal IPA.

"She didn't mean that literally." Her words and laughter
scattered as dark brown eyes zeroed in on her face.

Aubrey couldn't draw a proper breath with her pulse racing
like an overcaffeinated squirrel's. She never went drool-faced
over a man, even a gorgeous specimen such as the tall, muscular stranger in front of her.

"It's our award-winning IPA. My pride and joy," her friend said, noting Aubrey's sudden loss of speaking abilities with a barely suppressed laugh.

It had to be because she didn't expect him to be Asian American. Tara and Aubrey were two of six Asian locals, and her friend's family made up the other four. The odds of meeting a hot Asian American man on a weeknight—Tara's two older brothers excepted—were slim to none in Weldon.

"Spank Me it is, then," he replied to Tara as his eyes flickered to the name tag on her shirt. "Thank you, Tara."

"You're welcome," she said, and turned away to fill his order with a playful wink at Aubrey.

"I'm Landon," he said, turning his full attention to Aubrey. Her jaws went slack, and her tummy dipped and swerved at the appreciative gleam in his eyes. He took a seat semi-next to her, leaving a barstool between them. She fought down the smile tugging at her lips. Too many men invade a woman's personal space without a thought. But not this one. *Well done, Mr. Landon.*

"Aubrey." She sounded as breathy as Marilyn Monroe in her JFK birthday serenade. It was totally unintentional and massively embarrassing.

A knowing grin spread across his face, all cocky and sexy as hell. Then she just about died when a dimple tucked into his left cheek. *Note to self: Going without sex for a year makes you susceptible to gorgeous men with dimples.*

"What are you having?" He cocked his head to one side and a lock of jet-black hair fell across his forehead. Her fingers itched to brush it away.

"Buzz Off." As soon as the words left her mouth, she cringed and jumped to clarify herself. "The blond ale. That's the name—Buzz Off. I wasn't telling you to leave or anything."

And just like that, she made everything worse. Much, much worse.

"I'm relieved to hear that, because I'd like to buy you a drink." His laughter, low and rumbly, spread through her like warm brandy, and she forgot to be embarrassed. "May I?"

That voice. That laugh. That dimple. Aubrey could only manage a nod as heat and awareness flooded her.

—

Landon's eyes roamed over the striking woman in the Cookie Monster T-shirt, greedy to drink in as much of her as he could. The sight of her provided the perfect antidote to his frustrating day, which had been a parade of bad luck.

He'd enjoyed a thrilling ride into a ditch when his tire blew on the freeway, but that was tame compared to his trip to Weldon in the rustiest tow truck in existence. While Weldon's auto shop/gas station/mini-mart was the closest business that could replace his tire, it was closed for the day at eleven thirty. In the morning. *Don't small-town folks need gas or some cherry slushy in the middle of the day?* If he hadn't had over three hours of driving left, he would've risked driving on a spare.

Instead, he'd checked in at Lola's Trattoria and Inn and wandered through the pedestrian-friendly town, exploring the picturesque slice of Americana. An eclectic mix of stores filled the streets without a chain store in sight. That was quite a feat when he couldn't even stroll the cobblestoned villages of Europe without passing a Starbucks or a McDonald's.

He couldn't remember the last time he'd walked without a destination. There was no rush to *be* somewhere or to *do* something. The brief break from his hectic life had felt utterly foreign, and it had taken him half an hour to relax into it. As his steps became lighter and a smile tugged at his lips, a delectable smell wafted toward him. The aroma of freshly baked bread, butter, and sweet spices beckoned him to search for its source.

His nose led him to Comfort Zone, a bakery hidden between a barbershop and a pet store. The warmth and ease of the place ensconced him as soon as he stepped inside. It was lively without being loud and full of people without feeling crowded. Whether they were engrossed in a book or guffawing at someone's joke, the customers looked completely at ease, like they were hanging out at their best friend's house. Immersed in the atmosphere, he'd experienced a rare moment of peace, which was interrupted before he could properly savor it.

Landon was enjoying a cup of rich, dark coffee and a whole chocolate Bundt cake, the bakery's special of the day—soaking in the sun from the bright outdoor seating—when he'd choked on a gummy worm hidden within the thick, clingy peanut butter filling. His eyes and nose running from his coughing fit, he dumped the cake in the trash bin and walked away. He'd escaped asphyxiation, but he was angry as hell.

There were plenty of inedible cakes in the world, but the bakery and the Bundt cake had brimmed with potential. The chocolate cake itself had been beautiful—light, moist, and perfectly bittersweet. The cream cheese and peanut butter filling had tasted improbably delicious.

The baker had talent, but throwing in the gummy worms exhibited arrogance and callousness. And showcasing the Bundt cake as the daily special without alerting the customers to the unusual filling? That was wrong. A rebellion without a cause. It was an unfortunate pitfall for some talented chefs. Was it frustration? Boredom? Whatever prompted the addition of the gummy worms, the cake shouldn't have been served to a customer. Experiments should stay in the kitchen until they were perfected. Comfort Zone had used its customers, including him, as test subjects.

Landon had been on his way to review a three-starred Michelin restaurant in Mammoth, but his overnight stay in Weldon meant that well-laid plan wasn't happening. He had to fly out the next afternoon for his monthlong assignment in East Asia, which meant he had to drive back to Santa Monica at the crack of dawn. He was counting on the auto shop/gas station/ mini-mart to open at 6:00 A.M. as the sign promised.

It was unplanned and a bit impulsive, but Weldon's very own Comfort Zone was going to be critiqued in *California Coast Monthly*. As aggravating as the experience had been, excitement stirred at the prospect of writing a review he was emotionally invested in.

"So what brings you to Weldon?" Aubrey said, licking off the foam mustache her blond ale left behind.

The flash of pink jerked Landon out of his thoughts, and he zeroed in on the alluring woman in front of him. "Bad luck."

"That sounds ominous."

When she smiled, her almond-shaped brown eyes tilted up in the corners, adding to her ethereal beauty. Her cropped black hair capped her delicate head, and her petite body dipped and flared in all the right places. He could imagine her as a mischievous woodland faerie, clothed in gossamer wings.

"Nothing that exciting. My car blew a tire, but the auto shop is closed till tomorrow morning, so here I am."

"You're right. Not exciting at all." Aubrey munched on a pretzel, amusement curving her lips. "Next time, try throwing in a helicopter, some churning water, or an active volcano somewhere in your story."

"Maybe I'll add a femme fatale."

The bridge of her nose crinkled as she laughed, and her

cupid's bow mouth curved in an impish smile. Regrettably, her tinkling laughter caught her friend's attention, and Landon nearly cringed. The brewery had a large enough crowd to keep a single server more than busy, and Tara was bustling about like a woman possessed by a tornado. Every time she stopped by the bar, she threw a subtle glare his way, telegraphing a simple but effective message.

One false move and I drown you in a beer barrel.

She was one fierce cockblocker. Her loyalty to Aubrey was inexplicably endearing to him, but her concern was misplaced. Landon was all about consensual fun. He put on his best Boy Scout face to put her at ease, but the brewer's eyes widened in alarm. He'd actually never been a Boy Scout. Perhaps he should've gone for a laid-back expression instead. *Fuck it.* Landon smiled and nodded politely to her, and then stood from his seat.

"Why don't we find ourselves a table?" Well meaning or not, he wanted Aubrey to himself.

"I'd like that." She smiled at her friend and tilted her head toward the dining area. "Tara, we're gonna grab a table."

"How's this?" He'd chosen a small table at the back corner. When Aubrey nodded, he pulled out her chair and took a seat across from her.

Their proximity and relative privacy made the air between them hum with electricity. Their knees brushed every time either of them shifted in their seat, sending bolts of desire through him. A sharp intake of breath and a parting of her lips revealed Aubrey wasn't immune to their magnetic attraction.

Landon had dated his fair share of beautiful women. There was no reason to act like a gawky teenager, but his roaring heart and churning stomach said otherwise. He couldn't remember the last time he'd felt nervous around a woman. Her hand was resting less than four inches away from his, but he broke out in a cold sweat working up the nerve to brush his knuckles against it.

He started when Aubrey traced her fingers across the back of his hand with a shy smile. "So, Landon from out of town, what's your dream?"

His blood had gone south at her touch, leaving nothing for his brain, but he was even more dumbstruck by her question. The woman threw him off balance on all fronts.

"Not big on making small talk, are you?" He managed to keep his voice steady despite his spinning head and hardening body.

"If I'm going to have a chat with a complete stranger, I might as well have an interesting one." A deep blush stained her cheeks, and her lashes fluttered to hide her eyes. "Besides, you're leaving tomorrow. I was hoping we could pack a lot into tonight."

Landon sucked in a sharp breath. Her shy and earnest declaration moved him, and he fought the urge to pull her across the table to kiss her senseless. Instead, he lifted Aubrey's hand and brushed a kiss on her pale inner wrist. A wolfish grin spread across his face when she gasped at his touch.

"My dream was to open my own restaurant." To his shock, the truth stumbled out of him. A truth he'd refused to face for the past decade. Maybe he was desperate to give her an interesting conversation. A memorable one. "Someplace spacious and comfortable where people can enjoy a delicious meal without pretense or a six-figure salary."

"That sounds amazing. What kind of food are we talking about?"

"Whatever inspiration strikes me. If I had to label it, New American–slash–Korean fusion will have to do."

"I love Korean food. I would totally eat there." Aubrey sat forward, her eyes round and sparkling. "So you're Korean? I am, too."

"Yes, I'm Korean, and you would be more than welcome to eat at my restaurant."

"Are you a chef?"

"No, but I trained to be one. Have you heard of the CIA?"

"The Central Intelligence Agency? You learned to cook for undercover agents while dodging bullets and jumping out of airplanes?" She cocked her head to the side and gazed at him with solemn interest.

"I . . . um." Landon was fairly certain she was messing with him, but insulting her wouldn't be the best way to seduce her. "It's . . ."

Aubrey's pale skin turned from pink to crimson before she erupted into laughter, her frame trembling like a 6.8 earthquake. She held up a finger, gripping her side, pantomiming she needed a minute. He crossed his arms over his chest and leveled her with a steely glare, which wasn't an easy feat considering her infectious mirth.

"I'm s-sorry, but you had to see your face. You couldn't decide whether a small-town girl like me knew about the Culinary Institute of America or whether I was pulling your leg."

Mischievous little fox. He needed to get her back for that.

"Actually, that's incorrect." He drew closer to her, his lips close to her ear, and lowered his voice to a deep, gritty whisper. "I was debating whether or not I should tell you the truth, because if I did, I'd have to terminate you."

Aubrey stared at him in silence for a second, and then a delighted grin spread across her face. "This is fun."

"Yeah, it is." Landon was surprised to find he meant it. He couldn't remember the last time he'd had *fun*. He certainly had pleasant and interesting times, but fun times? No, this felt alien.

His earlier hesitation forgotten, he ran his knuckles down

the side of her face, relishing the feel of her warm, silky skin. Aubrey leaned lightly into his hand, and her eyes slid shut. She was so responsive to his touch. Landon's mouth went dry, and all he could think was *more*. He wanted to make her laugh again. He ached to make her fall apart in his arms with her swollen lips calling out his name.

"You're beautiful," Landon murmured, unable to look away from her.

"So are you." Aubrey's lips curved into a barely there smile that squeezed his heart.

He'd gone to the brewery for a pint to wash away the bitter taste of his sorry day, but he'd discovered something far more intoxicating—something potent enough to tip him off-balance. Aubrey made his blood sing and his rational thoughts melt away. The floor seemed to grow solid and strong, and his body settled heavily into his seat like he'd dropped anchor across from her—as though she had a gravitational pull all her own and he was helpless against it.

He'd led a nomadic life for a decade. He didn't know how to stay still for long. The smart thing to do would be to run the hell away from this woman, whose mere proximity made it unimaginable to even leave the table.

But *smart* wasn't part of his vocabulary at the moment. Greedy, feral, and desperate passion overwhelmed all else. He stood abruptly from his seat, and Aubrey's mouth parted in surprise. Then he grasped her hand and raised her to her feet.

"Do you want to get out of here?" His eyes bored into hers, his desire and urgency displayed for her to see.

"Yes."

2

Aubrey woke with a start.

She hadn't meant to fall asleep. Landon had been sexy, demanding, and irresistible, and they'd thoroughly worn each other out. But even now, his parted lips beckoned her to taste him, and her center ached with renewed desire.

They'd walked to his room in silence with their hands entwined—awareness and anticipation sizzling between them. As soon as the door closed behind them, they had torn off their clothes and made love with raging-hot hunger, too far gone to savor and taste each other. Landon reached for her again just as the sweat on her skin began to cool. With the edge of their desire placated, he traced and kissed every dip and curve of her body with curiosity and fascination, and held himself in check while she explored him with greedy fingers. Gasps of surprise and moans of pleasure had filled his room until exhaustion led them off to sleep.

Fortunately, Aubrey woke up before Landon. When it came to relationships, short, lighthearted flings were her modus operandi, but one-night stands were rare. She usually needed a few dates to trust and respect someone enough to share her body with him. But with Landon, she'd somehow known he would be a considerate lover and would treat her body with respect. More than that, she knew he would make her *feel good.*

And her instincts had proven spot-on.

All work and no fun had made Aubrey cranky and exhausted. She hadn't taken a vacation since Comfort Zone opened its doors. Running a bakery was a full-time job and then some, and all the money she'd earned in the first couple years went straight back into the business. She chose to open her bakery in Weldon for its affordability but also for its awe-inspiring surroundings. Unfortunately, the majestic mountains were a mere backdrop to her life, beautiful but untouchable.

The day before had been a wake-up call that she was hanging on by a thread. It was a tough day, no doubt, but she had been way too close to losing her shit. That wasn't like her. She'd built Comfort Zone and gained her independence with her focus, determination, and cool-under-pressure disposition. She'd needed a release. Badly.

Hopefully, last night had done the job. Landon was not only a considerate lover but a skilled and creative one. She would be sore and achy in some places later, but if he wanted to go for a fourth round, she'd jump him. Which was precisely why Aubrey had to get out of there.

What if he was annoyed to find her in bed the next morning? What if *he* sneaked out on her? The best-case scenario would be a nice-meeting-you and an awkward handshake-or-hug dance. She could imagine herself closing in for a hug and being impaled by his outstretched hand. *Death by mortification.*

Aubrey prayed for strength and tore her gaze from his mouth

only to be ensnared by his lush eyelashes. *What business does he have with lashes like those?* She tried glaring at the beautiful man lying next to her, but she only succeeded in ogling him.

A tiny yip escaped her when those ridiculous lashes fluttered as though preparing to unveil the deep, dark eyes beneath. She'd be lost if she looked into them again. Bracing herself on her elbows, Aubrey inched toward the edge of the bed. His arm slid across her bare back as she extracted herself from his embrace, and the innocuous caress set her skin alight. Even after last night, her fiery reaction to his touch flustered her.

By the time she'd crawled down the bed with awkwardly placed limbs, a thin veil of sweat filmed her upper lip. She spotted her bra and crawled over to the coffee table to retrieve it. En route, her knees collided with her shoes. Aubrey pulled on her lacy white bra and grabbed her champagne-colored ballet slippers while scanning the room. She found her shirt and jeans by the armoire, and she slipped her top on with shaky hands. *Where the hell are my panties?* Getting more nervous by the second, she gave up on her favorite pink undies and pulled on her jeans without them. *Ugh.*

Aubrey stuck her shoes in the back pockets of her jeans for extra stealth and tiptoed out of the room after a lingering look at Landon. She slipped on her shoes at the end of the hallway and crept out of Lola's like a cat burglar, careful not to run into anyone. Her clammy skin prickled in the early-morning chill, and she wrapped her arms tightly around herself. She wasn't ashamed of spending the night with Landon, but she also didn't need any town gossip.

The Eastern Sierra Nevada towered beyond the rooftops of Weldon, and Comfort Zone waited for her in a sleepy corner of town. It wasn't far from the inn, but she picked up her pace so she wouldn't be late.

She unlocked the rear door at four o'clock, right on schedule. She sighed as she tied a long, white apron around her waist, wondering what delicious mess would end up on it. She soaked in the warmth and security of her kitchen. *This is it.* She had everything she wanted—a quiet, solitary life doing what she loved most.

Landon's sleeping face sneaked into her thoughts, and Aubrey shook her head to scatter the image. She was probably still high from the multiple orgasms. Their night together had been amazing, but it was over. She had work to do.

Aubrey dug her hands into a mound of pudgy dough and sighed. She was home. When she baked, nothing could break her concentration. She lost herself in a cocoon of cinnamon, cocoa, and butter. Morning dawned as the sweet aroma of pastries filled the bakery, and Aubrey poured herself a cup of coffee and soaked in the moment.

Just as she unlocked the door to open shop, Tara marched inside. *Damn it.* It was too early for the Spanish Inquisition.

"Spill it, Bree." She hopped onto the nearest stool and pinned Aubrey with her don't-bullshit-me stare. Tara was still in her clothes from the day before. She must've closed shop and then brewed all night. "If I were a gambling sort of gal, I'd bet my mom's Korean fried chicken recipe that you went home with that smoldering sex-on-legs last night."

"Your mom would turn over in her grave if she knew you were throwing around her secret recipe like common poker chips. But wait. She's alive and well. What kind of daughter are you?"

"You are dodging the question," Tara said, pointing her index finger at her. Then her eyes widened, and her nostrils flared like they smelled blood. "You *did* take him home. You slept with him? You finally ended the longest drought in the history of Weldon . . ."

"Oh, shut up." Aubrey's cheeks caught on fire. "It hasn't been that long."

"Yeah, right. I was worried your girl parts would close up like neglected pierced ears if you didn't get some soon."

"Can you be more explicit, please? Your subtlety confounds me," Aubrey said with a pointed look at Tara. "I didn't take him home and sleep with him. We went to his room at Lola's, and I didn't sleep much at all. Though I did watch him sleep for a while before I sneaked out."

"I beg your pardon. I was way off the mark." Her best friend had the eye roll down to an art. "You went to a hotel with a gorgeous stranger and made love to him all night, then you stared creepily at him instead of sleeping."

"I won't see him again." She shrugged, her blush deepening. "I was just getting my fill."

"So you let him *fill* you all night?" Tara grabbed the counter so she wouldn't fall off her stool. She was laughing so hard she had tears in the corner of her eyes.

"You have the maturity of a twelve-year-old boy." Aubrey bit the inside of her cheek to stop herself from cracking up. She'd say her maturity level was on par with her best friend's.

"Then why did you run out on him without so much as a *so long, sucker?*" Tara inhaled shakily, her arms wrapped tightly around her ribs. "Why not get his number?"

"He isn't from around here, and I don't have time for a relationship. We enjoyed each other for one night, and that's that."

"That's all fine and well." Tara's expression softened as she brushed a lock of hair from Aubrey's eyes. "Are you sure you're okay? You look like a faded rag doll."

"You're merely witnessing the aftereffects of what earth-shattering, bone-liquefying sex does to a woman." Aubrey wiggled her eyebrows, unable to resist messing with Tara.

"Yowza." Tara's jaw dropped. "Details, Please?"

"Drop it, you perv," Aubrey said, even though she'd brought it up first. "I don't kiss and tell. At least not in detail."

"Hello, ladies." One of her regulars stood grinning at them, a few steps from the counter.

"Hi, Joe." Aubrey smiled through gritted teeth, willing herself not to die from embarrassment. *How long has he been standing there?* "What can I get for you, hon?"

As Aubrey busied herself preparing his order and ignoring Tara's anime leer, Comfort Zone filled with the sound of its morning crowd. When she finished plating the red velvet waffle and pineapple muffin, she held them out to her friend, jutting her chin toward the tables.

"Could you take these over to Joe?"

"What? I worked my tail off at the brewery last night, and you want free labor from me?" While her mouth grumbled, her hands grabbed the plates. "I'll let you take advantage of my kindness *and* cease the interrogation due to my benevolence. But at least tell me his name. Otherwise, I'll have to refer to him as Mr. Hot-Piece-of-A—"

"Landon." Aubrey blurted louder than she'd intended. She cleared her throat and lowered her voice. "His name's Landon."

Several things happened at once. Tara's eyes nearly popped out of her head, but no sound came from her gaping mouth. Silence saturated the air and she stood as though time had stopped. At last, Tara came back to life and gingerly placed the plates on the counter. Her mouth opened and closed, but still, no words came out. That was alarming. Nothing rendered her friend speechless. Nothing.

"Okay. Now you're scaring me," Aubrey said, nerves knotting her stomach. "What's gotten into you?"

"*Landon?* Oh, my God. I thought I recognized him from somewhere when I was giving him my death glare at the bar, but I couldn't place him. He looked so different in jeans and a T-shirt with his hair all tousled. By the way, he should always wear his hair all tousled. It's a good look for him."

"Focus, Tara. Tell me what's going on."

"Your handsome stranger? He's *the* Landon Kim. The celebrity food critic and blogger."

"Oh . . . What?" The air whooshed out of her lungs. *Were we seen together?* "A celebrity food critic? You *know* him?"

"I know *of* him. You're the one who *knows* him. Intimately." Tara winked and playfully pushed Aubrey's shoulder. "It really isn't a big deal. It's not like you're going to run into him again. I just got overexcited by our encounter with a star because I'm a total dork."

"You're not a *total* dork." She grinned, shaking off the weirdness of it all.

Visibility was a sensitive point for her. She'd run away from home when she was eighteen and had kept her whereabouts a secret from the people she'd left behind. She'd stayed in touch with her mom with their biannual phone calls and birthday cards, but Aubrey wanted nothing to do with her father. Having him find out about a one-night stand with a celebrity would be a humiliation she hoped to avoid.

"Wait." Tara sounded panicked again. "Landon Kim came to the brewery. What if he was there to review it? Did he order any of our small dishes? What if he hated everything?"

"Hush, babe." It was her turn to reassure her friend. "He told me he ended up in Weldon because of a blown tire. I think he was on his way to some other restaurant, so he couldn't have been here to review Weldon Brewery."

"But still. Let's do a quick recon." Tara dug out her phone and thumb-typed a search with blinding speed as Aubrey peeked over her shoulder. "Oh, look. He was named one of this year's most eligible bachelors. He's so hot and successful. He totally deserves it." After a peek at Aubrey's incredulous face, Tara swallowed the rest of her fangirling. "But we don't care about that. Okay, here's a good blurb. 'Food critic Landon Kim is renowned for his sharp, droll observations and sometimes brutal reviews. But his opinions are accurate, fair, and highly regarded in the food community.' More of the same. The same . . ."

"Put your phone away. He was an accidental tourist passing through Weldon. That's all. Let's move on as though he were never here."

—

Landon lifted his foot off the gas when he realized he was pushing one hundred. He raked his fingers through his hair and growled in frustration. He didn't know what he was expecting in the morning, but it wasn't to find her gone. His first instinct had been to feel used and discarded. Then his conscience butted in. He'd left many lovers' sides in the middle of the night. If this was how he'd made them feel, then this might be his comeuppance. A humorless laugh filled his car.

Aubrey didn't owe him anything. The unspoken decision to keep it a onetime deal had been mutual. They hadn't even exchanged numbers. But he'd changed his mind as the night wore on. He fell asleep with her warm, smooth body pressed against him, looking forward to making love with her in the morning. He hadn't thought much beyond that except for wanting to see her again. She, on the other hand, did not have a change of heart. Rather than walking the streets of Weldon and shouting her name into the sky, he'd decided to respect her wishes and leave as soon as his car tire was replaced.

Lost in his musings, he almost missed the exit to his office in Santa Monica. He signaled right and pulled into the exit lane, and several cars leaned on their horns. It was a relatively tame lane change with sufficient cushion, but West Los Angeles drivers weren't the most patient lot. They blared their horns if someone sneezed wrong. He shouldn't judge, though. *Who wouldn't be irritable with a diet consisting entirely of kombucha and green juice?*

Landon parked the car in the space reserved for the editor of *California Coast Monthly*, and rode the elevator up to the twelfth floor. He nodded his greetings to the receptionist and walked into Craig Blake's office.

"Heads up." He tossed the car key to his editor, who barely looked up in time to catch it. "And thanks for nothing."

"Hey, my car is perfectly maintained." Craig motioned for him to close the door and stood from his chair to lean against the edge of his desk. Landon had called to give him an update on his detour when he'd checked in at Lola's. "You must've run over some broken glass or something."

"Either way, it was a waste of time, and I don't have a real review for you this week."

On his drive back, Landon had decided not to rain down his wrath on Comfort Zone. It was a small operation, and his review would be incomplete without having tasted other items from the main menu. Then again, even if the other items were good, serving that cake deserved some tough criticism. The memory of the pastry chef's arrogance still rankled him, but he could let it go.

"Unfortunately, I need a review from you before you leave for Hanoi."

"You mean in less than two hours," Landon said incredulously.

"Yes." Craig scratched the back of his neck, looking sheepish. "I agreed to print Gary's exposé on a truffle oil conspiracy during our Christmas party last year."

"Gary from marketing? Did you get shit-faced?"

"Of course I did. Why would I stay sober with free top-shelf liquor flowing? Anyway, I told him I really liked him and it's not because I was drunk." He paused to grin when Landon slapped his knee and guffawed. "Then we sobbed in each other's arms about the USC football team's decade-long struggle. My lovely wife captured the moment on her phone and pulls it up whenever she needs a good laugh."

"That's fucking priceless. But truffle oil? Is *California Coast Monthly* moving toward satire?" Landon covered a yawn with his fist. He hadn't gotten much sleep last night. Remembering the reason for his lack thereof both turned him on and pissed him off. "Besides, what does all that have to do with my review? I told you I don't have one, and there isn't time to visit another restaurant."

"You know very well there's no way in hell I'm printing an exposé on truffle oil," he said. "Wipe that cocky smirk off your face. Gary's a decent guy, just misguided. His article is well written, and all his references check out, but his conclusions rival the aluminum-foil-helmet-wearing sort. I ran out of excuses, and I have an issue going to print. I've already bribed an anonymous designer in Layout to be ready for the switch, so you just need to fill Gary's spot. I don't care if you review the downstairs cafeteria. Just get it done in two hours."

"Screw you, Craig."

"I love you, too, man. Looking forward to your piece."

Craig was his friend, and Landon didn't want to hang him out to dry. Besides, Landon was in an abysmal mood. Venting about the gummy worm that almost killed him might be cathartic. It would be an allegorical piece reflecting on his trip to Weldon entitled "The Pitfalls of Brilliance."

"Well, you're going to have to do all the fact-checking and background research," he said. "I'm not missing my flight for your bromance gone wrong."

———

His head was floating a few inches above his neck, and only three of his four limbs seemed fully awake. But Landon embraced his jet lag like a light hangover, an inevitable part of his lifestyle. Gulping a sip of his venti coffee, Landon rolled into *Cal Coast's* parking structure in his new ride. He'd had his assistant pick up the Alfa Romeo Giulia and park it in his garage for when he returned from Asia.

He traveled eight out of twelve months for his job. It made no sense to invest in a car only to have it sit in the garage for a better part of the year. His condo was largely unfurnished for the same reason. "Home" was just a forgettable rest stop before he was on the go again.

Landon had chosen his profession because of the ever-changing landscape and the freedom it offered. When he'd given up his dream of becoming a chef, the nomadic lifestyle had lured him like the call of never-never land. He'd led an itinerant life for more than a decade, and it had never bothered him before. But this last trip had been different.

He'd gone through the motions of visiting eclectic villages, towns, and cities with their scenic beauty. He'd had the privilege of sampling unique, mouthwatering food at local institutions, as well as new, innovative restaurants, but none of it had moved him. None of it had been *fun*.

Had he spent all his wanderlust? Landon swiped his hands down his face. He had no idea, but nothing felt right anymore. He'd been on edge during the entire trip, and the only thing that had settled him was impulse-buying a car online.

Landon entered the building lobby, appreciating its welcome familiarity, and hopped on the elevator with a light step. Flying home this time had meant something different. He came home because he'd missed it, and it felt good to be back. Walking into the office and sitting at his desk gave him a quiet satisfaction. He turned his gaze out the window, letting his lips curve in a content smile.

Craig threw a stack of email printouts on Landon's desk, jolting him out of his reverie. "For your reading enjoyment."

"I got back from a monthlong assignment in Asia less than *twelve hours* ago. Can't a man have some peace and quiet around here?"

"And by *around here*, you mean your *place of work?*" His editor arched an eyebrow at him.

"Precisely." Landon grinned and picked up the first email. His smile disappeared, and he sat up in his seat. "What is this?"

"It's an email from the owner and baker of Comfort Zone, Aubrey Choi, requesting a second chance. She claims the cake you ate was a special order for a little girl's birthday, but her part-time employee accidentally served it to you."

Aubrey. She had continued to invade his thoughts while he was abroad. She was bold, sweet, and bursting with life. The sex was amazing, but their conversations in between had been equally memorable. He'd been seriously considering returning to Weldon to find her, but Craig saved him from that potential disaster.

Aubrey Choi, the owner of Comfort Zone, and his Aubrey, the goddess in bed, were one and the same. Panic filled his throat. Had she seduced him to get a positive review? It wasn't the first time a restaurateur had tried to bribe him. He'd rejected every last one of those overtures, because *what the literal hell?* Those people had demagnetized moral compasses.

He took a deep breath through his nose. As his initial shock receded, logic regained control of his mind. Aubrey never once mentioned Comfort Zone or her profession. She couldn't have known he was the customer who'd eaten the peculiar cake. And he definitely hadn't seen her at the bakery. As farfetched as it sounded, they had met by pure chance. A food critic and a baker. It was fucking serendipity.

Even so, they'd slept together, and he couldn't address the unfortunate cake mix-up without putting his reputation on the line. Landon never got involved with a subject of his review. He'd worked too hard and sacrificed too much to risk compromising his professional reputation. The opinion of a critic who could be bought—with money or sex—held no value. If he reviewed Comfort Zone again, his readers would know he'd broken his no-second-review rule, and that would draw unwanted attention to him and Aubrey, which would beg the question of why her and why now.

"I put you on the spot to write that review, so I didn't bother you with it, especially since these kinds of complaints usually die down after a while. But in this case, every sugar-loving citizen in Weldon must've emailed me. This is not going away quietly." Pulling up the nearest chair, Craig dropped a stack of files to the floor and sat down in its place. "I know you don't review the same restaurant twice even if the magazine's policy allows it."

"You're right." Landon sighed, dragging his fingers through his hair. "I never review the same place twice."

"But Ms. Choi's story is pretty compelling. With a six-year-old girl and a teenage part-timer to corroborate it? *California Coast Monthly* could become the Grinch who stole Weldon's favorite baker."

"This isn't the first time we've had restaurateurs beg for a retraction or a second chance. The magazine will have no reputation to save if it backpedals on every negative review."

"If you're willing to take another trip to Weldon for a second review, I'll write an editor's note, explaining that it's a onetime exception to the rule."

"That's only going to create a slippery slope. We'll be bombarded with complaints regarding the exception. *You did it that time, why not us?*"

"You were reluctant to write the review in the first place. Why are you being so stubborn now?"

"I have my reasons." The last thing he needed was to embroil *Cal Coast* in a scandal because of his personal life.

"Be reasonable, Landon. I looked into her story, and it checks out."

"I can't." He hated not being able to retract his review. Aubrey was an amazing woman, and she deserved better. He could only hope his review would fade from everyone's mind soon so she could go on with her life.

"This isn't a request, Kim." Iron laced Craig's voice. He rarely pulled rank on him.

"My answer is still no. It won't do the magazine any good." Landon arched his eyebrow and allowed a cocky grin to touch his lips. "Do you need my resignation?"

"Asshole," Craig said, dropping his boss voice. "You know you're too damn good to lose."

"Just trust me on this."

"At least tell me why."

"No." Landon wasn't dragging his friend into his moral dilemma. His headbutting emotions were already more than he could handle.

3

Aubrey was losing hope along with her customers. At two o'clock, people should've been scrambling into Comfort Zone for their sugar fix. But with the drizzling rain outside, even the locals took their goodies to go, and only the strains of her favorite eighties' music filled the empty bakery.

She plopped into a cozy stuffed chair, exhausted from taking inventory of Comfort Zone's new location before opening the shop in the morning. Ed's Diner, a Weldon institution, served its last short stack six months ago. Aubrey was devastated when Ed decided to retire and hang up his apron, but he'd encouraged her to expand Comfort Zone and relocate to the diner. She was scared at first, but her excitement had grown until there had been no room for fear.

The diner was clean and well maintained, and she could use most of the appliances included in the lease—like the stainless-steel countertop and sink, the stove top, the double-door fridge and freezers, and the dishwashers. But she still had to add a couple triple-stacked convection ovens, two stainless-steel worktables with casters, a dozen full-sheet bakery racks, and a load of commercial-size cooking tools to supplement her existing ones.

The money she'd set aside for the new kitchen was enough to cover the appliances and part of the contractor and labor fees, but she had counted on the profit from the current store to help pay for the remaining expenses, as well as fund some light interior renovations for the storefront.

With diminishing out-of-town customers and a nearly complete stall of her online sales, she might not have the funds to finish the renovations in the ninety-day tenant improvements period. Once she hit the ninety-day mark, she had to start paying rent, according to the contract, even if the shop wasn't open. Except there was no money. She was going to lose her security deposit, and Comfort Zone would be finished.

Spread thin and torn around the edges, Aubrey couldn't stop herself from pulling out the tattered pages of *California Coast Monthly* from her apron pocket. *It's like pressing and prodding a burned spot on the roof of your mouth with your tongue.* Worrying the spot made it hurt more, but she just couldn't leave it alone.

The Pitfalls of Brilliance
By Landon Kim

Traveling for work is never a vacation—that is, until you blow a tire on the freeway and live to tell your story.

This story has a simple beginning. My time at home was dwindling away, and I wanted to visit one more restaurant before going abroad again. Rumors of a restaurant rising out of the mountains, graced with the shimmering stars of Michelin, called me. I borrowed a friend's poorly maintained car (more on that soon) and headed for the mountains. It was supposed to be me, the car, and the open road for a half-day drive.

My friend fate's fickle nature manifested itself when one of the tires blew in the middle of the freeway, sending the car skidding. Fortunately, I was able to maneuver it off to the side, and no one was harmed as a result of the incident.

After a harrowing ride in the world's most ancient tow truck, I found myself in the hidden town of Weldon, California. With repairs unable to be completed until the next day, I had no choice but to spend the day in the picturesque town.

For the first time in what seemed like years, I had *free time* on my hands. I didn't know what to do with myself. I checked into a charming trattoria and inn and went for a *walk*. Yes, a leisurely stroll, if you will. The small, tidy streets of down-town Weldon had a warm, inviting feel to them, and I, by all means, accepted their invitation to explore.

I was lost in the delights of the colorful mom-and-pop stores when the sweet, seductive fragrance of baked goods beckoned me. Led by my trusty nose, I soon found myself in front of Comfort Zone, a quaint bakery sandwiched between an old-fashioned barbershop and a pet store.

The outdoor seating consisted of a couple wrought iron tables, with black-and-lavender parasols shading the customers from the sun. The simple but dramatic color scheme blended perfectly with the bright white storefront trimmed in gray. All this, combined with the alluring scent of fresh bread and cakes, and I was sold on the spot.

When I stepped into the shop, the interior did not disappoint my heightened expectations. From the plush couches and mismatched chairs to the clusters of black-and-white photos on the walls, the bakery essentially hugged me in welcome. The customers looked well at ease, whether they were laughing with friends or snuggled into overstuffed armchairs with their noses buried in books. I couldn't wait to join them.

The display case was a wonderland of cakes, pies, cookies, and pastries. The choices weren't overwhelming in number, but each was presented with such care and affection that it was impossible for me to choose. When I find myself in such delightful conundrums, I always go for the daily special. Something the chef was excited to share with me. A personal recommendation. Plus, it happened to be one of my favorite desserts, chocolate Bundt cake.

The polite but sullen young lady at the counter asked for my order—sliced or whole—and I went for the whole cake. With a cup of Sumatra coffee. I'm not a complete glutton, mind you, but I *was* on vacation. There is something wickedly decadent about digging your fork into an entire cake or your spoon into a whole tub of ice cream. I took my first bite of the cake, and my eyes slid shut. It was better to narrow my senses to focus on experiencing the cake without distraction. The chocolate cake was moist, not quite dense, and just the right amount of bitter and sweet. It was a perfect balance of the devil and the angel.

When I dug deeper into the Bundt cake, I discovered it was filled with a creamy, caramel-colored filling and specks of what I suspected were dried fruit. Intrigued, I forked up a small mountain and stuffed it carefully into my mouth. The filling was not caramel but some sort of a cream cheese and peanut butter filling. Other than its overuse and cloying texture, it tasted surprisingly delicious. However, the "dried fruit" pieces were unchewable, so I swallowed my mouthful.

And promptly choked.

Aided by the thick, sticky peanut butter filling, the translucent bits of colorful *what-the-hell-is-this* got lodged in my throat. With teary-eyed coughing and gulps of scalding-hot coffee, I escaped near asphyxiation.

So what were those odd bits of un-masticate-able health hazards?

Gummy worms. Chunky bits of chopped gummy worms.

What were they doing in the chocolate Bundt cake? And why?

Utter, egocentric arrogance.

The small-town baker/pastry chef has awe-inspiring talent. But it's the kind that has led to unbearable arrogance. An unfortunate pitfall for some brilliant chefs. It could have been frustration or boredom that led to the creation of the peculiar cake. Who can know for sure? Whatever prompted the addition of the gummy worms, the cake should not have been served to an unknowing customer. Experiments should stay in the kitchen until they are perfected. Comfort Zone's pastry chef used its customers, including myself, as test subjects, which was unforgivably selfish, and a senseless rebellion against the core value of chefs everywhere.

A true chef would never have done something so hurtful, disrespectful, and reckless. I take the arrogance of the act as a personal affront. And for that, I strongly advise my dear readers against ever entering the menace known as Comfort Zone.

You. Deserve. Better.

His review was humorous, lively, and even complimentary in parts, and she had to concede he was fair about the oddness of her cake. But he was completely wrong about her. Making

her customers happy with her sweet creations was her raison
d'être. Arrogance and boredom? *How dare he!* His sweeping
presumptions and scathing judgment of her as a chef based on
one gummy worm–filled cake was unfair and hurtful.

But he'd been so gentle and sweet during their night together.
Gah. Stop thinking about that. This *has nothing to do with* that.
She crumpled the tattered magazine pages for the twentieth
time and stuffed them in her pocket.

Aubrey wished the critic had been a small, thin man with
chalky skin and greasy hair. Someone who didn't know how to
bake or cook, sitting stooped over his computer in a cold, win-
dowless office. Hating on people who did their best to create
something lovely for others to enjoy. She could scoff at a man
like that and console herself that her life was fuller and happier
than his.

A long sigh leaked from her lips. *Yeah, right.* Scoffing wasn't
her thing. She'd probably feed the poor imaginary critic some
sweet buns to cheer him up.

It might actually be easier to scorn Landon Kim, an arrogant elitist. He was a tall, muscular specimen of male perfection with fan-freaking-tastic hair who happened to have a
degree from a little place called the Culinary Institute of America. The celebrity food critic and blogger could ostensibly cook
and critique—the perfect package. *Life is so unfair.* He was going
to breeze through life being rich, famous, and buff, while she
lost her bakery and was forced to work at a chain doughnut
shop that didn't even make their wares in-house.

She couldn't reconcile the funny, sexy man she'd taken to
bed with the cocky, judgmental food critic with a stick up his
ass. Well, maybe he couldn't *not* be judgmental—it was his job
to critique restaurants. And despite his mocking tone, his review of Comfort Zone was witty and well written. *Aubrey Choi,*

are you making excuses for him? She had lost her mind. That was it.

All of this was a rotten joke fate decided to play on her. *What were the chances of me picking up a food critic? A critic who happened to eat the most outrageous cake I've ever made?* It could only happen in a perfect shit storm so rare that it came just once in a billion years.

Her phone rang, bringing her back from her dismal thoughts. She stared at the screen with a confused frown. It was her mom, but it wasn't her birthday or Christmas.

"Mom?"

"Hey there." Her voice was soft and soothing. "How are you holding up?"

"What do you mean?" Aubrey frowned. She'd left her parents' house ages ago. Why would her mother be worried about how she was doing after all this time?

"Comfort Zone. I read that horrid review a month ago. I'd brushed it aside as nonsense when I first read it, but I've had this bad feeling recently. Are you in trouble?"

She covered the phone mic to take a huge breath. She and her mom never spoke about anything beyond the niceties—like the weather and royal weddings. It felt oddly wonderful to have her mom worry about her. "I'm okay. We've lost most of our out-of-town customers in-store and online, but the locals are still loyal. I'm sure the review will fade away soon. Comfort Zone can hang on till then."

That was a total lie. The impact of the review seemed to hit Comfort Zone harder and harder every day. Aubrey had written to the food magazine's editor in chief explaining that the chocolate Bundt cake indeed had been filled with gummy worms, cream cheese, and peanut butter, but it was a special order for her favorite mini-customer. However, despite Aubrey's many-flavored pleas, the editor gently and firmly refused to give Comfort Zone a second chance.

"Thank goodness," her mom said, the relief palpable in her voice. Aubrey didn't regret her white lie. "But for the time being, are things difficult for you? Is there anything I could do to help?"

I could use some money. Ha! Like she would ever ask her mom for money. Aubrey knew who the money would come from, and she would rather starve than accept his help.

"I'm okay, Mom. Everything will be okay. Thank you for calling, though."

"Are you sure? I could—"

"I'm sure. I'll call you if I need your help."

"Good. I'd really like that." Her mom paused as though wanting to say more, but she sighed softly. "Bye, Aubrey. Hang in there."

Talking to her mom left her listless and melancholy. Aubrey had never been there for her. It wouldn't be fair to accept her help no matter how dismal things looked. With a forlorn sigh, she stepped through the swinging kitchen doors, and the ancient hinges screeched in protest. They needed a spurt of WD-40. Everything needed WD-40 or Krazy Glue in her shop. Comfort Zone had outgrown its tiny, old home months ago.

That was part of the reason why Aubrey had decided to lease the diner. It had been a good year for the bakery, and it was generating a steady profit. Most important, her gut told her it was time, so she put away everything she could for the expansion. It took her months, but she finally paid the security deposit two months ago, spilling a barrel of happy tears.

Landon Kim's review came out only two weeks after the building owner handed her the keys to the place.

The foot traffic had decreased instantly. There were no early-morning lines out the door. The out-of-town customers trickled down to nil. If not for her loyal customers, she'd already be packing her bags, and their patronage alone couldn't keep the bakery afloat for long. Aubrey blinked away the bitter tears that rose too readily to the surface. This couldn't be the end of Comfort Zone. This could not be the end of her independence.

Her father's parting words still rang in her head. *You're going to fail, because that's what you do. Don't worry. I'll clean up your messes like I always do, but when you come crawling back, I expect you to be a very obedient and humble daughter.*

She would never crawl back to him. As a failure three times over. As a family embarrassment, who left home at eighteen, never attended college, and bankrupted her small business. She just couldn't do it.

It was sink or swim, and Aubrey could not sink. Cold sweat broke out on her scalp, and she clenched her eyes shut. She refused to lose her dream because of one scathing review. She would get a bank loan. Or sell off some equipment. Something. She couldn't sit back and watch her life crumble apart.

———

Landon heard a small commotion in the lobby before a red-faced teenage girl ran up to his desk.

"You can't just barge in there, young lady." Craig's secretary was tugging at her arm.

"Please," the girl sobbed. "I just need a minute of Mr. Kim's time. This is all my fault. Please."

Craig rushed out of his office and took stock of the situation. He nodded at his secretary to leave them and gently led the distraught girl into his office, motioning Landon to follow. She sat in one of the guest chairs. Landon leaned against the closed door and crossed his arms.

"What's this about?" he asked gruffly.

He'd been tense and restless since he'd learned that Aubrey was the recipient of his scathing review. He wanted to fix it, and his inability to help was eating away at him, but that was no reason to be short with a kid.

"Christ, Landon. You're scaring her." Craig shook his head at him and turned to the girl with a kind smile. "Okay, young lady. We do need to know who you are and why you're here, but go ahead and catch your breath. Would you like some water?"

The girl shook her head and made an effort to breathe normally. After several seconds, she squared her shoulders and faced Landon.

"My name is Lily, and I work part-time at Comfort Zone."

Landon groaned and ran his hand down his face. He belatedly placed where he'd seen her before.

"What my friend means to say is"—his editor paused to glare at Landon—"please continue."

"Mr. Kim, that day you came to Comfort Zone. I was the one who gave you the wrong cake. It was for Andy's birthday party, but I screwed up. Aubrey is an amazing baker and a wonderful person. Everyone in town adores her."

"Lily, I understand the cake wasn't meant for me, but what's done is done." He did his best to soften his tone. "I never review the same place twice, and I can't make an exception."

"Just try this." She plopped a small white box on Craig's

desk with a plastic fork on top. "It's Aubrey's pretzel bread pudding. It's better warmed and served with vanilla bean ice cream, but it's incredible on its own. Just try it."

It was a pointless exercise, but he didn't want to upset her again, so he obliged. The moment the pretzel bread pudding hit his tongue, he was enveloped in a perfect harmony of flavors and textures. It wasn't an explosion of sugar and spice. It was much subtler than that. The familiar flavors of cinnamon, nutmeg, and vanilla wove through the bread with the added smokiness of the pretzel dough. The salted caramel with the faintest hint of espresso added a modern edge to the classic.

"Damn." Landon had detected Aubrey's talent even when it was buried under peanut butter and gummy worms. But this? It was extraordinary.

"What? Is it that good?" Craig forked a big morsel and popped it in his mouth. "Holy shit. I mean, crap. Sorry, Lily."

It was the most delicious, creative, and masterfully executed bread pudding Landon had ever had. For the first time in a long time, he was at a complete loss. He might have ruined the career of a promising pastry chef with his review. The strange cake deserved his scorn, but Aubrey and Comfort Zone didn't. But nothing had changed. If he wrote a second review and their fling was discovered, both of their reputations would be shredded.

"You see? She really is an amazing baker and boss." Lily was practically bouncing up and down in her seat. "You'll give Comfort Zone another chance, right?"

Landon squeezed the back of his neck and resisted the urge to let loose a parade of profanity in every language he knew.

"Look, Lily. That is one of the best bread puddings I've ever tasted." He held up his hand when the girl opened her mouth to interrupt. "But the situation is more complicated than you think. I can't bend my policy without my readers questioning my objectivity. Besides, the entire town of Weldon seem to be fans of Comfort Zone. Business will go on as usual soon with my review long forgotten."

"No. You don't understand. Weldon has a tiny population. The bulk of Comfort Zone's customers were online or travelers stocking up on their way to the mountains and the lakes. Aubrey was always busy filling online orders on top of running the shop, but I haven't seen her send anything out since the review." Lily leaned forward in her chair, gripping the edges of the seat. "The bakery is going out of business because of your review. I think Aubrey spent a whole lotta money on a lease to move Comfort Zone to a bigger location. I don't know what's going to happen now, but when I mention the other store, Aubrey just looks sad. And scared."

Expansion? The kid had to be exaggerating. Could the situation truly be worse than he'd imagined? Landon scowled in frustration, and Lily shrank in her seat.

"You must be exhausted, Lily. It was a long drive from Weldon, right?" Craig led the kid, who was sobbing again, out of his office with a menacing glare at Landon. "Why don't we order you some food and let you recharge? Our employee rest area is quite comfortable."

Landon returned to his desk and sat facing the windows, his logic and emotion duking it out with each other. His rational side wanted to walk away from the whole mess—Aubrey, her talent, and her bakery. His human side wanted to write a second review for Comfort Zone. She was so special, and taking her talent away from the world would be a crime.

"Fucking hell." He raked both his hands through his hair as he crossed the hallway to reach his office. Several coworkers peeked at him but quickly ducked back to their work when he glowered at them.

He probably looked deranged. The whole situation was a fucking mess. Landon didn't do messes. He planned, calculated, organized, and exercised iron control over his life. Impulsive dreamers like his dad were the ones who made messes—shitting everywhere they pleased and expecting others to clean up after them. Landon had cleaned up his father's messes and swore to never be like him. So how had everything gone to hell? It was unacceptable.

His cell phone vibrated, and he ignored the infuriating buzzing until it stopped. When the buzzing resumed not a second later, Landon picked up his phone to throw it out a window, but he answered the call after a glimpse of the caller ID.

"*Mio dio*, Landon," Aria said, not bothering with something as mundane as *hello* or *how are you?* "I just finished a walk-through of our location. They made me wear a hard hat. A putrid, yellow hard hat. Can you believe that?"

"Unbelievable." Landon rubbed a hand down his face, and his expression relaxed into his resting bitch face. "How dare they protect you from a head injury at a construction site."

"The construction is crazy, by the way." His friend didn't acknowledge his dry response with so much as a snort. "Dust and noise *everywhere*. I'm surprised I didn't get impaled during my walk-through. But the point is—"

"Yes, Aria. It'll be great if you can get to the point."

"Shut up. If you don't behave, I'm going to start all over."

Landon sighed, both amused and exasperated. "Do you like it or not?"

"I love it. It is perfection." Her Italian accent, which was nothing more than a melodic lilt in her voice, grew a shade thicker when she was emotional. "I can't wait to start filming."

"That's fantastic," he said with a genuine smile. Aria had a keen eye for television, which was one of the reasons she rose to the highest ranks of celebrity chefdom. If she approved of the location for her wine country special, then it meant her audience would love it. "I'm glad you like it."

But his happiness for his friend reminded him of another talented chef who might never get a chance to shine. An image of Aubrey, sitting in a dark, empty bakery, flashed through his mind, and his stomach lurched. *For God's sake, Kim. She's not destitute.*

"What's going on?" A new sharpness entered Aria's voice. "Tell me before you break down and wail like a baby."

In another lifetime, he and Aria had interned at a world-renowned kitchen in Madrid—a wonderland of gastronomical research and food science. Each of them, something of a prodigy in their respective culinary institutions, had tied for first in an international cooking competition. The coveted three-month summer internship was extended to both of them. They worked grueling hours, gluttonously absorbed everything their brains could contain, and became rivals and then friends without conscious effort.

Considering their long friendship and Aria's uncanny ability to read people, there was no point pretending nothing was wrong.

"Have you read my last review? 'The Pitfalls of Brilliance'?"

"The one about your near-death experience from a gummy worm?"

"Yes, that one. Well, it turns out they'd accidentally served a special-order cake to me. It was meant for a six-year-old girl's birthday party."

"Well, that's a shame, but you stayed true to your personal experience. Serving the wrong cake shows they have issues with their service."

"Thanks for supporting me, but I shouldn't have passed judgment on the bakery after a single sampling. They made one mistake, and I basically shut them down for it." Landon gave her the short version of his dilemma, leaving out the night with Aubrey. "She doesn't deserve to lose her business over a common mistake her high school part-timer made."

"That's one hell of a mess."

"You think?"

"I do," Aria said sweetly. "So tell me the rest."

"What?" *Damn.* She was like a bloodhound when it came to sniffing out trouble.

"It's a terrible shame your review is having such a devastating effect on her business. The timing couldn't be worse for her. I get all that." She paused before she went for the kill. "But that doesn't explain why you sound like your world is going to hell. Who is she?"

"I ran into her at a bar in Weldon the day I got stranded." He sighed in resignation. He had to come clean if he wanted her help. Besides, it would help her to see the whole picture. "I had no idea she was the owner of Comfort Zone, and she didn't recognize me. Something just drew me to her. She was special, and we connected."

"Oh, my." The beginnings of real concern entered her voice.

"We spent the night together." He sounded wistful, and Aria sighed long and loud. "It was meant to be a one-night thing, but when I found her gone the next morning, I was . . . disappointed. We didn't even exchange phone numbers, but I wanted to see her again."

"Have you seen her since?"

"I probably would've gone looking for her after my trip to Asia, but I found out my Aubrey was one and the same as Comfort Zone's Aubrey Choi as soon as I got back. So, no. I haven't seen her since." Landon massaged the back of his neck. "Besides, there's no way she would want to see me after this fiasco."

"So, to recap, you want to set things right, but you don't want to bring attention to the whole situation because people might discover you slept with her. Plus, you don't want her to hate you. Does that sound about right?"

"Bloody, fucking hell." How had he messed up so badly?

"I take that as a *yes*. Well, I may have just the right solution for your mess."

4

The bell above the shop door trilled cheerfully as the man of her nightmares strode into Comfort Zone.

"You." All the shock, hurt, fear, and devastation of the past months saturated the single word. "Get out."

"Hello, Aubrey." His unflinching gaze cut into her like chips of onyx, but she willed herself not to glance away.

"Get. Out," she snarled through gritted teeth.

How dare he come here! He and his magazine had ignored the pleas of her townspeople, as well as her own, for over a frigging month. She didn't know when he'd learned who she was, but he had to have known after her first twenty emails to his editor. They had a one-night stand, which didn't mean he owed her anything, but what they shared hadn't meant *nothing*. Didn't he have any regrets about his review? Not even when he realized the cake mix-up was a mistake?

And now, there he stood, looking irresistibly sexy in her dying bakery. After everything he'd done, did he want to frame her for murder as well? The bakery was empty, so there would be no witnesses. It was tempting. Much too tempting.

Her outrage multiplied when his eyes swept across her neck, chest, and the length of her legs, reminding her he'd touched every inch of her that night. Heat spread through her treacherous body, and humiliation followed in its wake. Standing on the brink of losing her dream, she still wanted the man.

"I'm not here to resume our affair, if that's what you're worried about."

"What?" she whispered in disbelief, her mortification mounting. *"What?"*

She clapped her mouth shut and stood shaking with helpless rage. Silence was infinitesimally more dignified than screeching like a banshee. *Resume our affair?* Even if he draped himself across her bed in all his nude glory, she wouldn't so much as nudge him with her toes. *Gah.* She was determined to hate him, but the thought of him naked on her bed stalled her brain.

Her chance for a clever retort lost, Aubrey watched Landon through narrowed eyes as he perused her shop. He absently ran his hand over a leather chair and then paused in front of a photo on the wall. One of her favorites. A handful of her regulars were piled onto a single love seat, laughing themselves to tears. She fought the impulse to throw herself in front of it. Landon Kim didn't deserve their smiles.

He strolled to another set of pictures, his hands loosely clasped behind his back. Despite his relaxed posture, he permeated the shop with nervous energy, and his silence filled her with unease. Whatever he was there to do, he needed to do it and leave. His presence confused and hurt her.

"Do you often revisit the restaurants you've ruined?"

"I fucked up." She startled when he spoke from the other end of the shop. "That cake was beyond weird and a potential health hazard, but it was careless and unprofessional of me to write a review based on a single sample. I don't do careless and unprofessional. That's not the way I work. Usually."

"Do you want me to absolve you of your sins?" It had probably taken him a few hours to write the review that destroyed what she'd built in four years. Comfort Zone wasn't just a bakery to her. It was her home, her dream, and her freedom. Hot tears burned behind her lids, and she bit her lip till she tasted blood. If she cried in front of him, the last scrap of her pride would burn to cinders. "Come see me when you and I are the only survivors in a postapocalyptic, zombie-infested world. Maybe then . . . *may-be*. Who am I kidding? You can go straight to hell."

"I'm not here to apologize." He dragged a hand through his hair, showing signs of frayed nerves. "And I can't write a second review."

"Can't or won't?" Aubrey slumped into a chair, suddenly too tired to give a fuck.

"Won't." A hint of remorse flickered in his eyes. "Did you know who I was when you slept with me?"

She listened to her breath whooshing in and out, dumbstruck once more. Too bewildered to filter her thoughts, she said, "No, I did *not* know who the bloody hell you were. What the fuck are you implying?"

"I had to ask." His long, thick lashes fluttered like the wings of a moth who'd strayed too close to the fire. "I had to be sure you didn't sleep with me to extort a good review."

"I slept with you for a *good* review? Are you out of your mind?" She shot out of her seat and reached him in a single, rage-fueled bound—close enough to spit on his handsome, arrogant mug. "News flash, asshole. You didn't give me a good review."

"Will you listen?" He leaned in so close that she had to

tilt her head back to continue glaring at him. "I had to ask. I needed to be certain before I could help you."

"Help me? You. Ruined. Me." Grabbing fistfuls of his shirt, she jerked him in time with each word. But she was the only one who rocked back and forth, while he stood like a stone wall. She roared with frustration. "You wrote a review that *destroyed* my life. Just how did I benefit from sleeping with you?"

"You didn't." He raked his fingers through his hair, looking pained. "You said you didn't sleep with me for a good review, and I believe you."

"How very kind of you to acknowledge that. Now, turn around. Walk through that door. *Disappear.*" She released his shirt and shoved him toward the entrance, putting her weight into it. He stumbled back a step. "You are done insulting me."

The cautious vulnerability that entered his eyes stopped her from knocking him across the head. The man was hopeless—a cynic and a clueless idiot—but she could tell he'd been used that way before. *Well, tough shit.* He was still an asshole.

"But the fact is we did sleep together," he continued as though she hadn't spoken. "If I write a favorable second review and someone finds out about that night, our reputations will be wrecked beyond repair. No one will believe it was a coincidence."

"How will anyone find out?"

"Writing an unprecedented second review alone will raise suspicions. And . . ." He cringed a little, the tip of his ears turning pink. "And I've had some paparazzi ambushing me lately. They seem overly interested in my private life."

"Is this about you being one of the most eligible bachelors of the year? Oh, my God. It is." She *had* to choose a celebrity food critic and most eligible bachelor to have a one-night-stand with. *What shitty luck.* "Can't we just deny it? I don't think anyone has proof that we slept together, right?"

"And we don't have any proof that we didn't sleep together. It's impossible to prove a negative. Besides, we did sleep together." He threw his hands up in frustration. "Gossip spreads like wildfire on social media and gossip sites. Unfortunately, celebrity gossip is presumed true until proven false. We won't be able to convince anyone otherwise until it's too late to salvage our reputations."

Exhausted, Aubrey sat down once again. She understood the logic in his decision, but it changed nothing. "Just tell me why you're here, then leave."

"I'm here to make things right." Any sign of regret, doubt, or vulnerability had disappeared, and his voice rang with steely determination. "You're not going to lose Comfort Zone. Not without a fight."

"I'm not? How?" She couldn't feel her lips move. She reversed her posture and straddled the high-backed chair before she slid to the floor. He was going to write a second review after all.

"I tasted one of your other menu items, and I was blown away by it." Landon ran his hand down his face.

"When?"

The fluttering in her stomach was *not* happiness. She didn't care what he thought of her baking. She was supposed to hate him. He'd implied she'd seduced him for a good review. But her indignation wavered when she remembered the flash of worry and vulnerability in his eyes. It was still a dick move.

"Lily came to my office with your pretzel bread pudding. She said she was the one who'd made the mistake and begged for a second review. The kid really looks up to you."

"Oh, Lily." Her hand flew to her mouth, and she blinked away sudden tears. "I can't believe she did that for me."

"If all goes well with my business proposal, you could give her a big, fat raise."

"Your business proposal?" Confusion and curiosity interrupted her attempt to radiate hostility.

"I want you to guest star on my friend's cooking show," he said in a low voice, studying her intently.

"A cooking show? On television?" She sounded dumb, but her wit had gone on leave without notice.

"That's the usual medium for a cooking show nowadays." His tone was dry, but his eyes twinkled with amusement.

Great. Now he's laughing at me. "I've never been on TV. I don't even watch TV. I wouldn't know what to do or say. I'm going to make a fool of myself." Aubrey clamped a hand over her mouth and breathed noisily through her nose.

"No, you won't. If it makes you feel any better, it'll be filmed on a closed set, so you won't have a live audience." A corner of his mouth quirked upward. It wasn't a full-blown smile, but it was enough to make his dimple wink at her. That dimple was the root cause of her predicament. *Darth Dimple. Dimple of Doom. Count Dimpula. Oh, shit. He's still talking.* "—and the writers and directors are there to make sure everything goes smoothly. Besides, Aria would never let her guest chef look foolish on her show."

"Aria? As in Aria Santini?"

Aria was America's favorite celebrity chef, known for her simple, delicious Italian dishes that viewers could actually make at home. Aubrey owned every one of her cookbooks and had even watched a few of her YouTube videos. She was stunning—a tall, statuesque brunette with warm, brown eyes—and an amateur mezzo-soprano on the side. Almost too perfect to be real.

"Yes, that Aria. She's an amazing chef and a cooking show veteran. You'll be in good hands."

"And she's your friend?" Aubrey couldn't believe it. Aria seemed so sweet and Landon was so . . . not.

"Hard to believe, isn't it?" Landon arched a sardonic brow as though he'd read her thought bubble. "We've been friends for close to a decade."

Plenty of time for him to have tainted her. He'd probably turned Aria into a diva from hell to complement his arrogant bastard image. And he wanted Aubrey to be on her show? She didn't want anything to do with Landon Kim or his BFF. But he was offering his help, and she had a chance to save Comfort Zone.

Is my pride worth more than my dreams?

———

The blood had drained out of Aubrey's face when Landon brought up Aria. When his friend had explained the plan, she'd instructed him to mention it was her show. She'd hinted it would be a big selling point. He'd given her grief for her narcissism, but he'd secretly agreed with her. Most young chefs would kill for an opportunity to work with Aria Santini. But he also understood how intimidating it could be.

"The exposure you get on TV will be worth a hundred restaurant reviews. And you'll be well compensated. You could continue with the move and have the new location renovated while you're filming in the Central Coast."

Suddenly, he was desperate for Aubrey to accept his offer. He could help her, and it would fix the whole mess and maybe erase the haunted expression from her face.

"How do you know about the move?" She studied him with narrowed eyes.

"I always do thorough research before I make any business offers. It's the smart thing to do," he said, carefully leaving Lily out of it. He wouldn't have known about the expansion if it hadn't been for her, but he didn't want Aubrey to get upset with her well-meaning employee for oversharing.

Aubrey mumbled something unintelligible, and then her gaze snapped to his face. "Wait. You said I could do the renovation while I'm filming in the Central Coast? Exactly where and how long are we talking about?"

"Bosque Verde, California. At least three weeks."

"Bosque Verde is fine, I guess. It's only three hours from here. But three weeks? That's too long to be away from my shop."

"Yes, being closed for three weeks is scary for a small business, but not if you think about the big picture here. You could save Comfort Zone with *just three weeks* of your time. You'd be investing a few weeks away to establish a secure future." Landon had never worked so hard to convince someone to work with him. People generally came to him with offers, from which he picked and chose. "Aubrey, will you guest star on Aria's show?"

"Yes." Her answer was barely above a whisper. She didn't like asking for help, and she hadn't asked for his help, but here she was accepting it with grace. "Only because it'll give me a fighting chance to save Comfort Zone. Your proposal might take care of my problems for now, but there's no guarantee that starring in Aria's show will magically fix everything."

"It'll give you more than a fighting chance, Aubrey." Relief coursed through him, surprising him with its force. He had a chance to put things right for Aubrey, and he would succeed. "Aria's star power and your sunny personality will convince my readers that my review is flawed. And once the viewers try your recipes, they'll be your fans for life. Besides, fixing your current problems is the biggest hurdle. Ultimately, your talent and hard work will 'fix everything.'"

"My sunny personality? You gotta be kidding me. It's more like a thunderstorm when you're involved." Her short dark hair drew his eyes to her delicate features. She was still breathtaking, but the bruised shadows beneath her wide brown eyes and the pallor of her skin bore testament to the havoc he'd wrought on her life. "I hope you know what you're talking about. My future depends on it."

"I don't walk away from my mistakes. I'll set things right."

"You own up to your mistakes. Just not publicly." Aubrey's brows furrowed in thought, and then a ghost of a smile touched her lips. "But I do appreciate you coming here today. You didn't turn your back on my predicament. At least, not for *too* long. You might not be a *complete* bastard after all."

"I wouldn't go that far." He grinned, her almost-friendly tone putting him at ease.

"Maybe you're right." She surveyed her nails as though considering where he belonged on the bastard scale. "Are you planning to apologize for accusing me of selling my body to get ahead in the world?"

Landon cringed as her acerbic words bit into him. That had not been his intent. He knew in his gut they had met by chance and neither of them had a clue about the other's profession. But he needed to be certain she hadn't slept with him to bolster her business, knowing who he was. He couldn't entwine their lives further until she denied it with her own lips.

"Well?" Aubrey sat, tapping her foot with increasing speed.

"I was an idiot to believe for even a second that you'd faked your . . . enthusiasm."

"Yes, you were." She blushed a fiery red, but her expression remained placid. "I never doubted yours. Although you sounded so pained when you said I was killing you. I actually worried for a second."

Landon choked on air and coughed until his eyes bulged.

"You all right there?"

"Yes. Completely fine," he wheezed when he could drag in a breath without coughing.

Her words taunted him, but boldly affirmed her passion had been real. Ridiculous pride surged through his veins. He wasn't sure what aroused him more, her sexy retort or the memory it awakened in him.

God, you're killing me. Her small, curious hands had explored his body until raging desire threatened to consume him. When their bodies joined, he'd felt pleasure so intense it had bordered on pain.

The silence stretched on, and tension, thick and hot, stirred the air between them. Landon's throat worked to swallow, and Aubrey's triumphant smile revealed she knew just how turned on he was. He shifted on his feet and forced his body to relax.

Lesson learned. *Do not engage in sexual banter with Aubrey. Ever.* It was a foolish thing to do in the first place. He'd come back to rectify a wrong, not to create more problems. Their one-night stand had passed notice, but they couldn't take any further risks.

He dragged his hands through his hair. Why was he even thinking about *further risks?* She was the owner of a restaurant he'd reviewed, and she was about to appear on a show he was coproducing. Their relationship couldn't be anything but professional. Breaking eye contact first, he stuffed his hands deep in his pockets and cleared his throat.

"Let's go get a drink." He desperately needed one. "We should discuss the details of your deal."

"Weldon Brewery okay with you?"

"Sure. I'm game for anything."

And thus, he thought, *begins the greatest gamble of my life.*

5

Tara was in a foul mood, dealing with the crowd four hands short—her twin older brothers, Jack and Alex, were attending a beer festival—but when she saw Aubrey walk in with Landon, her expression shifted from frazzled to thunderous. Her unspoken question rang loud and clear: *What the hell is he doing here?* Aubrey rolled her eyes and shrugged, hoping it said, *Still figuring it out. Don't kill him—yet.* Her friend had murder in her eyes after she'd read the review. Aubrey had had to sit on her to keep her from storming Landon's office. Once she calmed down, Tara settled for writing a scathing email.

He led her toward the back of the bar, placing his hand lightly on her back. She should've shaken him off, but she was too busy peeking over her shoulder to see if there was a trail of steam behind her. Her skin sizzled like butter on a hot pan where he touched her. She mentally slapped herself, annoyed as hell at her body's reaction to him. He was the bringer of destruction. The pusher of her rage buttons.

She didn't realize until they were walking to the brewery

that he hadn't apologized. He'd admitted his mistake and called himself an idiot but had never said the magic words. It was as though *sorry* wasn't in his vocabulary. His intent was plain. He'd come to own his mistake and to make amends, but after all that, he couldn't utter the words *I'm sorry.*

What a strange, arrogant man.

Aubrey released her breath when he broke contact to pull out her chair. His manners remained impeccable even after obliterating Comfort Zone in "The Pitfalls of Brilliance." The table wasn't much larger than a round stool, so his long legs rested on either side of her knees, radiating bone-melting, masculine heat. Not that she noticed. But the brewery really needed some bigger tables.

"I think you'll like the location. They're renovating a hundred-year-old schoolhouse for the filming. It's run-down, but it has unbelievable potential." He rested his forearms on the table and leaned toward her. His open expression was a far cry from the tense, cold mask he'd worn earlier. "The surroundings, the view, everything is amazing."

Aubrey nodded, reminded of the charming stranger with the beautiful smile. He sounded like a kid showing off his favorite LEGO set. This Landon was adorable. *Full stop.* She forced her brows low into a brooding frown. In the last hour, she'd gone from hating him, to realizing she still wanted him, then to kind of accepting his non-apology. Her head spun, and she needed to get a grip.

"Most of the original structure was salvaged—Douglas fir flooring, board-and-batten walls, and even the chalkboards."

"That sounds lovely," she said, imagining *Little House on the Prairie.*

He awarded her with a smile. The one where his eyes

crinkled in the corners and his dimple burrowed deep into his cheek. *The* Smile. Her heart struggled against her ribs like a magician trying to escape from a straitjacket.

Hold it right there, Aubrey Choi. He suspected you of sleeping with him to get a good review. He obviously has major trust issues there. No. Sex. Allowed. Sex could ruin your professional reputation forever. Sex is bad. Don't even think about heavy petting.

They were discussing the details of his *business* offer. *Look serious. Not horny. Serious.* She adjusted her features into a somber mask and willed herself to concentrate, but Landon shifted in his seat, and his legs accidentally brushed against hers.

"Excuse me for a minute," Aubrey squeaked, bolting out of her chair. "I'm going to grab some beer. Would you like some?"

"Sure. I'll go—" Landon stood as if to accompany her.

"No." She cleared her throat and lowered her voice. "I can get us free beer. Just wait here."

"Sure." Confusion crossed his face, but he sat back down. "Thank you."

Aubrey dashed for the bar and ducked under it, grabbing two mugs from the freezer. She almost dropped them when Tara blocked her path.

"Sweet heavens, ninja woman. You came out of nowhere." Not trusting her shaky hands, Aubrey placed the mugs on the counter.

"I was standing here the whole time." Tara crossed her arms. "You just didn't notice because you were too busy ogling Landon Kim—who, by the way, was trying to burn your clothes off with his laser vision."

Aubrey burst out laughing with an undeniable note of hysteria. His review had nearly destroyed her dream—it still might—but she couldn't stop lusting after him. There was even a term for it. *Sleeping with the enemy.* Was it an actual thing? *It must happen often for there to be a coined term for it.* It was all wrong, but she felt helpless against the attraction. *No, I am not helpless against anything.* She was off balance because her enemy unexpectedly replaced her devastation with hope. Her wild emotions would settle after she had some time to absorb what happened.

"There won't be any burning of clothing." Aubrey heard the wistful longing in her voice and bit her cheek. "We're here to discuss business."

"Business? What business? Does it involve lost kittens?"

"What? No." She squinted, wondering what she'd missed. "What lost kittens?"

"Then why do you look so troubled?"

"Because I slept with a stranger who wrote a restaurant review that took Comfort Zone to the brink of extinction. Now he's back to help fix things, and I don't have any better options, so I have to swallow my pride and accept his olive branch."

"Deep breaths." Tara put her arm around Aubrey's shoulders. "So how does he plan to fix things?"

"He wants me to guest star on Aria Santini's new show. I'll be 'well compensated' enough to continue with the move and the renovations."

"Holy guacamole. And Aria freaking Santini?"

"I know. Right?" Aubrey pushed her palms into her eyes. A mean headache was gathering behind them.

"You're really going to do it?" Her friend filled four mugs using expert flicks and taps to create the perfect creamy head.

"I have to do it. You know I have to pay the contractors, and complete the renovations in the next couple of months. Or else I won't be able to open the shop in time, but I'll still have to pay the monthly rent per the lease agreement," Aubrey's panicked words spilled out of her mouth until she ran out of breath. She shrugged helplessly. "Tara, Comfort Zone will go bankrupt before it reopens its doors. I'd be crazy to say no."

"If that's your final decision, then I have your back, but sometimes 'crazy' could be the right answer."

"I don't know. The last thing I want is another wealthy, egocentric man in my life, but Landon said this was strictly business."

Tara stared bug-eyed at her, mouth agape. Minutes seemed to pass that way, and Aubrey fidgeted and scratched her neck. She broke under the stare attack. "I doubt I'll see him around much."

"You're my best friend and I love you, so I'm duty bound to smack you on the head if you believe the crap spewing from your mouth." Aubrey opened said mouth to protest, but Tara held up her palm—to silence her or to smack her, Aubrey didn't know. "If you're doing this, I want you to go into it with your eyes wide open."

"Doing what? Shooting a couple of episodes of a cooking show?"

"Quiet, child. Neither of you will be able to stay away from each other. The sexual tension is visible like a glowing crimson aura." Tara circled her palms around Aubrey like a fortune teller. "So by *this*, I mean having a relationship with Landon Kim."

Aubrey didn't have anything dumb left to say, so she asked

the question expected of her. "And what would I see with my wide-open eyes?"

"Fireworks and enough heat to generate electricity."

"No, please, no. I'm going to rip my clothes off before this is over, aren't I?" She covered her face with her hands. "No, wait. Do you love me?"

"Hell yeah. I love you like mad. Why do you ask?"

"You have to kill me. If you sense that I'm about to go to the Horny Side, you must kill me. If you love me, then you will do this for me. Sleeping with him again will be the ultimate humiliation, and it could ruin our reputations and careers. It could ruin everything *forever.*"

"Shut up and act cool," Tara whispered. "Darth Sexy approaching."

"Hello, Tara. It's good to see you again." His lips hooked to one side, hinting at his dimple. Aubrey wanted to trace the indentation with her tongue. "But I'm guessing I'm your least favorite customer tonight."

"Back for more of my spectacular brew?"

"How could I resist?" Landon chuckled, the corners of his eyes crinkling with amusement. The Smile. *Please, no. Not the Smile.* If Tara had taken her seriously, Aubrey would already have a lightsaber sticking out of her chest.

"May I suggest some of our seasonal specials?" Tara said in an overly courteous voice. *Crap.* Aubrey recognized the killer gleam in her best friend's eyes. "Buzz Off is a personal favorite—so sharp and bitter—it might bite you on the way down. The Witch's Brew is a close second. Don't be fooled by the smooth, rich porter. The brew is hexed to make unfeeling jerks permanently impotent."

"I have our beers right here," Aubrey said in a rush, picking up their mugs. "Let's go back to our table."

"Always a pleasure." Landon tapped two fingers to his brow in a playful salute to Tara and then tucked a couple of twenties in the tip jar. Turning away, he took the mugs from Aubrey's hands and lowered his head to speak to her. His warm breath tickled her neck, and her toes curled in her shoes. "Your friend wanted to give me the boot, not free beer. I was worried you two got into a brawl."

"Ha ha," she mumbled, not meeting his eyes.

Enough heat to generate electricity. She could probably power the Vegas strip with her restless energy. Back at their table, she took a sip of beer before peeking at him through her lashes.

"As good as I remember," Landon said, setting his mug down.

"Mm-hmm. Tara's amazing."

He settled back into his seat and stretched out one of his legs. His calf pressed into hers, and an electric jolt shot up to her head. *Zing.* His eyes glazed over for an interminable second before he snatched his leg away. Aubrey angled hers away as well, but they were still within inches of each other under the tiny table.

Her nerve endings were zinging across her skin like sparklers on New Year's Eve. The double barrier provided by his slacks and her jeans weren't thick enough, and the only business she could think about had the word *monkey* in it—monkey business, monkeying around, hot monkey sex . . .

"I want you to create two dessert recipes featuring wine from Bosque Verde. Your portion of the filming shouldn't take more than a week, but you'll need an additional two weeks in the front end of your trip to sample the local wines to use in your recipes. There are more than two hundred wineries to choose from, and I doubt you would want to rush things."

She stared at him, her face as blank as her mind. *Ooh ooh ah ah?*

Aubrey?"

She was understandably impatient for their meeting to end, but her blank expression nettled him. It took superhuman strength for him to concentrate—being so close to her that he could smell the vanilla and spice off her skin—but he'd promised to help her. To do that, she had to commit 100 percent to the show.

"Are you still worried about closing the bakery during the filming?" Landon frowned at her stubborn silence and then shook off his frustration. He'd fucked up royally, and he was lucky to have her on board at all. "I'll take a look at the show's budget and see if we could compensate you for any lost revenue."

"Comfort Zone is already running at a loss, so don't worry about that." Aubrey straightened in her seat, emerging from whatever fog she'd been in. "And I already said I'm in. I'm not questioning your logic. A few weeks in exchange for a chance at a promising future, right? I get that."

"But you shut down as soon as I brought up the three weeks."

"It wasn't . . . That's not . . ." Aubrey blushed and fidgeted in her seat. He studied her closely, cocking his head to the side. He couldn't figure out what was going on in her head. "Comfort Zone isn't just a business to me. It's my dream. I can't imagine going away for so long, but that doesn't mean I'll half-ass my way through the show to finish early."

"I can understand that." Relief washed through him in

waves of giddiness. *Huh.* Setting things right for Aubrey meant even more to him than he'd thought. "And you wouldn't be at the peak of your craft if you hadn't given it your all. I doubt you're capable of half-assing anything."

"Thanks. Okay." Splashes of pink bloomed on her cheeks. She was lovely. "So where will I stay? I'm going to need a full kitchen to work on my recipes."

"I've arranged for a villa, and I'll make sure you have everything else you need."

"Everything? *You'll* make sure?" Aubrey's eyebrows climbed to her forehead. "You got me the guest star opportunity through Aria, right? Your job is done. Shouldn't the show take care of everything else?"

"Aria came up with the idea of inviting you on her show. I'd like to take care of everything else for you as the show's executive producer."

"The executive producer?" She sank down in her seat when heads turned at her raised voice. "You didn't tell me that. Why didn't you tell me?"

"I'm telling you now." He scanned her pale face. There was panic in her wide, darting eyes. "It's a minor detail to our business arrangement, and it won't affect your work. Other than hiring you, my duties won't intersect with yours in any way. I've been on plenty of food shows as a judge, but this is my first time producing one, so my involvement in the show isn't widely known. Aria is my coexecutive producer, and she's the face of the show, not me."

"But does this mean you're going to be in Bosque Verde, too?"

"On and off," he hedged as he analyzed her reaction.

Then the puzzle pieces slid into place. She hadn't realized she would be spending time with him. She looked terrified at the idea. Landon couldn't blame her—he had been an asshole—but her reaction stung. Which went to show he was out of his mind.

If she found out he would be in Bosque Verde for the duration of her stay, she would bolt out the door. He couldn't let that happen. The show was the only way he could help her. To fix what he'd inadvertently stolen and nearly broken.

But he couldn't stay away from the filming. Some might think him neurotic, but he wasn't ready to relinquish control until he decided the production was running smoothly. He planned to monitor the construction and stay until the first few episodes were shot. They were filming in a brand-new kitchen, which was no more than a blueprint and some tile samples at this point. With all the variables, he'd be shocked if nothing went wrong.

"How much on and how much off?" Aubrey seemed to be holding her breath, waiting for his answer.

"Which would you prefer? More on or more off?" He grinned wolfishly before he caught himself. Flirting with her was the dumbest move he could make, but he'd forgotten himself for a moment. She was distractingly beautiful.

"Why would I have a preference?" She huffed and crossed her arms over her perfect breasts.

Goddamn it. I need a cold shower.

"I was only asking as a professional courtesy."

"I'll be at Bosque Verde as long as necessary to make sure everything goes smoothly." He managed to sound professional but vague.

"Okay, then. We're in agreement, and everything is set." Aubrey shot to her feet. "I really need to get going."

"Not interested in how much you'll be making for the two episodes? Or when you start?" He should have let her go, but he wanted her to stay just a bit longer.

"Sure, I'm interested." She plopped back into her chair, the tips of her ears turning red. "Go on, then."

When he told her how much they were offering, Aubrey's mouth dropped open. Landon grinned despite himself. If he wasn't certain before, he was now positive she hadn't approached him with an ulterior motive. She didn't seem capable of subterfuge.

"Just so we're clear," he said, "the show will get equal rights to the copyright on the two recipes, including online reproductions and potential cookbooks."

"Yeah. I'd figured that since I'm going to share the recipes with all the viewers. When do I start?"

"Next week."

"That soon? I don't know if I can take care of everything by then. Well, I guess it depends on when I get paid." She pressed her lips together and glanced down at her hands. "Not to seem money hungry or anything."

"This is business. We would be remiss to ignore the details, especially the money. The show would pay you in thirds. You'll get a third on signing, before you leave for Bosque Verde. Then a third on completion of filming, and a third when your episodes air," he said. "The bulk of the guest talent contract is boilerplate, but HR and the legal team will explain everything in more detail. And you'll have a full week to review the contract and ask as many questions as you'd like."

"HR and *legal?*" Aubrey scrunched up her nose like she'd smelled something foul. "You've gotta be kidding me."

She seemed so genuinely appalled, he couldn't help laughing. "I'll read through everything and have my personal attorney take a look as well to make sure the station doesn't take advantage of you."

"Who's going to make sure *you* don't take advantage of me?"

Her tone was flippant, but she scrunched her eyes shut a second later. "That came out wrong. I didn't mean it in a weird way."

"It's fine," he said softly despite his beating heart. "I would never take advantage of you. In any way."

"Good." Aubrey nodded and lowered her lashes to the table. "Yeah, that's good. Thank you."

6

Aubrey could not believe it was happening. She folded a pair of jeans and tucked them into her suitcase. With the generous compensation from Aria's show, she was able to make her second down payment and had enough left to pay Lily during the filming and close a day early for a long-awaited camping trip. She hoped her special spot had stayed the same while she was attached at the hip to Comfort Zone.

"Don't your cheeks cramp up when you smile nonstop like that?" Tara asked from her perch on Aubrey's bed.

"I'm just so excited." Aubrey's tireless cheeks held up fine even when her grin widened. "Wait, where's my tent?"

"For the seventh time, you already loaded it in the Jeep along with the rest of your camping gear. Sleeping bag, extra blankets, butane burner, flashlights . . ."

"That's right. I did." She'd packed her camping gear last night. She just had to remember to grab her provisions from the fridge before she left. *Chill, Aubrey.* She blew out a long breath and glanced around her bedroom. "I think I have everything."

"You're only taking two carry-ons? You haven't even packed any dresses."

"Two is more than enough. They do have a laundry machine at the villa." She twisted her lips to one side. "Hmm. Do you think I'll need dresses?"

"Take a couple of your cocktail dresses and cute sundresses just in case. You still have plenty of room in your luggage."

"Good idea." Aubrey stuck her head back in her narrow closet and riffled through her dress selection. "Are these good?"

"Yup. You look adorable in those." Tara pointed to the two dresses in Aubrey's left hand, then pointed to her right hand. "And those look sexy as hell on you."

After double-checking she'd packed everything on her list, Aubrey zipped up her bags and stood. Hot tears prickled her eyes, and her voice was thick with emotion when she said, "That's it, then. I'm off to Sequoia, then onto Bosque Verde."

"Think of it as a well-earned vacation, you workaholic." Tara wrapped her in her arms. "You're going to do great, and things will be fine here. Have a ton of fun, and keep me posted. In detail."

"Yes, ma'am." Unable to stop herself, she added, "I'll miss you."

"Of course you will." Tara sniffed daintily. "Now go already. I have beer to brew."

Her best friend walked her to her car, pulling one of her carry-ons. When she continued to hang on to her hand, Aubrey gently squeezed it. "I'll be fine, you big softy."

"I know, I know." Her ferocious Tara stood biting her bottom lip, the tip of her nose turning red. "I'm just so proud of you, Bree. You're really doing this."

"Thank you." She really had to leave before they started

bawling in the middle of the street. "I'll text you when I get to Bosque Verde."

Aubrey jumped onto her seat and drove away, her Jeep feeling heavier with her luggage and camping gear. She checked her rearview mirror again and again until Tara was only a speck on her driveway.

It was a gorgeous, blustery day with the sky an endless blue and the air bright with a hint of chill. Growing excitement thawed her nerves, and Aubrey shivered with anticipation. Even one night in open nature would do wonders for her stress and exhaustion. *Ugh.* She still couldn't believe how close she'd come to losing everything. *No, no, no. Go away, ugly thoughts.*

With the windows rolled down to let in the crisp wind and the ancient speakers blasting eighties' rock, Aubrey sang and danced all the way to the mountains. Her spirits were up in the clouds.

Entering the national park felt like coming home. The trees stood tall and proud like they were reaching for the sky. Driving on the well-worn dirt track into the park was smooth and easy, but Aubrey wanted to put her four-wheel drive to the test. She drove on until she found a familiar dirt path and turned into it. The ride took all her attention as her Jeep jumped and tilted on the rough terrain, and she loved it.

"Woo-hoo!"

Freedom tasted so very sweet until her Jeep emitted a wet belch and then a choking, metallic cough. When it started making weird Willy Wonka candy-machine noises, Aubrey had to face the facts. She carefully steered to a stop. Not a second too early, because it *putt-puttered* and died in the same instant.

"Crap! Crap! Crap!" Aubrey pounded her steering wheel in rhythm with her curses, but the dense redwoods swallowed her screams. With a ponderous sigh, she hopped out and took in her surroundings.

She'd suppressed her apprehension and doubts into a dark, dusty corner of her mind and convinced herself she was looking forward to her three-week adventure. Denial was working out swell until the relic known as her Jeep did the unthinkable. It chose *the* worst moment to puff its last cloud of smog.

The picture-perfect day mocked her as she stood with her hands on her head. She'd wanted to unwind and take some time to prepare herself for whatever lay ahead. Now she was stranded on the way up to the giant redwoods with no internet access and one flickering bar of phone reception. Her attempts to call Tara proved useless.

It was barely past noon, so she had plenty of sunlight left. She could either hike up or down to search for the nearest ranger station, or she could sit tight and wait for someone to spot her. The latter option wasn't very sound since she'd driven off the main road, opting to use the dirt trails that led to her favorite camping spot.

Aubrey yelped when her phone rang and scared away some poor birds. Her forehead creased when she saw who was calling.

"Landon?"

"Why haven't you been answering your phone?"

His low growl made her back stiffen, and a sharp retort formed on her tongue, but then she remembered her predicament. The fight shuffled out of her in a single-file line.

"I picked it up every time it rang, which is, like, this once." She sighed—a small, forlorn sound in the vast mountains.

"What's going on?" Landon wasn't growling anymore, but the edge in his voice still could've sliced metal. Fortunately, the reception cut in and out, so she didn't feel too intimidated. "Your phone has been going straight to voice mail for the last hour. I finally called the brewery, and Tara told me you left a day early. Where are you? Are you okay?"

"It's hard to say for sure. I'm somewhere in Sequoia National Park."

The pause lasted several seconds. Aubrey frowned at her screen, but the call hadn't dropped. Landon saved her from saying *hel-lo-oo* in the nick of time.

"You drove to Sequoia in your ancient Jeep?" He took care to enunciate each word.

"How do you know about my ancient Jeep?"

"I saw it parked in a designated space for the Sugar Goddess at Comfort Zone. I'm assuming that's you." The static made him sound worlds away. Worlds away and frustrated. "And you're avoiding my question."

"Yes, I drove my Jeep out here." Pushing her poor old car up a mountain wasn't the smartest call, but his tone grated on her nerves. "I decided to take a detour to enjoy a night outdoors. Do you have a problem with that?"

"Yes, since you don't even know where you are," he said.

Aubrey chewed her lower lip, annoyed at her outburst. Logic dictated that it wasn't his fault she was stranded in the wilderness. She considered not telling him about her situation, but being petty wouldn't help anyone, especially her.

"Calm down, Landon. I know where I am, but I can't draw a map and mark it with an X." She hopped into the driver's seat with her feet sticking out the open door. "I've encountered a small problem."

"What is it? Are you okay?" The genuine concern in his tone made her heart gallop offbeat.

"Why do you keep asking if I'm okay? Of course I'm okay. Everything's fine." Aubrey gulped some mountain air. "Except that I'm broken down on a dirt trail in the middle of the forest."

This time, the silence lasted longer.

"Hel-lo-oo?"

"Do you have water? Anything to eat?"

"Yes and yes." Just because she'd gotten herself into a stupid situation didn't mean she was stupid. Temper crept into her voice. "I have all my camping gear with me. I could live happily as a wild woman for weeks if I wanted to."

"Okay. Stay put, and I can . . . Shit. I can't come for you until I know where the hell you are."

"Wait. We're talking on the phone," she said with relief and excitement.

"I'm aware of that," he said flatly.

"It means I finally have reception." She pulled her phone away from her ear and went into her map app. "Bingo. Here, I'm sending you my GPS location."

"I got it." They both sighed into the phone. "I'll be there in three hours."

"You can just send a tow truck tomorrow. I'm okay to stay the night."

"I'll be there in two hours and forty-seven minutes."

"Fine. I don't have plans to go anywhere."

Her wry response was met with silence. They'd been disconnected. If she'd lost connection three minutes earlier, she might've been stranded indefinitely. A shiver jerked its way down her torso. That was a close call.

Aubrey went to dig through her trunk for a paperback she'd seen rolling around. She'd probably read it already, but a good romance deserved multiple reads. Once she knew help was coming, the day went much better. The birds forgave her and came back to sing. The breeze rustled through the leaves in harmony. Aubrey had always loved the mountains. Her surroundings filled her with serenity, and she was quite content to sit on the roof of her Jeep, munching on some white chocolate cranberry cookies.

Aubrey looked up from the book as the sun yawned after a long day and the shadows stretched their tired limbs. The beautiful love story had fast-forwarded time. Putting aside her book, she inhaled the mountain air, appreciating her serene surroundings until a steroid-overloaded muscle car came roaring toward her, barely missing her Jeep.

She gagged and spat out her lovely snack as a dust storm engulfed her. Between her *peh-peh-peh* and stinging eyes, she didn't see Landon until he grabbed her by the waist and lifted her off the roof. She reached and clung to his shoulders.

"What the hell's the matter with you?" he said, his eyes dark as the night forest.

Her feet dangled as he held her hostage in the air. Angry Landon was downright intimidating. He'd probably welcome a throwdown with a mama black bear to burn off his fury. His face was inches from hers, and his rough breathing heated her skin.

She was so turned on.

Aubrey wasn't right in the head, but lord have mercy, she wanted him. His lips were pressed into a straight line, and she wanted to kiss them until they resumed their usual shape— wide, generous, and *nom nom* on the bottom.

Her tongue flicked out to wet her lips, and she clasped her hands around his neck without conscious thought. Landon's eyes widened, the anger and relief behind them withering in the heat of desire. His palpable yearning entwined with hers, leaving her winded.

Without breaking eye contact, Landon lowered her to the ground, letting her body slide down his. She bit her lip to stop from moaning. He leaned in, and her eyes fluttered shut. For a long moment, there was only silence and stillness. Aubrey opened one eye to see what was going on, and her cheeks heated up. Landon had pulled away and was staring intently at her. Was he wondering why the hell she had her eyes closed? She quickly stepped around him to create distance.

"What's the matter with *me*? Nothing. Except you tried to kill me with your dust storm–generating muscle car and insane stunt driving." Aubrey rubbed her face with her hands to pull herself together. "You scared the crap out of me, and you almost flattened my Jeep."

"It's an Alfa Romeo Giulia, and it's nowhere near your car."

"Is she an old flame?"

"What?" He looked thoroughly flummoxed.

"You named your car 'Julia.' I figured she was your first love or something."

"Giulia with a G, not—never mind." A vein near his temple was pulsing ominously, and Aubrey was enjoying herself immensely.

Of course it was an Alfa Romeo Giulia. She'd recognize that V-shaped grill anywhere. When she was a teenager, the Alfa Romeo 159 had been her favorite vehicle to steal from her father for a joyride. He'd collected cars like he collected women. There were never enough, and a new model always caught his eye.

She hated how her father intruded her thoughts at random moments, casting a heavy net of loss and bleakness around her. And as irrational as it was, she really hated Landon having anything in common with him. Even a stupid car.

"Thank you for coming for me," she said, shoving aside her irritation.

"You're welcome," he said softly, surprise and shy pleasure marking his features. "So where do you want to set up camp?"

"What?" Aubrey shook her head as she fought the effects of the Smile.

Her brain did a hard shutdown in preparation for a reboot. *Bing, bing. Reboot complete.* Landon had found her. He'd barreled down the road, yelled at her, and done a bit of the caveman thing, but hadn't kissed her. Her eyes narrowed with renewed annoyance.

"You said you wanted to camp before going to Bosque Verde." He jammed his hands into his pockets and smoothed his expression into a loaded blank. "Show me where you were headed. I want to see this place you'd endangered yourself for."

"For the record, I did not endanger myself. I know these woods well, and my Jeep doesn't make a habit of dying on me." *Since I don't drive it more than five miles a day.* She should stop explaining herself. It made her sound guilty. "Speaking of my car, I can't just leave it in the woods."

"Why not? It looks as though it belongs here—a primeval relic revered by the forest."

"Feeling poetic, are we?"

"I made arrangements to have it retrieved." Landon shrugged. "It'll be repaired and returned to Weldon."

"A tow truck will ramble up the mountain to find it in the middle of nowhere?" Aubrey smacked her forehead with her palm. "It's so simple."

"Yes, it is." His raised brow accentuated his arrogant, perplexed expression, and her lips pressed into a thin line.

Cocky bastard.

"Could you pop the trunk?" he said as though they were done with the topic. She complied wordlessly, and he grabbed her bags and headed toward his car. *Seriously?*

"I can't afford to have someone come all the way up here and then drive out to Weldon." She hefted her tent onto her shoulder and grabbed her duffel bag. Landon reached out to take her load, but she marched past him and dropped them into his trunk. "It'll cost a fortune."

"I took care of it," he said over his shoulder as he went for the rest of her stuff. She followed him. "Getting you to Bosque Verde on time and in one piece is more important to me. To the show, I mean."

"Okay," she nearly yelled, throwing her hands up in the air. "Fine."

He chose to "take care of it," and she couldn't undo it, and she certainly didn't have the money to repay him. She and Tara read during their recon that he'd sold a food blog for millions of dollars in his twenties. He probably had money to burn. Besides, he could expense it to the show as "guest chef rescue fees."

Aubrey gathered all the blankets under one arm and carried the grocery bag in her free hand. When Landon pulled out the cooler, his back and biceps flexing, her trunk was empty at last. She dropped off her armload in his trunk and hid her keys in the Jeep's glove compartment, then hesitated. She doubted anyone would happen upon it, but she took her vehicle registration and insurance documents just in case.

"Which way?" Landon said once they were both seated and buckled up.

"You see that fork in the road a few yards away?"

"No, I see trees and dirt."

"Fine." She sighed a short *ha*. The universal sound of forbearance. "You see where the trees thin a little in two directions? Go left and follow the road."

"Are you sure we won't drive off a cliff?"

"No," she said morosely. "Prepare to plunge to your death."

Landon's laughter filled the car as he maneuvered through

the narrow, bumpy path, and Aubrey couldn't hold back her smile. She was in a ridiculous situation of her own making, and being surly to the man who'd dropped everything to come to her rescue was plain rude of her.

"Wait," she said in a hushed tone, her pulse kicking into a sprint. His intent didn't dawn on her until they reached the campsite. "You're not planning on staying, are you?"

"How else are you going to get to Bosque Verde tomorrow?" His brows dipped low over his eyes. He was obviously reassessing her IQ.

Aubrey frowned back, questioning her intelligence herself. He had the only working car between them. Of course he was staying. He stepped out of the car, and she did the same before he could come around and open the door for her.

A campfire dinner with stars spilling out of the sky. A shared conversation—softened to a whisper in deference to the majesty of nature. Knees brushing, fingers tangling, and . . . *Sweet Lord.* She could *not* endure a night in the woods with him.

"Do you even have camping gear?" she asked.

"I didn't exactly have time to pack before coming to rescue you."

"Rescue me? Oh, please." She couldn't pull off her blasé attitude since he did kind of rescue her. "Either way, you don't have any camping gear. No gear, no camping. Let's just drive to Bosque Verde now."

"You and I drove close to three hours to get here. Why waste a perfectly good opportunity to unwind?"

"But . . . but . . ."

"Do you have a tent?"

Aubrey nodded while trying to figure out what game he was playing.

"I'm sure you could fit one more person in it." Landon

squinted at the sky. "We should set up before the sun goes down."

"It could get into the forties at night," she said, her voice pitched louder than necessary. "You'll freeze to death without a sleeping bag."

"I doubt you'll let me die." Landon perused her body from head to toe and then back to her warm face. *Is he planning to use me as a heat pack?* He held her gaze for a second too long before turning away. "I saw you bring a stack of blankets from the Jeep. Those should do fine."

"Fine," Aubrey huffed. If he wasn't nervous about being squished into a tent with her, then neither was she. Well, she was, but she could stop anytime she wanted. Just click off the nervous switch. There. Done.

You are not irresistible, Landon Kim.

———

Where the hell are these supposed to go? Landon stared down at the two tent rods in his hands.

"Let me guess. You weren't a Boy Scout," Aubrey said, her laughter trilling like silver bells. "I told you I'll pitch the tent."

He glowered at her. "I'm trying to contribute."

He'd never slept in a tent before. Growing up by the beach, he could ride the waves and scuba dive like a semiaquatic mammal. He was also an excellent skier. All in all, he was athletic and outdoorsy—just not a freaking Boy Scout. *Does preferring a comfortable bed make me a wimp?*

He sneaked a glance toward Aubrey. She'd stopped laughing, but the corners of her mouth trembled suspiciously. For the twentieth time, he wondered what had possessed him to insist on camping. It was rash. Impulsive. He didn't do rash or impulsive. Not anymore. That was his old self. A chip off the old block. Bitterness-like crushed aspirin-filled him. He blinked rapidly, pushing away uninvited thoughts of his father.

"You can contribute by making dinner." Aubrey bit her lips then tucked her chin, doing a very poor job of hiding her amusement.

"With pleasure," he said without hesitation.

Despite his wounded pride, Landon grinned. He enjoyed her laughter even though it was at his own expense. Scraping up what was left of his dignity, he sat on a nearby stump to watch Aubrey work.

I'm going to cook for her. The realization sneaked up on him with the swiftness of a pickpocket. It happened so quickly, he wasn't sure how to feel. All these years, he'd refused to cook for anybody, including himself. His sudden decision to upend his self-imposed rule should've left him shaken to the core, or maybe come with a life-altering epiphany. Instead, he felt calm as though cooking for Aubrey was the most natural thing to do.

While Landon processed his decision, Aubrey had the tent set up in fifteen minutes flat. He whistled under his breath. "I can see you've done that a few times."

"When I was little, my dad used to whisk me away for impromptu camping trips." She stilled for a second, then shrugged. "And living in Weldon, it's hard not to take advantage of the outdoors. It's practically in your backyard."

Landon pursed his lips. *Another one with daddy issues?* He shelved away the question for another day to address a more pressing issue. The tent was about the size of his coat closet with a lower ceiling.

"Do you think I'll fit in there?" he asked. He didn't mind squeezing into a tiny tent with Aubrey, but keeping his hands off her would be torture.

"Don't worry. Guys bigger and taller than you have slept in it without trouble."

He gave himself whiplash, snapping his head toward her. Her profile told him nothing of her intent, but imagining Aubrey with big, tall men rubbed him the wrong way. Rubbed him raw. *Goddamn it*. Was he jealous? No, because that would be ridiculous.

"If you say so." He contorted his face into what he hoped was a smile. "Thanks for saving me from sleeping like a pretzel in my car."

"Sure thing, I guess. You sort of invited yourself." Her grin softened the bite of her words, and his lips spread into a genuine smile. They stood grinning at each other until Aubrey abruptly broke eye contact and glanced at the sky. "We should get the campfire going. It'll get dark soon."

"On it."

He went to his Alfa Romeo and grabbed a bundle of firewood Aubrey had brought. She tugged out a small folding table beside him. After scouting for a spot, she set up the cooking gear on the table for their makeshift kitchen. Meanwhile, Landon rummaged through the rest of the provisions and grocery bags with feigned nonchalance. He couldn't find the lighter for the campfire.

Her brows drawn together, Aubrey stood from her log as though to help, and Landon's search grew frantic. He'd rather rub two damp branches all night than ask her for the fucking lighter. His humiliation quota was filled for the day. Then he saw it. The damned thing was hidden between some popcorn and marshmallows. When he straightened with a handheld lighter wearing a Howdy Doody grin, Aubrey doubled over with laughter, pretending to have a coughing fit.

"I could find you a flint and a rock, if you'd prefer," she said, her voice hoarse.

After glaring at her with as much indignation as he could muster, he bent to light the fire to hide his grin. He was going to get her back for that. Later. He was busy at the moment. Utilizing his common sense, he crumpled up some newspaper and nestled it inside the piled wood and lit it. After a few minutes, the campfire crackled and burned robustly, and he took a moment to congratulate himself.

Time to prepare a dinner for two.

"I could make cassoulet," he said, digging out chicken and sausage from the cooler.

He rummaged through the grocery bag and grabbed a couple of cans of beans. There was a random carrot, slightly past its prime, half an onion wrapped in plastic, and a bulb of garlic at the bottom of the bag. She must've cleaned out her fridge for her time away from home.

Landon washed and trimmed the vegetables next to his makeshift cutting board and then reached for the knife. *Let's hope I remember how to use this thing.* It was the first time he'd held a kitchen knife since he'd given up his dream. The outdoor setting somehow made the moment feel less intimidating. Campfire cooking was about having fun. There was no reason to take a trip down memory lane. He didn't need fanfare for his comeback.

Then he was back. It was where he was meant to be. His hands knew exactly what needed to be done, and he moved without hesitation, grabbing this and throwing in that. When he stopped, a pot of cassoulet was ready to go on the fire. Except for the most important ingredient.

"Aubrey, you said you had red wine, right?"

"Yes." Her voice was breathy, and her cheeks appeared pink. Wordlessly, she ducked into the tent.

Did he do something wrong? *Shit.* He hadn't said a word to

her for twenty minutes, lost in his own world. Aubrey returned and handed him a bottle of red. He opened his mouth to apologize for ignoring her, but she spoke first.

"I'm starving," she said, her eyes roaming his face and then dropping to his hands. Then her gaze jerked up and landed on his mouth.

Oh, God. Did watching him cook turn her on? *I should cook something else. Right now.*

"For food. I want food. Not other stuff."

Landon stirred some wine into the pot, pretending not to know what she'd meant. He hoped the falling dusk hid his hard-on and that the moment would pass. But Aubrey stood transfixed, her breath coming in quick puffs, and his gaze slid to her parted lips. They were impossible to ignore when he was famished himself. He craved to taste her. *Just one kiss.*

"I'd better put the blankets inside for you," she said with urgency worthy of an alien-invasion announcement. He watched her duck inside the tent with desire twisting his stomach into painful knots. If she'd stayed a second longer, they would've been doomed before the first shoot.

7

The sun began its slow descent, blanketing the interior of the tent in its muted twilight. Grateful for the seclusion, Aubrey heaved a deep breath but choked before she could exhale. She'd forgotten to bring in the blankets from Landon's car.

Crap. She gnawed on her bottom lip and paced the entire four-step length of the tent.

There was no way she was going back out there. That would be equivalent to announcing she was a horny idiot. *Hey, I made up the blanket excuse to get away from you, but I was so turned on that I forgot to grab them.*

With her hands on her hips, Aubrey surveyed the tent as though all her marbles had spilled inside it. After a few deep breaths, she reached a decision. She hated to do it, but there was no other choice. As her father would say, it was the civilized thing to do. Her skin crawled at the thought of the man, but she had to channel the socialite she was raised to be. Chin held high, she lifted the flaps and glided toward the campfire. Landon straightened from the bubbling pot to watch her approach.

"Do you need some help?" she said.

That's right. She was going to pretend nothing happened and hide under the comfortable quilt of politeness. *What sexual tension?*

"No, thanks. It just needs to sit and simmer for a few more minutes." Landon responded with equal politeness in contrast to the knowing smirk playing around his mouth. "Wine?"

The stars were taking stage in the sky, preparing to steal the night. The crisp mountain air played with the tendrils of her hair and caressed the nape of her neck. One false step and her clothes would melt off. Throwing wine into the mix would be the stupidest thing she could possibly do.

"Sure. Why not?" *Yup.* She was a dumbass.

Aubrey took tiny, measured sips of wine as Landon stood to ladle the cassoulet into some wide mugs. He handed one to her and settled next to her with the other.

"Be careful. It's hot."

She breathed in the decadent aroma of wine, thyme, and rich, stewed chicken and veggies. The sausages added a smoky layer to the hearty stew, thickened with soft beans. Her mouth watered, and her stomach urged her to face-dive into the bowl. At the risk of burning her tongue, she blew on a heaping spoonful and filled her mouth with cassoulet.

"I had to improvise quite a bit and make do without some ingredients." Landon watched her with shy anticipation. "Do you like it?"

"Ooh me gah," she groaned as her eyes slid shut. She couldn't handle more sensory input. The bite of cassoulet burst with a rainbow of flavors and textures that required her undivided attention. Warm, creamy, fragrant, and just a touch salty. It was wonderful—kind of like sublime butter except she could eat bowls of it without censure. "I can't believe you made *this* out of the random ingredients I brought. I call dibs on licking the pot clean."

"I'm going to take that as a yes," he said in a warm, intimate voice. His blush melted her heart, and the Smile blinded her.

Satiated with wine and cassoulet, the campfire lured Aubrey into a sleepy stupor. When Landon put his arm around her and pulled her close, she yawned and tucked her head against his shoulder. His thumb drew small circles on her shoulder, and she nearly purred. *Dangerous?* Probably, but nothing short of Armageddon was going to make her leave the fleeting haven by his side.

"Should I tell you a scary story?"

Aubrey bolted upright and covered both ears. *Or a scary story.*

"No. Never. Absolutely not."

"Okay. Okay." Landon chuckled, tugging her hands down. "I just thought that's what people do when they go camping."

"Well, I don't." She rubbed the heebie-jeebies from her arms. "I watched *The Exorcist* when I was ten, and it scarred me for life. I haven't been able to watch or read or listen to anything *evil* since then."

"I'm with you there. *The Exorcist* is the creepiest movie ever made."

"Right? The kid who could see dead people has nothing on the vomit-spewing, head-spinning girl." Aubrey shivered. "Now stop talking about it. Or I won't be able to sleep for weeks."

"Sure. Let's just enjoy the fire."

With a soft sigh, Aubrey reclaimed the prime real estate she'd just vacated. Landon draped his arm around her shoulders, tugging her closer.

"When I was in high school, a bunch of my friends went camping and took a picture of their bonfire." His voice was deep and soothing. Aubrey relaxed against him. "But when they developed the picture, there was a man standing inside the flames—"

"Oof!" Aubrey shoved him away and socked him in the arm. His full-blown laughter sounded delicious and warmed her all the way down to her toes. So she threw another punch at his shoulder for being so freaking hot.

Before she could pummel him some more, Landon caught one of her wrists in each hand. His grip wasn't tight but firm enough for her to feel the strength he held in check. She tugged and pulled to test his hold. Futile. Her only two options were headbutting him or biting him. As though he could read her game plan he grinned and wrapped her arms behind her back. Thanks to the momentum of their tug-of-war, Aubrey fell into his arms with a small yelp.

His laughter and smile faded, and the tenor of their battle shifted, sending a thrill down her spine. The chemical reaction of skin against skin burned their teasing and flirting into ashes, and desire whirled around them. She willed her eyes to shoot poison daggers at him, but they kept trying to flutter shut. Heat spread up her neck and face, and bolts of electricity shot through her veins.

Landon drew her closer to him, his expression stark and hungry. Releasing her hands, he pulled her flush against him. She should have pushed him away, but she sat transfixed. Inches apart, they breathed each other in—frustrated and desperate. Heady forces drew their lips closer, and she closed her eyes, overwhelmed by her need for him. And as spontaneously as their chemistry erupted into the atmosphere, it shattered with a sharp crack of a splitting log.

He dropped his hands and shot to his feet, turning his back to her. The fire had shifted with the wood collapsing on itself, and the dancing flames wove surreal shadows between the trees. He crossed his arms tightly over his chest, and the muscles in his shoulders and back visibly tensed.

"I'm going to turn in," Aubrey said in a small voice. She'd wanted him to kiss her, which was reckless and stupid. *You know what's worse?* She was hurt he'd had enough control to stop the train wreck, and disappointment overshadowed the relief she should've been feeling.

Landon pivoted toward her and raised his hand as though to touch her, and her breath caught in her throat. But he dropped his arm to his side, and Aubrey trudged away and slipped inside the tent—churning, contradictory emotions twisting her up. She zipped the entrance shut and sat uncertainly, not knowing what she should do next.

Her brain finally instructed her to go to sleep. After rubbing some toothpaste on her teeth and scrubbing her face with Cetaphil, she crawled into her sleeping bag and shut her eyes, expecting to toss and turn for hours. But before her mind grew loud with impossible questions, fatigue dragged her into a blissful, dreamless sleep.

The sun flitted through the green walls of the tent. Aubrey cracked open an eyelid and then closed it again, huddling deeper into her sleeping bag. She yawned with lusty abandon and stretched her legs to her tippy toes. Last night had been freakishly cold for the time of year, and the mountain air had frozen the tip of her nose. She loved it. Hiding from the morning chill in her cozy cocoon felt decadent.

Wait. I'm not alone. Memories of last night rushed back. She bolted upright like a mummy awakening from a sarcophagus.

Her warm haven morphed into a constricting bond as she fought to free herself. There was no sign of him in the tent. All she saw was a mountain of blankets.

Hang on a second.

Landon must have brought in her blankets to use last night, but she certainly didn't have enough to make a mountain. Aubrey scooted over on her bottom and peeked under the mound. Landon was curled up in a ball, wearing his socks, parka, and hood. *Oh no.* The jumble of throws was no match against the freezing temperature.

Curious to see if he was alive under there, she prodded his side with her toes. When he didn't budge, she knelt beside him and searched for his buried face. Faster than she could screech, he pinned her under him.

"Sleep well?" he growled.

"Umm." She cleared her throat, her heart pitter-pattering. "It got a little colder than I'd expected. Were you okay?"

"Yeah. Sure. The only part of my body I can feel are my jaws, thanks to my chattering teeth, but otherwise, I'm swell."

"I told you we shouldn't camp without proper gear." She reached out and put her hand on his cheek. His eyes widened, but she was too distracted to feel self-conscious. "Okay. Let's thaw you out."

Aubrey climbed over him and burrowed into the blankets. Landon stiffened, which was impressive for a block of ice. Without allowing herself to ponder his reaction, she pressed herself against his broad back and wrapped her arms around his waist. He was much too tall for her to spoon properly, but it would do. She buried her nose in the crook of his neck and tucked her hands inside his parka, flattening them across his chest.

"What are you doing, Aubrey?" His husky question rumbled against her palms.

Getting revenge? He'd succeeded in getting her hot and bothered the night before. He deserved a generous sample of sexual frustration. Aubrey grinned with devious delight. But no. She'd hardly planned this—for revenge or otherwise. He was freezing, and she wanted to share her warmth. Like a Saint Bernard but without the mini-keg of whiskey.

After a while, the tension ebbed out of his back. She breathed him in and sighed into his neck. He smelled delicious—all man, wood, and fire. Landon dug his hands into his jacket, clasping them over hers. Aubrey squeaked at the cold touch, but he tightened his grip and pulled her closer.

He thawed in her arms, and she melted against him. Aubrey refused to analyze the warmth and security the moment wrought. *Happy* was too simplistic a word to describe what she felt, but maybe happiness was meant to be this overwhelming.

Her smile slipped when Landon shifted and she found herself blinking into his eyes. Before she could figure out what was happening, he grasped the back of her knee and drew her leg over his hip. His hard length pressed against her stomach, and her breath caught in her throat.

He stared at her with undisguised desire, and her insides tightened in response. But when he lowered his face toward hers, her mind filled with a fog of confusion. Aubrey startled and placed her hands on his chest, but couldn't quiet summon the will to push him away.

"Don't," she whispered, sounding as unsure as she felt.

Landon stopped with his lips only an inch from hers. Reckless desire gripped his features, but he slackened his hold, giving her the choice to break contact. Seconds ticked by in slow motion, and she teetered on the edge of giving in. He lay absolutely still as her eyes darted across his face, her indecision pushing toward panic.

Releasing a shuddering sigh, he kissed the top of her head and gently set her away from him. Then he pushed himself off the ground and walked out of the tent without a backward glance.

The lighthearted mood they'd shared the night before evaporated in the morning sun. They packed up early and left for their journey to Bosque Verde. The silence in the car smothered Landon like a thick blanket, heavy and suffocating. Time dragged as if it were wading through thick batter. The three-hour drive would feel like a decade if they kept this up.

Aubrey had been polite but quiet all morning, and he played along with the make-believe that nothing had happened in the tent. It was technically true. Nothing irreversible had happened. *Keep telling yourself that, and maybe you can convince yourself that you're not screwed.*

Landon pretended to give the highway his undivided attention. He lounged in his seat, pushed far back to accommodate his height, and rested one hand lightly on the steering wheel. He was the picture of relaxation except for the muscle in his jaw that had been ticking nonstop for the last forty miles.

He stole a sideways glance at Aubrey, who was busy wringing her hands and worrying her lips raw. His efforts to appear nonchalant were overkill. She was lost in her thoughts and wasn't even aware of his existence. He wanted to hold her hands still and swipe his thumb across her bruised lips. Landon doubted she'd appreciate his ministrations when she was so skittish around him.

It hit him that he had to spend weeks working with the *irresistible* woman and he had to resist her at all costs. And if this morning was any indication, he was in serious trouble. With their careers on the line, he had to get his shit together. He refused to tarnish Aubrey's professional reputation. His plan was about righting mistakes, not creating more. His lack of control was unacceptable. But his chances of success were so bleak, it would be funny if the cost of failure weren't so high.

"This looks brand new." She broke the silence so suddenly, Landon shot her a surprised glance. He raised an eyebrow—because he didn't think he could speak without his voice breaking—then returned his gaze to the windshield. He hoped she thought he was being aloof, not nervous enough for his knees to knock together. "The Alfa Romeo. Is it new?"

"Yes."

"What happened to your old car?"

"My old car?"

"Yeah, the one that blew a tire on the freeway?"

"Oh, that was my editor Craig's car." Landon shrugged. "I haven't owned a car for almost ten years."

"Really?" Aubrey stared at him with her nose crinkled. "Why? How did you survive in California without a car?"

"I travel eight months a year for work. It didn't make sense for me to buy one only to have it sit in the garage."

Aubrey nodded as though digesting the new information. "Then why did you get this one?"

"I changed my mind. It's a damn nuisance not to have a car for the four months I'm home." Landon smiled a little, ridiculously flattered by her attention.

"So true," she said, her expression earnest. "And it only took you ten years to figure that out. No wonder you're so successful."

He burst out laughing so hard his seat belt locked and restrained him from bumping his head on the steering wheel.

She grinned at his reaction, relaxing for the first time all day. They shared a brief, less stifling silence as the scenery changed outside the car.

"Maybe you want to come home," she murmured almost to herself.

Landon glanced at her before answering glibly, "I *am* thirty-four. I guess it won't hurt to embrace stability."

"Are you sure you're up for it?" Mischief glittered in her silver eyes.

She's fucking adorable.

"Well, let me know if you ever need any advice."

"You want *me* to ask *you* for advice about adulting?" he said, not bothering to hide his grin. "What are you? All of twenty-three?"

"Why do people get uppity about being older than somebody? Is aging a personal accomplishment?" Her tone chilled by ten degrees. "I'm actually twenty-seven, and I have plenty of advice for someone like you."

"Someone like me? How do you figure?"

"A man who gallivanted around the world for a decade without so much as a car waiting for him. I'd say you've been living in never-never land."

"So I'm Peter Pan and you're Wendy, all grown up?" He forced out a strained chuckle to hide his unease. Her teasing had hit too close to home.

"Precisely."

"Well, you must've collected some crazy anecdotes in your long life."

"Oh yes. Especially from the good ol' days." She patted his shoulder, empathy oozing from her solicitous frown. "I'm here for you, kid. Anytime. Just ask."

8

The sound of Landon's deep, rich laughter lifted the weight that had been crushing Aubrey's chest. Optimism lifted her spirits. *Maybe he and I could be friends.* Yes, he'd been her hot one-night stand and her mortal enemy, but now could he be an ally? A friend? With the first third of her compensation, Aubrey had paid her general contractor to get Comfort Zone's expansion on track. He resumed the renovations and would obtain the necessary permits once all the appliances were installed. If Landon was right, the TV appearance would bury the negative review and bring more customers than she'd lost. It was hard to be enemies with a man who was hell-bent on helping her.

Spending time in the wine country to create new recipes sounded like a dream. Her portion of the filming would only last about a week at the end of her stay, so she wasn't going to worry about that too much. If she could forget about her infatuation with Landon, she would have an amazing time at Bosque Verde. As simple as that. Once they became friends, everything would be wonderful.

To start off Operation Friendship on the right step, Aubrey

turned and smiled brightly at Landon. He returned her smile, briefly taking his eyes off the road. *There. That wasn't so hard, right?*

They drove in sufficiently comfortable silence, only stopping once for an In-N-Out Burger and restroom break. Her animal-style cheeseburger—with extra melted cheese, grilled onions, pickles, and dressing—was messy, juicy heaven. Their conversation was on the bland side but not too weird. Comfortable was good. Bland was great. All she'd needed was a game plan and a positive attitude.

Once they were back on the road, Aubrey was surprised at how quickly the rest of their drive went. The streets leading up to the hills grew narrower and narrower until Landon turned onto a nameless dirt road.

"We're almost there," he said, glancing briefly at her.

They were halfway up the long, curvy road before she spotted the gorgeous hacienda sitting on the hilltop like a bright, sun-drenched haven. She couldn't look away from it. When they pulled into the driveway, there was a silver Land Rover parked out front.

"Here we are," Landon announced unnecessarily and unfurled his long frame from the car. Aubrey was still admiring the stunning villa when he opened the door for her. "I'll get your bags and meet you at the door."

Too tired to object, Aubrey murmured her thanks and made her way to the entrance. She raised her hand to knock, but the door swung open before her knuckles reached their target. Her hand still poised midair, she blinked as her eyes adjusted to the relative darkness of the interior.

"Please come in," a handsome silver-haired man with a slight French accent urged. "You must be Aubrey."

She only had time to smile her thanks when Landon called

out from behind, "Lucien, I hope we didn't keep you waiting too long."

"No, no. Not at all. I got here only a few minutes ago." Lucien pumped Landon's hand and slapped his back enthusiastically. The bro hug. "It's good to see you, my friend."

"It's been too long." Landon craned his neck and surveyed the villa. "Where's Aria?"

"Come," his friend said without answering Landon's question. "Let me show you to your rooms."

Rooms? The men walked ahead of Aubrey, speaking in lowered voices to each other, leaving Aubrey free to gawk at the beautiful interior of the house. Everything in it was obviously expensive, but it still felt rustic and welcoming with a cream, yellow, and brick-red interior.

Their voices remained muted, but the conversation grew fast and heated. Landon nearly knocked a ceramic vase off a side table, gesturing with hands full of her luggage. They were whisper-screaming, so Aubrey couldn't make out what was being said, but Landon looked murderous. A mountainous cactus sporting head-to-toe spikes would shrivel at his expression. Lucien improbably maintained an air of sophisticated ennui while facing his friend's fury.

At the top of the stairs, they turned into a wide hallway. She stole a peek at the nearest suite with a spacious bedroom, attached bathroom, and private balcony. Landon's broad shoulders rose and fell in a sigh as though preparing for an unpleasant task. He turned in slow motion to face her, and she got the awful feeling that the unpleasantness somehow involved her. Lucien shrugged apologetically and strode a few steps away.

"You could pick," Landon offered after a cursory look around. "Both suites are on this floor. I don't have a preference."

"What?"

Aubrey glared mutely at Landon, who dropped her bags and mussed his hair with both hands like he was trying to shake out a spider.

"Look, Aubrey. I don't like the situation any better than you do. It isn't how I'd planned our lodgings, but there's nothing I could do about it at this point. We're two reasonable adults. I'm sure we can share a three-thousand-square-foot villa without trampling each other."

"Reasonable adults? Sure. Why not?" She threw her hands out and nearly smacked Lucien, who'd quietly joined them again in the face. She was too worked up to stop and apologize. "We were perfectly reasonable during our campout, so this pro-tracted living situation shouldn't be a problem *at all.*"

Landon lifted his index finger and opened his mouth as if to argue and then wisely closed it. *That's right, buster.* He had nothing to say because she was right. He frowned instead, so she frowned back at him. They pretended they hadn't almost kissed, *multiple times,* in the mountains, because they weren't supposed to be in such close quarters again. But they were wrong. They were going to share a private villa for at least three freaking weeks. Just the two of them. With complete privacy. *How can he stand there and bullshit me about being reasonable adults?*

When the stare-off continued, Lucien cleared his throat. "I'm sorry, Aubrey. I'm afraid it's all my fault. My other villa became unexpectedly occupied."

"And by 'unexpectedly occupied,' he means Aria asked if she could stay in his villa, and he said yes, rolling over for a tummy rub." Landon snorted rudely, his anger subdued but close to the surface. "You promised that room to me, Lucien. Sure, Aria is, well, Aria, but damn it, man. You can't just give her everything she wants. Especially when you won't give her—"

"Aria had legitimate concerns about sharing this villa with Aubrey," Lucien interrupted with an icy mask that rivaled Landon's furious face on the terror-inducement scale. Aubrey might have made some noise at his statement, because he rushed to clarify, "Concerns about sharing the kitchen. She wants Aubrey to have unfettered access to the kitchen. It makes sense for each of them to have their own practice kitchen, so they don't need to worry about inconveniencing each other."

"What about inconveniencing us?" Landon waved his hand from himself to Lucien.

"Us? Who cares about us pushovers?" Lucien chuckled and then his smile turned sly. "If it would make you feel more comfortable, I'd be happy to switch places with you."

"Fuck you," he said glumly.

Ha ha. They were so fucking funny. *What an adorable bromance.* Seething, Aubrey raised her eyes to the ceiling and counted to ten. *This is happening. I'm going to be roommates with Landon for the next three weeks.* Her shoulders rose and dropped with a sigh of doom.

"I have dibs on the best room. Which one is it?"

"Well, if I were you, I'd pick the one farther down the hall." Lucien's voice was warm and sincere. "The patio faces the woods, and on some mornings, you can see visiting deer and rabbits."

"Thank you." Aubrey managed a small smile. "That sounds lovely."

"Not as lovely as you." Lucien bent to kiss her hand, and Aubrey blushed with shy pleasure.

"Even after thirty years in the States, we can't seem to knock the French ways out of you." Landon casually pulled Aubrey's hand free and led her down the hall to her room.

"Couldn't you find someplace else?" Outside of their host's earshot, Aubrey made a last-ditch effort to preserve her sanity.

"I could go back out after the three-hour drive and find myself a roach motel, but do you really think it's reasonable for me to do that when there's an open suite in *my friend's* villa?"

"Can't you at least sleep downstairs?"

"On the sofa?"

She felt a twinge of guilt. "Yes."

"I don't think that's a good idea."

His answer efficiently extinguished her guilt. "Why? It's huge. Two people could sleep on it."

"I sleep naked. Are you sure you want to walk down the stairs to find me sleeping on the sofa?"

Aubrey gasped, and her eyes nearly crossed as her brain flashed one sinful image of naked Landon after another. "No."

"I agree. It doesn't seem very professional." He dimpled at her. *Stupid. Evil. Dimple.*

"I really should stay with the rest of the crew."

"They're staying at an inn near the schoolhouse. Unfortunately, they don't offer a full kitchen. You still need a kitchen to work on your recipes, correct?"

"Fine," she ground out. "I'll sleep on the sofa."

Landon's eyes narrowed, and he took two long steps toward her. It took all her willpower to stand her ground. "And what do you wear to bed?"

"Excuse me?" Her voice was a mousy squeak. She wore satiny shorts and cami sets. They were a splurge, but she wanted to enjoy what little sleep she got. From a man's perspective, though, sexy bits of fabric could be more provocative than nudity. "Hmm. The thing is . . . Yeah."

Excuse me. Where's the nearest wall I can bang my head against? Instead of voicing her thoughts, she laughed—a lame, I've-dug-myself-into-a-hole laugh. Then Landon flared his nostrils like an angry bull and clenched his jaws tight enough to crack a molar. *What? Did a bee sting his ass?*

"You probably want to freshen up. I'll make us a light dinner so we can have an early night." He abruptly changed the subject in a stoic voice. Then he headed for his room without waiting for her response.

Aubrey walked into her suite and shut the door behind her, allowing her panic to rush through her. Landon's cool, detached demeanor left her baffled and oddly disappointed. Maybe she'd imagined his burst of temper. More than anything, her yearning for the man scared the bejesus out of her. Blood rushed to her head, and her heart beat out an ominous march. She couldn't stay here.

Would he notice if I sneaked out right now? She could steal his Alfa Romeo and make a run for it. *Brilliant.* Then, she could spend the night in the slammer with some interesting cellmates. They would probably turn out to be nice, ordinary people. *Grr.*

She was stuck. Stuck in a beautiful villa in a ridiculously romantic vineyard with a steaming hunk of man-beef. Her stomach growled loudly, and Aubrey rolled her eyes. *I didn't mean literal beef, you brainless organ.* But another, much more insistent brainless organ told her there was no way in hell she was going to keep her hands to herself. The most disturbing part was she wasn't entirely certain she wanted to.

Aubrey pushed herself off the door and walked farther into the room. She ran her fingertips over the Egyptian cotton bedding and thought of the four-post canopy bed she'd had as a little girl. She grew up surrounded by gratuitous opulence. Living in her cramped two-bedroom rental showed her how much she'd taken for granted. She sometimes missed the luxuries she'd left behind, but freedom was too high a price to pay for marble floors and crystal chandeliers.

When her paternal grandmother was alive, her father ran the family's upscale Korean markets from the corporate office. She had lovely memories of her early childhood. Her *hal-muh-nee* lived with them, and they were a close-knit family. Her parents were affectionate and always full of laughter. Aubrey was their only child, and she was adored by her parents and grandma.

It was when her grandmother passed away that things began to change. Her father worked longer and longer hours, and she sometimes wouldn't see him for days. But whatever he was doing, he was successful at it because they soon moved into what felt like a fairy-tale mansion. Aubrey loved the princess dresses and the elaborate parties she attended with her parents.

But gradually, her parents' angry, raised voices invaded her room night after night, and the laughter faded from their home. As she grew older, she stopped going to the parties. The dresses felt more like uniforms, and the parties were performances she didn't feel prepared for. Her father didn't seem to care whether she went or not. He grew aloof and distant, and her mom faded away. In the fog of their unhappiness, Aubrey grew invisible and was forgotten.

But that was all in her past. Aubrey left home to pursue her own life and never looked back. And she planned to do everything in her power to keep her dream alive.

She washed her hands and face in the bathroom, which was bigger than her bedroom in Weldon, and used a soft, thick towel to dry off. After hesitating for a second, she grabbed her lip gloss from her purse and quickly dabbed some on before going downstairs. When she walked into the spacious gourmet kitchen, she was surprised to find Lucien gone and Landon busy at the stove. Her heart fluttered.

It was just the two of them.

———

Lucien's cellar has better wine than most restaurants, but the man thinks eggs and cheese are the only relevant food components." Landon beckoned Aubrey to take a seat when she hesitated at the entrance. "We could go to the market tomorrow, if you'd like. But for tonight, I hope you're okay with a cheese omelet."

"As long as you're cooking. Eggs are so obedient when I'm baking, but they turn on me when I try to cook them any other way." She hopped onto a stool by the island. "Besides, we wouldn't want your CIA degree to go to waste."

"God forbid." He chuckled under his breath.

"So are you and Lucien close?"

"We *were*." Landon huffed through his nose.

He chopped the shallots with more force than necessary. He and Aubrey weren't roommates by accident. It stank of Aria's signature meddling. Her pretty excuse about kitchen-sharing was bullshit. He could've made them a simple time chart, for fuck's sake.

Landon regretted telling Aria about his night in Weldon. He wanted to explain why he couldn't have any further personal interaction with Aubrey. Perhaps Aria decided to ignore his logic because his voice betrayed his longing whenever he spoke about Aubrey. Whatever the case, she hadn't wasted any time initiating her matchmaking scheme.

The whole point was to fix his mistake, not add to it, and

this setup was not helping. *His* plan had been to stay at Lucien's place on the other side of the hill, but Aria had apparently highjacked his room. Lucien, of course, couldn't refuse Aria anything, even if it meant throwing Landon to the wolves.

When Aubrey cocked her head at him, he forced a smile. "We've been friends for years. Lucien owns Le Ciel vineyard and a winery in San Miguel. He recently had this villa built to use as a luxury bed-and-breakfast and an additional tasting room in Bosque Verde. When I mentioned you needed a place to stay with a full kitchen, he insisted you stay here."

"I wish I had friends who could lend me their fancy villas at the drop of a hat. I only get free beer." She snorted at her own joke.

"Free craft beer of the highest caliber. You have nothing to complain about."

"You're right. Tara spoils me." She sighed happily.

He chopped chives, whisked up eggs, and flipped omelets like he'd been unchained. The joy. The freedom. It all flowed back to him. After a few minutes, he noticed the quiet still-ness in the kitchen. Aubrey hadn't stirred or spoken while he cooked.

"Is that why you haven't followed your dream and opened your own restaurant?" she murmured as though she was think-ing out loud, her gaze far away.

"Is what why?" Landon wasn't sure he'd heard her right. Her lashes fluttered, and she focused her brown eyes on him.

"You didn't want to turn something you love so much into the dreaded four-letter word—*work*."

Landon's hands stilled at her words. *Something you love so much.* She saw so much of him in something as inconsequen-tial as tossing together an omelet. He couldn't decide whether he felt *seen* or exposed.

"People say when something you enjoy becomes your full-time job, the joy gets sucked out of it."

"You may be onto something," he said, avoiding her question.

"Well, those people don't know diddly-squat. Nothing could take away your love for cooking as long as you don't lose sight of what's important. Every time you cook, you have to remember you're nourishing people. Making them happy." She scrunched her nose as though searching for the right words. "If you cook for your customers with that in mind, then your love for cooking won't be stifled. *Work* only becomes a vile word when your goals change to money or fame or whatever else the world entices you with."

Even family.

He'd *had* to give up his dream—he'd had no other choice. Money and fame were never part of his goals, but life had stifled his love of cooking. He flinched as flickers of resentment against his family wove through his thoughts. *No.* His mother and Seth were not to blame for his choices. It was his decision, and he refused to regret it.

"I'm completely humbled, Ms. Choi. You truly are full of wise, grown-up advice." Hurt flashed in her eyes at his cynicism before she blinked it away. *Damn it. What the hell is wrong with me?*

Aubrey winked with forced humor. "You're learning, Grasshopper."

Her gentle teasing chastised him more effectively than a long lecture. Aubrey really was the grown-up between them. He opened his mouth to apologize for being a dick, but she wasn't done with him.

"Why did you stop cooking, Landon?" Her wide, calm eyes bored into his soul.

"We, my family, immigrated to the States when I was three. My father wanted more for his family." He swallowed, trying to hold his words back, but he couldn't stop the truth from spilling over. "A few years later, my parents bought a small house with a backyard. It had a big, sturdy tree to one side where my dad hung a swing. I spent all day in that backyard, becoming permanently muddy and scruffy. Then my little brother came along, and my life was perfect."

"You had a beautiful childhood." Aubrey waited for him to continue, wearing a wistful smile. She didn't seem to mind that his response didn't answer her question, and she realized he had more to say.

Landon brought out a bottle of chilled chardonnay and raised it in question. Aubrey shook her head and pointed at her sparkling water. He poured himself a glass while he gathered his thoughts.

"We had everything we needed, but my dad still wanted more. He dreamed up one scheme after another. 'To hit it big,' he'd say. Whatever he did, right or wrong, I hero-worshipped him. He was this strong, handsome man with faraway eyes and a booming voice filled with promises. I thought he made the world go around. *My* world, at least." Landon twirled his wineglass and watched the pale, gold liquid spin into a micro tornado. "Of course, his plans never panned out. They just got more expensive and outrageous after each failed attempt. Still, I believed that he would set everything right."

"Oh, Landon." She covered his hand with her own. Her sympathy washed over him like warm, tropical rain, improbably melting away layers of loss and guilt.

"By the time I was in high school, I worked odd jobs at restaurants to help out. My mom was working herself to an early grave to provide for our family while my father spent every cent she managed to save." The usual burn of betrayal and disappointed tore through him, but he felt stronger against it. Almost as though he could drown it out someday. "But I was lucky. I ended up falling in love with cooking. I worked as a line cook and moved up quickly, and then I created a food blog, writing about the chaos of a restaurant kitchen and the beautiful dishes born from its depth. I did well enough to give my mom a few hundred dollars a month and support myself through the CIA."

"Balancing all that must've been draining." Her hand tightened around his.

"It was worth it." After everything, it had truly been worth it. The memory brought a fond smile to his face. "By the time I finished my degree, the stars lined up for me. My blog was doing well, and I was offered a sous chef position at David Ferrand's restaurant in Oregon. It was a dream come true."

"What happened?" she whispered.

"My old man. He piled up debt as high as Kilimanjaro. Our house was mortgaged out, and with his latest bust, we were about to lose it. I couldn't bear to watch the house being taken away from my mother. She loved that house. She talked about growing old in it and having me and my brother visit with our own families someday." Landon found and held Aubrey's gaze, letting her anchor him. "I searched for ways to keep the house, but I found out my dad had dug himself into a hole too deep to crawl out of. He knew it, too, so he took off and left us to clean up his mess."

"Your hero should never let you down so thoroughly. You must've been devastated. I'm so sorry, Landon."

"I couldn't afford to feel sorry for myself. Mom and Seth needed me, so I did what had to be done. I refused Ferrand's offer and sold my blog to the highest bidder. I made enough money to pay off my father's debts and buy the house outright for my mom. That's how I traded in my kitchen knife for a mighty pen." His old wound seeped blood, and his voice came out a hoarse whisper. "I haven't cooked since then. For anyone."

Except you. His unspoken confession rang out between them, but his emotions were too raw and muddled to face *why*.

"Well, you have to make up for lost time." Aubrey said with a tremulous smile. "My dinner, please, Chef."

"Coming right up," he said as a boulder slid off his chest.

Relief coursed through him, and a stupid grin took over his face. He didn't understand his feelings, but at least he knew how to feed her. *Because that's what chefs do.*

9

Since Landon walked into Weldon Brewery, Aubrey's nights had been filled with vivid dreams of him, which left her spent. She'd all but forgotten what a good night's sleep felt like. *Well, it feels fan-freaking-tastic.* She remembered her head touching the down pillow last night, and when she opened her eyes, it was morning. She'd gotten eight hours of dreamless sleep.

"I just saw the most beautiful doe right outside my patio." Aubrey strode into the kitchen and found Landon slouched over a steaming mug in the kitchen. He grunted and waved in the direction of a coffeepot. "Woke up on the wrong side of the bed?"

He glanced at her with bleary eyes and gulped down his coffee like it was tequila after a hard day. Aubrey shrugged and maneuvered toward the coffee, giving him a wide berth. Humming under her breath, she searched the cupboards for a nice, big mug. She was filled to the brim with optimism, and she was ready to tackle anything that came her way—including a grumpy Landon.

"Do you really have time to chauffeur me around today?" Aubrey studied his hunched form. "More importantly, are you even capable of it? You can't seem to hold a civilized conversation, much less drive a motorized vehicle."

"For the love of God, woman. It's not even eight," he grumbled. His eyes dropped back to his mug as though his outburst had taken too much out of him.

Not a morning person, eh? In her giddy mood, she almost joked she'd made a narrow escape that night by sneaking out on him before he woke up. She stopped short, horrified at her own callousness. She hid her troubled expression under the awning of her lashes and silently chastised herself.

"Damn it." Landon raked his fingers through his hair. By the remorse on his face, he'd misread her expression and thought he'd hurt her feelings. "I didn't get much sleep last night. I promise to be better behaved once I finish my coffee."

"You're fine." She waved aside his apology, pouring herself a steaming mug of coffee and topping his off as well. "It's gorgeous outside. Let's drink our coffee on the porch."

Without further protests, Landon followed her outside and settled his six-foot-three-ish frame into a yellow-and-white chaise. Sinking into its twin, Aubrey sighed and soaked in the vast otherworldly hills spread out before them.

Compared to the dense green mountains surrounding Weldon, these hills appeared stark and desolate. They sizzled under the unforgiving sun by day and shivered against the coastal winds by night. The resilient way the stringy trees and the waving fields of grass persevered commanded respect as much as the grapes they cultivated within their depths.

"Tomorrow, I'll bake some sweet buns for breakfast." Eyes

sliding shut, she inhaled the steam rising from her mug and then took a sip. "This coffee deserves some company."

"Does that mean you'll wake up even earlier?"

Ooh, a complete sentence.

The caffeine seemed to be kicking in. He even managed a crooked smile.

"Ha ha. I'll do most of the prep work tonight so I can just pop them in the oven tomorrow morning. Wait and see. Even Oscar the Grouch would turn into Mr. Sunshine after some of my sweet buns."

"Are you always this humble?"

Aubrey stuck her tongue out at him. "I'm proud of my family legacy. It's my grandma's recipe."

"Your grandma?" Landon's gaze strayed to her lips as though waiting for another glimpse of her tongue.

Without conscious thought, she wet her suddenly dry lips and watched his pupils swallow the brown of his eyes. *Gah.*

"Mm-hmm." She cleared her throat, unnerved by the charge in the air. "My grandma taught me everything I know about baking."

"Comfort Zone's an amazing place. She must be proud of you."

His voice was a husky caress. Nervous energy fluttered through her, heat blossoming on her cheeks. Landon abruptly shifted his eyes to the horizon.

"She would've been, I think. I couldn't have opened Comfort Zone if it weren't for her."

"How so?"

"I used to travel a lot, too. Not as fancy as yours, but I'd visit a country and live there for a few months working odd jobs until I saved up enough money to move on to a different place. It was wonderful, but exhausting. It got old after a few years, but I didn't know how to come home."

"I know exactly what you mean," he said softly.

A flutter of happiness tipped the corners of her mouth. *Don't ask why I'm happy about that.* He mirrored her smile, and she forgot to breathe.

"Well, I finally came back because my grandma got sick," she continued, slightly out of breath. "In a lot of ways, I was closer to her than to my mom. I wanted to be by her side to send her off. When she passed away a few months later, she left me some money with a message."

"What kind of message?"

"Oh, something very short, but profound. 'Time to get baking, girlie!'"

"Sounds like you had the world's coolest grandmother."

"No doubt about it."

"Are you going to use the sweet bun recipe for the show?"

"Hold your tongue, devil. Didn't you hear me? It's our family legacy. That one's staying in my mind vault." And no smooth-talking, executive producer was going to extract the sweet bun recipe from her. "I already have some other ideas for my new desserts. That's why I wanted us to go wine tasting today. Mostly, ports and dessert wines. I have to make sure I can find the wines I imagined for the recipes."

She had a lot of work to do if she didn't want to embarrass herself on national television. Aubrey pinched her bottom lip and squished it between her fingers. A nervous habit.

"While the early bird may get the worms, there are no such advantages for humans when it comes to wine." Landon gently drew her hand away from her mouth and gave it a squeeze. Some of her panic subsided at his quiet reassurance. "Most tasting rooms don't open until 10:00 A.M. Let's go get some breakfast. You're going to need some food in your stomach to absorb all the alcohol you'll be consuming today."

Aubrey had been swishing a sip of red wine in her mouth for the last two minutes, waiting for Landon to turn his head. Her teeth were probably stained purple. While the spittoon was widely used in the tasting rooms, she was too embarrassed to spit in front of him. But she couldn't swallow either.

As luck would have it, this particular wine made Aubrey queasy. It wasn't bad wine. Objectively speaking, she had to admit that it was very good wine, but the bouquet held too much tobacco for her taste. It was like breathing in fumes from an exhaust pipe.

When he stepped away after an eternity, she spat the luke-warm wine into the spittoon. *Blah.* She poured herself a cup of water from the communal jug and rinsed her mouth before chugging the rest of it down. Her nausea soon passed, and she moved on to the next wine on the tasting list.

Landon hadn't been exaggerating. They were only on their third winery, and Aubrey felt a bit warm, even though she'd been spitting out the wine. The stress and exhaustion of the last couple of months must've taken a physical toll on her. She was wiped out. It was awesome how generous the pours were, but her alcohol tolerance was nonexistent at the moment.

"Ready?" Landon was by her side again.

Aubrey gave him a closed-lipped smile and a nod, and he guided her outside with a hand on her back. She was light-headed and way too warm. Could she get tipsy from the wine residue left from her tastings? That didn't make sense.

By the fifth winery, she utilized the spittoon without re-straint. She'd rather have Landon see her spit than give her mouth extra time to absorb the wine. When they were done with the tasting, the light pressure of his hand on her back said it was time to head to the next winery. She almost asked him to take her home, but she had too much work left to do.

Something felt off when they stepped out of the tasting room. *Why is it so bright?* Aubrey squeezed her eyes shut. Forgetting her eyes were closed, she kept walking and then stumbled on some steps.

"Whoa." Landon caught her by the arm so she didn't face-plant onto the sidewalk. She was mystified. Those steps came out of nowhere. "Are you okay?"

"Just peachy. Thank you."

She lifted her foot to step down the last stair, but her foot hit the ground too soon. Aubrey repeated the motion a few more times with the same result. Her face scrunched up as she stared down at her feet in consternation.

Oh. She was already at the bottom of the stairs. Aubrey giggled into her hands. She'd been toeing the ground like a horse scraping its hoof.

Landon cupped her elbow and tugged her toward his car. *He is so handsome.* She sighed and smiled dreamily at him, waiting for his dimple to appear. She pouted when he didn't deliver, and his brows knit together. *His frowny face is scorching hot.*

"Should we call it quits, or do you want another go after lunch?"

"There are more than two hundred wineries here, and you said you have meetings set up for the next couple days." Aubrey gave Landon her sternest look. Well, she tried to give him a stern look, but he kept circling his head around and around. *How is he even doing that?* She couldn't believe he was messing around at a time like this. This wasn't a vacation. She was going to be on TV, for heaven's sake.

"I know you're going to be on TV. I'm the one who asked you." He was suspiciously placating.

Wait. How does he know what I'm thinking?

"Because you're thinking out loud."

"I have to taste as many wines as possible *today*," she said out loud since he could read her mind.

"Your professionalism and dedication are admirable," he murmured as he gingerly lowered her onto the passenger seat. She had no idea how they'd teleported to his car.

Something about his droll comment made her think he was making fun of her, but the whole situation was so hilarious she burst out laughing again. He swiped his hand down his face.

"Food and lots of water. That's what you need."

Aubrey avoided Landon's eyes as she diligently worked on her flat iron steak. She hoped the protein would soak up the alcohol in her system. There couldn't be much, but her spent systems thought it was enough to get her light-headed and goofy.

She didn't even know where they were. Landon had brought her to the restaurant while she'd dozed in the car, and by the time the fog of sleep cleared from her head, they were having lunch in a domed wine cellar. It was a lovely place. Cream-colored ceramic tiles covered the walls, and warm sconces of muted light surrounded their table.

Landon had ordered the plat du jour—flat iron steak with chimichurri sauce and roasted fingerling potatoes—for the two of them. She bristled at his high-handedness but didn't object because she'd been planning to order the same thing.

The tender steak was perfectly marinated and cooked medium rare. The chimichurri sauce was fragrant and bright with fresh parsley, garlic, and exquisite local olive oil. Rosemary and garlic coated the roasted potatoes, which were crisp on the outside and creamy on the inside. Aubrey tucked it all in with relish, gulping down tall glasses of ice water.

"How's the steak?" His expression was bland, but his lips wobbled suspiciously as he sipped his iced tea.

"It's delicious. Thank you," she said primly.

She couldn't afford to be annoyed with Landon. Despite his insistence, she'd been too excited to eat a good breakfast and had nibbled on some toast instead. Thanks to her empty stomach and overworked body, the wine took a shortcut to her head and switched on her tipsy antics. She could see that Landon was dying to tease her about it, so she had to tread very lightly and not give him an opening.

"Are you sure you want to do more tastings today?" he asked once their plates were cleared away.

Aubrey narrowed her eyes at him but relented at the genuine concern on his face. "I wouldn't go so far as to say I *want* to, but I really don't have a choice. I can't work on the recipes without the wine."

The food and water managed to clear up her head a great deal, but she hoped she found her wine soon. She wasn't sure how many more wineries she could handle while maintaining any semblance of professionalism.

"I could push back my meetings tomorrow."

"No, please don't do that." She swallowed her trepidation. "I'll be fine."

Landon didn't look convinced but dutifully chauffeured her to the next tasting room. Aubrey swished and spat her way through the rest of the wineries, powered by determination. Until the seventh winery of the day.

"It's our signature fortified wine," said the server.

"You mean port?" Aubrey asked.

"It *is* port, but we can't call it that anymore. Only port made in Portugal can use that designation now. What we have is *fortified wine*," he said, pouring her a glass.

"Like the whole *champagne* and *sparkling wine* thing."

"Exactly. Whatever we call it, go easy with it. It has a 22 percent alcohol content." The friendly, knowledgeable server leaned across the bar and rested his forearm on the counter, studying her closely. "How many wineries have you visited today?"

"This is my seventh." Aubrey slurred the last word so it sounded more like *my sieves*. She didn't even think it was the alcohol anymore. She was simply dead on her feet.

"Wow. That's quite an accomplishment." He chuckled. "Your face is a bit flushed. Just remember that even if you spit out the wine, you'll still absorb some of the alcohol."

"Tell me about it." Aubrey pressed her hands against her cheeks. Her limbs were pleasantly heavy, and she felt toasty down to her toes. *Shit.*

"Do you have a designated driver with you?"

"I—"

She didn't get a chance to say *I do*, because Landon appeared out of nowhere and placed a strong arm around her shoulders. "Yes. She'll be riding home with me."

Did he just? *What the literal hell?* They were business associates and maybe friends. Nothing more. And yet, he'd just figuratively peed on her. *Like I'm a fucking fire hydrant.* She should be pissed. Furious. But she couldn't even muster enough indignation to shrug his hand off.

"Good." The server straightened from the counter and shot Aubrey a rueful grin. "I don't think she should be driving tonight."

Landon nodded at the other man and pulled Aubrey closer

to his side. Instead of extracting herself, she snuggled against him. *Business associates. Pfft. Friends, my ass.* The weight of his arm wrapped her in a cocoon of security, and she wanted to savor the sensation. She'd been on her own for so long that she'd forgotten how it felt not to be alone. It felt good. Really good.

"Have you tasted this yet?" Landon reached for her freshly poured port and breathed in its bouquet before taking a thoughtful sip.

"Nuh-uh. How is it?"

Aubrey accepted the glass from him and took a dainty sip, planning to spit it out like the rest. But no. She swallowed the nectar of the gods. It would've been a sin to waste the glorious wine. *This is it.*

With its perfect blend of spice and vanilla notes, leading into a fresh mélange of berries, it was perfect for her strawberry shortcake. She could see Tara rolling her eyes. *Wine snob.* Aubrey smiled and inhaled the bouquet again and again, practically bouncing on the balls of her feet.

"This is wonderful." She sighed. "This is it."

"Congratulations, Chef," he said, grinning broadly.

"Thank you."

"We're done with today's adventures, then?" He watched her flushed face warily.

"Yes, please. As soon as I buy a couple bottles of this."

She hurried to the wine display and reached out for a bottle and then screeched to a hard stop. *Yowza.* The secret was out. They knew this stuff was gold and were charging accordingly. But this was *the* wine. Now that she'd tasted it, nothing else would do. Gulping in a fortifying breath, she reached for the bottle.

"I got this," Landon said, staying her hand. Aubrey opened her mouth to protest, but he held up his hand. "It's for the show. Don't worry about it."

"Okay." Masking her relief, she "gave in" with a shrug. "As long as you can expense it."

"Of course." He graced her with an arrogant sideways glance before humoring her. "I'll be sure to submit a reimbursement form in the morning."

"Excellent."

She'd maxed out her good credit card in the last couple of months, and she would've had to use her highway robbery card for the fortified wine. The sound of her interest accumulating would've kept her up all night. Her second payment from the show would go straight to the contractors, but hopefully by the time she received her third payment she could pay off the card.

But none of that mattered. Her head was humming with the fragrance of the fortified wine and the flavors of her dessert, and it was beautiful. Getting something just right felt so good. She couldn't wipe the goofy grin off her face.

The bottles purchased and carefully wrapped, Landon guided Aubrey to the parking lot, his hand on its customary spot in the curve of her back. Strange how perfectly it fit against her body, as though he'd molded her with his own hands and carved out a nook for just that purpose.

Warmth spread through her faster than she could control. Confused and vulnerable, she quickened her steps to escape his touch. Landon matched her hurried steps but didn't try to reclaim her back. When they stopped at his car, he reached around to open her door, and his chest nudged her shoulder. She shivered with awareness.

"Cold?" Landon frowned. "Get inside. I'll turn on the heater."

"Thank you." But she just stood there like an idiot while he waited for her to sit down. *Gah*. Spurred on by embarrassment, she dove into the seat with the grace of an orangutan.

Her mind raced like a hamster on its favorite wheel, making everything blurry. Aubrey closed her eyes so the world would stop spinning. Exhaustion blanketed the cacophony of emotions in her head, and her limbs grew heavy and limp. The car shifted softly as Landon settled into the driver's seat, and then there was nothing.

Landon drove at a snail's pace so he wouldn't disturb his sleeping passenger. Aubrey was curled up like a child in her seat, her expression soft and peaceful. His chest clenched at the sight. She was so beautiful, it hurt to look at her. Yet he couldn't stop staring.

He'd reached for her again and again that night until he'd drifted off into an exhausted slumber. If he'd stayed up to watch her sleep, would he have let her walk away? *No.* The answer came unbidden, shocking him. A surge of possessiveness had taken over when he'd made love to her. In that moment, there had been no time—no past, no future. Only the two of them. He didn't think beyond that. He couldn't. And the next morning, she was gone.

He'd convinced himself it was for the best. She'd been a fantasy—a mirage his starving soul had conjured. But here she was. Real, warm, and so damn close. Tightening his hands around the steering wheel, Landon stepped on the accelerator. He had to get her to the villa before his daydreams got out of hand.

Dust clouds whirled on the dirt driveway when he screeched to a stop in front of the villa. He bolted out of his seat and nearly ripped the passenger door off its hinges. He was rock hard and aching. The exquisite torture had to end for his sanity's sake.

Despite the unceremonious way her door was jerked open

and the way crisp night air rushed against her, Aubrey didn't so much as twitch. She was out cold.

Goddamn it.

Landon hesitated for a second and then lifted her out of the car. With a soft sigh, Aubrey snuggled against him and wrapped her arms around his neck. Then she tucked her head against his shoulder, warming the side of his neck with her sweet, moist breath. His aroused body responded predictably to her proximity, and he felt dizzy with the desire flooding through him. He had to get her out of his arms as soon as humanly possible.

When he reached the front door, he wanted to scream in frustration. *How am I going to press the security code with Aubrey in my arms?* Landon kicked the solid wood door. It made him feel marginally better, so he kicked it a couple more times. With some juggling and a lot of cursing, he finally got the door open.

His breath was coming fast and short from a mixture of physical exertion and good old-fashioned lust. Completely oblivious to his struggles, Aubrey whimpered something in her dream and drew closer to him, bringing her lips to rest on the pounding pulse on his throat.

"Fuck," he groaned.

Landon stomped to the staircase and climbed up steps two at a time. When he reached her room, he dropped her none too gently on the bed and then got the hell out, locking the door behind him for good measure.

"God, help me."

He slid down to the floor with his back against Aubrey's door, too weak to support his weight for another second. Landon drew his shaking hands through his hair and fought to get his breath back. His hands clenched and unclenched helplessly on his thighs, bereft of the soft body they had held a minute ago. His skin still burned where their bodies had touched. He'd

hardly slept last night, much too aware only a single wall separated them. Now that he'd held her in his arms again, there
would be no sleep for him tonight.

When Lucien had thrown him under the bus, Landon
convinced himself it wouldn't be difficult to be roommates with
the most tempting woman in the world. He wasn't going to waste
time finding a new place to stay, especially since he would be
in and out of Bosque Verde on business. The villa was the most
practical option. Simple and convenient.

He was an arrogant, delusional jerk. It wasn't convenience
that kept him there. It was her. *Call me a masochist*, he thought,
laughing without humor. Sharing the villa with her wasn't difficult; it was nearly impossible. He couldn't have her and it was
killing him, but he'd be damned if he gave up a single minute
with her.

Landon dragged his hand down his face. Self-control was
an art he'd mastered over the years. He was a grown man with
responsibilities, but he wanted Aubrey with a desperation that
made him want to forget all that. But the day he allowed passion to rule his life would be the day he became selfish and
weak. Like his old man.

His mood grew dark knowing another sleepless night
awaited him. Getting out of her room wasn't enough. He had
to get out of the villa. Making up his mind, Landon changed
into his swimming trunks and headed out to the pool. Maybe
he could exhaust himself enough to catch a couple hours of
shut-eye.

10

Aubrey lifted her arms high above her head and twisted her torso as if she were wringing herself dry. The petal-soft sheets caressed her skin, and she luxuriated in the endless bed. *Petal-soft sheets? Endless bed?* Her twin-size bed had humble, three-hundred-thread-count sheets.

She sat upright as her sleep-muddled mind grasped that she wasn't in her bed. She wasn't even home. She was in Bosque Verde. *With Landon.* Burying her hot face in her hands, Aubrey fell back into bed. *Did he think I passed out drunk? What else could he think?*

People weren't kidding. *Stress really is your body's worst enemy.* Her stamina had dropped to nil in the last couple months. Her immune system was crap, too, if her recurring sore throat were any indication. She should take better care of herself. Comfort Zone wasn't going to run itself when she went back.

And how did I get to my room? Landon must've hauled her ass to bed, and she'd slept through it. Despite her embarrassment, goose bumps spread on her skin. He'd held her in his arms, pressing her against his hard, broad chest, and she couldn't remember a stitch of it. *What a waste of glorious skin to skin.*

Aubrey groaned and flipped onto her stomach. *How am I going to face him tomorrow?* It was catastrophically mortifying. What if she'd drooled in her stupor? *Oh, God.* Before her panic could reach its peak, an idea popped into her head. She would make it up to him *and* buy his silence by baking him her sweet buns. No matter how exasperated, annoyed, and/or angry he might be, Landon wouldn't be able to stay that way after a taste of the delicious morsels. She clapped her hands together and grinned, unintentionally reenacting the scene where Sister Maria decides to sew play clothes for the von Trapp children out of old curtains.

Aubrey headed to the bathroom, humming "Do-Re-Mi" and stripping off her wrinkled clothes. Steam filled the shower in an instant thanks to the villa's fantastic water pressure, and she stepped beneath the water with a lusty sigh. When she could afford it, she would totally spring for top-notch plumbing.

The long, hot shower washed away her tension, and she stepped out shrouded in a perfume of lavender and citrus. Feeling infinitely calmer and in control, she tugged on her black cami and matching shorts.

She pressed her ear against her door and held her breath. The house was quiet. Landon must have been asleep. Throwing on an emerald kimono, Aubrey tiptoed down the stairs. Other than the moonlight streaming in through the windows, the villa lay in darkness. With a sigh of relief, she padded into the kitchen and switched the light on.

Getting her hands messy with flour, sugar, and spices never failed to chase her worries away. The scent of rising dough and butter filled the air and brought a smile to her heart. Aubrey hummed an unknown tune as she laid out pieces of pudgy round dough on the baking sheet. She loved the pale innocence of uncooked dough—plump and squishy as a baby's cheeks. She would let them proof overnight, then brush on some melted butter and sprinkle them with turbinado sugar in the morning.

When the buns were tucked safely in the fridge, she tidied the kitchen with practiced efficiency. Satisfied with her midnight project, Aubrey took off her apron and reached for the kimono she'd thrown over a stool. Her hand froze midair when Landon strode into the kitchen wearing a towel slung low on his waist. A good sneeze would've dislodged the loosely tied towel. *Where the hell is the pepper shaker?*

His broad chest glistened with drops of water, and damp curls of jet-black hair fell across his forehead. She'd forgotten how beautiful he was. If she'd only seen a photo of him, she would've bet her bakery that the picture was photoshopped. The definition on his abs was absurd.

Her heart lodged itself in her throat as Landon stepped toward her, his face feral and hungry. Or maybe he was just thirsty for some water. *Who knows?* The desire roaring through her befuddled mind, but she knew denial wasn't the answer.

They were standing in the same room, half-naked. It was a recipe for catastrophe. She had to create some space between them and cover up some skin. She fumbled to pull on her kimono, missing the armhole twice. *Shit.* Even when she succeeded in donning her robe, the scrap of silk barely hit the curves of her bottom.

As Landon took slow, measured steps toward her, Aubrey's panic rose. He was going to kiss her. She could see it in the heat of his gaze. If he kissed her, she'd be lost. Her body was screaming for his touch. She wouldn't be able to hold back if he so much as laid a finger on her. He was less than five steps from her, and she had to do something.

"Sweet buns!"

Her voice screeched and bounced off the kitchen walls. Landon stopped short, his eyebrows drawing together in puzzlement. The plan had been to make small talk about preparing some sweet buns for tomorrow's breakfast. Regretfully, her brain was too busy dreaming about nibbling on his bottom lip to transfer adequate information to her mouth.

"I hope you're not commenting on my anatomy, because I'm kind of shy." Landon's lips twitched as humor infiltrated his lust-glazed eyes. "And for the record, I have swimming trunks under this towel, so my sweet buns are decently clothed."

"Oh, shut up," she snapped, equal parts annoyed and turned on. "Or else I'm not sharing a single morsel of my sweet buns with you."

"Now, when you say *your* sweet buns, are you referring to the ones peeking out of your . . ." He waved a hand in her direction. "Robe?"

"Grow. Up."

He only laughed harder.

You wanna play like that? Fine. Aubrey pivoted on her heels, giving him an eyeful of her half-bared bottom. When Landon choked on his laugh, she tossed a Cheshire cat grin over her shoulder and sashayed away from him.

How do you like them sweet buns?

She went up to her room and drifted off to sleep a few minutes later, still wearing that smile.

———

Early the next morning, Aubrey set the freshly baked sweet buns on the kitchen counter and brewed a fresh pot of coffee before retreating to her room. When she heard the front door shut, she tiptoed into the hallway and risked a peek outside the window.

Landon left for his meeting dressed in a fitted gray suit that accentuated his broad shoulders and narrow hips. He looked the part of a successful businessman—powerful and in control. Aubrey's breath caught in her throat, and her heart sprinted as if she were the final runner in a tight relay race. *Am I ever going to get used to my reaction to him?* Her attraction was becoming harder and harder to quell.

Aubrey sighed and turned away from the window once the dust settled on the driveway. She checked the platter of sweet buns she'd left for him and was equal parts pleased and peeved to find every last piece of the bread gone. Her baker's ego danced while her empty stomach growled, but she shushed both of them. A small white sheet of stationery occupied the empty platter. Anticipation skipping on her nerve endings, she opened the folded note with not-so-steady hands.

Thanks for the sweet buns. See you tonight.
—Mr. Sunshine

Her heart attempted a triple flip but crashed after a two-and-a-quarter turn. With a tremulous smile, Aubrey traced his words with her fingertips. His handwriting was surprisingly neat, but bold and decisive like its arrogant creator. Warmth and a spark of happiness burst in her core. The moment felt more intimate than anything she'd experienced before.

No, no, no. Aubrey threw the note back on the table. After staring at it for three seconds, she pushed it away a little farther. *Do not pick that up again.* Being with Landon felt far too good. Far too right. It scared the shit out of her. She couldn't let her guard down. Last night had been a close call—she'd been a few seconds away from climbing him.

Aubrey squeezed her eyes shut. What would she have done

then? *Give myself to him and pray I'll be enough for him? Hope he won't cast me to the shadows?* That was plain dumb. Relationships failed. Even when couples committed their lives to each other, they only had a fifty-fifty chance of staying together.

Love was a gamble. *How much would you bet on a game with fifty-fifty odds? For me, a hundred bucks, tops.* That was her cap for how much she could lose at a casino. But love demanded the ultimate all-in. *You can't divide your heart and bet a safe portion.* Aubrey wasn't a gambler. She had to fold.

She couldn't stray from Operation Friendship. It was best to keep this a friendly business arrangement. That was the only way no one would get hurt. Aubrey took a big breath and put her fists on her hips, superhero-style. *I'm going to get Landon out of my mind.* How?

Two. Words. Strawberry shortcake—with port-macerated strawberries. *Well, six if you count the description.* A familiar excitement hummed through her as she imagined her new dessert. *Damn it. It's fortified wine, not port. Seven words.*

If she wanted to bake the perfect dessert, she needed to shop for the perfect ingredients. Fortunately, these ingredients didn't involve alcohol. Aubrey got ready in record time, jumped on a pretty beach cruiser bike—courtesy of Lucien—and pedaled toward the small enclave of stores down the hill. A soft breeze ruffled her hair as she sped across her beautiful surroundings with gleeful abandon. By the time she arrived at her first destination, she was breathless and laughing.

The produce shop was filled to the brim with colorful local produce, from artichokes to zucchini blossoms. Aubrey's palms itched to touch and buy everything, and she barely managed not to drool.

"Eureka," she breathed. In the midst of the bounty, she spotted a small row of gorgeous scarlet strawberries.

"Fort Laramie."

"What?" Aubrey spun to face a giant of a man, her hand pressed to her chest. She craned her neck to take in his height and barrel chest.

"The strawberries," he said. "They're the Fort Laramie varieties. Not Eureka."

She released a breathy laugh, her momentary surprise fading. "I was saying, 'Eureka!' as in 'I found it!'"

"I see. California gold rush slang. Sorry, it's been awhile." His weathered face crinkled with amusement. "I've never seen someone so excited over strawberries—even Fort Laramies!"

"They smell so intense." She reached out to touch one. "And they're heavier than they look. They must be juicy little buggers."

"Mmm-hmm. They're the sweetest strawberries around, too." The man stuck out a porterhouse steak–size hand. "I'm Jorge. Welcome to Central Coast Produce."

"Hi, I'm Aubrey."

He freed her hand and offered her a sample. The tender bulb exploded in her mouth in a symphony of flavors.

"I love your Fort Laramie strawberries."

A warm, baritone chuckle permeated the air, and Aubrey realized Jorge was a teddy bear despite his formidable size. "Well, join the club, but I love all my beauties equally."

"I need a dozen quarts." Then she bit her lip. "I'll be cleaning you out, though. Is that all right?"

"I'm a farmer, but also a businessman. Getting cleaned out is a good thing."

Aubrey's jaw dropped open again. "You grew all these?"

"Yup." His teeth were dazzling white against his weathered skin. "Except for the flowers, olives, and grapes, these are all from our farm. My wife and son usually man the shop, but they went to some fancy organic farming seminar."

"How wonderful."

"Can I get you anything else?"

"Eggs. Do you have eggs?"

"Only the best eggs you'll ever taste."

"Eureka."

Aubrey was panting and sweat-drenched by the time she returned to the villa a couple hours later. It was freakishly difficult to climb uphill with the sun pounding down on her. She'd had most of her supplies delivered to the villa, but the bike moved as though it were pulling a carriage via her leg power.

The sky-blue tank top she'd donned this morning was stuck to her like a second skin, and her underwear was soggy with sweat. She was going straight to the pool and jumping in with her clothes on.

When she saw a red Mercedes parked in front of the villa, Aubrey groaned out loud. She wasn't expecting anyone and felt the opposite of hospitable. Then her groan descended into a miserable moan.

Their unannounced guest was as stunning in person as she was in the pictures. Tall, statuesque, and glamorous. *How can the woman look so perfect on a sweltering day like this?* While Aubrey would never be able to compete with her in the looks department, she was mortified that her first meeting with Aria Santini would be at her stickiest, smelliest moment.

Aubrey considered running for the bushes, but Aria spotted her from across the driveway. With no other choice, she dismounted the beach cruiser, almost falling flat on her face when her exhausted legs buckled. She righted herself like a gangly camel and manipulated her red sweaty face into what she hoped was a nonchalant expression. *I so am not fangirling.*

Aria hurried toward her with a shining smile, her hands

clasped in front of her perfect bosom. Before Aubrey could utter a laid-back *hey*, Aria drew her into a firm embrace, profuse perspiration and all.

"Oh, *mio dio!*" Aria said in a lyrical voice. "It's so good to meet you."

Aria was not a diva from hell as Aubrey had feared. Her voice, her smile, and her genuine warmth made Aubrey's awkwardness melt away.

"Um . . . hi. Aria Santini, right?"

"Just Aria." She linked her arm through Aubrey's and led them toward the villa. "I'm sorry to drop in without notice. I don't have your number, but I thought I'd still come and introduce myself. I've been dying to meet you."

"Me?" Aubrey was still dazed, but she belatedly remembered her manners. "Well, it's lovely to meet you, Aria. Let's go inside before we melt into a puddle out here."

———

When Landon walked into the villa, tugging at his tie, he was hit with the sound of melodic laughter and mouthwatering aromas. Having spotted the red Mercedes out front, he wasn't surprised. Good food and booming laughter followed Aria wherever she went. Her love for life and cooking was highly contagious. Landon had known Aria for almost a decade, and she was one of his closest friends. Unfortunately, she also had a penchant for occasional mischief. She might be perpetuating some on him right now.

Groaning inwardly, he strode into the kitchen. Aubrey's expression flickered mid-laugh, and she quickly lowered her lashes. *How much has Aria been grilling her?* When Aubrey glanced back up, he searched her eyes. *Too quiet, too guarded.*

Not bothering to hide his irritation, he walked over to Aria and leaned down to place a light peck on her cheek. "Aria."

"Well, hello there." Humor shimmered in her eyes. "I was just getting acquainted with my guest chef."

Landon glowered at her. Grown men cowered when faced with his anger, but Aria shrugged and lightly tossed her hair with a *bite me* grin. *Why am I still friends with the woman?* he wondered.

Then Aria returned her attention to the subject of her curiosity, who was watching their interaction with a faint smile.

"Now that Landon's here, we should open that bottle of champagne and celebrate properly."

"Celebrate what?" Landon asked cautiously, not knowing what scheme his impetuous friend had brewed.

"Her new dessert, of course. It's simply divine." Aria was brimming with excitement.

"I wouldn't go that far," Aubrey said, her cheeks turning a lovely pink.

"I'm sure it's that and more," he said.

Landon was so in awe of her. Her sweet buns—something she'd baked for him and only him—were amazingly good. It was nothing short of magic how she could make something so simple into something extraordinary. A couple seconds lapsed in silence before he realized he was staring at Aubrey again. He tugged at his collar.

"I'm a little overdressed for the celebration. I'll join you ladies in a few minutes."

Aria, who hadn't missed the longing in his gaze, crossed her eyes at him. With a warning glare and more than a little trepidation, Landon headed for his room.

After splashing some cold water on his face, he studied his reflection. His hair stood up on spiky ends from dragging his fingers through it repeatedly. He'd driven back to the villa filled with restless excitement, knowing Aubrey would be here. It felt like he was coming home to her. It was a terrifying thought. He had no home. Aubrey was not his. And still, he hoped and yearned.

Exhaling roughly, he turned his back on the mirror. Landon didn't like himself too much at the moment. He couldn't touch her even though his body was screaming for her. If he gave in to the wild attraction between them, people could paint her as a woman who'd slept her way to success and bury her with sick glee. He wanted to punch a hole through the wall, but he opted to pull on a black T-shirt and well-worn jeans to rejoin the celebration in the kitchen.

"You took your sweet time." Aria smirked. "Did you have to shave your legs?"

Aubrey choked on her bubbly water.

"You didn't expect me to show up to a party with hairy legs, did you?" Landon managed to keep a straight face, but he felt heat climbing up his neck. He actually did shave, not his legs but his five-o'clock shadow.

"Now, children. Be nice." Aubrey grinned, her voice gritty from her coughing fit.

"Okay, Mama," Aria said. "But someone had to wipe that smug grin off his face."

Aubrey nodded solemnly. Landon cleared his throat.

"If you ladies are finished having fun at my expense, why don't we start the celebration?" He smiled at Aubrey, and she blushed sweetly, making his heart lunge against his rib cage. "And I expect a sample of the reason for the celebration."

11

Every night since she'd arrived in Bosque Verde, Aubrey had fallen asleep as soon as her head hit the pillow. But as she climbed into bed after their impromptu celebration, she doubted she would get any sleep at all. Her heart still pounded like a bass drum beating out a battle march, and her sensitized skin felt every brush of her silky pajamas and the smooth sheets like a caress.

Landon's eyes had followed her every movement, and she'd felt ridiculously hot in the air-conditioned kitchen. While Aria's bright humor and warm presence had eased the tension between them, a stolen glance or an accidental brush of their skin had set Aubrey back on fire. The only thing that stopped her from ogling and panting after Landon all evening was observing Aria and Landon's easy friendship.

Aria teased him relentlessly, and he gave back as good as he got. They didn't pull their punches either. Even when Aubrey cringed at their bawdier jokes, thinking they'd gone too far, they only laughed harder at themselves and at each other. Watching Landon with his guard down—laid-back and playful—made her heart twist with something bittersweet. Aubrey had probably seen more of his true personality in one evening than she would've if she'd spent weeks with him as a business acquaintance.

She sighed and tossed onto her other side, fluffing her pillow. Landon was considerate, funny, and intelligent, and she genuinely liked him. If she could push aside her wildfire attraction to him, Operation Friendship could be a huge success. Becoming his friend would be wonderful—not to mention far less complicated than a fling—and, with any luck, lasting. With the flickering hope of having Landon in her life, Aubrey slid into sleep.

The next morning, she couldn't get her eyes to open. She knew the sun was out through her closed lids, but they were heavy as iron curtains and refused to budge. After a minute of half-hearted struggle, sleep overpowered the morning person inside her.

When Aubrey dragged herself out of bed, it was past ten o'clock in the morning. The villa was silent when she descended the stairs after a shower. Landon seemed to have left for work, and she stood alone in the kitchen, sipping a mug of strong coffee. Her strawberry shortcake had turned out well last night, but she wanted to play around with it a little more. There was room for improvement, especially with the texture of the cake after the macerated strawberries were poured on.

Aubrey enjoyed a quiet day on her own, experimenting with her new recipe, but by sunset, she found herself glancing out the windows facing the front and listening for tires crunching against the driveway.

She wasn't sure how this roommate thing was supposed to work. Were they going to have dinner together? Should she cook something and wait for him to come home? No, not *home*, the *villa*. Her cheeks warmed up at her slip. Before she could

fluster herself any further, her phone chimed to announce a
new message.

> Landon: I thought I'd pick up some Thai for us. Does
> that sound okay?

Her chest hurt as though it had fallen asleep like a lazy foot
only to wake up to prickling pain. He was picking up dinner.
For us. She couldn't breathe.

> Landon: Or I could cook if you'd like.

She gave her head a quick shake and typed out a response.

> Aubrey: Thai sounds wonderful.

> Landon: Great. I'll see you around 7:30.

> Aubrey: Okay, see you soon.

She stared at the screen for a long while, scared to look
away. Her heart still fluttered like the wings of a dragonfly
taking flight, and her blood hummed—*this.* A few words and
suddenly she didn't feel alone. Her thirsty soul soaked in the
joy of having someone come home to her. Business associate.
Friend. It didn't matter at all. She was going to tuck away every
moment of her time here. While she was in Bosque Verde, she
wouldn't be alone. She would have Landon.

Seven thirty was more than an hour away, and Aubrey didn't
want to drive herself crazy, waiting for him by the door. She
trailed her fingers along the books in the living room bookshelf
and chose a Julia Child biography. Curling her legs under her,
she sat at the corner of a leather sofa and read the first page over
and over again by the light of a table lamp.

The sound of a car driving toward the villa had her rushing

to the door and pulling it wide open. Landon parked near the entrance and stepped out of the vehicle. Surprise registered on his face before his lips spread into a warm smile.

"Hi," she said breathlessly.

"Hi."

"Hi," she repeated because she couldn't think of anything else to say.

Landon hadn't moved from his spot by his car, but her second greeting seemed to nudge him into action. He jogged over to the passenger side and pulled out two enormous paper bags with handles. One was a brown shopping bag, and the other was a plain white one. She'd never been to a restaurant that recycled random shopping bags for takeout.

He turned sideways to get through the doorway with his load, and Aubrey belatedly stepped aside so he could get inside.

"Did you order their entire menu?"

"Not quite," he said with mischief in his voice.

"You should go change out of your suit. I can set the table."

"No, I'm fine." He placed the bags on the kitchen counter and pulled his tie off. "What I would like for you to do is get a nice, cool drink and hang out in the living room for a few minutes."

"What are you up to?" She glanced sideways at him with narrowed eyes. But instead of answering, he gently pushed her out of the kitchen, handing her a bottle of sparkling water.

"Trust me. It'll be worth it."

About fifteen minutes later, Landon came into the living room and offered her his arm. She looped her arm through his with a shrug. He looked adorably excited, and she didn't want to be a party pooper. When they stepped into the kitchen, she saw the table overflowing with beautiful food.

"Oh, my gosh. How did you do all this? I thought you were picking up takeout."

"It is takeout, but I didn't want you to miss the restaurant's amazing presentation. I know the owner, so I asked them to pack the food for me in their serving wear. I promised to return everything tomorrow."

Aubrey sat down, pulling her chair forward. "Okay. Tell me what I'm looking at."

"This dish," Landon said, pointing to a twelve-inch-wide plate with an indentation in the center the size of a soup bowl, "is the two-hundred-years pad thai. A recipe passed down for generations. That split langoustine on the side isn't just for decoration. It's so sweet and fresh, it's one of the stars of the dish."

"What are those little mounds?"

Pointing to each, he said, "Salt, chili flakes, and crushed peanuts."

"And that's a carrot rose? It's as detailed as the roses I make for my cakes. I build mine petal by petal. How the heck did they carve a carrot into that?"

"Very carefully." Landon chuckled, obviously pleased by her appreciation. "The food's going to get cold. Let me move on to the rest."

There were tamarind prawns nestled in a fresh pineapple bowl, sliced lengthwise; steamed fish in lime sauce in a steel, fish-shaped bowl; and red curry with rambutan, a close cousin of lychee, per Landon, stuffed with ground shrimp in a shallow golden pot with large handles on each side. It truly was a feast for all senses.

"I'm going to eat *all* of this," Aubrey said fervently, her eyes never leaving the table. "Just kidding. I'll let you have a little."

Landon tossed the bean sprouts, chili flakes, and crushed peanuts into the pad thai and then finished with a splash of

lime. Aubrey dug in as soon as he served her a generous portion. If ever there were a perfect bite, this was it. The dynamic
scent blended into the flavors that first met her tongue—tart,
sweet, and salty with a hint of nuttiness. Then there was the
texture. The not-too-thick rice noodles were so chewy but not
sticky, the sauce adding just the right amount of moisture.

She insisted they split the langoustine, pulling the succulent
flesh out of the shell. She was delighted by the taut, crunchy
outer texture, proof that it was fresh and perfectly cooked. And
the sweetness. It wasn't dessert, but it certainly was satisfying
for a main dish.

Aubrey loved the addicting flavor of the tamarind shrimp,
and the lip-puckering lime sauce and fresh cilantro on the tender steamed fish was refreshing. The red curry with rambutan
was the most unique and novel Thai dish she'd ever tried. The
rambutan has a firm texture similar to dried mangoes but a little
softer and meatier. The ground shrimp inside had a meatball-
like texture and added plenty of salt to the sweetness of the
fruit. The spicy red curry with the creaminess of coconut milk
rounded out the dish beautifully. Add in some jasmine rice,
and she could have probably eaten a basinful in one seating.

She was so full her stomach was stretched tight, and she
felt slightly light-headed. All her blood was rushing to her overstuffed stomach to assist with the digestion, leaving little for her
brain.

"That was the most fascinating thing I've ever seen," said
Landon.

Her butt nearly shot off her chair. She'd forgotten about
Landon in her delirious gluttony. *Oh, my God.* "Did I actually
eat all of this? Please tell me you ate enough, too."

"I've seriously never seen someone eat a meal with such intensity and bliss before."

"Did. You. Eat?" Mortification was washing over her in hot waves.

"Yes, yes." He swiped his hand through the air as though her question were a pesky fruit fly. "So what made that happen? I've eaten with you before. This was definitely new."

"Well, I love Thai food, obviously, and I was famished. But it was really the impact of the gorgeous presentation and the surprising combinations of flavor and texture that did it." She blushed to the top of her hairline. Maybe her head was steaming a little at the crown. "Thank you so much for dinner, Landon."

"It was my absolute pleasure. Your joy made my meal more delicious as well."

They chatted awhile longer and then cleared the table and washed the dishes in comfortable silence. That evening allowed her to ease into a lovely routine without overthinking things. Operation Friendship was in fine shape.

<hr>

Preparations for the first shooting had the production team running around in a flurry of activity, and Aubrey and Landon's cozy evenings came to an end. He seemed to be in the thick of it all, which meant she hardly saw him at the villa. In the last few days, he went to work before she woke up and came home after she fell asleep.

Her days were far less exciting without him. Aubrey sighed listlessly. Less exciting was a good thing. A safe thing. In fact, if she thought with her brain instead of her girlie parts, she would remember she had her heart and Comfort Zone to protect.

She shook off her melancholy and got herself ready for work. Her portion of the filming was scheduled to start in a week, and she still had one more recipe to create. That meant she had to hit the tasting rooms again. The perfect Moscato remained elusive even after several days of wine tasting. Even though light dessert wines were far less potent than fortified red wines, nausea rolled through Aubrey's stomach. She would swish and spit every wine, and stop when she got tired.

After her decision to take things easy, the wine tour promised to be relaxing and enjoyable. And the tour provided pickup and drop-off service, so it was perfect for her current car-less situation. Her group was made up of a friendly middle-aged couple with their college-age daughter and a lovely older couple on vacation from Germany.

Michael, their tour guide and chauffeur, was a sun-bronzed Californian with a brilliant smile and an endless supply of jokes. The college girl laughed hysterically at every witticism, and Aubrey worried the poor girl might crack her ribs.

"Aubrey, you get shotgun." Michael took her elbow and led her to the front passenger seat.

"Me? Are you sure?" She couldn't help glancing at the younger woman, feeling guilty even though she'd done nothing wrong. But the girl glared at Aubrey with narrowed eyes, and her guilt evaporated. *Glare at him, not me.*

"Yes, I'm sure. Everyone else is here with someone." He winked. "I'll keep you company, so you won't be lonely."

She shrugged and climbed onto the front seat.

The off-the-beaten-path wineries Michael took them to were all beautifully situated and had an abundance of the white and dessert wines the group had signed up for. Aubrey spat and rinsed after every tasting. So far, the wines were lovely, and she was holding up fine.

"Hey," she protested when Michael casually took her glass from her hand.

"This one's exquisite," he said, inhaling deeply from the glass.

He made a point of holding her gaze so she wouldn't miss he was referring to both her and the wine. Inner Aubrey rolled her eyes, but tourist Aubrey humored the guide and offered a bland smile. He was, after all, giving them an excellent tour. But when he took a small sip of her wine, Aubrey had to draw the line. She didn't mix spit with strangers. *Gag.*

"Give that back. You're the designated driver." She snatched her glass back. Michael guffawed like she'd made some adorable joke even though she was frying him with her death ray.

The next winery had a stunning view of the valley, so Aubrey forgave Michael's prior wine theft. As the day wore on, the gorgeous vineyards and easy company relaxed Aubrey enough to let go of her stress. Finding a half a dozen candidates for her second dessert didn't hurt either. At the end of the productive tour, the sway of the van lulled Aubrey to sleep as Michael drove the group back to their lodgings.

"Rise and shine, Sleeping Beauty." She heard a faraway voice calling her. She struggled to wake up, her eyelashes fluttering against the weight of sleep.

Aubrey's eyes shot open, remembering she was in a tour van. In fact, she was the last one in the van, and Michael was standing beside the open passenger door wearing his white, toothy grin. He offered his hand to help her off the van, and she grasped it to make sure she didn't bury her drowsy nose into the driveway.

She tested her land legs and was relieved to find them sturdy, but when she tried to withdraw her hand, he held on. Suppressing her annoyance, Aubrey smiled stiffly and tugged harder at her hand.

"Sorry about keeping you. Thank you so much for a lovely tour."

Michael relaxed his death grip, and she retrieved her hand, but he didn't leave as she'd hoped. Now that she was fully awake, Aubrey was impatient to get started on her recipe.

"Are you sure you don't need me to help you inside?" He gave her what had to be a well-practiced puppy dog face.

Cute . . . but not that cute. She sighed and opened her mouth to shoo him away, but her words caught in her throat as strong hands wrapped around her waist.

"Thanks for the offer, but I can take it from here." Landon spoke quietly from behind, but the icy steel in his voice propelled Michael into action. He scampered to hand over her wine to Landon and drove away in a cloud of dust.

Aubrey spun out of Landon's hold and gaped at him. His high-handedness infuriated her, but his possessiveness lit a fire in her pants. Fury and lust wrestled inside her with no clear winner.

"Enjoying the locals?" Landon raised an eyebrow and regarded her with a humorless smirk. "So this is how you've been spending your days."

What the blazing hell? "Why, yes, I do enjoy meeting the locals." Aubrey's temper burned through any lingering confusion. She was her own person, and *no one* controlled her choices. "There are so many lovely, interesting people here."

"Is that so?" His icy voice sent a shiver down her spine.

"More importantly, it's none of your business how I spend my days. Or with whom."

"Like hell it isn't."

"I agreed to guest star on Aria's show with two original recipes. I went wine tasting to find the Moscato for my second dessert, because it's a part of my job, if you recall." Her flight instinct had a slight edge over her fight instinct, but she held her ground and pulled back her shoulders. "I don't go frolicking in the fields when you leave the house, asshole. I take my work very seriously."

"Fuck." The fight drained out of Landon in a blink, and he scrubbed his face with his hands. "That was uncalled for. I was way out of line."

"It was, and you were." As she stood glaring at him with her arms folded across her chest, she noticed for the first time how exhausted he looked. Her brows drew together as concern overshadowed her anger.

"I didn't like it," he said, holding her gaze. "I didn't like seeing him touch you. Looking at you that way."

"Landon," she whispered. His words wrapped around her heart and squeezed tight. "You can't say things like that."

"I know." His regret and yearning were palpable in the moment, and his vulnerability made Aubrey ache to hold him.

Landon squeezed the back of his neck and closed his eyes for a few breaths. When he opened them again, all his emotions were in check. The moment had passed. Gratitude, disappointment, and regret filled her.

"It looks like you've had a rough day." Her voice shook only a little.

"The construction on the schoolhouse is delayed by days. Every damn thing is leaking and short-circuiting. Then, the production manager's wife went into labor five weeks early, so he had to fly home today. The baby was in a rush to meet his parents, I guess." He ran his fingers through his hair, looking sheepish. "So yeah. It's been one hell of a day, but it's no excuse for being a jerk."

"No, it isn't." Aubrey's tart response was half-hearted. He

needed to rest, not stand in the middle of the driveway arguing with her for no good reason. She held out her hand with a
no-hard-feelings smile. "With all that going on, I'd be a little
cranky, too. Truce?"

His brows shot up to his forehead, and then a relieved grin
spread across his face. He clasped her hand, but instead of shaking it, he lifted it to his lips for a lingering kiss. Her toes curled,
and her legs threatened to wobble.

"Truce."

Landon took heavy-footed steps up the stairs, and Aubrey
headed for the kitchen. A shower and a nap should do him
wonders, but she had a feeling his version of rest consisted of
stretching his legs out in an armchair and reading his emails.

By the time sunset flooded the kitchen with its orange glow,
Aubrey was banging around like a raccoon raiding a trash can.
She could taste the smooth Moscato sorbet in her head, but the
cold glob in her mouth only bore a passing resemblance to the
one in her imagination. When she was happy with the flavor,
the texture was not quite right, and when the texture came out
just so, the flavor was underwhelming. Alcoholic beverages were
notoriously hard to freeze properly, especially in ice cream con-
sistency. Frustration knotted her stomach.

At least her cherry and walnut cookies were exquisite. The
local olive oil added a brisk, floral flavor to them, and the lightly
sprinkled pink Himalayan salt drew out more of the subtle layers
of flavor.

Aubrey loved chewy and crunchy cookies equally, but for
this recipe, she went for a delicate, crisp exterior and a moist,
chewy center. The cookie held a savory note from the olive oil
and a hint of saltiness, but it was sweet. No baked good had a
right to call itself a cookie without being sweet. And the cher-
ries added a zing to keep things fun.

The cookies were about the size of her palm, so she could build a full-size ice cream sandwich. The crispy, chewy texture wouldn't crack apart at the first bite, and its density would keep it from soaking up the ice cream and getting soggy.

Unfortunately, the latest batch of sorbet was unworthy of being hugged by such awesomeness. She had to get the recipe right. Comfort Zone's future could depend on her two recipes for the show. All she needed was a goddamn perfect Moscato sorbet. Was perfection too much to ask for? Her frustration boiling over, Aubrey balled up a dish towel and threw it across the kitchen.

"Whoa!" Landon caught the towel an inch from his face. "I thought we called a truce."

"I'm so sorry," she mumbled through the hands covering her startled mouth before she dropped them to her sides. "But you weren't standing there when I threw it, so you technically got in the towel's way."

"Okay. My mistake." Landon chuckled and swaggered to the island, where she'd set up her working station. "Now tell me what's going on."

"Oh, nothing," she said breezily. "I just can't seem to get anything right."

He snatched a cookie off the cooling rack and bit into it. "You're insane. What could possibly be wrong with these?"

"*They're* not the problem." Aubrey's cheeks warmed at his compliment, but there was no time to preen. "The sorbet won't behave."

"Could I help?" he asked, taking stock of the island.

Aubrey shooed him away, mumbling to herself. "Maybe I can create a simple syrup with the Moscato. That way the flavor can be intensified."

She didn't come up for air until a new batch was spinning

in the ice cream maker—kind of like a puppy chasing its tail. *Why are desserts so cute?*

"Be a good little blob." She wagged her index finger at the ice cream machine, her expression stern to match her words. *Wait a minute.* Being bossy wouldn't get her anywhere. She was, after all, at the mercy of the tail-chasing blob. "I'm sorry. I didn't mean to be bossy. I'll say please. Pretty please."

A hoot of laughter made her jump and scream long and loud. Landon nearly toppled from the stool, startled by her horror queen performance. *Was he watching me the entire time?* Aubrey patted her hair to make sure it wasn't a spiky mess. *Because having tidy hair will make Landon forget I was talking to the sorbet like an insane person.*

"Sorry. I didn't realize you were here," she said.

"It's not the first time. Being completely ignored by a beautiful woman helps build character." Landon recovered from his near fall and winked at her. "Besides, I wasn't here the entire time. Come on. Follow me."

"Where are we going?" She narrowed her eyes at him but didn't pull away from his gentle hold on her arm.

"Nowhere. Just upstairs," he said with a smile in his voice.

Only when he led her to her room and took a step inside did she dig her heels in. "Wait a minute. This is my room."

"Yes, it is." He gave her a little tug, and she followed him inside, curiosity getting the best of her.

Her hands rose to her chest as she gasped at the sight of her giant bathtub, filled to the rim with snow-white bubbles and surrounded by lavender-scented candles. The smell was enough to make her swoon, but the fact that Landon had drawn a bath for her jellified her bones.

"Oh, Landon," she whispered. "You did this for me?"

"I thought you might want a break from your sorbet. I could

tell how much getting it right was stressing you out. And I only thought it fair to do something in return for the honor of watching a master pastry chef at work."

"I'm not a chef, much less a master." But she couldn't quell the flush of pride warming her cheeks.

"You're wrong about that." His voice was soft, but it carried a ring of conviction that made her heart pound against her ribs. "I'll leave you to your much-deserved bath, then."

"Landon, wait. You wanna . . . Could you keep me company?" When his eyebrows burrowed into his hairline, she blushed furiously and waved her hands in the air. "No, no. Not like that. Once I'm in the bath and hidden under all that bubble, you want to stay and chat? It would help take my mind off the disaster waiting for me downstairs."

What the hell am I doing? It still totally sounded "like that."

He nodded mutely, licking his lips as though they had gone suddenly dry. She stared at him for a few seconds before he startled. "Uh. Right. I'll be right outside. Let me know when it's safe to come in."

Looking over her shoulder as though Landon was about to burst through the door without warning, Aubrey quickly stripped out of her clothes and stuffed them into the laundry bin. Then she rushed back to the tub and lowered herself into it. *Mmm.* She couldn't hold back her moan of bliss.

"What was that?" said Landon's muffled voice.

Her eyes widened, recalling the situation she'd put herself in. "Umm. I'm ready."

The door swung open the second the words left her mouth, and Landon hefted in an ottoman from her sitting area like it weighed nothing. *So. Hot.* Her body warmed in ways not related to the heat of the bath, but she snapped herself back to attention. It wasn't about their attraction. It was about their friendship. Friends talked, and she'd been enjoying her conversation with him too much for it to end. That was all.

She cleared her throat and talked all friendly, like. "I'm perfectly content with being a small-town baker, you know."

"*Content?* That's a loaded word." His gaze shot to her face. "Some people search for a lifetime never finding it. Twenty-seven is hardly a lifetime."

His eyes darted to her shoulders above the bubbles and then down the length of her body to the toes peeping out at the other end of the tub. Until then, he'd been staring at his hands, which were clasped between his knees. Aubrey bit the inside of her cheek to keep a satisfied smile from touching her lips. *Friendship? What friendship?* Her mind was doing so many flip-flops, her eyes swam.

Landon coughed, swallowed, and cleared his throat, and did it all over again before he continued. "How could you be certain you don't want more?"

Aubrey hesitated. His question touched a nerve, resonating deep within her. *Am I content with my life as Weldon's favorite baker?* She had been, but now she wasn't at all certain. With a suddenness that stole her breath, a gaggle of dark-haired, brown-eyed munchkins skipped across her heart. *A life with Landon. No.* She shook her head so hard the beautiful children ping-ponged around in her head and disappeared.

"It'd be nice to travel the world again. I would love to explore Asia and experience the different flavors, smells, textures, and colors of each country. It would help me continue to grow as a baker." She forced her mind to focus on work so she could ignore the aching loneliness and the longing for *more* he'd ignited in her.

"You should. Why box yourself in when you have limitless potential?" Landon cocked his head and regarded her thoughtfully. "Wanting more isn't a bad thing. Not always. *You* should want more. Have more."

"Maybe."

She'd been working for hours, thanks to the sorbet crisis, and exhaustion engulfed her. Closing her eyes, Aubrey rolled her bunched-up shoulders and massaged her neck with one hand.

"Turn around." Landon stood and approached her.

She should've said "No, thank you," but Aubrey was too sore and tired to argue. She turned in the tub and offered him her back, gathering more bubbles to ensure her girls weren't visible. His hands were strong and warm against her, and she moaned deep in her throat as he worked out a stubborn knot. *It hurts so good.*

Landon stilled behind her at the sound and then blew out a slow breath. When he resumed his gentle ministrations, the tenor of his touch had changed. Her body's response was instantaneous. Aubrey pressed back into him and shivered when his hands slid up and down her wet, slick arms.

With her heart slamming against her rib cage, Aubrey turned to face him and held his hot gaze. She couldn't think straight, but she wanted this. She wanted this so much. Landon lowered his head and she leaned toward him, her hands lifting to his hair and her lips parting in anticipation.

The chime of the doorbell jarred Aubrey out of her trance, and she hid back under the bubbles with a sharp gasp. Landon didn't budge and continued to hold her gaze. She shut her eyes and stopped breathing.

Saved by the bell.

She didn't dare look at him. If he chose that moment to

flash the Smile at her, she would drag him into the tub fully clothed and have her way with him.

—

"I'll get that," Landon said after a moment's hesitation.

Aubrey nodded, lowering her lashes to hide her eyes from him. If it weren't for the rapid rise and fall of her magnificent breasts—or the bubbles covering them—and the rosy blush on her cheeks, he might've believed he'd imagined the moment.

He stalked to the front door, grumbling under his breath as he pushed up his wet sleeves. Aria and Lucien stood outside with their arms loaded with brown paper bags. Landon itched to slam the door on their clueless, grinning faces.

"Great timing," he said dryly.

Aria rolled her eyes and pushed past him, but Lucien cringed, scratching the back of his head.

"Did we interrupt something? I insisted we call first, but Aria . . . Well, you know Aria. I think her exact words were, 'Oh, poof.'"

"I know her all too well," Landon said, stepping outside. He needed a moment to collect himself after seeing Aubrey nearly naked. "Come on. Let's take a walk before dinner."

Lucien gave him a sideways glance as he easily matched Landon's long strides. "You okay? You looked crazed when you opened the door for us. Something wrong with the production?"

"No. Nothing's wrong. I'm perfectly fine."

"Hmm. If you insist," his friend said while his expression called bullshit.

Landon raked his fingers through his damp hair as they veered onto the small path that led into the wooded hills. He nearly groaned when his body hardened again, remembering how it had gotten wet. Her naked arms had felt like warm silk under his hands, and the bubbles had clung to her breasts like seashells on a mermaid. A strategic breath from him would've dislodged the tenacious foam. He had to walk off his hard-on if he wanted to return to the villa. He didn't want to leave Aubrey alone with Aria for too long.

"How are things with you and Aria?" Landon said. "Are you still being a stubborn ass?"

"There's nothing going on between us, and I've been a stubborn ass for forty-seven years. I have no incentive to change at my ripe old age."

"You're exhausting, do you know that? If you shut Aria out, you'll regret it for the next forty-seven years. The tragedy is she'll hurt right along with you. If it comes to that, I'll beat you to a pulp. She's my best friend, man."

Lucien replied with something between a groan and a scoff. A cop-out. He knew Landon was right.

By the time they walked into the kitchen, the women were in deep conversation. Based on her crinkled nose and wildly gesticulating hands, Aubrey was probably relaying her frustrating attempts to make Moscato sorbet.

"Well, one thing's obvious," Aria said, "you've been at it too long. Let's have loads of delicious food and fabulous wine and not spend a single minute thinking about work."

"How's that even possible?" Aubrey laughed. "Food is your work."

"Oh, poof."

Aria covered the dining table with a board of savory charcuterie—a slice of *jamón ibérico* was calling Landon's name—and several excellent cheeses, a harmonious mix of soft and creamy, sharp and pungent, and hard and nutty varieties. Ripe, late-summer berries and juicy, deep orange cantaloupes added splashes of color to the white tablecloth. Aria set down fresh, colorful salads, one after the other—curried Israeli couscous; balsamic-glazed arugula and strawberry salad; and pear, goat cheese, and walnut salad. It was Aria's signature feast.

"Did you and Lucien clean out the delicatessen?" Landon reached for a spear of truffle gouda, but Aria slapped his hand away and made a fist in his face. "Fine. I'll wait."

Aubrey giggled at his side, and he raised an eyebrow at her. "Amused, are we?"

Ridiculously aware he was showing off, he swiped a fig from the table and held it up as his trophy. He tossed the ripe bundle into the air, intending to catch it deftly in his mouth, but Aubrey's hand shot out and intercepted it. With a smug grin, she bit into the fruit and then licked the sticky juice from her lips. Landon's breath caught in his throat, and blood rushed south.

Does she have any idea of the effect she has on me?

By the playful twinkle in her eyes, she had no clue how sexy she looked eating that fig. Only when he grabbed her wrist and brought the other half to his mouth did her eyes widen with awareness. He was careful not to let his lips touch her fingers because that would've sent him over the edge. But Aubrey's lashes fluttered as a shiver ran through her, and he reached out to throw her on the table.

"Should we start with one bottle, or should I just open all three?" Lucien's musings pulled Landon out of his lust haze. Barely.

"All of them." He badly needed a drink. He turned on his heels and strode to the kitchen. "I'll get the glasses."

Aria shot him a narrow-eyed glance. His voice probably sounded as strangled as he felt. He'd nearly ravished Aubrey on the dining table. In front of his friends. He would be shocked if he sounded normal.

Even his complete loss of control didn't douse his desire, and the effort it took to not ogle at Aubrey nearly gave him an aneurysm. It wasn't until they were well into their second bottle of wine that Landon trusted himself to look her way.

Her head was thrown back in full-throttle laughter at something Aria was saying. Her eyes were scrunched shut, and little ridges formed at the bridge of her nose. She was radiant. Landon chugged another glass of wine.

Everyone was coaxed into a languid mood, and happiness laced through the idyllic evening. Landon finally allowed himself to relax. His wine-addled brain reasoned that he'd had it all wrong from the beginning.

Of course we could make love to each other. It wouldn't ruin their careers because no one would know. He would have her— their attraction couldn't be fought—but he would protect her by keeping their affair a secret. *Simple.*

Weeks of frustration released its death grip from his lungs. Leaning back against his chair, Landon watched Aria for a few seconds as she sipped her third glass of wine. Then, he brought his lips to Aubrey's ear.

"I think she's ready."

"Ready for what?" Aubrey whispered.

"Just watch and enjoy." He grinned and turned to the other side of the table and did his best impression of a medieval king. "The night is young, and we must have music."

"*Absolument.* We must have the greatest of all music." Lucien joined in without hesitation, winking at Aubrey. "Opera."

"Idiots, both of you." Aria rolled her eyes and leaned toward Aubrey. "They think they can make me perform like a parrot whenever I get tipsy. But I'm far from tipsy tonight."

"Will flattery work, then?" Landon said. "Signorina Santini, your sublime voice will make us mortals weep and the heavenly angels sigh."

"Your voice is as beautiful as you are, *ma chérie*. It's indeed a gift from God," Lucien said, grasping Aria's hand to shower it with adoring kisses. She laughed and slapped at the Frenchman's shoulder.

"I'd love to hear you sing." Aubrey's soft request was shy but sincere.

"Fine. It's a democracy, no? Three to one means I must sing." Aria smiled at Aubrey but narrowed her eyes at Landon and Lucien. "Pick a song for me."

"How about 'Un bel dì vedremo' from *Madame Butterfly?*" Lucien suggested.

"Well, I guess you can never go wrong with Puccini." Aria shrugged, giving in with a grin. "It's one of my favorite pieces. It pushes at a mezzo's range, but I love to sing it."

Landon caught Aubrey's hand in his and smiled. "Now let's enjoy the fruit of our efforts."

12

The fruit of their efforts was breathtaking.

At first, Aubrey was too distracted by the warmth of Landon's hand holding her own, but soon, the performance sucked her in whole. The vivacious woman disappeared, and sorrow bled into Aria's rich, velvety voice, and the soulful music pulsed in Aubrey's heart and seeped into her veins. When the last note faded, the air vibrated with energy and then stilled into a silence so clear and pure that Aubrey was afraid to break it. She was awed and humbled by the beauty of the music, and helpless tears streamed down her face.

"You're beautiful, Aubrey Choi," Landon whispered, smoothing his thumb across her wet cheek.

With her heart brimming with joy and vulnerability, Aubrey's feelings for him broke through the surface and shone on her face. She should look away. *Hide.* But his dark, heated gaze drew her in deeper and deeper until everything else fell away, leaving the two of them in their own world.

She jolted out of the trance when she heard Aria shuffling about, haphazardly piling her purse and cardigan into her arms.

Tears trailed her cheeks as well. Maybe she was overwhelmed from putting so much of herself into the song. The longing in her voice had felt so real. As though she truly waited for the day when her lover would return to her.

"Are you leaving?" Aubrey placed her hand on Aria's arm. Aria nodded without meeting Aubrey's eyes as she stirred the contents of her purse. "Thank you so much. It was beautiful. I'll never forget it."

Aria managed a wan smile, but it disappeared in an instant when she saw Lucien approaching her with his hand outstretched. Her graceful features contorted with pain and fury.

"Aria," Lucien said, dropping his hand to his side. "Please don't."

"Please don't what?" She glared at his distraught expression and laughed bitterly. "You can take your sorry excuses and take a flying leap into hell."

With angry steps, Aria sped out the door. With distracted nods to Aubrey and Landon, Lucien ran after her shivering figure as it faded into darkness.

Aria and Lucien? Aubrey didn't want to speculate, especially since Aria was so unhappy. She just hoped they could work things out. They were both such amazing people. Landon heaved a sigh beside her as he watched his friends leave. Then he closed the door with a soft *click* and faced her.

Aubrey's throat worked to swallow the sudden lump in her throat. *Okay. So where were we?* They'd been burning off the oxygen in the room with sexual tension. *Right.* Something seemed to have shifted in him this evening. All through dinner, Landon had found ways to touch her—their shoulders brushed, their elbows rested side by side, and their knees pressed together under the table. Even now, his expression was hungry and unapologetic. Operation Friendship was in trouble. Big fucking trouble.

Run.

"Good night," she said, much louder than necessary.

When Landon's eyebrows drew together, Aubrey ran for her room without a backward glance. Then she locked the door behind her and fell face-first into bed with her limbs sprawled inelegantly. Aria's singing had stripped her bare, and the scared, insecure girl inside her had stood shivering in front of Landon. That girl would've begged. For love. For forever.

While her defenses were down, a breath of freedom had enticed her with glimpses of hope, but her survival instincts kicked in and yanked her back to reality. *Love ends. Then what? You'll be cast aside. Forgotten and alone. Don't you remember how much it hurts? Please, you must never risk your heart.*

Using the words imprinted on her soul, Aubrey cajoled the lonely little girl back into her fortress. But the woman who remained needed *something.* She didn't want love and forever. But she wanted the right-out-of-the-oven, burn-your-fingers hot man downstairs, who looked at her like he wanted to eat her up. The man she had feelings for. *Yes, I have feelings for him. Shit. I have feelings for him.* This was not good, but she couldn't hide from it anymore. Aubrey had more-than-friends, more-than-sex feelings for Landon.

She reached for her phone and emergency texted Tara.

Aubrey: Code Shit Fuckity Shit.

Tara: I thought our emergency code was Shit Shit Shit.

Aubrey: No, we decided to use this one.

Tara: Fine. Not important. What's going on?

Aubrey: Help.

Tara: Do I need to load Jack and Alex in the car and head on up there?

Aubrey: Yes. No. Landon activated his laser vision and nearly incinerated my clothes. I think he wants me.

Tara: . . .

Aubrey: I mean, he isn't even pretending not to want me. Remember the "business only" deal? Well, he means business, but not business business. He means the kind of business that happens in the bedroom.

Tara: And the shower, the kitchen, the office, the back of a car, etc. You have to broaden your horizon, my dear. So what's the emergency?

Aubrey: You know what the damn . . .

She speed-dialed Tara. It would be much more satisfactory to shout at her with her mouth rather than her thumbs.

"You know damn well what the emergency is. Laser eyes and burning clothes? He wrote a shitty review about Comfort Zone, but now he's trying to set everything right. If we sleep together and people find out, they'll think he's only doing it because I'm screwing him. Ring a bell?"

"And how are people going to find out? You guys have a whole private villa to frolic in. It's the perfect setup for a secret fling. Just don't make out in public."

"You." Aubrey sighed. "Are. The. Worst."

"How is being realistic and logical *the worst?* I told you this would happen. Eyes wide open. Remember?"

"You were supposed to skewer me with a lightsaber before something like this happened."

"Oh, God. That sentence is a treasure trove of puns."

Aubrey hung up on her cackling friend, but Tara called right back. "Listen. If you really don't want this, you need to address it head-on and bring it to an end. No more running. Talk to him. And *be honest.* You want him but not enough to risk your reputation and your dream. Right?"

"That's the whole point. I don't know what I want anymore. I have feelings for him, and I'm scared of wanting more than a frolic or a fling. The only thing I'm sure of is that I don't *want* to want more."

"Oh, Bree. I can't help with that part. You know that, right?"

"Yes, but I'm so damn confused."

"I know, babe, but you can do it. Figure out what you want, then make it yours."

After they hung up, Aubrey tried to sort through her feelings, but the cacophony of *what-ifs* and *buts* in her head wouldn't leave her alone. She longed for some sweet buns, which was crazy considering the amount of food she'd stuffed her face with earlier. *Oh no. The food.* She hadn't cleaned up any of it. Not only was she a coward, she was a stinking slob.

Aubrey tiptoed back to the kitchen imagining the leftovers strewn across every usable surface. She growled and stomped her foot like a petulant kindergartener. The kitchen. The dining room. Everything looked immaculate. Landon had tidied up while she was freaking out upstairs, making her the rudest guest ever. With slumped shoulders, she trudged toward the stairs then stopped.

Her sorbet. She'd forgotten all about it. With a burst of

anticipation, Aubrey unlocked the lid and peeked into the ice cream maker. The sorbet rolled smoothly into a ball against her small spoon, and she gingerly brought the dollop to her mouth.

By everything holy and sacred. It was the best sorbet she'd ever tasted. The Meyer lemon and honeysuckle in the Moscato shone through without overwhelming the flavor of the Muscat Blanc grapes. The texture was spot-on, firm without being icy and smooth without being gloppy, and the sweet morsel melted against her tongue into a smooth liquid without a hint of cloying stickiness.

On autopilot, she made for Landon's room, taking two steps at a time. She rapped on his door, her knuckles mimicking a famous woodpecker, then she shifted from foot to foot, unable to stand still. If he didn't answer soon, she was going to start bouncing on the balls of her feet.

When he finally opened his door, Aubrey's knees turned to jiggly pudding. *Gah.* The sight of Landon shirtless and barefoot made her mouth go dry. He was dressed, or undressed, in his charcoal gray slacks and nothing else. His chiseled body could've been carved from marble, but her body remembered the heat of his skin, and he was anything but made of stone.

She lifted her gaze from his naked torso and swallowed. Or tried. A cold drink would come in handy. *Ooh.* Her sorbet would be perfect to cool her down. Excitement blooming again, she grabbed Landon's hand and tugged him down the stairs.

"What—"

"Just come." Aubrey couldn't tone down her ear-to-ear grin.

Looking bewildered, Landon followed her the rest of the way without protest. Then he saw the tub of sorbet on the kitchen counter, and his confused frown transformed into a broad smile.

"You did it, didn't you?"

Aubrey dipped her finger into the bowl and offered him a

taste. Landon's eyebrows rose as he stared at the sample. She reddened to the top of her head.

"Sorry." She tried to draw back her hand, but Landon caught her wrist and brought her finger and the sorbet to his mouth. He savored both until moist heat warmed her chilled finger.

Lust burned through her body. She spread her other hand on his chest to stay upright, but the feel of his hard, bare chest did nothing to steady her.

"Let me." Her voice was a husky croak, and she coughed to clear it. "Let me make you an ice cream sandwich."

Landon held both her hands captive, one against his chest and the other still a breath away from his lips. He seemed to consider her offer for a moment before releasing her, then he leaned against the island to watch her move about the kitchen.

Putting a little bit of space between them and focusing on the dessert allowed Aubrey to find some semblance of composure. With a melon baller, she added three scoops of sorbet on a cookie and then gently pressed another cookie on top. She studied the proportions and nodded in satisfaction. After making its twin, she handed Landon his ice cream sandwich and then lifted hers in a mock toast.

"Here goes nuthin'." They bit into their sandwiches at the same time.

"Oh, my God." Landon moaned, savoring his first bite. He took a second bite and shook his head slowly. He was lost in his own world—just a man and his dessert.

He made ultimate sexy noises until his ice cream sandwich was gone. Aubrey watched intently, knowing she would pull out this memory again and again on long, lonely nights. When both of them were finished, they stood in the middle of the kitchen grinning at each other. Landon was the first to move. He came straight for her and enveloped her in a bear hug.

"You, Aubrey Choi, are a genius," Landon said with earnest intensity. "That's one of the most perfect things I've ever eaten." "Thank you." Happiness warmed her with its rosy glow. The quiet joy of the moment shook her more than the carnal desire that raged between them. "That means a lot to me."

With her hands on his shoulders, she rose to her tiptoes and kissed his cheek—a light, fleeting touch. But his muscles jerked and tightened beneath her hands. Awareness and triumphant pride burst through her, and she stepped back with a startled gasp. The taste of power made her tremble with need, and she wanted to wield it again.

She whispered, "Good night," and then retreated to the security of her room. Aubrey wished she could lock the door from the outside. She could easily get addicted to the heady feeling of power, and she didn't trust herself not to march downstairs to see what else she could do to him. She squeezed her thighs together and moaned. *Get. A. Grip.*

Putting her game face on, Aubrey strode to the shower and turned it on full blast. She stripped down, leaving her clothes in a careless heap, and stepped into the freezing cold spray. She squeaked before slapping her hand on her mouth. Still, she stood shivering under the water until her body went numb. She couldn't succumb to the hunger that consumed her.

If she did, her heart was as good as lost.

———

Landon stared after Aubrey as she'd made a run for her room for the second time that night. A mixture of longing and helplessness wrung his gut. He wasn't accustomed to women running away as though he were a live grenade, and he certainly never chased anyone who didn't want him. But his desire for

Aubrey wasn't something he could turn off with a snap. He wanted her more than anyone he'd ever met—his desire was something pure, raw, and powerful—and not having her was pushing him to the edge of sanity.

With a resigned sigh, he reached toward the light switch when he saw Aubrey's sorbet and cookies on the counter. He couldn't let her hard work go to waste, so he transferred the ice cream to the freezer and stored the cookies away in an airtight container. Then he trudged to the wine cellar and grabbed a random bottle of red to keep him company while he brooded.

The minute he stepped into his room, Landon filled his wineglass to the rim and chugged it dry like some post-workout Gatorade. Lucien would be horrified at his mistreatment of the fine wine. Landon didn't give a damn. He had no intention of spending another night wide awake and aching.

Having rationalized his decision to rekindle their relationship, he faced the next obstacle preventing him from ravishing the woman. Aubrey herself. She was ensnared by the same manic attraction that consumed him. He could see it in her fleeting glances and her soft gasps to his touch, but she held him at arm's length. His gut told him it wasn't only about her reputation. He sloshed more wine into the glass and gulped half of it down. She was afraid. Of what, he hadn't the slightest clue. All he knew was he couldn't bulldoze through her defenses. Hurting her was the last thing he wanted.

Landon had to make the first move. Show her his hand, laying everything out in the open. He would tell her everything. Then she would have full control to decide as she wished.

With anticipation lifting his spirits, Landon resolved to spend the entire next day charming Aubrey. The choice was hers, but that didn't mean he wasn't going to stack the odds in his favor.

13

Moonstone Beach?" Aubrey squinted. "Today? I thought you're up to your neck with work."

"The construction isn't finished, and our production manager is gone for the time being. I don't need to roam around the set like a pest when there's nothing I could do about the delay." Landon scratched the back of his neck. "I think you and I could both use a breather."

"Moonstone Beach. It does sound beautiful." Aubrey hesitated even though the idea of a fun day with Landon was eroding away her caution. "Where's this place again?"

"In Cambria, a small town about an hour from here. I think you'll like it there. It reminds me of Weldon but it's set along the coast rather than a river." With amusement twinkling in his eyes, Landon laid down what obviously was his trump card. "And I don't think you'd want to miss their olallieberry pie."

"Olallie-what?" Aubrey burst out laughing.

"Oh, it's just about one of the best pies in the state."

"I'm intrigued." Resisting Landon was hard enough, but

when pie was added to the equation, she didn't stand a chance. "Okay, I'm in."

"Good choice. I'll see you downstairs in a few minutes. And don't forget to grab a jacket. It's about thirty degrees cooler over there."

As they neared Cambria, Landon switched off the AC and opened the windows to let in the salty air. He wasn't kidding about the thirty-degree difference. The brisk wind spread goose bumps on Aubrey's arms. She tugged on her cardigan without taking her eyes off the panorama. Gray clouds hung above Moonstone Beach as if signaling an impending storm, and the bleak beauty of the coastline squeezed at her heart.

"Do you think it'll rain?" Aubrey leaned forward in her seat to peer out the window.

"Nope. Those clouds are permanent fixtures in these skies." The conversation in the car dwindled as a pensive mood overtook them. The waves were breaking mercilessly against the jagged cliffs surrounding the beach, and the morning fog layered a poignant sadness to the scene. Even after parking the car, they sat ensconced in the warm silence for a few extra minutes.

"Ready to find out why they call this Moonstone Beach?" Landon asked.

Aubrey shook herself out of her reverie and beamed at him. She was suddenly giddy with excitement. A *whole day with Landon*. And what an amazing start to their day.

Moonstone Beach was covered with colorful coin-size stones that glistened and beckoned to them as the waves washed over them. The spell of the poignant beauty refused to release her, and Aubrey stood staring out at the ocean, watching the soft break of the waves on the beach. Despite her light jacket, she couldn't stop shivering against the chill of the breeze.

When Landon put his arm around her and pulled her close, Aubrey nestled against him, unwilling to fight the wonder of the moment. They stood still with the gusty breeze tousling their hair, and she felt at one with him—as though their connection was as ancient as the ocean and the stony cliffs carved by the waves.

A force greater than her insecurity was at work between them, and she couldn't fight against it anymore. At the very least, she had to face the truth—she yearned for more. Aubrey wanted to share moments like this with Landon year after year. She wanted him to be hers and hers alone.

Want. Want. Want. More. More. More.

The little seed of *more* planted itself deep in her heart, and the contentment she'd forced on herself withered and crumbled. Even if she did nothing with her newfound truth, she would stop running from herself.

"Do I have time to pilfer some of these moonstones?" She forced a carefree smile on her face.

"Take all the time you need."

She collected the beautiful stones—pink heart-shaped stones, clear azure stones, warm bronze stones, and a myriad of others in amazing colors. Soon the stones started toppling out of her cupped palm, and Aubrey frowned in frustration. When her attempts to rebuild the stone tower failed, Landon took the stones from her hand, chuckling low in his chest.

"I had no idea you're so greedy."

Aubrey rolled her eyes at him. "I'm only greedy when it involves pretty, *free* moonstones."

She returned her focus to the task at hand and didn't stop until both of Landon's jacket pockets were weighed down with her collection. "Okay. I think I'm done."

"Good." Landon pointed to his drooping jacket. "My pockets have reached maximum capacity."

"Moonstone picking is hard work." Aubrey stood up with a sheepish grin and stretched her back. "I'm starving."

"I know the perfect remedy." Landon took her arm and led her to the car.

At first glance, the restaurant looked about as big as a walk-in closet at the villa, but when the hostess led them to their table, Aubrey saw that there was a whole garden at the back dedicated to serving its patrons alfresco.

Abundant green foliage wove through the pergolas and arches, and sunlight streamed in through the dense leaves. The garden was decorated with shimmery giant butterflies and chubby colorful mushrooms, giving it a dash of whimsy.

Taking her seat at the table, Aubrey smiled at Landon. "I see you've brought me to an enchanted garden."

"And you fit right in," Landon said with an appreciative glance.

"I'll take that as a compliment." When she had her blush under control, she took another good look around the garden. "Maybe I should just drink some morning dew for lunch."

"I'd expect nothing less from a fay." His tone was light, but the heat in his gaze made her shiver with awareness.

Then her stomach rumbled uproariously as though saying *She is no ethereal fairy, mister.*

"My tummy disagrees with the whole dew-for-lunch idea."

"We'll have to find you something more substantial."

Her rich salmon bisque and the brightly flavored lamb curry burrito were definitely more substantial and satisfying than morning dew. While she'd never drunk morning dew, she assumed it tasted pretty much like condensation on a glass of a cold drink.

The bite she snagged from Landon's lobster enchiladas was

also amazing. The generous bites of lobster were chewy without being rubbery, and the enchilada sauce had a smoky kick to it to prevent the dish from becoming too rich.

"This trip was a great idea. I don't think I'll forget it anytime soon." Sitting with a full stomach in the sun-warmed garden turned Aubrey into a happy Buddha.

"Well, it's not over yet. You still haven't tried the olallieberry pie."

"Don't tell anyone I said this, but there's no way I could fit pie into my stomach right now."

"Okay, then. Let's make like tourists and check out downtown Cambria. I'm sure we can burn off our lunch and make room for pie."

"Could we take a nap first?"

"Up you go, lazy buns." Landon lifted her by her arms, and happy Buddha had no choice but to waddle along beside him.

Downtown Cambria reminded Aubrey of Weldon, but it had a slightly more laid-back, beach-town feel to it. Fewer diners and more cafés with outdoor seating. She'd forgotten how fun it was to be a tourist. The streets were studded with stores full of local art, wines, and olive oils and everything else Cambria. She was particularly drawn to a quaint shop with delicate handblown glassware. As she browsed the shop, soaking in all the lovely globes, jars, and bottles, Landon gestured to her that he'd be outside to take a call.

She was roaming down the aisles when a row of graceful glass bottles caught her eye. The teardrop-shaped bottles had oversize globe stoppers that gave them a bold, startling look. They felt kind of *off*—just enough to draw her attention—but not *wrong*. The odd proportion and balance of the bottles gave them a unique beauty that entranced her. She gasped a little at the price tag, but she just couldn't walk away from them.

They'd be perfect for her moonstones, and she wanted to give one to Landon for the wonderful day trip.

Well, you only live once. Aubrey picked out a green bottle for Landon and a light blue one for herself. She marched with determination to the cashier but had to take a deep breath before she could actually put the bottles down for her to scan and wrap.

"I didn't mean to neglect you for so long. We might actually start shooting as scheduled if the stars line up for us." The bottles were safely packaged and stored in a sturdy shopping bag when Landon walked in with an apologetic smile. "Been shopping? What did you get?"

"Oh, just a small souvenir."

Landon cocked his head at her but didn't pry. He took the shopping bag and linked his fingers through hers. They strolled hand in hand, glancing at the shops lining the street. Aubrey couldn't help her heart from fluttering from the simple pleasure. He'd been incredibly attentive and sweet the entire day and found ways to touch her every chance he got—holding her hand, guiding her by the small of her back, tucking a lock of her hair behind her ear. All the while, Aubrey's heart beat—*more, more, and more.*

"So are you ready for your olallieberry pie?"

"Yes, please." Anything to stop this day from ending.

He chuckled softly while his eyes lingered on her face and his thumb traced a circle on the palm of her hand. She exhaled a quiet sigh. He wanted time to slow down, too.

___

The famous olallieberry pie was famous for a reason. The bakery was housed in a converted two-story cottage that was bursting with cozy charm and pie-hungry customers. Their table was on the second floor, overlooking a trinket shop that Aubrey wanted to clean out. It was cuteness overload.

"There you go," their server said, placing two picture-perfect slices of pie in front of them, then bustling off to serve the other slices of pie balanced on her arm.

"Wow," Aubrey said. "Their definition of a slice is a quarter of the pie?"

"Trust me. It's the perfect size. A wimpy one-eighth slice would leave you licking the plate, consoling your stomach's unfulfilled need for more pie."

Aubrey laughed and broke the golden, flaky crust to scoop up her first bite. She stopped laughing. She stopped talking. It was all about the pie as she savored the intensity of the tart and sweet filling and the richness of the buttery, short crust. Olallieberries looked similar to a blackberry but had the soft skin and delicate seeds of raspberries, so the deep, royal-purple filling had a fun, slightly chewy texture.

When she finally glanced up from her plate, Landon was watching her with the Smile. Of course she smiled back. She couldn't stop herself even though she suspected her teeth were tainted purple and dotted with olallieberry seeds.

"Good?" he said.

"So, so good."

Aubrey exercised a heavy dose of restraint at the gift shop and kept her purchases to an olallieberry refrigerator magnet for Tara and a jar of olallieberry jam for herself. Landon casually strolled the shop, stopping here and there, then lined up at the register. She waited for him by the door, dying to know what he'd gotten, but she kept her curiosity to herself in case he asked her about her purchases from the glass store.

Landon tucked her into the passenger seat, then slid into his seat and turned to her. "You want to see what I got?"

"*Yes.*"

He pulled out his find with a flourish and dangled it in front of her nose.

"What is that?" Aubrey said, drawing back to get a better look. Then she burst into a belly laugh. "Is that an olallieberry pie air freshener?"

Grinning broadly, he broke open the plastic packaging and hung the cartoony pie behind his rearview mirror. He looked so mischievous and gleeful that Aubrey bit hard on the inside of her cheek to stop from mooning over him. This adorable and carefree Landon might be worth risking everything for.

The stars filled the sky, and a sliver of a crescent moon lit the road on their drive back, and Aubrey retraced the details of the day, committing them to memory. Landon drove at a leisurely pace. Perhaps he wanted to prolong the day as much as she did. It really was a perfect day, and a part of her wanted it to lead into a perfect night.

Unable to shake off the dangerous path of her thoughts, she stole sideways glances at Landon, turning away with a blush only to look back again. Every time he caught her staring, he made her heart perform acrobatics with his sexy dimple. He could probably see what she wanted plastered across her face, but she couldn't stop staring.

When his cell phone rang, she jumped as though she'd been caught being naughty. Aubrey's heart plummeted when she heard Aria weeping on the other side.

"Landon, please. I need to talk to you."

Before she could hear any more, Landon transferred the call to his handheld.

"Where are you?" He paused and nodded as though Aria could see him through the phone. "It's okay. I'll be there soon."

When the call ended, tension blanketed the quiet happiness that had permeated the car. Landon seemed distracted, and Aubrey pulled on her lower lip, torn between concern and curiosity.

"Is everything okay?" she asked hesitantly.

"Yes." He glanced at her and then turned his eyes back to the road. "No. She needs someone to talk to, but she'll be okay."

"Let me know if I can do anything to help."

Landon smiled a little and gave her knee a squeeze, but his mind was elsewhere. Aubrey wished they could've enjoyed the rest of their evening together and then immediately felt like a brat. She'd only known Aria for a little more than a week, but Aria was her friend and she needed Landon's help. Aubrey couldn't believe how selfish she was.

The remaining drive to the villa dragged on for what felt like hours. The car had barely rolled to a stop when Aubrey jumped out and ran for the front door. If she lingered, she might want to hold on to him. Besides, he'd never leave Aria in tears to stay with her. Their one night together wouldn't—and shouldn't—trump ten years of friendship.

Too busy lecturing herself, she didn't hear Landon behind her and jumped when he grasped her arm.

"Are you okay?" A frown creased his forehead.

"Yes, yes. Of course. I'm just tired."

"Get some rest, then." But his gaze bored into hers, seeking the truth behind her transparent lie. "I'll be out for a while. Will you be okay?"

"Yes, I'll be fine," she said, tilting her chin up. "Good night."

"Hey, wait." As she stepped toward the door, Landon tugged her into his arms. "I had a wonderful time today. Thank you for coming with me."

"You're welcome." Her smile wobbled in the corners. "It was lovely."

They stood with their gazes locked, and his arms loosely wrapped around her waist. Their smiles dimmed as the space between their bodies became hot and charged like a stormy night in the tropics.

"I should go," he said, but he made no move to leave and stared at her lips.

"Yes, of course." She tried to step back, but his hands tightened on her waist. Aubrey cocked her head to the side. She really hadn't wanted to keep him from Aria. "Landon?"

His eyes darted around her face, tortured and frantic. He was going to stand there all night, fighting an inner battle. *Oh, for God's sake.* She rose on her tiptoes and tugged his head down and then kissed him. It was soft and lingering, and he sighed into her mouth. His tongue traced her bottom lip, coaxing her to let him in. Her lips started to part before she remembered Aria, and she pushed against his chest.

"You have to go." She sounded winded. *Gah.* She was in trouble. "I hope Aria's okay."

"Me, too." He shoved his hands through his hair and took a backward step. "Good night, Aubrey."

"Bye."

Long after Landon drove off, Aubrey stood exactly where he'd left her, blinking like an owl. The chill in the evening air nudged her to action, and she stumbled into the dark villa.

She already missed him.

14

Their lovely day together had filled her with energy, and Aubrey paced her room, twitchy with cabin fever. Nothing made sense where Landon was involved. She was in a perpetual haze of conflicting desires—want him, can't have him, fuck it, be practical. It was time to make up her mind, and there was only one wise choice. No more kissing. No more testing the line. They were going to be friends. With *no* benefits.

She heaved a loud sigh and parked her bottom on her bed, but her feet danced around the floor, enchanted with angst. *How am I supposed to still this restless energy? Oh yes.* The villa's lovely swimming pool.

She hadn't brought a swimsuit, but it shouldn't matter; the pool was surrounded by trees and hills as far as the eyes could see. As for Landon, he'd be gone for God knew how long. *Will he want to continue our kiss when he gets back?* The wayward thought made her want to kick something, preferably Landon. It was unfair. She was a strong woman, and her brain, not her lady bits, ruled her actions. No man should be so irresistible. Taking a deep breath, she crammed serenity down her throat.

Swim. Now.

The late-summer night held hints of the autumn chill, but the sun-warmed water felt luxurious on her naked skin. Despite the accent lighting glowing out of the pool, the stars poured down from the sky, outshining the artificial lighting. Even the grace of the crescent moon seemed to pale in comparison to the brilliant diamonds blinking in the heavens.

The rhythmic laps around the pool calmed Aubrey's clattering mind and released the tension from her body. Soon her heart resumed its steady beat, and the soothing balm of nature spread peace through her. After a while, Aubrey lay floating on her back, stroking one arm and then the other, making herself circle slowly around the pool. Her mind wandered lazily until it settled on Landon—the dark intensity of his eyes, his full, sensuous mouth, his firm, muscular chest, and his long, strong legs. In her calm, relaxed state, thinking of Landon made her mouth curve into a lazy smile.

The quiet scrape of the pool chair shattered her reverie, and Aubrey stood up in the pool, clumsily splashing water in her hurry. Landon sat a few feet from the pool, his arms crossed over his chest. He was apparently waiting for the second act of the show. His face was partially hidden in the night, so Aubrey couldn't read his expression.

On the contrary, she was in a glowing pool with the moonlight shining down on her—her nudity spotlighted from top to bottom. Embarrassment flaming her face, Aubrey stopped treading water to cover her breasts with her arms. When she started sinking, she released her arms to tread water again.

"Go away."

"Not on your life."

"Then at least have the courtesy to look away," she snapped.

"I'm not feeling particularly well mannered at the moment."

"Well . . . I . . ." She clamped her mouth shut to stop sputtering.

Aubrey couldn't see his face, but she felt his gaze follow her across the pool. She had nowhere to hide, but creating some distance was better than nothing. By the time she reached the far end of the pool, her mortification had morphed into anger.

He had suddenly shown up in her life, unreasonably attractive and amazing in bed. But he'd written a judgmental review, which still might cost her Comfort Zone. Then, he unilaterally announced he didn't want to resume their affair, then made her a business proposal. *It'll be strictly business. Blah, blah, blah.* They were starting to become some sort of friends, and they had gone on a lovely day trip. Now, here he was, watching her like a man dying of hunger. Hunger for her. He had no right to confuse her like this.

Indignation doused her fury with fuel. The fire burned her modesty and inhibition into ashes. Aubrey spun around to face him and draped her arms over the edge of the pool. Her breasts jutted forward, the top curves breaking water. She held her position for a long minute, daring him to explore every last inch of her.

Then she kicked off the wall and swam to the other end. She didn't rush and enjoyed the caress of the water against her sensitized skin. Slowly and deliberately, she drew close to her sole audience. Landon sat motionless in the shadows. She dove under at the last stretch and broke through when she reached the edge. Tipping her head back, she let the weight of the water smooth her long bangs back.

"If you won't look away, the least you could do is help me out of the pool."

Landon was so still, he could've been a statue, and Aubrey's courage faltered. Then, with a suddenness that nearly knocked the chair over, he stood and reached the edge of the pool in two long strides. Uncloaked from the darkness, his eyes blazed with desire, and her body caught fire in response.

When he reached out, Aubrey wanted nothing more than to put her hand in his so he could pull her into his arms. She wanted to press her wet, cool body against the hard heat of his and kiss him with all her pent-up desire.

There was nothing she wanted more. Maybe except for this—

Once she had a firm grip of his hand, Aubrey planted both of her feet on the wall and leaned back with all her strength. She heard rather than saw Landon land in the water. While he remained stunned for a split second, she pushed herself up and out of the pool.

The thick towel she'd brought dwarfed her, leaving only her feet visible. Grateful for the armor, she glanced at Landon from under her lashes. He was resting his chin on his forearms, leaning out of the lip of the pool. He wore an amused grin on his face, but his eyes raked over her like hot coals. She was afraid he'd singe the towel off her.

Now would be the time to make a pithy remark and trot away. But all her anger and bravado had seeped out of her, and she stood trembling. In fear or desire, she couldn't say.

"Run, Aubrey," Landon warned quietly. "If you're still there when I get out of here, I guarantee you won't be going to bed alone tonight."

She knew she should do as he'd said, but her legs refused to take her back to safety. *Just take one step. The next ones will be easier.* Even when Landon pushed himself out of the pool, his wet clothes clinging to his hard body, all Aubrey could manage was a wide-eyed gasp.

He stalked toward her with measured steps—his large body

taut with control and dangerously graceful. His face was a mask of lean hunger, and she *wanted*. She wanted him with a fierce desperation that stole her breath.

She'd shared one night with him, and the memories were seared into her mind. But it was nothing—*nothing*—compared to the carnal fever that seized her now.

He stopped mere inches from her, and his heat engulfed her. "Look at me."

Helpless against his command, she stared into his eyes. It was going to end in heartbreak, but she had no choice. Fighting what raged between them was a slow death. When Landon lowered his head, she tilted her face and parted her lips to receive his touch fully. It was surrender. It was freedom.

She pushed her body against his and fisted her hands into his hair. Answering her unspoken demand, he deepened the kiss with a shuddering groan. Hunger eclipsed sanity, and she plunged her tongue into his mouth and tugged his head down, struggling to get closer to him.

Aubrey writhed against him and bit his bottom lip hard. With a low growl, he wrenched the towel from her body and pressed her against him. His hands were rough and hot on her bare skin, and a muffled moan escaped her.

Still not close enough.

Frustrated with the barrier between them, Aubrey tugged at his damp shirt with fumbling hands. She whimpered in protest when his lips left hers for the second it took to pull his shirt over his head.

He's so beautiful.

Spreading her fingers wide on his chest, Aubrey buried her lips in the hollow of his throat and traced open-mouthed kisses along his jaw to capture his lips again. Their touch held no gentleness—only rough urgency. Landon drew his hands up the side of her body and cupped her breasts. When he grazed his thumbs over their hard peaks, Aubrey whimpered and rocked her hips against him. He released her mouth to taste her neck, sucking and nibbling on the sensitive skin.

"God, I need you." His voice was a husky plea. "All of you."

Landon's words pierced through the fog of passion and buried themselves in Aubrey's mind. She jolted awake from her dream. She couldn't do this. She couldn't risk her livelihood. Her future.

But it was more than that. She was falling for him.

Her parents' wreck of a marriage had convinced her love and forever weren't for her. *If he grows tired of me, I'll become invisible even when I'm by his side. I'll disappear like Mom.* She couldn't risk becoming a ghost, floating through life, unseen and unheard.

———

He was consumed by fire. He had no consciousness other than need and desire. Their hot breath mingled as one, and he couldn't get close enough to her. At first, he didn't notice at all. Then through the haze, Landon realized Aubrey was pushing against his chest. Bewildered, he lifted his head just enough to focus his eyes on hers.

"I can't." Her voice broke on the second word.

"Why?" He held her gently by the shoulders. "Don't pretend you don't feel this. We can't fight it. I'm sick of fighting it."

"Nothing has changed. If anyone finds out we've slept together, all the time and money I invested to expand Comfort Zone could be lost. Even my appearance on Aria's show could backfire on us." Her voice was thin and hesitant. "I won't be that person who'd do anything to get ahead, and you can't be the man who could be bought."

But she was wrong. Everything had changed.

Aubrey hurried inside the house, buried under the white towel, and he watched her disappear up the stairs. Landon didn't know how long he stood at the foot of the staircase. He forced his steps to lead him to his room, and then he changed into his running clothes.

Landon sprinted on the dirt trails circling the property until he tasted blood in his throat. Then he ran some more. His lungs burned, and his muscles screamed, but he couldn't erase the memory of Aubrey in the pool, wet and naked. She took his breath away. He ached for her. But the fear and vulnerability in her eyes haunted his mind even after his body cooled.

When she'd sneaked away from his hotel without a word it had stung his pride. He'd laughed at himself for feeling used and discarded. It had hardly been his first one-night stand. Still, he hadn't been able to stop thinking about her. Wanting her.

He had to face the fact that making love to Aubrey had marked his soul. Burying himself deep inside her had satisfied a hunger he hadn't known was there, but it made him starved for more. He'd been a coward to leave Weldon without finding her. He'd denied the unsettling emotions she'd awakened in him because it was easier that way.

Well, *easier* could go to hell. He no longer cared that a relationship with Aubrey would complicate his life. The wild need inside him demanded to be fulfilled. If he didn't heed the deafening call to make love to her, he would burn to cinders.

Landon had to discover the source of her fear and assuage it with everything in him. Aubrey was a warm, sensual woman, so full of life. A woman like her shouldn't be locked behind a defensive wall.

But until she was ready, he had to respect her wishes and give her the space she asked for.

15

The next morning, Aubrey couldn't bear being alone with her thoughts, so she decided to take a stroll. Downtown Bosque Verde was charming and small enough to navigate on foot. The locals busily traversed the tidy streets, greeting one another as they passed, and the cluster of tiny shops beckoned with their warmth and charm.

But she didn't see any of it. Not really.

Why? Landon had asked.

She might be a coward, but she was an honest one, and it was time to start facing some facts. *Yeah. Why, Aubrey?*

When her cell phone rang, relief flooded her at the reprieve, but then she saw who it was and her gut twisted with familiar anxiety. Her father rarely called, but when he did, he expected her to answer on the first ring. She let it ring five more times. If she sent him straight to voice mail, he'd probably have his secretary call her every five minutes until she picked up. Aubrey stared at her cell and considered smashing it against the sidewalk, but she couldn't afford a new phone.

Grrr. Let's get this over with.

"Yes."

"Too busy to talk to your old man?" His voice was smooth and silky as a snake, and an involuntary shiver shook her.

"Say what you have to say. I'm not in the mood for chitchatting."

"I see your manners haven't improved. I can't say I'm surprised." He sighed impatiently like he'd grown tired of the niceties. "You're coming home."

"Oh, I'm going home—to Weldon—but not for another week."

"Stop being a child. I've been more than patient in allowing you to play Little Miss Baker for the last few years. It's time you grew up and accepted your responsibilities."

"My responsibilities?" Aubrey's fingers tightened around her phone, and she forced herself to breathe through her nose. "You want to marry me off to clinch a business deal? You always said that was a daughter's duty to her family."

"You flatter yourself. You think all it takes is a pretty face and a high school diploma to marry well?" he said. She'd applied for every college he'd chosen for her and had been accepted into all of them. Then she'd refused to attend any of them and left home to travel and gain real-world experiences. Years later, her decision still seemed to infuriate her father. "Only the most accomplished of your friends were able to make advantageous matches. Without my name and money, you're nothing more than *good time* material."

Aubrey swallowed the expletive tickling her tongue when a young family strolled past her. "You and I obviously don't share the same definition of *friend*."

"Would you say Landon Kim is your friend?"

She'd just reached her bicycle when the ground rolled under her feet. Gripping the handle for balance, Aubrey hissed into the phone, "Stay out of my life."

"You prefer to be a media clown's plaything than a good man's wife?"

She blanched at her father's crude words and hated herself for letting him get to her.

"You will come home this minute. If you continue down this path, even my money and reputation won't be enough to save you. I won't stand by and watch you sully our family name any longer."

"I lost count of how many mistresses you've had over the years." Her laughter held an edge of hysteria. "There's nothing left for *me* to sully, Father."

"My personal business is my own. No one would dare question me. Even your mother turns a blind eye," he said smugly.

Aubrey covered her mouth to stop her horrified gasp from escaping. To think, she'd once longed for this man's love and approval.

"If you don't come home of your own accord, then I'll have no choice but to disown you." He delivered his threat in a purr.

"Don't hold your breath." Realization hit her. His excuses about her bringing shame to the family were exactly that. Excuses. Maybe he really needed to marry her off to someone for his shady side business. Unfortunately for her father, she frankly didn't give a damn. "As far as I'm concerned, I disowned you when I walked out of your house nine years ago."

"Your mother will be very disappointed in you."

"I've been disappointed in her for years," she said, and then cringed at her knee-jerk reaction to her father's meanness. She wasn't disappointed in her mom. She never had been. It hurt her to see her mom stay with him and be hurt again and again. But that was her mom's decision, and she wouldn't question her anymore.

"I'll be sure to tell her that," he said.

Goddamn bastard. "She'll know I didn't mean it." Aubrey pushed the heel of her palm against her eye.

Her father was the monster. Not her mom. When Aubrey was younger, she'd resented her mother for not leaving him. She'd shunned and lashed out at her mom. As she got older, Aubrey understood she wasn't angry with her. She just couldn't bear to watch her hurt so much. But the damage had been done, and she didn't know how to close the rift she'd created between them.

I'm so sorry, Mom.

"Come home, or else I'll—"

She hung up on her father's ranting and turned off her phone. Her brief conversation with him eradicated all hopes of enjoying her day out, so she returned to the villa to work on her ice cream sandwich. That was why she was in Bosque Verde, after all.

While she found a semblance of peace practicing her recipes, she ran out of steam in a few hours. The sun was slinking down the horizon, and Aubrey shook herself out of her stupor and went to the kitchen to jostle up some grub. Gone were the days of cozy breakfasts and relaxed dinners with Landon.

She poked around in the fridge and settled on a plump white peach for supper, and then she trudged back to her bedroom like a coward. There really wasn't any need for her to hide since Landon had been avoiding her as if she were the latest strain of the flu virus. She had no right to be hurt by his absence, but her heart wouldn't listen to reason.

She mumbled insults at herself and tore into the juicy flesh of the peach. *What did I expect after what happened?* She finished her dinner and walked over to the bathroom to dispose of the pit and wash her sticky hands. Then she studied herself in the bathroom mirror, hoping her reflection could clue her in about what to do next.

One thing was certain. Things couldn't continue like this. The taut tension between them was suffocating, and she was certain something was going to snap from the palpable strain. Aubrey sat at her balcony and stared into the pastoral landscape stretching out before her. Despite the peaceful scene, her heart and mind raged war against each other. She couldn't run from herself except in circles, the truth bashing into her face every time she fled from it. Even so, she stubbornly ran until her overworked brain threatened to short-circuit. Aubrey clenched her eyes shut.

"*Fine,*" she snapped at the voice in her head. *Goddamn it. I have a voice in my head?* Things were worse than she'd thought. "Fine, I'll talk to him."

Of course, she'd known what she needed to do. She wasn't stupid. Just chicken. Landon was right. Their mad attraction wasn't about to peacefully ride off into the sunset. Aubrey sighed. Hiding behind her defensive wall no longer held much appeal for her. The peace and security it once provided now felt claustrophobic. She was suffocating in her own fear.

Aubrey wanted Landon. She liked him—more than anyone she'd ever been with—but that didn't mean she was going to fall stupidly in love. Her heart thumped an odd rhythm. He wasn't looking for love or commitment either. He probably wanted to let their crazy attraction run its course. Just like she did.

Knowing what she had to do and actually doing it were two different beasts. But the man she'd spent the day with in Cambria was full of laughter and warmth. There was no need to be intimidated by Landon. They would talk like two adults and lay things out in the open. She wasn't going to wait until she lost control of herself and make excuses later. She was going to do this with her eyes wide open and own it.

Aubrey tossed restlessly in bed, waiting for Landon to come

home. *Home.* It was so easy for her to imagine him coming home to her. Her tired mind spun into happy dreams when the sound of gravel crunching in the driveway jerked her awake. Blood pounding in her ears, she held her breath and listened for Landon's footsteps.

When his bedroom door clicked shut, Aubrey scrambled for the door before skidding to a stop. She was only wearing a lacy gray slip. While it was her favorite nightie, it probably wasn't suitable for having a serious conversation. She dug through her drawers and found a boxy T-shirt that came halfway down her thighs. Pulling the shirt over her head, Aubrey marched straight to Landon's room.

Well, straight to the front of his door. She stood there for interminable minutes gathering the courage to knock. Her palms were slippery with sweat, and her breath came quick and shallow.

You got this.

She rapped her knuckles smartly against the wood. There was no turning back now. When Landon opened the door, she sucked in a sharp breath. He wore a pair of jeans slung low on his hips with a plain white T-shirt on top. A lock of damp hair had fallen across his forehead, and she wanted to smooth it back for him.

Landon said nothing and studied her with a wary expression. He didn't seem angry. Just unsure of what to do. Maybe this wouldn't be as bad as she'd feared.

"Can we talk?" Her question emerged as a husky whisper.

He didn't say or do anything. Aubrey wondered if he didn't hear her when he finally stepped aside to let her in.

"Sure," Landon replied, leaning against the wall with his arms across his chest. The hint of amusement in his voice loosened the knot in her chest.

"I owe you an apology."

When she fell silent again, he pushed himself off the wall and dragged his hand through his hair. "You care to tell me what you want to apologize for?"

Aubrey narrowed her eyes at him. "I'm getting to that."

His mouth twitched once. Then he gave her a flowery bow. "By all means. Please, do go on."

"You're being an ass. You know that?" She glared at him when he shrugged. *Focus. You need to have an adult conversation.* She inhaled through her nose and tried again. "At the pool, I know I gave out mixed signals. I shouldn't have run off and left you in that . . . um . . . condition. I didn't mean to do that."

"Since when does calling someone an ass count as a sincere apology?" He arched an eyebrow.

"That wasn't a part of the apology." She bristled at the wry twist of his lips. "Besides, you *are* being an ass."

"No more games, Aubrey." Landon stalked toward her, and his tightly reined strength compelled her to retreat until she backed into the opposite wall. "I want to touch you. Hold you. Kiss you. Not being able to is driving me crazy. I wish I could go back and unwrite that review so we didn't have these obstacles between us."

Gah. Her chest rose and fell as his words and the sweet vulnerability in his eyes buried themselves in her heart. "Me, too. I wish there were nothing stopping me from running to you, but there are so many."

"I've decided you're worth every risk." Her heart stopped and then thundered back to life. Landon stood inches from her and held her chin between his thumb and forefinger. "What do we do now, Aubrey Choi?"

The warmth of his breath brushed against her cheeks, and

her body grew limp with the need to press herself against him. He wanted her despite everything. He wanted to risk everything for her. What could she do?

"Let's jump those obstacles." She smiled as excitement fluttered in her chest.

No more running.

Landon blinked and forced air into his lungs.

Fuck me.

Her sexy, mischievous grin plowed into his gut and spread scorching heat through him. He traced her flushed cheek with his thumb and lowered his head toward her. His heart was bruising his ribs, and blood pounded in his ears. Still, he hesitated before brushing his lips against hers. He'd wanted this for so long, wanted her so much.

Her achingly sweet response stole his breath, and he tilted his head to better taste her. She moaned and slid her hands down and then spread them out on his chest. Desire, hungry and raw, gripped him, and he buried his fingers in her silky hair. His mouth devoured hers greedily, and he only wanted more. Needed more.

Landon pulled back and took her hands in his and wordlessly led her to his bed. He stretched out in the middle and tugged her down next to him. Aubrey tucked herself into the crook of his arm, breathless and trembling, and he held her against him. Her soft curves conformed to the hard planes of his body, and he sighed deeply.

He held his body still and stared unblinkingly at the ceiling until his eyes stung. He would probably go insane before the night was over, but he wasn't going to make love to Aubrey tonight. Landon had given her space the last few days because he'd sworn not to push her into something she wasn't ready for. If he'd stayed near her, he would've begged her to have him.

But she'd come to him tonight, opened up to him and made herself vulnerable, and he wouldn't take advantage of her. He had to be sure it wasn't lust and adrenaline motivating her. *Tomorrow morning.* If she was still by his side the next morning, then he could be certain she wanted to be with him.

"So." His voice caught on the first word. His throat worked to swallow, and he succeeded on the fourth try. "How did you come up with the name *Comfort Zone?*"

Aubrey lifted her head from his shoulder and stared at him like he was crazy.

Yes. Yes, I am.

"You want to talk about that now? Like, right now?"

"Absolutely. Right this second. I must know."

"Oh-kaay." She laid her head back on his shoulder. "I left home to travel the world when I was eighteen. When my grandma died, I lost the one person I could call home, so I decided to create my own home—Comfort Zone. Somewhere I would never feel alone, a place I could always be myself."

Something shifted in his core at her faraway voice. Landon had spent the last decade running away from everything that meant anything to him. Anything that reminded him of home. He had so much to learn from this amazing woman.

"Eighteen is pretty young to leave home," he mused out loud. Most Korean Americans were expected to live with their parents until they were ready to build their own families. Landon had left home about ten years ago but still felt guilty about leaving his mom.

"The only reason I didn't leave earlier was because I didn't want my mom to be alone."

He blinked, startled by their similar train of thought, but it was the pain in her voice that made his chest feel hollow. "Tell me."

"When I was little, I was in awe of my father. He was so handsome and charming. Everyone seemed to like and respect him." She was quiet for a moment. "My parents dressed me like a princess and took me everywhere they went. All the grown-ups would pat my head and tell me how adorable I was. I was so proud. I thought I was special."

"You are special." He frowned at the implication that she was anything but.

"You're corny." Aubrey winked at him. "And trust me, I don't want to be anything like him. My father became distant and cold, and my mom didn't smile anymore. His ego grew with his bank account, and he started collecting mistresses. The best his money could buy."

"How did you find out?" He hated this. She was hurting, and he couldn't do anything about it.

"I found out when I was thirteen, but it had been going on for much longer, I'm sure. Woman after woman. I ditched school one morning and followed him." Aubrey lowered her eyes, her voice quiet and childlike. "I don't know where I found the guts—I'd always been terrified of him—but I confronted him. He didn't even bother removing his hand from the woman's waist. He told me if I skipped school again, he'd send me away to a boarding school in another country. That was it. No explanation. No apology. I was the one in the wrong."

All Landon could do was brush a featherlight kiss on her lips and hold her tighter. Her piece-of-shit father didn't deserve a daughter like Aubrey.

"The thing is, he'd already been wanting to send me off to boarding school before then. When he couldn't show me off at social events and I proved mediocre in academics, he lost interest in me. He wanted to sweep me under the rug like a dirty secret."

Landon cursed under his breath, unable to hold back. *God.* If it could stop her from hurting anymore, he would shoulder her painful past with his own and carry it for the rest of his life. No matter what happened between them.

"When I begged my mom to leave him, she refused. She said I was too young to understand. She actually made excuses for him. I told her I hated her. That she was a coward." Aubrey sucked in a shaky breath and burrowed deeper into his embrace. "God, I was so cruel."

"You were *thirteen* and hurting."

"She was hurting, too. I should've been there for her. Love broke my mom, and she drifted through life like an empty shell. And I just let her fade away." He kissed her again and rubbed her back in soothing circles. "It wasn't all bad. I was a teenage nightmare and wreaked havoc on his pretty social life. Once, he had to get me from the police station because I'd wrapped his Lamborghini around a tree."

"How old were you?" He chuckled, imagining young Aubrey with fight and rebellion in her eyes.

"I was fifteen."

"That's my girl." He hugged her tightly and kissed the top of her head.

"My turn," said Aubrey, looking up at him. "Tell me about your family."

"Well, I have a younger brother. He's a photographer. A pretty good one. My mom's a painter, so he probably got the artistic genes from her."

"A painter and a photographer? That's awesome. Are you artsy?"

"Not in the least. My drawing skills are limited to stick fig-
ures."

Instead of laughing, Aubrey traced the contours of his face
with her fingertips. "Your food is your art."

Her words at once gave him courage and scared the hell out
of him. He tightened his arms around her. This time, he drew
strength from her.

"If you keep that up, I might actually take the plunge and
open a restaurant."

"Well, you can't be a celebrity food critic forever." Aubrey's
expression was suspiciously bland. "When your looks go, you
won't have a choice. They'll banish you to the kitchens."

An affronted laugh burst from him, and he kissed her up-
turned nose. "I think I'll blacklist you from my restaurant just
for that jab. I don't know if my ego will ever heal."

"Fine. Just cook for me at home." She yawned, tucking her
chin against his chest.

Home.

"I'd love to," he whispered. "I would love nothing more
than to cook for you at home."

Aubrey answered with the steady rhythm of her breathing,
asleep in his arms.

16

A coil of something strong and heavy was wrapped around her midriff. The sensation was unfamiliar but pleasant, and she smiled in her sleep. When Aubrey twisted to the side, stretching her back, she found herself pressed flush against Landon's warm, hard body.

"Oh." Her eyes flew open to their maximum capacity.

His arm, which had been lying across her stomach, was draped over her waist now, and his hand rested precariously close to her bottom. Her lungs shrank to the size of marbles, forcing her to resort to short, shallow breaths, and her pulse skipped at the base of her throat.

She drank in the sight of his sleeping face, wonder filling her. He was beautiful. Holding her breath, she lifted her trembling fingers and traced his dark eyebrows, broad forehead, and cheekbones. She stopped at his parted lips, softened by slumber.

Aubrey swallowed, fixating on his mouth. He looked tastier than a chocolate lava cake. *What's the lovers' protocol for situations like this?* She rose up on her elbows and then leaned over to stare at his sleeping face. She worried her bottom lip, deciding what to do. He'd been working so hard, and she wanted him to rest. Despite her selfless intentions, her face kept creeping closer to his. Her lips were only a few millimeters away from his lips when Landon smiled.

"Good morning," he murmured without opening his eyes.

She drew back with a startled gasp, but he stopped her with his hand in her hair and kissed her. She closed her eyes and joined him in the lovely dream.

The first caress of his lips was gentle and fleeting, but she mewled in frustration and urged him to deepen the kiss. His breath caught in his throat, and he plunged his tongue into her mouth. He tore her T-shirt and shift off with an impatient tug, and his hands were everywhere at once, greedy and rough.

She caught fire in his arms and touched and tasted him with hunger and desperation. She had waited too long and was too starved to savor their reunion. Next time, she would drive him a little mad before she gave him release, and he would love every minute of it. But this time, they satiated their hunger with raw, animal instinct and came hard and fast in each other's arms, shouts of pleasure filling the room. They slowly returned to reality, breathless and languid.

"I wish I could keep you in bed all day." Landon leaned his forehead against hers.

"We'll have tonight." Aubrey smiled, cupping his cheek for a quick peck. "For now, you need to get out of bed and into the shower. Didn't you say something about you having a small part in the production of a cooking show? Or were you just trying to impress me?"

"I can't decide whether you're an imp or a siren." He kissed the tip of her nose, his laughter vibrating against her breasts. "And just to clarify, are you impressed?"

"*Very* impressed," Aubrey said, and she ground her hips against him.

"Siren. Definitely a siren."

With a helpless groan, Landon claimed her lips again, and she kissed him right back despite her best intentions. Before she was swept too far adrift, she squirmed and pushed against his chest. He growled in protest and titled his head to nibble her neck.

"You need to go," she said in between helpless moaning.

Landon reluctantly lifted his head and glanced at the clock. He rolled to the side and swiped his hands down his face.

"Tonight," he said.

With that promise, he headed for the shower, giving her an excellent view of his delicious bottom. When he ran the water, Aubrey tugged her slip over her head and headed downstairs to fix them some breakfast. They both needed sustenance.

She rummaged around in the kitchen and set about making some croque-madames. Grabbing a brioche loaf, she cut four slices from it, appreciating the fresh bread smell. She missed Comfort Zone and the warm smell of the kitchen in the mornings.

I'll be back there soon. The thought made her pause with the brioche poised over the hot pan. *Where does that leave Landon and me?* She shook her head and pushed the thought aside. She'd done enough worrying where they were concerned. She just needed to *be* for now.

There was nothing like making some béchamel to quiet her mind. Aubrey whisked and whisked the flour and melted butter over low heat until a smooth ball of roux formed, and then she slowly added in the hot milk.

"Please don't break. Please don't break."

Relieved to have the thick, creamy béchamel finished, she

heated up the frying pan, scooping a generous pat of butter onto it. The bread turned golden, and the gruyère oozed out between the ham and bread. Then she set about frying some sunny-side-up eggs with which to top the sandwiches. It looked and smelled heavenly, making her mouth water. Although it was heavy with butter and cheese, they'd burn it off tonight. Even as she blushed at her naughty thought, anticipation knotted her stomach.

She finished pouring fresh coffee into two mugs when Landon walked into the kitchen. He was on the phone, and his lazy and somnolent expression was nowhere to be seen. While his voice never rose, his cold, clipped words communicated his displeasure quite clearly. Aubrey felt bad for whoever was on the other end of the call, and a little chill ran down her spine. Landon wasn't a man to be trifled with.

"That was the contractor. They've run into yet another problem with . . ." His words trailed off as his eyes traveled down her body. "Is that what you were wearing under your shirt? I don't think I'd have forgotten seeing you in that."

"I think you took it off before you opened your eyes this morning, so you technically didn't see me in it," Aubrey responded primly. He didn't have time to be distracted by her. "Now, sit and eat before your sandwich gets cold."

"Thanks for cooking." Landon swooped down for a quick, hard kiss before sitting down.

Aubrey touched her lips with her fingertips, holding on to the feel of his mouth. She missed it as soon as it left hers. *Why did he stop?* She vaguely recalled he had a good reason, but she wasn't pleased to be left aching and hungry.

"This looks great."

He smiled across at her, but when he witnessed her lust-glazed stare, his eyes turned dark as night. Before she could remember why they shouldn't go back upstairs, Landon lifted her in his arms and carried her to his room.

The sandwiches got cold.

———

With only a couple days left until the first shooting, Landon's schedule was brutal. Since he and Aubrey had gotten together, leaving for work had grown harder by the day, but it was especially difficult this morning.

She was in the kitchen wearing one of his white T-shirts without anything underneath. He could see the fabric shifting against her naked body, and he dreamed of more pleasurable ways to spend his day.

She's trying to kill me.

"Will you be writing out your recipes today?" Landon placed a soft kiss on her forehead and stepped back.

"Yeah," she said glumly. "I've never had to write a formal one like this. There are so many steps I need to include. I can't get too detailed because people might be like, 'Does she think I'm stupid?' But if I don't explain enough, the recipe might turn out wrong and they'll be like, 'Curse you, Aubrey Choi.'" She shook her fist for effect and then hung her head. "I wish I could just jot down the ingredients and measurements for the folks and they could figure out the rest."

"I know. But you'll be immortalizing your recipes for future generations, so cheer up." He pulled out a small package he'd hidden in his back pocket and held it out to her. "Here. Open it."

"Landon. You have to stop getting me presents." Despite her words, she took her gift eagerly.

"Don't you dare take that joy away from me. Besides, they're never extravagant."

"You put so much thought into them." She cupped his cheek in her warm, soft hand.

"Of course. They're for you." He needed to leave before he took her back to bed. "Come on. Open it."

With a happy smile, Aubrey unwrapped the package and then screamed with delight. It was a palm-size notebook with colorful unicorn sketches all over it. "I love it. It's perfect. Thank you."

"My pleasure," he said, leaning down to kiss her. Her goofy smile tasted delicious—sweet and floral. He deepened the kiss for a few seconds and groaned. He wouldn't be able to stop if he went on for a second longer. Dropping a featherlike kiss on the corner of her lips, he rested his forehead against hers, letting their breaths mingle as one.

Is this what home feels like? His chest tightened with wonder and panic, but he allowed the warmth and tranquility to wash over him. It was a stolen moment of happiness—isolated and timeless—and it imprinted itself permanently on his mind.

———

Aubrey was still grumbling and scribbling in the kitchen when Landon came back later that evening. She smiled distractedly at him.

"Hi."

"Hi yourself." Landon kissed the top of her head. "Have you been in here all day?"

"Mm-hmm," she answered without looking up from her notebook, chewing on the end of her pen.

Carefully taking the pen from her, Landon tipped her face up for a proper kiss. "You need to take a break."

"But . . ."

"No buts. Besides, I have somewhere to take you."

"Now? Where?"

"Yes, now. It's a surprise."

Aubrey squinted at him for a second. "Well, it had better be a really awesome surprise."

The schoolhouse was finally finished, and Landon wanted Aubrey to see it before the place was overrun by the crew and their equipment. He didn't stop to think why he wanted to show her the house. Or why he wanted to see her reaction.

He hadn't lived fully since his old man's disappearance. His dream had dangled in front of him, temptingly within reach. All he had to do was claim it. But Landon had walked away to take care of his family, the one his father had abandoned. *That selfish bastard.* Landon swore never to put his dreams before his mom's and brother's well-being. He refused to be like him.

He didn't resent his mom or Seth. It was his decision. His pain to bear. And he'd borne it by being a spectator in his own life. His brand and his reputation had dictated his choices. He hadn't owned a home or a car for the last decade. He chose to be a stranger passing through wherever he went. He didn't dream—he didn't *want*—and it had made him invincible.

But Aubrey had shifted something in him. Suddenly, he *wanted.* He reached for her every night, time and again, and made love to her like a man starved. Now that he finally had her, he wanted her to be his—only his—for as long as she would have him. He swallowed the fear that rose in his throat and pushed aside the thought of losing her.

When he saw the finished schoolhouse, it beckoned him. It whispered to him. *Home.* He'd convinced himself that Aubrey had nothing to do with it. That he'd grown tired of his nomadic life. But whenever he imagined home, Aubrey was in it—in the kitchen, in the courtyard, in his bed.

"Oh," Aubrey whispered reverently. "It does look like house in *Little House on the Prairie.*"

"*Little House on the Prairie?*"

"Yeah. That's what I imagined the schoolhouse would look like when you first told me about it."

"Do you like it?" He held his breath.

"It's perfect." She sighed. "It feels like a place where children should run amok, driving their parents crazy. But a happy crazy."

"You haven't even seen the inside yet." Landon played it cool even though his face was twitching to explode into a Howdy Doody grin.

"Well, what are we waiting for?"

Aubrey floated through the house as though she were in a trance, her fingertips tracing the walls, the doors, the furniture. The comforts of modern innovation had been incorporated seamlessly into the century-old schoolhouse, and its charming rustic vibe hummed uninterrupted throughout. He watched her face, wondering if she sensed it, too.

"Landon, this place is amazing." She sounded breathless.

He caught her hand and led her to the big open kitchen with high-end appliances hidden behind country-white panels mimicking the abundant cabinets. It was beautiful, but most of all, it was functional. It was a kitchen made for cooking.

In a house of their own, the kitchen would be the center of life. They would bake and cook together every evening and trade stories about their day. And they would laugh. There would be so much laughter and happiness.

"I don't think I want to share it with the rest of the world yet." Aubrey placed a gentle hand on the gray granite counter-top, as though she wanted to shield it from the prying eyes.

She feels it, too.

"Should we break it in before anyone sees it?" Landon's heart pounded in a wild, deafening rhythm.

"I'd love to." Aubrey clapped her hands together. "What should we make?"

"I wasn't talking about cooking." He rounded the island with steady, deliberate steps.

"What?" Her lashes fluttered against her flushed cheeks. "I don't think . . ."

"Don't think." Landon was already past rational thought.

Aubrey retreated a step but stopped when her back came up against the island. Landon reached her in two steps and placed his hands on either side of her. She squeaked and stared up at him with wide eyes. He bent toward her, chuckling against the side of her neck.

"Did I ever tell you you're irresistible when you get flustered?" He loved the color of her skin—warm and intimate—blossoming just for him. He brushed featherlight kisses from her neck to her shoulders, tugging aside her shirt to expose their delicate curve. "If I were a painter, I'd work day and night to blend the exact color of your blush."

"Why, Mr. Kim." Aubrey freed his shirt from his slacks and ran her hands over his bare back. His muscles clenched, and a shudder ran through him. He was helpless against her touch and she knew it, and her momentary shyness was nowhere to be seen. "I never knew you were a poet."

"Only with you, my muse."

17

The time to shoot her episodes came much too soon for Aubrey. She wasn't cut out for show business. There were way too many people, too many lights, and most of all, too much makeup. The thick mask they plastered on her face made smiling feel like weight lifting.

The only thing stopping her from running out the door screaming was the thirty-minute foot massage IOU Landon had left by her pillow this morning. But for now, she had to play dress-up with the scary stylist.

"I like the way you dress," Covergirl observed. "You have a pretty unique sense of style."

"But?" There was a big *but* coming.

"Well, let's give it an extra little pop." She scrutinized Aubrey like a butcher about to slice off a choice slab of meat. "I think we should go with an Alexa Chung feel."

"Alexa who?"

"Alexa Chung. Probably one of the most influential fashionistas in the world today." She was clearly appalled at Aubrey's ignorance. "Whatever she wears, it becomes the *hot now* trend. Casual chic, boho chic, city chic."

"And if she wore a potato sack, it would be called burlap chic." Aubrey laughed, which turned into an awkward cough when the stylist glared at her. Apparently, Alexa Chung was too sacred to joke about.

"Can you suck in your stomach a little?" She struggled to zip Aubrey's dress up.

"What?" Aubrey frowned but did as she was told.

With more grumbling from the stylist, Aubrey was zipped up, powdered, and made generally presentable. She pursed her lips as she studied herself in the mirror, twisting left and right. Her clothes did feel tight around her waist and bust.

She was probably bloated because her period was finally coming. *Wait. What's today's date?* After some quick math, Aubrey realized she'd missed two periods. *Oh, shit.* Of course, she knew she was late—just not that late. She'd gone through times when stress made her period stop for a month or two—like when she'd left home and when she'd opened Comfort Zone.

Since she'd been stressed to the max when she was on the brink of losing Comfort Zone—when things had felt hopeless—she hadn't thought anything of being late. But now . . . now she felt far less desperate. The move and the renovations were in progress. She had a real chance of saving Comfort Zone. Then why was her period still late? And why were her clothes so tight?

Aubrey forced down her panic before it could start. With the stress from the past few months, her hormones were understandably out of whack. Other than the double-the-bloating inconvenience, there wasn't cause for alarm. Landon had used condoms on their night in Weldon and every time since.

She must've put on a few extra pounds. It would be a mira-

cle if she hadn't gained weight since she'd been indulging herself with never-ending deliciousness the entire time at Bosque
Verde. It was the price of spending so much time with chefs,
foodies, and vintners.

With her doubts and worries close to the surface, Aubrey stepped into the line of fire and stood before a camera
for the first time in her life. Reality became eerie and blurred
with blinding lights and black-eyed cameras pointing at her,
their sharp intensity piercing and accusatory. *Wow us*, they
demanded. Sweat pooled between her breasts and down her
spine, and her mouth refused to form the lines written for her.

And the appalling scene repeated over and over again.

"*Cut!*"

Aubrey blinked. The director bolted out of his chair and
stormed through the kitchen. When the lights finally dimmed,
she recovered from her walking coma and realized she'd wasted
everyone's morning.

Wringing her cold fingers, she leaned over to Aria. "I don't
think he likes me much."

"Don't worry about Stan." Aria winked at her. "He can be
bad tempered, but he's a good guy for the most part. He'll come
around."

"Thanks. And sorry for wasting everyone's time like this. I
don't know why I just can't get the words out." Aubrey would've
buried her face in her hands if she weren't afraid of messing up
her makeup. Covergirl would kill her if she did.

"I got it." Aria snapped her fingers, and her brown eyes lit up
like lightbulbs. "That's the problem. You're struggling because
we're feeding you the lines. Reciting other people's words isn't
easy for everyone. We just have to roll with it, improv-style."

"Sounds risky." *And potentially disastrous.* "I don't want to
cause any more problems."

"Trust me." Aria was already walking out the way the director had run off. "I'll go talk to Signor Huffy Pants."

Aubrey avoided meeting anyone's eyes and shuffled off to grab some water. By the time she finished the bottle, Aria and Stan returned arm in arm. He was still red in the face, but he looked more alarmed than angry. The poor man had obviously been bamboozled by Aria.

"All right," he said, settling in his chair. "Use the script as a guideline, but you could use your own words for this episode."

When given the chance to be herself, Aubrey's passion for desserts spoke for itself. Aria was quick on her feet and was able to guide her along with great questions and perfectly timed comments. They were actually able to finish filming her first segment on schedule.

"Oh, thank goodness." Aubrey sagged onto the kitchen floor when they wrapped up for the day. "I honestly don't know how you do this. It's exhausting."

"It is, but it's so much fun."

"I can tell you're having fun." Aubrey didn't want to offend Aria, but it was about as fun as scraping burned cake off the bottom of a pan. "As for me, my part of the filming can't be over soon enough."

"Well, I think you did splendidly, sweetheart," Aria said with a warm smile.

Smiling back at her, Aubrey thought how fortunate she was to have Aria on her side. She genuinely liked the warm, vivacious woman.

"You're pretty awesome, you know that?" Aubrey said.

"Well, yes. Maybe a little." Aria's laughter twinkled in the air. "And so are you. Never doubt that."

"Thank you."

Aubrey stared at her hands. With less than a week left at

Bosque Verde, she was worried about the renovations at the diner. She'd been communicating with her contractor, but his team was running far behind. The old appliances were out, but the new ones hadn't been installed because the permits hadn't come through. It took multiple phone calls to have something done and more calls to have it fixed. She was bleeding money. The renovation costs could exceed her carefully planned budget, and it was only going to get worse, from the sound of things.

Aubrey glanced around her. The set kitchen looked beautiful, but it had taken a lot of wrong turns before coming together. She should've paid more attention to Landon's headaches with its progress. But her plate had been so full, she'd chosen to hide her head under the sand.

She hadn't mentioned her renovation nightmare to Landon. They hadn't discussed their relationship or where it was headed beyond their time in Bosque Verde. Aubrey wasn't ready for it to end, but Landon hadn't made any promises. If she told him about her troubles with the expansion, he might feel obliged to help and end up staying with her longer than he'd wanted.

Her heart bled, her head hurt, and her entire body ached.

"Is everything okay?" A warm hand covered hers.

"I've been struggling a bit with Comfort Zone's expansion." Aria was her friend, and no matter what happened with Landon, she hoped Aria would remain her friend.

"Oh, honey. Why didn't you mention this sooner?" Her friend listened attentively and asked insightful questions as Aubrey laid out her problems. "Is that all?"

Aubrey's eyes widened. "Isn't that enough?"

"Hang on. I can't believe you're having contractor problems. I mean, I can believe it, but your timing is unreal." Aria fished out her cell phone and dialed a number from memory. She spoke so rapidly, Aubrey couldn't quite follow her one-sided conversation. It sounded like she was discussing Comfort Zone's expansion, and it seemed to have gone well, because Aria turned to her with a wide smile. "I have a plan."

"A plan?" She'd just needed to unload. She'd never expected a *plan*.

"As far as renovations go, your problems are comparatively minor. I called in a favor with my close friend and favorite TV contractor. You know those guys who tear down buildings to studs then rebuild them in two days?" Aubrey nodded with her mouth gaping. "Well, he and his team are wrapping up a project next week. Once they finish, they could get your kitchen reno-vated and your dining area remodeled in about two weeks' time. They obviously need to see your place for more accurate time and cost estimates, but they'll be working for a steep discount."

"Is *fairy godmother* your side job?"

"Nope. You're just extremely lucky. He begged me to cook for his wedding reception a few weeks ago, and I couldn't say no." She shrugged as if to say, *Whaddaya do?* "The silly man offered to build me a cabin in exchange, but what am I going to do with a cabin? Renovating the space for Comfort Zone is a much better deal."

"How am I going to repay you?"

"You don't owe me a thing. We're friends, and I'm happy to help," said Aria. "And one more thing. You should tell the current contractor to wrap up what he's doing and clear out so our team can have a smooth transition."

"Okay. Of course. Thank you so much. If there's anything I can do, please let me know." Aubrey wrapped her in a tight hug, feeling the crushing weight lift from her. "You don't know how much this means to me."

"It's my absolute pleasure. Now release me. I can't breathe."

"Sorry." Aubrey grinned sheepishly. "And please don't tell Landon about Comfort Zone. I don't want him to worry any more about me and my bakery."

"Sure." She arched a graceful eyebrow but agreed without question.

"Aubrey? Aria?"

Aubrey started at the sound of Landon's voice, and Aria squeezed her hand in reassurance.

Then her heart nearly stopped. In the craze of her filming debut, Aubrey had briefly forgotten about her missed periods. Her anxiety returned in a rush. *What if I'm pregnant?* That wasn't possible. Stress always screwed up her cycle. There was no reason to freak out.

Landon chuckled as he came around the bend. "Why are you ladies hiding down there?"

"Oh, girl talk, you know," Aria said. She made collapsing from exhaustion sound mischievous. "Anyway, are you ready to go over the details of the last three episodes? The team should be coming back from dinner soon."

"Can't wait." Landon wearily massaged the back of his neck. When Aubrey covered a huge yawn, he studied her with concern. "You look beat."

"I'm fine," she lied.

"I heard you did great," he said, rewarding her with the Smile.

"Everyone was very understanding and patient." The compliment embarrassed her. She'd botched the first half of the filming, adding to everyone's work.

"Is she always this modest?" Aria smirked at Landon.

"No, she's unbearably egotistical." Aubrey stopped mid–eye roll to smother another yawn. Landon frowned. "You need some rest. I'll drive you back to the villa."

"Don't be silly. I don't want you to drive back and forth because of me. You don't seem all that perky either." Landon looked incredibly sexy with his mussed-up hair and five-o'clock shadow, but sexy or not, he was too tired to chauffeur her around. "I'll just wait here until you guys finish."

"That'll be hours later, and you won't get any rest with all of us making a ruckus. Knowing our director, there's bound to be some door slamming as well." His lips drew into a thin line, and he raked his hand through his hair. "I'll drive you over now. It's not a big deal."

"Absolutely not." Aubrey crossed her arms and glared at him. He was so stubborn.

"Oh, stop it, you two. If somebody saw you now, they would think you guys like, *like* each other." Aria placed air quotes around the second *like*.

Landon and Aubrey turned to glare at her.

"Here, Aubrey." Aria handed her the keys to her Mercedes. "You can take my car. I'll drive back with Landon to the villa when we're done and pick up the car from there. Problem solved."

"Don't mind if I do." Aubrey snatched up the car keys without missing a beat.

Aria and Landon stood gaping at her, surprised by her lightning-fast acquiescence. They didn't know she'd been eyeing the red lovely for a while now. She'd learned to appreciate well-engineered cars in her grand theft auto days, and she particularly enjoyed the smooth drive of a Mercedes.

Eager to get behind the wheel, Aubrey waved at Aria and Landon over her shoulder and fast-walked out to the driveway. She rolled the top down on the bright red car, preparing to enjoy the wind in her hair. The engine purred to a start. *Oh yeah.* Grinning broadly, she *vroom*ed away from the schoolhouse.

It was exhilarating. The powerful engine propelled the car to not-technically legal speed in mere seconds, but her body remained suspended in plush luxury. She could really get used to driving around in a fancy toy like this. *Not a chance, idiot.* It was a luxury she couldn't afford anymore. Freedom had a price, and she'd gladly paid it.

Aubrey glided to a stop in front of the villa and killed the engine with a satisfied sigh. After a lingering touch on the dashboard, she stepped out of the car and let herself inside the house. It felt empty, dark, and chilly with Landon away, and the thrill of the joyride faded into a dull gray. Feeling listless, Aubrey headed to her room.

Maybe she should draw herself a bubble bath. She wished Landon were there to join her. *Ugh.* This was getting pathetic. She could entertain herself for one evening without Landon. As she walked into her bedroom, the ominous shower music from *Psycho* played from her back pocket.

"Tara." It was her best friend's ringtone. "Man, I miss you."

"You miss me, my ass. If you miss me so much, why haven't you called in days? Hmm? Nothing to say to that, eh?" Tara snorted.

Her friend's ribbing made her so happy that tears welled up in her eyes. Aubrey suddenly ached for the familiarity of Weldon and Comfort Zone, and Tara's voice sounded like home.

"Sorry, sorry. There's just so much going on, and I have no idea what I'm doing. All I know for certain is that I'm not meant for show business." Aubrey couldn't stop her weepy blubbering. "I'm making a complete fool of myself. My new recipes turned out well, but what's the fucking point? The viewers can't even taste them."

"Chill, Bree. I'm sure you're doing great."

That pushed Aubrey over the edge, and she started sniffling

in earnest. "I'm sorry. I don't know why I'm crying. I'm just so happy to hear your voice."

The line went silent for three seconds. "Hey, is everything okay? Are you okay?"

No. I'm going to throw up. With a hand clapped over her mouth, she rushed for the bathroom and hurled into the toilet.

"Aubrey? Hello?" Tara sounded like a panicked ant, barely audible from the phone by her side.

"Hang on," Aubrey croaked, flushing the toilet. Then she dragged herself upright, rinsed her mouth, and splashed cold water on her face.

"What in the world is going on? Did you just throw up?"

"I think I love him." As the whispered words left her mouth, Aubrey knew it was true. She loved him, and she'd been too terrified to admit it to herself. *And I might be pregnant.* Tears streamed down her cheeks. "We've been together the last few days."

"Together? In what sense?"

"Together as in heart, body, and soul." Aubrey trembled and pressed the phone closer against her cheek to avoid dropping it.

"Heart and soul? That's quite a declaration coming from a commitment-phobe." Tara's words wobbled, but Aubrey could hear the smile in her voice. "I'm so happy for you, Bree. You deserve to have love and happiness in your life."

But loving him didn't guarantee reciprocated love or happiness for Aubrey. Not at all. It merely exposed her to loss and heartbreak. She tugged on her bottom lip, pinching it tightly between her thumb and index finger.

"Have you told Landon how you feel about him?"

"No, I didn't even know until now. Besides, we haven't talked about what happens after Bosque Verde." She gulped in mouthfuls of air as panic closed in around her. "He might not want to continue with this—us—after the filming is done."

"I will mess him up if he breaks your heart." Tara sighed and gentled her tone. "But you have to tell him, Bree. If you really love him, don't let anything stand in your way. I know it's scary, but this is a chance worth taking. You deserve to be happy."

"Thank you." Aubrey swallowed a fist-size lump in her throat. "I love you."

"I love you, too." Tara cleared her throat. "Now go on and do your thing. I already know which maid of honor dress I'm wearing at your wedding."

———

Aubrey was fast asleep by the time Landon got back to the villa. She was snuggled under the covers with her hand tucked under her chin. *She's fucking adorable.* Undressing quickly, he lowered himself on the bed and molded his body to hers.

She was wearing her gray slip, her body full and warm with sleep. *Did I say adorable? I meant to say sexy as hell.* He groaned, pressing closer to her. The scraps of silk she called pajamas were pure torture. But he reminded himself of the dark circles under her eyes that afternoon. She was exhausted and needed rest.

He carefully extracted himself from her side and pulled on a T-shirt and a pair of boxers to rein himself in before getting back in bed. He kissed the top of her head and held her tightly. He listened to her even breathing with his hand splayed over the smooth curve of her hip, and Landon wished they could stay like this forever. In a beautiful cocoon with only the two of them.

She meant more to him than any other woman he'd been with, and he couldn't imagine letting her go. But what choice did he have? Her portion of the filming would be over in days, and she would return to Comfort Zone and the dream she'd worked so hard for. Her path was set.

As for him, he didn't even know where he wanted to live or what he wanted to do after the filming. Should he continue traveling and critiquing restaurants? For how long? Or could he finally let go of his past and open his restaurant? The thought alone made his chest tighten with anxiety. His meticulously planned life was shaking at the core, and all he wanted was this woman by his side.

Even in the storm of his troubled emotions, exhaustion lulled him to sleep.

—

Muted light invaded the room through closed curtains, alerting him that morning had come. Landon instinctively reached for Aubrey, but she wasn't in bed. He frowned, impatient to have her . . . at least twice. He raised himself on his forearm. His scowl transformed into slack-jawed astonishment. She was on the floor beside the bed stretching like a languid cat, her breasts thrust forward and her sweet ass curved into the air.

"Damn, Aubrey." His growl of need and appreciation sounded feral even to his own ears. The cat startled and popped up to her knees—eyes wide and blinking. "Michelangelo wouldn't be able to sculpt a more perfect bottom than yours."

"More poetry?" Aubrey laughed. "And so early in the morning."

"While being presented with a premium view of your delectable behind is nothing to complain about, I'd much rather wake up to feel your body next to mine." Landon grasped her hand and tugged her back into bed.

"You were exhausted. I wanted you to sleep a bit longer." Aubrey scanned his face and nodded with approval. Apparently, he didn't look dead on his feet anymore. "Besides, I didn't want to wake up Grouchy Landon, your evil alter ego."

"You already know a very effective cure for that affliction." She gasped when he cupped her ass in his hands. "Sweet buns."

She kissed him with a smile on her lips, and the teasing banter ceased. His world shrank to this single moment, intense and vibrant. The feel of her skin, her sweet moaning, and his name on her lips. That was all. He made love to her with frantic desperation, because he yearned for her even when she was in his arms.

He buried himself in her warm core and set a pace that had her writhing under him, begging for release. When he didn't think he could hold on any longer, she came apart in his arms and he met her at the peak, their fingers threaded above her head. He stayed inside her as their breaths slowed and the tremors going through their bodies quieted. Then he rolled to the side, taking her with him, and drew her head against his chest.

"Best morning ever," Aubrey whispered.

His laughter was closer to a growl. Every morning with her had been the best in his life, and he didn't want them to stop.

18

Landon woke her up at the crack of dawn and surprised her with chocolate-dipped strawberries on ice. His intentions weren't all innocent, but the juicy, tart, and sweet strawberries made the best after-sex breakfast. The morning with him was the high point of her day.

It was her last day of filming, and he'd dropped her off at the schoolhouse before heading to his meetings. She welcomed and feared this day—excited to return to Comfort Zone and afraid to lose Landon. Aubrey walked inside, expecting to find Aria in the center of the chaos, but she was nowhere to be seen. Worry niggling at her, Aubrey went through the motions of being dressed and made-up. Still, there was no sign of Aria.

Feeling awkward standing around as the crew ran about, she escaped to the outdoor deck and found the person she was looking for. Aria sat motionless in one of the chairs, gazing pensively at the surrounding hills. Aubrey never thought she'd use *Aria* and *pensive* in the same sentence. Her eyebrows drew together as she walked up to the deck and sat beside Aria.

"Hey there."

"Aubrey." Aria seemed startled to find Aubrey sitting next to her. It was odd since she hadn't exactly tiptoed up to the deck. "When did you get here? Are they ready to go?"

"Not yet. We still have a few minutes."

Rather than start her usual chatter, Aria fell quiet, and her eyes drifted out toward the horizon.

"Is something wrong?" Aubrey asked.

"No. Yes. I don't know." Aria trailed off, choking on the last word.

"Do you want to talk about it? Maybe it'll help."

"Oh, you know, it's the typical stuff that Italian operas are famous for. Unrequited love, desperate yearning, and all that." Aria's tremulous smile made Aubrey reach for her hand. "I know he feels the same way I do. I can feel it in my bones, but he keeps pushing me away."

"You mean Lucien?" The words popped out before she could stop them.

Aria sucked in a surprised breath. "Landon wouldn't have mentioned anything. . . ."

"Of course not. I guessed something was there that night you sang for us."

"That obvious, huh?"

"It was the song. I couldn't stop crying." Aubrey squeezed the hand she held. "But Lucien. The way he looks at you and talks to you. I don't think your love is unrequited. Far from it."

"You are so sweet," said Aria, a sad but genuine smile lighting her face.

"I'm also right."

"It's time, ladies!" one of the crew members? yelled from the doorway.

"It was wonderful to chat. You have a way of making people happy." Aria linked her arm through Aubrey's, and they headed for the set.

Aubrey's second day of filming went much more smoothly than her first. She still couldn't stand the crowd, lights, and heavy makeup, but for the most part, she felt less like a train wreck. All in all, she couldn't wait to be done with her television career.

From the first "Ready. Set. Action!" there was no hint of sadness left in Aria as she threw herself into her show. She was a pro through and through. Aubrey's respect for her grew even more.

"Something smells marvelous in here. It must be your cookies." Aria turned toward Aubrey. "Should we take a peek at them?"

"I thought you'd never ask," Aubrey said, putting on her oven mitts. "Do you see how golden brown they are around the edges? They're ready."

"Mmm. They look and smell marvelous." Aria sounded genuinely excited as she watched Aubrey pull out the cookies from the oven. "I wonder how your Moscato sorbet is doing."

"Why don't we check?" Aria's excitement was contagious, and Aubrey opened the ice cream maker with a little flair. The stunt sorbet they scooped out of the ice cream machine was perfect per script. "It looks ready, but there's only one way to know for sure."

In real life, as she'd written in her recipe, the sorbet would need two hours in the freezer to be firm enough to hold their shape between the cookies yet soft enough to scoop. Television magic made perfection a few steps quicker.

"It's time to taste test the ice cream sandwiches." Aria clasped her hands together.

"Let's go to the assembly line." Despite it being part make-believe, Aubrey couldn't help getting excited about her Moscato sorbet sandwiches. "This batch of cookies was baked earlier in the morning so they're ready to be assembled. Be sure to cool your cookies to room temperature at home before you assemble the sandwiches."

It was so much fun putting together the ice cream sandwiches and chatting with Aria that Aubrey almost forgot she was being filmed. When they toasted each other with the finished product and took their first bites, they moaned in unison and dissolved into laughter.

"Cut! Great work, ladies." This time, Stan said it with a smile. "Now, I think the rest of the crew should enjoy some of those ice cream sandwiches."

To the cheers of the crew, Aria and Aubrey assembled the rest of the sandwiches and passed them out. Aubrey was filled with joy and pride. It was so gratifying to see the crew devour them with appreciative murmurs. Impressing them was no easy feat, considering these people were used to eating the fine cuisine that celebrity chefs prepared on their shows.

As she turned the corner to feed the rest of the crew, she heard Landon greet Stan and Aria. Her heart picked up speed with anticipation. She'd missed him all day, and she couldn't wait to see his face. Moving as quickly as she could, she made sure everyone had their sorbet sandwiches. But as Aubrey turned to walk back, something stopped her cold.

"Landon, do you have a minute?" The voice belonged to the director.

"Sure. What can I do for you?"

"I wanted to speak with you about some concerns."

She heard footsteps, and their voices drew closer. They had

moved into the hallway leading to the kitchen, on the opposite side of the wall from where Aubrey was standing.

In a hushed tone, Stan said, "There are some rumors circulating among the crew. Of course, I'm always the last to hear, aside from the star of the gossip."

"The suspense is killing me." Landon's words remained light, but tension underscored them. "Just spit it out, will you?"

"Some of the crew have been talking about your uncomplimentary review of Aubrey's bakery and why you flipped your opinion by casting her for the show. They're speculating your change of heart has something to do with your sleeping arrangement. Some of the jokes are turning bawdy." He continued when Landon remained silent. "If their gossip gets out, it wouldn't be good for the show and would be disastrous for your reputation."

"Thanks for bringing it to my attention. Perhaps you and Aria could run a refresher course on professionalism and discretion." She hardly recognized Landon's voice when he spoke. It was so tightly controlled, she couldn't find a hint of her Landon in it. "They're industry professionals who have signed nondisclosure agreements. They should know better than to spread rumors."

"If there is no truth to the rumors, I suggest as a friend that you cut ties with Ms. Choi immediately," Stan said solemnly.

"Thank you for your concern, but there is no truth to the rumors. Aubrey Choi is a talented baker that I casted for the good of the show. Apart from that, she is nothing to me."

The blood drained from Aubrey's face, and the tray in her shaking hands tilted precariously. She couldn't hear the rest of their conversation over the ringing in her ears. *She is nothing to me.* Her heart trembled and shrank back, searching for the safe place where even her father's disdain and indifference couldn't hurt her. But it was gone. She'd let Landon in too deep, and there was no place to hide.

Nothing? She meant nothing to him? Did he want to keep her around as his dirty little secret?

No.

Landon would never do something like that. He would never treat her like a plaything to be used and cast aside. She wouldn't give up on their relationship based on one overheard conversation. He cared about her and respected her. Aubrey knew that. She trusted him. And she would not crumble in front of the people who believed she would peddle her body for a step up in life.

Her pride and iron will reasserted themselves in full force. She had to pull herself together. Though the ringing in her ears receded, the shock left her limp and nauseous, but she'd crawl across a bed of rusty nails before she would let anyone see that. Filling her lungs with air, Aubrey returned to the kitchen with slow, measured steps.

"Whoa. Careful with these. It'd be a tragedy to waste them." Landon appeared at her elbow and took the tray from her limp hands. When he got a closer look at her, his smile froze on his face. "What happened? Are you okay?"

"Nothing. It's nothing." She shook her head to clear it. "When did you get here?"

"A few minutes ago. Just in time for dessert." He was smiling again, but he still watched her warily. "Are you sure you're okay?"

"Not really. I'm beat." Landon wouldn't believe her if she kept insisting everything was okay.

"Let's go back to the villa, then."

"Actually, I want to lie down for a few minutes." A little time and space should restore her equilibrium. "Can I use one of the guest rooms?"

"Of course," Landon said, gently cupping her elbow. Aubrey flinched away from him, and confusion and hurt clouded his expression.

"Sorry," she said with a tense smile. "We need to be more careful in public."

Landon put down the tray on the counter, and the crew swarmed around it like zombies dog-piling a human body. *Fucking pieces of shit.* The sight of them devouring Aubrey's ice cream sandwiches was vulgar. Even an imbecile could taste the genius in her creations. They didn't deserve her desserts.

He had to protect Aubrey.

Unless they wanted their careers to crash and burn, the crew wouldn't dare violate the nondisclosure agreements and publicly spread derogatory statements involving the show. The contractual damages were a slap on the wrist, but if word got out they'd breached the nondisclosure provisions, they would never find a job in the industry again.

But for how long could they hide their relationship? He'd flat-out lied to Stan and denied Aubrey meant anything to him. His first priority was protecting her reputation as a baker and ensuring that Comfort Zone's expansion and reopening wouldn't be derailed by nasty rumors. That had been the core reason which had held him back from writing a second review for her. That was why he'd offered her a spot on the show instead. To fix his mistakes without hurting her professional reputation. Without hurting his.

A slash of fear cut through his thoughts. His brand. His reputation. He'd sacrificed his dream to take care of his mom and Seth. He had worked day and night to build his reputation as a food critic. His reviews—his word—were worth something because he'd earned the respect of his peers and readers. One word of his relationship with a subject of his review could end that.

He had enough set aside to make sure his family would always be taken care of, but he couldn't let his entire life crumble over an affair. Landon couldn't throw everything away to chase his dream. To chase Aubrey. Losing his father had taught him that family, responsibilities, and security should always come first, and his infatuation with Aubrey almost made him forget that. *But what of it?* Letting Aubrey go wasn't an option. They just had to do everything in their power to keep their relationship a secret.

Landon caught a glimpse of her leaning against the far wall, waiting for him. Her face was drawn, and the pallor of her skin worried him. He buried his panicked thoughts. Aubrey needed rest. The filming seemed to have drained her, but he sensed there was something else. It bothered him that he didn't know what it was. If he knew, he could fix it and erase the hollow look in her eyes.

"I'll show you to the room I've been using," he said, walking down the hallway. "It's the farthest room from the kitchen, so the noise won't bother you as much."

"Thank you." She sounded distant, and the knot in his stomach tightened.

He breathed a little easier when her face brightened at the sight of the room. It was one of the smaller rooms in the house, but the robin's-egg wallpaper and the white wainscoting made it the most charming one. The bed was dressed in the same motif, and Aubrey sighed as she sank into it. Maybe there wasn't anything else. She really might be just tired.

"Sleep tight." Landon tucked her into bed and kissed the tip of her nose. "I'll come back when everyone clears out."

Long after the crew wrapped up and the stars filled the sky, Landon kissed Aubrey awake. Her wide eyes were cloudy with sleep, but a lovely smile lit her face when she saw him sitting on the edge of the bed. His heart clenched and warmth filled him. He was tempted to climb into bed with her, but he had a reason for waking her up.

"Hey." Landon leaned down and dropped a kiss on her forehead. "Feeling rested?"

"Mmm-hmm. What time is it?"

"Almost ten."

Aubrey gasped at his response, her mouth forming an adorable *o*. She'd been dead to the world for nearly five hours.

"Come outside. You should eat something before going back to sleep."

"Aren't we going back to the villa?"

"We'll stay here tonight. There's no filming until late tomorrow morning, so we won't be invaded by the crew."

"Ugh." She shivered. "The crew."

Landon shot her a sharp look, trying to discern whether she was kidding or not. Had she overheard him speaking with Stan? *No.* If she had, she would've confronted him about it already. He was being paranoid. Aubrey never enjoyed being swarmed by the crew, especially the makeup and dress-up part.

Besides, he planned to tell her about what Stan had said so they could discuss a long-term plan to keep their relationship a secret. But not tonight. Tonight, Landon only wanted to make her happy.

He helped her out of bed and led her down the hall. When she stepped out on the deck, her hand fluttered to her mouth. The fire pit glowed with crackling wood, and the strand lights beckoned like miniature moons. He'd set out fresh fruit, cheese, and crackers on a small table with white linen.

"Oh, Landon," she breathed. "This is lovely."

He tugged on his collar as heat washed over his skin. Grateful for the dim lighting, he gestured toward the table. "Should I pour us some wine?"

"Uh, you go ahead," Aubrey said. "I'm still a bit groggy. I don't want to doze off on you before I can enjoy this moonlight picnic."

They sat quietly on the deck, enjoying their dinner, but Landon felt his nerves fraying. They hadn't talked about what happened after Bosque Verde. Neither of them was ready for this to end, but how could they continue seeing each other in secret once they left the villa? He had to figure out a plan.

"Since you're done with your portion of the filming, are you planning to head right back to Weldon?"

She stared down at her feet for what felt like hours, and then she finally lifted her head. "I think it's time to get back to the real world."

Get back to the real world? Something about her tone made his gut clench.

"How about you? Do you have to stay here until they're done with filming?"

"No, there isn't much left for me to do. The production team and the crew are working well together, and everything's running smoothly." He glanced sideways at her, forcing his face into a smile. "It's best for me to get out of their hair for the time being."

"So you could leave anytime?"

"In a few more days."

"I see," Aubrey said, worrying her bottom lip.

Unlike the comfortable silence they'd shared a moment ago, a blanket of unease settled on them. Aubrey seemed to be miles away, and he wanted to join her wherever she'd gone.

"If you don't mind staying for two more days, I'll drive you back to Weldon."

Landon forced the words out even though they cut him like shards of glass. He didn't think he could stand being apart from her. Except there was no other choice. He would make it his top priority to find them a secluded place where they could meet as often as they liked without risk of discovery.

"I know you need to get back to oversee the expansion and relocation, but don't expect me to stay away for long."

"Landon?" Her voice was so soft he wasn't sure she'd spoken.

"Yes?" He cocked his head to the side.

Aubrey cleared her throat and then met his gaze with a grin closely resembling a grimace. "Oh, nothing."

"What is it?" His mouth suddenly went dry, and his heart pummeled his rib cage.

"Nothing, really." Her eyes were wide and vulnerable, and she spoke with a tremor in her voice. "I just wanted you to know that being with you makes me happy."

The tension flowed out of him, and he smiled at her with all the joy exploding inside him. "I'm happy when I'm with you, too."

19

Early the next morning, Aubrey drove Landon's Alfa Romeo into town. He wanted her to use it for the day since he could have someone drop him off at the villa after the shooting. She didn't need much convincing. It was nice to be on her own for a while.

Landon had made love to her with undiminished passion last night . . . and this morning. He made her happy. Their shyly spoken declaration on the moonlit deck shrouded her in warmth, and she was glad she hadn't mentioned the conversation she'd overheard. She trusted him, and that was that.

She is nothing to me.

But she couldn't get his words out of her mind. Aubrey took a shuddering breath and fought to ease the constriction in her chest. She understood they had to keep their relationship a secret to protect their reputations, but they couldn't sneak around much longer. Especially if she was pregnant. The more she'd thought back through the last three months, the more certain she became she was going to have a baby. Landon's baby.

Aubrey was done with hiding. She loved him and wanted

forever with him. Even if he didn't return her love yet, he cared deeply about her and wanted more than a fling. She wanted to proclaim to the world that she was his and he was hers. There might be an initial uproar, but they could tell the public what really happened the day she'd created Frankencake. They had the truth on their side.

She wandered listlessly through downtown Bosque Verde until her feet throbbed. It was time to face the pink elephant that had doggedly followed her all morning. Maybe she was getting worked up for nothing. It wasn't like they hadn't been careful. They'd used a condom every time. *Right. Stop being a chicken.* Aubrey marched herself to the local drugstore before she could change her mind. The pink elephant trudged alongside her as she purchased three different brands of pregnancy test.

Every time her foot got heavy on the gas, she took a deep breath and slowed down to the speed limit. Wrecking Landon's vehicle was the last thing she needed. Once she reached the villa, she sprinted to her bedroom and locked the door behind her. The elephant waited politely outside the bathroom as she peed in a cup and dipped each of the sticks into it.

She checked the time every five seconds, making the two minutes wait time stretch on like saltwater taffy. But when she reached the two-minute mark, Aubrey ran away from the sticks.

"I can't look. Oh, God. No, I have to look." She clasped her hands against her pounding chest and took baby steps toward her bathroom. *Ha! Baby steps. Pun totally not intended.* She choked down the hysterical cackle tickling her throat.

When she peeked at the results with one squinty eye, a shaky sigh rushed out of her.

Pregnant.

+

||

Aubrey picked up all three sticks and shook them again and again. *Still pregnant.* She sank down to the cold marble floor and hugged her knees to her chest. She tasted salt in her mouth and realized she was crying. *A baby? Landon's baby?*

She felt feverish and cold—afraid and elated. Aubrey wasn't ready to be a mom. Comfort Zone needed her. It was a crucial time for the bakery. How could she raise a baby and run a business? But Landon would be by her side. Right? She had no idea how he would feel about the baby, but he wasn't a man who would turn his back on a woman carrying his child.

"Fuuuck," she groaned, burying her head in her arms. "What am I going to do?"

When she raised her head, the sun was dipping behind the mountains, and her bottom was frozen from sitting on the cold marble for so long. She wanted to lie down, but if she did, she wouldn't have the strength to get off the floor. She had to *do* something. And she made a decision that was seriously counterintuitive for her. She called her mom.

"Aubrey?" Her mom's voice was warm but held a hint of worry. "Is everything all right?"

"No," she said, biting her lip. "I don't know what to do, Mom. What should I do?"

"Why don't you tell me what happened first?" Her mom was in her stone Buddha mode. She only did that when she was seriously worried—like the time little Aubrey was rushed to the hospital with appendicitis. She thought about hanging up. *Do I want to dump all this on her? She has enough to worry about.* "I'm here for you. I've always been. Tell me, baby. We'll figure it out together."

Aubrey wailed, furious at herself for pushing her mom away and regretting how she'd let so many years pass without doing anything about it. Her mom was there for her. It was time to let everything go and be her daughter. Maybe that was what her mom had wanted all along—to take care of her and for Aubrey to trust her enough to rely on her.

"Mom, I'm pregnant."

"Oh, honey." Her mom had to be shocked, but she held on to her calm. "Who's the father?"

Aubrey nearly lost it again. *Well, Mother.* She inhaled until she couldn't sip in any more air and then blew it out her mouth. "Remember the food critic who wrote that horrible review about Comfort Zone?"

"How could I forget that jerk?" Her mom stopped herself and continued in an even tone. "But you said he admitted the review was a mistake, and now you're filming that cooking show with Aria Santini. I think I've almost forgiven him."

"I guess that's good? Because he's the father."

"What?" Her mom choked on air and went into a coughing fit. "You know the risks of being involved with him. Don't you? How could you—damn it. I'm sorry. I have no right to judge."

"You have every right. You're my mom. It's in your job description."

"Oh, baby." Her voice trembled for a second. "Well, I trust you. I do. If you chose to be with him, then he must be worth it."

"He is worth everything. I love him so much. But I'm freaking out."

"Have you told him? Does he know?"

"No, I called you right after I found out."

"You are going to tell him, right?"

"Yes. Of course," she said with false bravado.

"Does he know how you feel about him?"

"I don't think so."

"Do you want him to?"

"I want forever with him and the baby. But I'm so afraid he'll break my heart."

"Then fight for them. You fight for the people you love. You can't give up without giving it your everything," her mom said with steel in her voice. "My biggest regret is not fighting for you and your father. I lost both of you. I couldn't stop loving him after his first affair. I thought he'd come back to me eventually, but he didn't. I was ashamed and afraid, and it became worse with every affair. I let my insecurities define me, and I pushed everyone away, even you, and I'm so sorry. But listen to me, Aubrey. Your father hurt me, but *I'm* the one who broke my heart. I'm the one who gave up without trying. I let myself disappear."

"Mom." Aubrey hurt so much for her mom. She had been so alone for so long. "You didn't lose me. You could never lose me."

"Oh, baby. I love you so much. You can do this. If he doesn't see how damn lucky he is to have you, then he doesn't deserve you. Don't be afraid of losing him. It'll be easier to bear than losing yourself."

"I love you, Mom."

After they hung up, Aubrey knew what she needed to do. She had to tell Landon she loved him and wanted forever with him. And tell him about the baby. Even if he wasn't ready to become a father, he'd make a great one. What mattered most was whether he wanted forever with her. If he wanted her like she wanted him, they could figure out everything else together.

Aubrey was going to fight for them.

—

After a long nap, which she finally understood was a symptom of early pregnancy, Aubrey prepared for the battle of her life.

She actually hoped it wouldn't be a battle at all. She would tell Landon she loved him, and he would tell her he loved her back. *Yay.*

Aubrey cooked balsamic-marinated chicken breasts and to-mato bisque, planning to serve them with crusty bread. She wouldn't be eating much, so she kept the menu simple. She washed her hair and dried it with care and put on light makeup to boost her confidence. Then she squeezed into a soft, pink dress and waited for Landon to come home.

The wax from the candle had melted and dripped into globs at the base of the holder. The minutes ticked by, and their dinner grew cold. And Aubrey's dress grew increasingly uncom-fortable. She checked the wall clock for the seventh time in fifteen minutes and jumped when her cell phone binged. A text from Landon.

Landon: Please have dinner without me. I'm putting out a fire. I'll be back late.

The unexpected delay deflated her like a punctured bal-loon, and her hands started to shake as the adrenaline faded from her system. Aubrey blew out the candles and put away the dinner with the speed and agility of an unoiled Tin Man. Once that was done, she found herself pacing around in the quiet house, unable to settle her nerves.

For a change of scenery, she climbed up the stairs to pace in her bedroom. After slipping out of the torturous dress, she took in a nice full breath and sighed, unconsciously placing her hands on her stomach. She'd only known for hours, but she loved the baby growing inside her.

Aubrey wanted Landon to know how much she loved him and how happy she was to be pregnant with his child. Even if he didn't love her in return, she wanted him in their child's life.

If he didn't want anything to do with either of them, she would have the baby without him. The thought petrified her, and a part of her still wanted to run away—to give up without a fight. It would hurt less than having him tell her he didn't want her or the baby.

Tired of all the pacing and the endless what-ifs, Aubrey went out to the balcony with a thick robe wrapped around her and plopped down in a chair to gaze at the stars shining down on her.

The sound of a car crunching up the driveway jolted Aubrey awake. She must've dozed off, which seemed to happen whenever she wasn't standing. Rubbing the chill from her arms, she walked inside and glanced groggily at the clock in her room. Past midnight.

It was too late for them to talk. She was half-asleep on her feet, and he had to be exhausted after such a long day. The sound of the front door opening made her squeak in alarm. She was too nervous to act normally, so she slid under the covers. She didn't need to pretend to be asleep for long. Thanks to the baby, she fell asleep soon after Landon came to bed and wrapped his body around hers.

The next morning, her eyes opened at the crack of dawn, and she didn't wait for Landon to wake up. She sneaked out of bed and headed for Landon's unoccupied room, grabbing some clothes on her way out. Once she was washed and dressed, Aubrey set out for a long walk down the hills.

All the courage and strength she'd scrounged up last night seemed to have evaporated into thin air. But she had to tell him. They were leaving Bosque Verde tomorrow, and she needed to know where they stood before that happened. She had to know she wasn't his shameful secret. That they could build a real future together.

She was blind and deaf to the beauty surrounding her, barely conscious that her feet were moving. When a hand grasped her arm, she jolted back to reality with a startled scream.

"What was that for?" Landon looked more alarmed than she felt.

"I didn't hear you coming. You scared me."

"How could you not hear me? I called out for you loudly enough to scare the birds out of the trees."

"Well, I didn't hear you."

"Fair enough, and I didn't mean to startle you." Landon raked his fingers through his hair, standing shirtless and barefoot in front of her. He must've scrambled out of bed to catch up with her. "Now, do you want to tell me why you're avoiding me?"

"Whatever made you think that?" Aubrey asked with a guilty flush creeping up her neck.

"You were pretending to be asleep last night. I wanted to talk to you in the morning, but you weren't in bed. I saw you walking down the driveway, so I ran after you. And you know the rest of the story." He heaved a deep sigh and mussed his hair some more. "What's going on?"

Aubrey stared at the ground and drew little circles on the dirt road with her Vans-clad toes. She wasn't ready to talk. Fear clamped its teeth into her, and she wanted to run. *Coward.*

"Damn it, Aubrey. Just talk to me. Something's been bothering you since your final shoot," Landon said. "Please don't shut me out. I need to know what's going on."

"Don't push me." She hated how petulant and pathetic her voice sounded. Where was her resolve and bravado now?

"You're the one trying to push me away." He stepped toward her. "Please tell me what's going on. I can't do this. I don't want to leave you in Weldon and be on my way. I don't want this to end. I want to be with you."

"You mean you want to keep me as your dirty little secret." The words flowed out of her before she could stop them. That wasn't where she'd wanted to start. Not at a place of hurt and fear.

"What the hell are you talking about?"

"I heard you." Her accusation hung between them. "I heard you talking with Stan after my last shoot. I heard you tell him that I'm nothing to you."

"Goddamn it, Aubrey. You know why I had to say that. How could you even think I meant it?" His voice cracked over the last words. He took a deep breath before continuing, "I know I should've brought it up first, but I wanted to find a good time to talk to you. In a calm, rational manner. But I wish you'd told me you'd overheard us instead of hurting like this."

"Are you telling me you're ready to go public with our relationship?"

Landon drew back as though her words were daggers flying toward him. "What are you saying? You heard Stan. We could stop the crew from leaking the rumors, but this is our wake-up call. If people find out about us, it could destroy both of our careers. The whole point was to restore Comfort Zone without destroying our reputations. That has always been the plan, and it still is."

"That was the plan before we got together. But now that we're involved, we can't go on hiding like this."

"We have no other choice." His lips pressed into an obstinate line, and his eyes snapped with frustration.

"Are you ashamed of being with me?" Her body trembled, unable to deny what he was telling her.

"*No.*"

"Then let's go public."

"Listen to yourself. You're not making any sense. Our careers are important to both of us. Discretion is a necessary precaution to protect our reputations. Our future."

"My future doesn't involve being anyone's secret." Holding her head up high, Aubrey spun on her heel and walked away from him.

Landon didn't try to stop her.

—

Aubrey had gone back to bed after leaving Landon on the street. She was awakened from her fitful sleep by the insistent ringing at the front door. The sun was beginning to set, and she struggled to fall back asleep—to forget and escape. But whoever was at the door refused to go away. Dragging her leaden body off the bed, she trailed down the stairs, bumping into the rails on her unsteady legs.

"Aubrey!" Aria nearly shouted in her face, bubbling over with excitement. But she took a step back as her smile slipped. "Aubrey? Sweetheart, are you okay?"

"Come on, my dear. Let's have some refreshments, shall we?" Lucien, who'd been standing beside Aria, exchanged a look with her and firmly took control. Aubrey followed him to the kitchen, grateful for his warm strength.

"What happened?" Aria prodded gently when they were settled in the cheerful breakfast nook.

Aubrey mutely shook her head and stared down at her fidgeting hands, and Aria didn't push her. After sipping the lovely iced tea that Lucien placed in her hands, she began to regain some of her bearing. The first thing she noticed was that Aria looked absolutely radiant. Next, her sluggish brain registered Lucien was also beaming with happiness. While they looked at her with concern in their kind eyes, they gazed at each other with breathtaking tenderness.

Aria was sitting across from Aubrey, and Lucien was standing behind her with his hand on her shoulder. Reaching up, Aria placed her hand over his. Her left hand. Aubrey's ears began ringing at the sight of the exquisite diamond ring on her finger.

"You two are engaged," Aubrey said in a raspy voice.

"Yes," Aria confirmed, beaming at Lucien. He bent his head and gently kissed his bride-to-be.

"We wanted Landon to be the first to know," Lucien said picking up the conversation. "I have a lot to thank him for."

"If Landon hadn't talked some sense into him, Lucien would've pushed me away once and for all, making ridiculous excuses like our age difference." Aria snorted softly and rolled her eyes. She turned to face Lucien and poked her index finger into his chest. "You being seventeen years older than I am doesn't make me a child. I'm a grown woman, and I know who I love."

Lucien's expression darkened as though remembering the pain he'd put them through, but the momentary cloud lifted when his eyes met her shining ones. "I know. You also know who I love."

They're so much in love.

Even through her anguish, Aubrey was thrilled about their engagement. They were wonderful people, and they deserved each other. She couldn't cast a shadow over their happiness. With dogged determination, she pulled herself together and wrapped Aria in a tight hug.

"Congratulations." It meant so much to Aubrey that her friend didn't have to hurt anymore. "I'm so very happy for you."

"What's wrong?" Concern returned to Aria's eyes. "Where's Landon?"

"Everything's fine. I think he went to run some errands."

"You're so pale, darling. Are you sure everything's okay?"

"Honestly, I'm stressing out a bit about returning to Weldon and facing all the work I have waiting for me." Aubrey managed a sheepish smile. "But that's being ungrateful. Thanks to you and Landon, I'll be able to finish renovations to the new location and open Comfort Zone again. I really am very lucky."

"I can't believe you're already going back. I'll miss you so much." Aria squeezed her hand. "But I have a feeling we'll be seeing each other soon to celebrate your engagement to Landon. He's crazy about you, you know."

Not enough to want a future with me. The calm façade Aubrey had put on began to crack at her friend's well-meaning words. They needed to leave before she fell apart.

"Come visit me in Weldon." Aubrey hurriedly stood. "I'll let Landon know you came by. Congratulations again."

After hugging Aria and Lucien, she gently sent them on their way. Even after she closed the door behind them, she didn't shed a single tear. She felt as though her soul had dried up.

—

Landon was grateful that his mind remained a clean slate, unfettered by thoughts or feelings. Even his breathing grew slower, subtler, like his body understood his need to play possum. The pain he was keeping at bay was too much for him to let in, so he just drove calmly and competently without a destination. Stop and go. Left and right.

He hadn't realized it was already dark until his headlights came on. Then he saw without really noticing that the scenery

looked familiar. His subconscious had led him back to the villa.
Back to Aubrey.

There was no more hiding from it. Dragging in a ragged
breath, Landon placed his head on the steering wheel. He
couldn't get the image of Aubrey's face out of his mind, determination and heartbreak mingling with her unshed tears.

He should've stayed and talked to her. Whether he'd meant
to or not, he'd hurt her. Strangers had scorned and judged her
because of who he was. He'd had to distance himself from the
rumors to protect their reputations and careers, but he'd also
done it to protect her. He realized this was only the beginning.
Gossip and rumors could get very ugly, very fast. If he didn't
deny their relationship, she could've been hurt more deeply.

Without warning, she'd become his dream. He wanted her
to be his and only his. Every time he touched her, made love
to her, he wanted more. He wanted—no, needed to know her,
and he was desperate for her to know him. All of him. Despite
everything, he wanted to hold on to her.

No. His hands wrapped tightly around the steering wheel,
turning his knuckles nearly blue. If he held on to her, she would
become another person he could fail. And lose.

He'd been daydreaming when he'd thought he could have
her. He'd been willing to risk his reputation, security, and his
duty to his family to have her. More egregiously, he'd been
willing to risk her reputation and dream to keep her by his
side. He'd allowed his selfishness and recklessness to taint his
decisions. No more. He refused to be like his father. Landon
couldn't go public about his relationship with her. He couldn't
put everything Aubrey had fought so hard for in jeopardy just so
he could hold on to her.

He couldn't bear causing her pain, but more than that, he
was afraid. That was his reality. He had to walk away. Pushing

himself wearily out of the car, Landon walked to the front door. He could've spent the night at the schoolhouse if he'd wanted, but he'd come back to the villa. Until now, he hadn't known he was a glutton for pain. His lips twisted into a bitter mockery of a smile.

With agitated stabs of his finger, he punched in the security code and let himself in. It was dark and silent inside as though it were unoccupied, and his stomach clenched with panic. Landon scanned the foyer and breathed a sigh of relief when he saw Aubrey's canvas backpack resting by the entryway.

That morning, he'd had a taste of what it would be like to lose Aubrey. A part of his soul had cracked. But by some miracle, the dream hadn't fully taken root in his consciousness. He could still survive this as long as it ended now.

20

Aubrey heard Landon drive up to the villa and took a bracing breath. A few hours after Aria and Lucien had left, she'd finally snapped out of her stupor and began thinking very, very hard.

This couldn't be the end. No matter what had happened that morning, she would fight for him. Her plan to confess her love had only been delayed, not derailed. She needed to apologize for flying off the handle earlier and tell him how much she loved him. Whatever held him back, she had to try to convince him to give them a chance.

Praying for courage, Aubrey took out the handblown glass bottle she'd gotten in Cambria and filled it with moonstones. With her hands shaking, she buried the first of the pregnancy tests deep inside and pushed the stopper closed. She walked to his room with fine tremors crawling down her spine and knocked. As she waited, she held on to the glass bottle for strength.

He opened the door and looked blankly at her as though he didn't even recognize her.

"Landon."

"Yes," he said stoically, not bothering to move back from the doorway. He hadn't turned the lights on in his bedroom. The only thing illuminating the hallway was the faint glow of her bedside lamp seeping out of her door. No matter how hard she searched, she couldn't see the expression in his eyes, and fear dug its sharp claws into her a little deeper. Suddenly realizing she'd been gripping the glass bottle with all her strength, she stuck it out to Landon.

"Here."

When he just stared down at the bottle in her extended hand, she was certain he wouldn't take it and almost lost the little hope she'd had. But Landon slowly raised his hand and took it from her, and Aubrey sighed with relief.

"I got it from the glassworks store in Cambria and filled it with the stones we gathered that morning."

"I can see that."

"I wanted to thank you for that wonderful trip. I'll never forget it." She fought on doggedly despite the lack of encouragement. "That bottle means the world to me, and I hope it'll mean as much to you—"

"Aubrey," he interrupted. "What are you doing?"

Cut off in the middle of her practiced speech, Aubrey froze and blinked at him. When his question finally penetrated her brain, she told him the truth.

"I love you."

His eyes snapped up to hers, and she felt the intensity of his gaze even in the dark hallway. Then his face became a hard mask. "Don't."

"Landon, please listen." Tears clogged her throat. Stark fear slithered down her back, and she realized she'd never felt real fear before. Not like this.

"This morning, you handed down an ultimatum. You

ordered me to choose between you and my career." She couldn't tell whether the tremor in his voice came from fear or anger. "There is no reason why we can't see each other in secret. For the good of our careers, it doesn't make sense to flaunt our relationship publicly."

"But I—" Panic thumped in her chest like in "The Tell-Tale Heart."

"I refuse to be manipulated. My career, my life, and my future are not inconsequential."

"I never meant to imply they aren't important. I meant quite the opposite. I love you, and I want to be with you. Forever. But I can't be with you in secret. I don't want to hide anymore. I can't live believing that the person I love is ashamed of me. Not again."

Something akin to anguish and desolation flitted across his face, but it faded in a second. "My career isn't only about me. I have responsibilities and duties to my family. The same responsibilities I would have for you, your career, and your happiness if we were together."

"I know it isn't going to be easy, but we could do it together. I want us to build a life together. Something real and lasting." Aubrey gripped his hand in both of hers as tears fell endlessly down her cheeks. She couldn't tell him about the baby yet. She didn't want to trap him into staying with her. Prey on his sense of responsibility and his drive to set things right. But she wanted him to know what they could have together. "We could build a family of our own."

"It's wishful thinking—as far removed from reality as a fairy tale." His harsh expression was cut in stone, and the bitter certainty of his words drove the point home.

"Please, Landon." Aubrey dropped his hand and retreated a step. "Don't do this."

"I have no choice." His voice was thick with emotion, and his eyes were almost pleading. "We have no choice."

Aubrey couldn't remember how she'd gotten back in her room, but there she was. She'd given up and walked away from Landon. But she'd fought for their love with everything she had. Right now, she felt as though she were being ripped apart strip by strip, but she would be proud of herself someday. She had no regrets.

She couldn't tell him about the baby. She couldn't trap him in a relationship he no longer wanted. Even if he chose to be with her, she would always know he'd stayed for the baby. She'd know he didn't love her. She could never live like that again.

She let her tears flow silently. There was no holding them back. It hurt so much. Landon didn't love her. He wasn't willing to give them a chance. The anguish threatened to overwhelm her until she wished it would consume her.

Aubrey sat on her bed until she was certain she could form comprehensible words. Then she reached for her phone and dialed.

"Bree? What time is it?" Tara's voice sounded croaky from sleep. *Ribbit-ribbit.* Aubrey felt hysterical laughter bubbling to the surface and quickly clamped down on it. If she lost it, she would never make it out of Bosque Verde.

"Almost three in the morning, I think." Aubrey was surprised that her voice sounded almost casual. "I need you to come take me home."

"Send me the address. I'll be there in three hours, tops," her best friend said without a moment's pause.

Aubrey placed her phone on the nightstand and lay down, hugging a pillow to her chest. She wasn't sure if she'd slept or not. When she was aware of her surroundings, almost two hours had passed. She had to pack. Her limbs didn't move properly, but she somehow placed two packed bags by her bedroom door.

As promised, Tara texted from the driveway in two and a half hours.

Aubrey stood and quickly scanned the room to make sure she hadn't forgotten anything. Then, pulling her suitcases behind her, she walked out to the hallway and stopped in front of Landon's door. It would be easier for her to sneak out, but she had to see him one last time. No matter how much it hurt, she didn't regret a single moment with him. He'd saved her from her solitary confinement. She'd lost him, but her love would always stay with her.

It was barely six, but she knew he'd be awake. When she knocked quietly, he opened his door as though he'd been waiting for her. He was still wearing the same clothes from last night, and the shadows under his eyes told her he hadn't slept. The eyes that searched her face looked almost wild, and when his gaze fell on her suitcases, blood drained from his face.

"I didn't want to leave without saying good-bye this time." Her words reverberated in her head like the echo of a gong. *Don't you dare cry in front of him.* "Tara's here to take me home."

Landon stepped out into the hallway, moving jerkily like a broken toy soldier. Taking the suitcases from her, he started down the stairs without a word. As soon as he had his back to her, she swallowed the painful lump in her throat and blinked her burning eyes. When she had her emotions in check, Aubrey followed him down.

At the foyer, he stopped and placed her bags on the ground. Then he turned his head away, his throat working frantically. She needed to leave *now.* She was seconds away from falling apart in front of him. As broken as she felt, she wanted to retain some of her dignity. She hurriedly grabbed her suitcases and headed for the front door.

"Good-bye, Landon."

Before she could take more than a couple of steps, Landon spun her around and pressed his lips against hers. He tasted like salt and sorrow. She stood still, refusing to respond to his kiss until he stepped back, his arms falling to his sides. His eyes searched her face frantically. For what, she didn't know and couldn't care. She turned her back to him and walked away. She couldn't bear to stay another second.

Tara stepped out of her car as Aubrey neared it and enveloped her in a tight hug. Then she tucked her into the passenger seat and stowed her luggage in the back. Once she settled in the driver's seat, Tara turned to Aubrey and handed her a box of tissues.

"Let's take you home."

It felt as though he'd been on his back staring at the ceiling for days. There was a hairline crack by the ceiling fan, and Landon thought he should let Lucien know. This place was much too new to have any cracks. His friend should hunt down his contractor.

At first, Landon thought he was hearing his pounding headache bouncing off the walls. But he heard two pairs of feet hurrying up the stairs and realized it must've been them knocking on the front door. Aria and Lucien looked down at him from either side of his bed, so Landon closed his eyes to shut them out.

"He looks like death." Landon cringed at the sound of Aria's voice. She might as well take a hammer to his head.

"He'd better not die in my villa." At least Lucien whispered.

Aria perched on the side of his bed. "Landon, sweetheart. Where's Aubrey?"

Resigned to the fact he couldn't will them away, he tried to answer the question. Maybe that would get rid of them. Tragically, he couldn't get the words past his parched throat. He couldn't remember the last time he'd had water. He couldn't remember the last time he'd done anything.

"Could you bring up a cup of water for him?" Aria asked Lucien.

Landon knew he couldn't keep his eyes closed when Lucien and Aria tugged on his arms to get him sitting upright, so he opened them to glare at Aria. Unfazed, Aria put the cup to his lips.

"Drink."

Glaring made him tired, so Landon closed his eyes again and tried to lie back down.

"Drink this water. Or, so help me God, I'll throw it on your face." Aria shook his arm sharply and shoved the cup into his hand.

Aria didn't make empty threats, and Landon didn't feel like changing out of a wet T-shirt. He grudgingly drank one sip, then gulped down the rest of the water, realizing how thirsty he was.

"She's gone." His voice was nothing more than a hoarse whisper despite the water.

"What?" Aria's voice rose an octave, and Landon clutched his head, cursing under his breath. "She didn't even say goodbye. What did you do?"

"Darling, maybe he doesn't want to talk about it right now." Lucien rested his hand on her arm.

"It doesn't matter. She's gone." Landon wished he could

return to his fascinating study of the bedroom ceiling. "There's nothing to talk about. Now or later."

"It doesn't matter?" Aria said with some heat. "You disappear for two days and we find you here looking like death, and you have the gall to tell us that it doesn't matter? If I were your mother, I'd box your ears right now."

"I'm just trying to survive," Landon clarified. *It's been two days. Only two days.* He recalled assiduously emptying all the wine in the villa to dull the pain in his chest, but for the life of him, he couldn't get himself drunk. He couldn't hide from the pain. She was gone. God, she was gone.

When he made to collapse back into bed, Aria slapped him sharply on his shoulder. "Don't you dare lie back down. What in God's name prompted you to let her go if you were going to fall apart like this?"

"She overheard me talking to Stan about the rumors going around," Landon said.

Aria squinted in confusion. "What rumors?"

"The one where the crew decided I hired Aubrey after my review because she was sleeping with me."

"*Mio dio,*" Aria breathed, then she slapped her thigh and stood up bristling with temper. "Don't they realize they're talking about real, flesh-and-blood human beings?"

"I told Stan she meant nothing to me and asked him to kill the rumor." He felt quite detached from it all. "And Aubrey heard me."

"What did she say?" she asked incredulously.

"She wanted to know if I'd meant what I said. I told her I had to say what I did to protect both of our reputations. Restoring Comfort Zone and her reputation was the end game from the beginning. We couldn't risk discovery." Landon pinched the bridged of his nose and squeezed her eyes shut. "She said she didn't want to be my secret anymore. She wanted to go public and weather the storm together."

"And?"

"I told her it was impossible, so she left."

"How could she have stayed after that? She wanted a life with you. What were you thinking?"

"Please, shut up. You're not helping."

"You need to hear this," Lucien said firmly. "I almost lost Aria because of my stubbornness until you talked some sense into me. Aria and I want to repay the debt."

"Landon, you're an idiot if you can't see that Aubrey loves you," Aria said.

"I know. She told me before she left," he replied.

"And you still let her leave? How could you be so stupid?" Aria threw her hands up in the air and muttered something rapidly in her native tongue.

"Letting her go was for the best." Landon wanted to run from the doubt seeping into him. "She wouldn't listen to reason. We've both worked too hard to lose everything now."

"I agree with my fiancée," Lucien said. "You're a fucking idiot."

Landon was starting to get annoyed at being called an idiot. He couldn't believe these were his friends. *Traitors*.

"Please close the door on your way out," he said politely and lay back down.

21

Tara pampered her for the first few days, letting her sleep and cry all day. But Aubrey knew the pampering was over when Tara plopped a trayful of food in front of her.

"Eat. It's your favorite, chicken *jook*. You know my *jook* is magic. One bowl of this stuff and you'll keep on going like the Energizer Bunny. And when you're done eating, call my mom and thank her for teaching me how to cook Korean food."

The steaming bowl of porridge brought more tears to Aubrey's eyes. Aubrey was touched by Tara's kindness, but she shook her head. "I can't."

"Do you want me to bring you a straw so you can drink the damn thing?" Tara said with a steely light in her eyes. "You'd better eat and get your strength back, because I sure as hell am not going to carry you to your ob-gyn appointment."

Aubrey's face blanched at Tara's words. "What? How? I didn't have a chance to tell you."

"You were so emotional the last few times we talked, and you've been throwing up at least twice a day since I brought you home. And honestly, your grapefruit-sized boobs are hard to ignore. So unless you got a boob job in Bosque Verde, my guess is you're pregnant." Tara's expression softened. "I don't know what happened between you and Landon, but you need to pull yourself together. You need to eat for the little munchkin's sake."

Pressing her lips together in a determined line, Aubrey nodded and dug into the chicken *jook*. The first bite was all it took to remind her she was starving. After two bowls of the piping-hot porridge, they made their way to the doctor's office.

The doctor said she was about twelve weeks along and a month overdue for her first ultrasound. As he performed the exam, he explained what they were seeing and hearing. Like the baby's heartbeat. It thundered from the speaker like a thoroughbred mustang, and Aubrey choked back a sob.

"It's the most beautiful sound I've ever heard," she whispered, too reverent to speak any louder. She spread her fingers on her tummy and listened to the life inside her.

"Bree, your jelly bean sounds like a choo-choo train," Tara said, her voice husky from tears. "Her whole tiny body is pulsing with her heart."

"I know. I can't stop staring." Aubrey traced her fingers over Jelly Bean's image. "I'm a mom, Tara. I have a little person growing inside me."

"A little girl," her friend corrected. "I bet you she's a girl."

"Well, your next ultrasound is at the four-month mark," said the doctor. "Would you like to know the sex of the baby then?"

"Yes. Yes, please." Aubrey thought her heart was going to burst. For a moment, she wished Landon could've been there, laughing and crying beside her. The pain of his absence stole her breath until she looked at her baby again.

She felt weightless with joy and paralyzed with fear. Who wouldn't be anxious about being a single mother? But she could do this. Aubrey couldn't wait to share her dreams with her child. They would make mistakes together, learn together, and laugh together. They would live to the fullest together. *Me and you, Jelly Bean, are going to be a family.*

"Is she real?" Aubrey said through her tears. "I can't believe she's really inside of me."

"She's so beautiful," Tara sighed, choking up with emotion again.

The doctor waited with a polite smile on his face for them to stop blubbering. He probably saw a lot of blubbering in his line of work. "Is this the first baby for the two of you?"

They paused mid-bawl and gaped at the doctor and then turned back to look at each other. When Tara wiggled her eyebrows at her, Aubrey burst out laughing.

Before the good doctor sent for their straitjackets, Tara grinned at him. "While that's really flattering, I'm just standing in for the baby daddy."

Hearing the word *daddy* almost pushed Aubrey into another sobbing fit, but she pressed her lips together.

Don't you worry, Jelly Bean. No more crying for Mama. I'm here for you, love.

—

Aubrey wouldn't have noticed the passing of time if it weren't for her growing belly. At five months, she was showing a respectable baby bump that her loose dresses couldn't hide anymore. Jelly Bean was doing fabulously, and Aubrey was a proud mama.

Thanks to the reality show renovation team Aria had rallied for her, the bigger, badder Comfort Zone was customer-ready literally two weeks after Aubrey came home. She freed herself from the blackhole of heartbreak after her first ultrasound, and threw herself into Comfort Zone's big comeback. Tireless in her generosity, Aria continued to support the reopening by posting about Comfort Zone's makeover and renovation progress on her blog.

With the new location and the hype Aria helped create, the bakery regained its out-of-town and online customers within a month of its grand reopening, while her regulars continued to be her loyal customers. Aubrey and Lily worked themselves to the bones during the first month, but couldn't keep up with the demand.

Even after the success of the opening month, the future of Comfort Zone remained uncertain. Still, Aubrey followed her instincts and chose to take a risk. She hired a sous chef, and it was one of the best decisions she'd ever made in her life. If Aubrey hadn't taken the risk, she would never have known how much and how fast Comfort Zone could've grown.

Now at the two-month mark, business was booming, and the daily bustle in the bakery electrified the air with spices and excitement. While her heart ached for Landon every time their daughter kicked in her growing belly, Aubrey was so proud of what she'd accomplished.

"How does this look?" Justine stared down at the whoopie pie in her hands. The humble dessert had been dressed to the nines with rolling blue ribbons and edible silver beads sprinkled across it.

"I'd lose the fondant ribbons and the bling-bling," Aubrey said, smiling at her sous chef.

"What? Just leave it plain?" she said with a doubtful expression. "But it'd look so plain."

"Exactly. A customer looking at the familiar appearance will expect the familiar texture and flavor. The chewy texture of the chestnut and sweet rice cake center will take them by complete surprise the moment they bite into the whoopie pie. It'll be a multisensory culinary experience."

"Wow. You're like a baked goods genius," Justine gushed and stared at her with dreamy eyes. Aubrey blushed, equal parts pleased and embarrassed.

She'd known Justine was *the one* even though she was only number three on her interview list. At barely twenty-one, Justine didn't have much practical experience, but she was a graduate of a prestigious cooking school, and Aubrey was truly humbled that someone with her potential wanted to work for her. Most important, Justine *loved* to bake. Her enthusiasm for her craft rivaled Aubrey's love of all things sweet and baked.

They worked incredibly well together in the kitchen, as comfortably and naturally as breathing. They moved seamlessly through each recipe, assisting and complementing each other without having to ask or instruct. Aubrey often thought they were twins separated at birth despite the fact she was seven years older than Justine, who was a svelte, five-foot-eleven redhead.

Everything worked out so beautifully with her sous chef that Aubrey was even able to hire a full-time cashier/server for the front as Lily began her new role as her apprentice. With more of her time freed up, Aubrey continued to create new recipes, and she planned to introduce the strawberry shortcake as a seasonal special in late spring. She stretched her back and cringed for the umpteenth time that afternoon. Her twelve-hour shifts were getting harder by the week.

"You've been doing that a lot lately," Justine said.

"Doing what?"

Lily rolled her eyes. "Grabbing your back and scrunching up your face like the Grinch."

"Gee, thanks. You try carrying an extra fifteen pounds on a

five-foot-two frame. My back literally feels like it's breaking by this time of the day."

"You know," her sous chef said hesitantly, "Lily and I could manage the kitchen till we close."

"What? But . . . ," Aubrey said with a confused frown.

"With all due respect, Justine is trying to tell you we don't need you here every minute of the day."

"*Lily!*" Justine gasped, shooting an alarmed glance at Aubrey. "Please don't get the wrong idea. Having you here is the best because you literally make every bake more amazing. But it's hard for us to watch you working through your pain."

"Yeah, what she said. We have it under control here," Lily said, softening her voice at Aubrey's stunned expression. "You need to take care of yourself and the baby. Just work eight hours like normal people for a while."

She was so touched by her colleagues' considerate words that a sob escaped her mouth, and she grabbed one of them in each arm and hugged the air out of them. "You guys are so incredible. Thank you for worrying about me."

"Does that mean you'll go home?" Lily asked in a breathless rasp.

"Yes. I really need to get off my feet."

After fussing and saying good-bye for twenty more minutes, Aubrey finally drove to her little cottage. It felt strange entering her house with the midday sun streaming through the windows. She didn't think she'd ever come home in the middle of a workday.

Aubrey was dead on her feet, but she had the wherewithal to grab herself a carton of Ben & Jerry's before plopping down on the sofa. She put her feet up on the coffee table and played her favorite playlist. Being home so early felt like she was playing hooky, and she let the goofy fun times roll.

Digging into her Cherry Garcia, she belted out eighties'
tunes at the top of her lungs in between bites. She almost
missed the knocking at the door during her rendition of "Take
on Me." Aubrey wiggled her butt to the edge of the couch before she hefted herself to standing with a grunt. Getting out of
a chair was going to get very difficult in a few more weeks.

When she pulled open her front door, her jaws dropped and
dangled from their hinges.

"Hello, baby."

Her mom stood on her front porch with two small suitcases
by her feet. Aubrey didn't hesitate. She launched herself into
her mom's arms and held her tightly. She had no intention of
wasting any more time to close the gap between them. With a
sound between a sob and a laugh, her mom hugged her back,
being careful not to squish her granddaughter.

"Mom. What are you doing here?" she said, picking up one
of the bags and tugging her mother into the house.

"I left your father. He *forbade* me to help you. Ha! My baby
is having a baby, and he tells me I can't help? I won't let anyone keep me from you." Her mom dragged in a shaky breath,
straightening her shoulders. "I stayed away these few years because you needed to make your own way. But now, you need
my help even if you don't know it. I'm not letting you do this
alone."

"Thank God," Aubrey said with a heartfelt sigh.

The *everything will be fine* mantra Aubrey had been hypno-
tizing herself with flickered and showed its cracks. She'd been
doing this on her own, but it hadn't been easy. She was con-
stantly afraid, sad, and so alone. But not anymore. She didn't
have to do it alone. Her mom was with her to love her and take
care of her. The relief liquified her knees, and she sank onto
the nearest sofa.

"I'm here, baby. Everything is going to be fine." Her mom sat down beside her and enfolded her into a warm, healing hug, and Aubrey sighed into her arms. "If your father dares come between us, I'll expose his secret overseas accounts."

"I've always thought the Korean markets were a front for something more sinister, but overseas accounts?"

"Your father is very good at keeping secrets, so I don't know the details either. All I know is it involves powerful politicians in Korea and possibly money laundering."

"Money laundering?" Aubrey gasped. She'd known her father was a scoundrel, but finding out he was a hard criminal shocked her to the core and destroyed any lingering hopes for a reunion.

"Before I left, I broke one of his passwords. I was afraid to take any photos on my cell phone, so I copied out as many account numbers as I could."

"Wow. So this is the real you." Aubrey giggled and hugged her again. "You're a total badass."

"Yeah," her mom said as though she were savoring the thought. "You and I both. We get that from Grandma."

Aubrey's laughter was smothered by a yawn she couldn't hold back.

"Why don't you go take a nap? I'll keep myself busy."

"Busy?" She quirked her eyebrow. "There isn't much to do in the house except to settle in. That sage-colored room straight ahead? You could use that room. It's a bit cramped with all my cook books and baking toys, but the bed's comfy and cozy."

"I'm sure it'll be perfect."

Her mom kissed her on the forehead and headed to her room. After another huge, teary yawn Aubrey shuffled her slippered feet to bed. One of her pregnancy superpowers was to fall asleep the moment her head hit the pillow. Even the happiness

and anticipation of having her mom with her didn't diminish
her power.

———

When Aubrey's eyes opened to a dusky room, she remembered hearing her grandma singing in her dream. She swung
her feet to the floor and then paused, struggling to get her
bearings. Her house smelled just like Grandma's. Confusion
marring her forehead, Aubrey padded out to the living room,
following the aroma. She stopped in her tracks when she
reached the kitchen.

"Mom?"

Her mom was wearing a slim pair of jeans and a pullover
with her hair tied loosely at the base of her neck. She looked
younger and more relaxed than Aubrey had ever seen her. And
she was baking. Linda Choi did not bake.

"Hi, sweetie. My St. John's suit felt like a weighted vest, so
I borrowed one of your sweatshirts." Her mom blushed as she
glanced down at herself. "I hope you don't mind."

"Of course not. I'm glad we wear similar sizes. You can bor-
row anything you need. I made the switch to maternity clothes
a few weeks ago," Aubrey said, tugging on the stretchy material
at her tummy. The stomach panel was made of a magical material that stretched way out and supported the bump without
squeezing it. "These leggings are crazy comfortable; I don't
think I'll ever wear regular tights again."

"Oh, my baby. You're so beautiful," Mom said, going to
Aubrey and place her hand on her stomach. Sniffling away her
tears, she tested the secret panel and whistled. "Wow. I wish
they'd had those when I was pregnant with you."

Aubrey beamed at her, warmed by the shared moment, and her mom ushered her to the table, bustling around with joyous energy. Soon, a small feast lay before her.

"This looks amazing, Mom." Aubrey lowered her head, close enough to feel the steam coming off the goodies, and breathed in heaven. "The kitchen smells exactly like Grandma's. I had no idea you knew how to bake."

"It's been so long, you might break a tooth on that biscotto."

"Oh, my God." Aubrey's words were muffled because she was stuffing another bite of said biscotto into her mouth.

Jelly Bean loved the almond biscotto and fluttered in her tummy. It was perfection. So were the lemon bars and sticky buns. Aubrey was too stuffed to try the cherry upside-down cake, but she knew it would taste just like Grandma's.

Her mom sat across from her and fiddled with her fork. "You've always been braver than I have."

Aubrey stared at her with a mouthful of lemon bars. Even if she could speak, she wouldn't know what to say. This new mom not only knew how to bake a mean biscotto, she'd just initiated the Big Talk. She was going to stick with staring for now.

"I was very young when I met your dad, and I never got over the feeling that he was way out of my league. The more I fell in love with him, the more afraid I became of losing him." Linda glanced down at her hands and took a shuddering breath. "I was only twenty-four when I first found out about your father's dalliances. I confronted him, and he wept at my feet. He promised it would never happen again, but it did."

"Why didn't you leave?" The question that had been burning at the back of her throat for years broke free in a fragile whisper.

"I did, but I only stayed with your grandma for a few weeks

before I went back to your father." Her mom lifted her gaze and bit her trembling lips.

Then Aubrey knew, and it felt like a punch in the gut. Her mom had her when she was twenty-five. "You found out you were pregnant. You went back because of me."

"That's what I told myself. That I went back and stayed with your father for you." Tears were streaming unchecked down her mom's pale cheeks. "But that's not true. I was afraid of being alone, of struggling to provide for you. I had already lost myself by then. I was a scared shadow of my old self with no hopes or dreams of my own. I used the pregnancy as an excuse to go back."

"Mom."

"Let me finish. You need to hear this. I need to say this." She wiped her face with her palms and straightened her back. "I know I wasn't there for you. I shut everyone out, drowning in my nightmare. I failed you. I failed myself. I know I could never make it up to you, but I have to try. Will you let me?"

"Mom, you don't need to ask. I was a horrible teenage brat, and adult me wasn't much better. I wish I'd been there for you, too, instead of hurting you and making you feel more alone." Aubrey's tears weren't of sorrow but of freedom and peace. "You and I, we let Father's toxic influence break us apart. Break *us*. Never again, Mom. No one will take away our confidence and shove us in a corner."

"Never again." Her mom's eyes were bright with tears and determination.

Yes." Landon drummed his fingers on the steering wheel. "Twenty percent."

"That's too big of a risk," his financial advisor sputtered on the other end.

"It's just 20 percent of one portfolio."

"It's still a huge amount of money."

Landon was fighting the madness clawing at his mind by focusing on his investments. His advisors thought he was taking unnecessary risks, but he knew exactly what he was doing. Taking calculated risks for high payouts. He studied the market for hours on end. It was the most effective way to distract himself from the gaping hole in his chest. Drinking was a shitty excuse of a crutch. It only made him feel as physically miserable as he was inside.

"Don't worry, Stu. The payout is worth the risk."

His financial advisor made a choking noise on the other end.

Landon's brief spurt of amusement left him. "Do it."

"I can't stand back and watch you bankrupt yourself."

"Stop being dramatic. I don't have all my eggs in one fucking portfolio. Do it."

Landon hung up on him without waiting for a response and dialed his property manager. Unlike his finance guy, his property manager didn't question Landon's requests even when they seemed reckless. After five minutes of listening to "Yes, Mr. Kim," Landon grew tired of the call and the property manager. He made a mental note to replace the yes-man. Stu cared enough to argue with him. He was irritating, but he had a backbone. Landon couldn't work with someone who let him make seemingly stupid decisions without a fight.

Not that his plans were anywhere near stupid. He wasn't like his father with his unrealistic schemes. Landon worked his ass off to accrue his wealth. It gave him the power to protect his family and his future. He wouldn't do anything to risk that.

He drove in silent contemplation, pushing his car far beyond the speed limit. His fingers resumed their restless drumming on the steering wheel. It wasn't enough, though. None of it was enough. His cell phone rang, and Landon answered without looking to see who it was. He figured it was another one of his frustrated advisors.

"Landon." His mom's warm voice traveled through the lines.

"Is something wrong?" His question came out gruffer than he intended.

"Why do you ask that every time I call?" his mom responded in Korean. "Can't I call my son to say hello?"

"Of course, you can." He ran a hand down his face. "Hi, Mom."

"Hello, baby."

Landon could feel her smile, and he was suddenly homesick. "But seriously. What's wrong?"

"I don't know. You tell me."

Did Seth say something to Mom?

"There's nothing to tell." The now-familiar burning spread in his chest. The pain tore at him as he fought to push away thoughts of Aubrey. "I'm fine."

"Seth says you're behaving like a madman. Like you're trying to destroy yourself." His mom's voice trembled. "Landon, whatever it is, come home."

"I don't—"

"For me. If you don't want my help, that's fine, but I need to see for myself that you're okay."

His heart clenched at the helpless worry in his mom's voice. "I'll be there in about four hours."

Landon changed routes and headed toward his childhood home. He'd flown his mom out to Europe or had her stay at his

place in Santa Monica, but he'd avoided going home for several
years.

———

Landon arrived at the house and sat in the driveway as the sun
set behind it, and he understood why he'd avoided it for so
long. The house reminded him of how wonderful life had been
when he'd cared, and how much it had hurt to lose the things
he cared most about.

As soon as he stepped out of his car, the porch door swung
open, and his mom bounded toward him. He met her halfway
and lifted her off the driveway in a bear hug. She laughed and
cried and laughed, and warmth thawed his frozen heart.

"Come on." After a long while—but not long enough for
Landon—his mom pulled back and tugged on his hand. "I
made your favorite."

His stomach growled vociferously. Everything his mom
made tasted incredible, but her spicy fish soup had no equal. He
couldn't wait to fill himself up with it. But when they walked
into the kitchen, he saw a precarious tower of sandwiches on
white bread without the crusts.

"Peanut butter and marshmallow sandwiches," said his
mom, doing a decent Vanna White impression. "Your favorite
snack."

He grinned as happy memories flooded him. He'd been
about ten or eleven when their neighborhood had a long black-
out that lasted a good fifteen hours. He and Seth had been
arguing over what to watch for their family movie night when
everything went dark. They stopped arguing—both happy the
other hadn't gotten to watch the movie he'd wanted—and shared
an unforgettable meal, watching the fire dance in their toasty

family room. Peanut butter, banana, and mini-marshmallow sandwiches. It tasted like the food of the gods, which they consumed faster than their mom could make them. Even their father had seemed content that night, although he'd refused to eat a single sugar-loaded sandwich.

"Mom," he said, reaching for a sandwich. "You're awesome."

Landon finished the entire plate while he and his mom chatted about his mischievous childhood.

"You were such a curious child," she said. "There wasn't a science project you couldn't blow up. You would tinker with the ingredients until you got a bigger, better reaction. Then you pushed for more."

"Yeah. Always wanting more is a Kim family trait."

"You say that like it's a bad thing." His mom gave him a long, sideways glance. "Always wanting more is different from never having enough."

He let his mom's words sink in. They'd said so much without bringing up the real topic. Landon was terrified of becoming his father. As a kid, he already had his dad's callous confidence, endless ideas, and drive for more. He even looked like him. If he didn't keep himself in check, he would chase after *more* until he let everyone down.

But his recent dreams to open his own restaurant, to find a home, and to share his life with Aubrey now felt like the beginning of something lasting rather than the end of everything he'd built up. Not a rash gamble but a choice he would cherish forever.

Landon glanced away from his mom to hide the panic reaching out to suffocate him. He walked into the kitchen with her close behind. "When you said my favorite, I thought you meant *meh-oon-tang*."

"The sandwiches were your favorite snack. The fish soup is

for dinner." Her smile held a trace of sadness, but she let him change the subject. "How many hot peppers do you want in the soup? I have serrano and jalapeño."

"Serrano. At least three. I want the steam-sauna effect." He rolled up his sleeves. "Where's the fish? Would you like me to clean it up for the broth?"

"Landon, we haven't cooked together in so long." His mom cleared her throat, her eyes wide. "It's in the garage fridge. Red rock cod. Make sure you don't nick the roe and the liver."

"Give me some credit, Mom. I did graduate with honors from the CIA and am still a respected food critic. They're the best part of the soup. I'll make sure to extract them in pristine condition."

The kitchen was small but well appointed, and he worked on the fish at the big sink, while his mom drew water for the broth from the island sink. When the base broth of kelp, onion, ginger, and garlic was ready, she added the chunks of fish Landon had cleaned. While that boiled, he sliced and then added some white Korean radish, green onions, and tofu to the soup. His mom had the fresh perilla leaves and crown daisy ready to add at the end.

Saliva was pooling in his mouth when the soup was finished. His mom laid out the *banchan*, small dishes of kimchee, seasoned bean sprouts, steamed spinach, and pan-fried zucchini. When she placed a bowl of rice, filled past the rim, in front of him, Landon dug in. The fish soup was boiling hot, and the spice level was volcanic. He wiped away the sweat beading on his forehead and upper lip and ate seconds and thirds. He only came up for air once he'd finished.

"Mom." He slouched back in his chair, feeling like he'd purged all the toxins from his mind and body. "That was the best."

"Just a reminder of what you're missing, son."

Landon spent the night in his old room and actually managed to sleep a few hours. As expected, the pain had rolled in with the dark. *Aubrey*. Her name moved through his bloodstream, scorching and gutting him, but he didn't try to hide from it.

Something had shifted with his homecoming. Letting himself be taken care of—allowing himself to become vulnerable— freed a part of him that he'd chained and thrown into the dungeon. Even the pain was better than the empty numbness Aubrey's absence had left.

The next morning, he stood by the front door, knowing he was done running.

"Mom." She had a death grip around his waist. "I'll come visit soon. I promise."

"I love you, baby. Please don't hurt alone anymore."

"Mom."

"Don't deny it. You loved your dad, but you didn't even get to grieve his loss properly. You were so hard on yourself. Giving up more than I would ever have dreamed of asking you."

"I didn't want to be like him. I wanted to take care of you and Seth."

"You are like him, though." Landon stiffened, but she held on. "So passionate. So talented. But you're stronger than he was."

"I'm not so sure about that."

"Well, I am. Even as a kid, you always owned what you did, good or bad."

"I—" A rush of pent-up emotions choked him. "I was so scared when Dad left. I couldn't lose you and Seth, too."

"You gave us everything money could buy, but you kept yourself distant." She pulled back and gazed at him with pain shadowing her face. "I thought you resented me for having to give up your dream."

"Not for a single moment." Landon shook his head, horrified his mom had blamed herself all these years. "I walked away from my dream—from my life—because I didn't think I could survive losing anything else I loved."

"If you keep hiding, then you won't have anything to lose, because you'll have nothing worth having. It's time to start living your life, son."

"I know."

"Well, then. You'd better go and get back the woman you love."

22

When Tara came by for their weekly dinner, Aubrey's eyes were nearly swollen shut.

"Ye gatz!" Tara cringed away from her. "What happened to you?"

"I . . . I . . ."

"Hello, Tara." Her mom's serene voice broke through Aubrey's wailing. Despite the pregnancy dramas, they'd been getting along surprisingly well.

"Hey, Mama Linda. How long has she been like this?"

"Oh, on and off since she woke up this morning."

Aubrey stopped crying to listen to their exchange. They were talking about her like she wasn't there. She blew her nose loudly to break whatever invisibility spell they'd cast on her.

"What now, Bree? Did one of your cacti die? Or do you miss the fuzzy dice you had when you were twelve?"

Linda giggled behind her hand, and Tara inclined her head in acknowledgment. Aubrey glared at the two of them, switching to her irritated mood.

"Can't you ever be serious?" she snapped.

"Only on very special occasions."

Her mom actually snorted. Very unladylike. Tara was a bad influence on her. She didn't blink an eye at the daggers Aubrey was shooting at her.

"Well, this is important," Aubrey said.

"What is it?" Tara's eyebrows shot up, alarm creeping into her voice.

"I'm fat."

"Good heavens." Her friend face-palmed.

"No. Seriously. Look at my feet. They look like Fred Flintstone's." Aubrey sniffed ominously, warning of another torrential storm. Her mom rushed over and frantically rubbed her arms, trying to ward off the wails. "And I have sausage fingers. I feel like a giant ogre when I handle the dough."

"Don't be ridiculous." Tara poofed and rolled her eyes. "You're all stomach. The rest of you is tiny. People can't even tell you're pregnant from behind."

"Really?" A tentative smile tugged at her tremulous lips.

"Absolutely. It's only when you turn around that they say, 'Whoa. Careful where you point that thing.'"

"Thanks for nothing. Some friend you are. Taking cheap shots at a pregnant woman."

Linda made a choking sound and trembled, but managed to suppress her mirth. "Now, girls."

Tara wasn't as diplomatic. As her best friend chortled at her own witticism, Aubrey contemplated strangling her. Just a teeny bit. But she settled for hurling a cushion at her head.

"Hey. Watch it, preggers. I will take you down. I won't take it easy on you because you've swallowed a basketball."

"Shut up, or else I'll sit on you." Aubrey couldn't stop herself from bursting out with laughter. "You're all kinds of horrible. Just wait till you're pregnant."

"You're welcome. Now that you've found your sunny disposition again, I want you to listen and listen good. You're
more beautiful than ever. You're glowing from inside out."
Tara smiled mistily at Aubrey. "I'm so proud of you, Bree. Your
strength and courage are blinding, and I think you're ready to
take on the world."

"She's right, honey. I know the changes are hard, but you're
doing a brilliant job growing a small person inside of you." Her
mom tapped Aubrey on the tip of her nose. "And your pudgy
fingers still bake the best pastries in town."

"Oh, you guys."

Weepy group hugs were the best.

———

Landon wanted to realize the dream Aubrey had solidified for
him during their first night in Bosque Verde. He longed to cook
food for people to enjoy and be nourished by—simple, approach-
able gourmet that wouldn't require a second mortgage. The
only reason he couldn't decide where to open his restaurant was
because he wanted Aubrey to be part of his dream. Maybe he
still had a chance of making the restaurant *their* dream.

But he'd hurt her so much. Destroyed her fragile trust.
How could he convince her he loved her after what he'd done?
Landon drove into Bosque Verde just as the sun began to set.
Being in the schoolhouse that made him dream of making
a home with Aubrey at once soothed and tortured him. The
deck, the kitchen, the bedroom. Everywhere he looked, she
was there. There was nowhere to hide, but he didn't want to
hide from the memories no matter how painful.

Night settled around the hills, and he paced around in the
house, using every ounce of his willpower not to jump into his

car and go to her. In desperation, he stalked to his bedroom and took out the glass bottle Aubrey had given him. He held it against his chest and closed his eyes. *Maybe the stones were still warm from her hands.* It was madness, but that didn't stop him from opening the bottle and pouring the stones into his palm.

When the pregnancy test dropped out with the stones, Landon stopped breathing. It felt as though he was outside of his body watching himself. He flipped the stick over to uncover the result and then fell to his knees. In Aubrey's lovely hand, she'd wrote, "First encounter with parenthood." With stark clarity, their last conversation replayed in his mind.

That bottle means the world to me, and I hope it'll mean as much to you.

She'd been trying to tell him. She'd been was trying to tell him, but he wouldn't listen. No matter what his reasons were, he was the one who had turned her away. He'd turned away the woman he loved at her most vulnerable moment. He'd abandoned her when she was pregnant with his child.

The pain that sliced through his heart made him sense the boundary of his own sanity. He vaguely wondered what it'd feel like to let the ugly, black guilt consume him. But something pulled him back.

Our child. Aubrey was going to have his baby.

He had no right—no right at all—to feel the joy that coursed through him. A dream he never knew he held came true in that moment. His very own family. With Aubrey. For the first time since he'd watched her walk out of his life, his lips curved with hope.

He had to fix this, and he needed help. He impatiently waited for the sun to rise then called Aria at seven o'clock sharp, grateful that she was an early riser.

"I'm a fucking imbecile," Landon said without preamble when Aria answered the phone.

"I thought we'd already covered that." He could hear her roll her eyes on the other end of the line. "Yes, yes, you are."

"Aria, I love her so much." He paused to breathe, trying to still the tremor in his voice. "I need to bring her home."

"You're finally talking sense."

"She's pregnant," Landon blurted out.

He heard the phone clatter to the floor on the other end, and then there was silence. Landon wondered if he'd lost the connection.

"When did you find out?" Aria asked, her voice both excited and worried.

"Last night. The glass bottle she gave me had a positive pregnancy test inside. She was trying to tell me, Aria. She was trying to tell me, but I wouldn't listen." He couldn't hide his anguish from his friend.

"Oh, Landon."

"What should I do? How can I begin to make it up to her?"

"Well, first thing first," Aria said briskly, ready to take charge. "How do you feel about the pregnancy?"

"I'm so ridiculously happy," Landon said, a goofy grin spreading across his face. "I feel ecstatic every time I think about the baby. Our child . . . I'm a fuckwad and don't deserve her, but I need to bring my family home. I need it like my next breath. Nothing else matters."

"It's going to take some work, considering the mess you've made, but I guess I've an idea or two to contribute to the worthy cause."

"Anything. I'll do anything. I'll go crazy if I don't do something. Right now. I've been without her for over two months." He hadn't slept since he'd found the secret in the bottle, and he couldn't sleep until he had Aubrey back in his arms. "Is there any chance one of your ideas will bring her home today?"

"I have no plans to kidnap a pregnant woman, so no." Aria's voice softened as she continued. "Besides, you don't even have a 'home' to bring her to. And you're not ready, Landon."

She was right, of course. He was a wreck. If Aubrey saw him like this, she'd run screaming in the opposite direction. Landon swiped his hand down his face. "I need a shower, some food, and a few hours of sleep."

"Before you start pampering yourself, you need to slow down. This isn't happening in a day."

"No?" he asked helplessly.

"No, but you could get started today." Aria paused as though waiting for him to say something. When he remained mute, she sighed. "What do you need to do before you could bring Aubrey home?"

"Find a house." Landon blinked as his brain creaked and squeaked to turn the rusty cogs. "A place she would want to make our home."

And he would find a location for his restaurant. Landon would not be a spectator in his life anymore. He would chase his dreams. All his dreams. For Aubrey. With Aubrey, he could do anything.

23

Landon tossed a white envelope on Craig's desk and settled into a guest chair, legs stretched and ankles crossed.

"Since when do you write on paper?" his editor said, gingerly picking up the envelope between his thumb and index finger. "If this is a resignation letter, I'm not going to bother opening it. It's going straight to the shredder."

"How did you know?" The hair on his arms swept upright at his friend's apparent clairvoyance. Landon didn't want to abandon Craig or *Cal Coast*, but he couldn't travel around the world to write reviews when he would soon have a kitchen to run.

"Know what?" Craig asked, pulling out his letter and snapping it open. It only had three sentences. "What the fuck, Kim? Is this a resignation letter?"

"Yes, but since you've already opened and read it, there's no need for the shredder." Landon laughed with nerves and relief. He'd pissed his friend off, but he'd taken a major step toward his dream.

"Why the hell are you pulling this shit on me?"

"Sometimes, Craig, it's not all about you." He smirked at

the irate editor but continued solemnly, "This isn't about me leaving *Cal Coast*. It's about me opening my own restaurant. It's about me being a chef and not a critic. It's about me living my life again."

"It's about damn time. I am so proud and happy for you." Craig was on his feet and beside Landon in a flash, clapping his shoulder. "But goddamn it, I wish it didn't mean losing you here."

"You know I can't do both."

"Of course I know. But how am I going to find someone to fill your freakishly big shoes?"

"How about Gary?"

"Fuck you, Kim."

"Thanks." Landon rubbed the back of his neck as some of his amusement died down. "Before I go, I have a favor to ask."

"Let me hear it. I'll do everything in my power to make it happen."

"I want you to print my farewell article. In this month's issue."

"The one coming out next week?"

"Yes."

"The one that's all but ready to print, and making any alterations at this point would be a huge pain in the ass?"

"Yes."

"Sure. Consider it done."

"Thank you." Landon stood and extended his hand to Craig. "You can sit at the chef's table anytime."

It was masochistic of her, but Aubrey let herself hang on to a tiny connection to Landon. Every month, she bought a copy of

California Coast Monthly and read Landon's review until she memorized it. Then she could hear his voice in her head when she recalled his words later. It probably wasn't the healthiest hobby to indulge in, but she didn't care because she needed it.

This month's issue featured everything fall. It was her favorite season. The changing colors, the scent of wood and smoke in the air, and the comfort food overload. More than anything, autumn was the season of love and family to her.

She flipped through the magazine, skimming the recipes she wanted to come back to later, and looked for Landon's section. A tremor of unease fleeted across her when she found it. His column lacked its customary background and enticing food photos. The layout was as elegant as ever, but the stark black, gray, and white of the page felt somber even before she registered the title.

It's Not Farewell
by Landon Kim

For the past decade, you, my readers, have been my confidantes, friends, and heroes. Every bite I took for *California Coast Monthly* and the blog, I ate imagining what you would think. How you would feel. I was never alone because you traveled with me. Everything I saw and experienced, I thought, *Oh, the readers would love this* or *God, this would upset the readers.* Every word I wrote, I wrote with you in mind. My reviews and articles were pieces of me I shared with you, praying it would fulfill your expectations. To laugh at culinary disasters, to find the silver lining in a bad meal that redeems the restaurant, and to dream of the endless deliciousness the world has to offer.

Once. Only once. But still once. I failed you. I failed myself. And I nearly destroyed an amazing pastry chef's dream. I almost stole the gift she had to offer you.

Many of you might remember my article "The Pitfalls of Brilliance." In it, I rip apart a baker after eating a bite of her cake. I'm not reneging on my impression of the cake. It was sincerely alarming. Gummy worms and peanut butter do not belong in a chocolate Bundt cake. Of course, there is a big *but*.

But it didn't matter what *I* thought about the cake, because it was meant for another customer. The unusual filling was the brainchild of a six-year-old birthday girl, and I'd eaten her cake. The server had given it to me by accident, an understandable mistake considering the cozy shop had been bursting at the seams with hungry customers.

I discovered the real story behind the peculiar cake about a month after the issue was released, but I did nothing to correct my mistake. I refused to retract my review. My reasoning was that the cake I'd eaten shouldn't have been foisted on an unsuspecting customer, and my reaction was honest. I also refused to go back to the bakery to write a second review based on a more comprehensive, thoughtful examination of a wider variety of menu items. I had my reputation to protect, and that mattered more to me than a hole-in-the-wall bakery.

My ego, my arrogance, led me to give you, my readers, a superficial and incomplete review and almost pushed a small, overextended bakery out of business. That review was about me and my unfair judgment of the pastry chef. I did not experience the moment with you as I should have, and I did not write the review with you in mind.

I apologize from the bottom of my heart, dear readers.

I have always given you (except the fateful once) and give you now my complete honesty. Please take my opinion about the lovely bakery and its incredible chef with a grain of salt. While I meant every word I've written here, my opinion might be biased because I'm hopelessly in love with the pastry chef.

This is the last article I write as a food critic and blogger for *California Coast Monthly* and any other publication for the foreseeable future. But this isn't farewell. I am off to chase my dreams. All that means is I'll be seeing you from inside the kitchen, sharing more of myself with you.

Thank you for the unforgettable memories.

Aubrey stared at the pages long after she'd finished reading the words. *I'm hopelessly in love with the pastry chef.* Her brain shouted twelve questions at once, and she couldn't focus on any of them. It was too loud. Her heart squeezed and twisted, and she was sobbing, but the cacophony of her thoughts wouldn't quiet down for her to figure out why.

I'm hopelessly in love with the pastry chef.

24

Aubrey sat on her love seat—the only chair she could get up from without struggling like an overturned turtle—*not* thinking about Landon's latest article. She was indulging in her latest addiction—cookie butter. Tara's brothers, Jack and Alex, brought it back from their trip to one of San Diego's beer festivals, and she was completely hooked. It was the greatest culinary invention since ice cream.

Humming a little happy tune, Aubrey dipped her spoon in the cookie butter to eat it right out of the jar, but before she could lick the sinful goodness, her doorbell rang. A primitive growl rumbled in her chest. *This had better be important.* No one should be allowed to interrupt a pregnant woman when she was eating her cookie butter unless it was something very, very important.

"I've got it, baby." Her mom hurried from the kitchen, smoothing down her apron. She lived in there and baked like she was making up for lost time. Her sweet buns were even better than Grandma's.

"I love you, Mom." It wasn't the cookie butter euphoria

talking. Her mom was an incredible woman, and Aubrey was so lucky to be her daughter. "I'm so glad you're here."

"Me, too." Her mom's eyes glittered. When a second, tentative knock sounded at the door, Linda smoothed out her apron again with a delicate sniff and opened the door.

"Oh." The visitor sounded surprised. "I'm here to see Aubrey."

"Um . . ." Her mom hesitated and glanced over her shoulder. "She's indisposed at the moment."

"Could you tell her it's Aria? I really need to see her."

Aubrey swallowed a mouthful of cookie butter without tasting it. Her mind's screen saver lit up at the sound of Aria's voice. *I'm hopelessly in love with the pastry chef.* She didn't know what it meant, but it was a permanent installment in her brain museum. *Do not ask me why I don't understand those simple words. Just. Shut. Up.*

"Aria?" She heaved herself out of the chair and nodded toward her mom. "It's okay."

Her mom stepped back to let their guest inside. Then Aubrey glanced at her six-month-old baby bump and snapped her head up to see Aria's reaction. Even without her BUN IN THE OVEN T-shirt, there was no way of hiding her pregnancy.

"I kind of gained some weight." That was probably the stupidest sentence that ever came out of her mouth.

Aria rolled her eyes and smiled. "Stop being ridiculous and give me a hug."

"Oh, Aria." Aubrey hugged her tightly. She'd missed her vivacious friend so much. "It's so good to see you."

"I missed you, too." Aria squeezed her back, being careful not to crush Aubrey's tummy. Stepping back, she placed a warm hand on Aubrey's stomach. "How are you two doing?"

"We're doing well. Really well."

"Yes, you are." Aria appraised Aubrey carefully. "You're absolutely gorgeous."

"I'm huge."

"Please don't get her started." Her mom approached them with her hand outstretched. "Hi, I'm Linda, Aubrey's mom."

"I'm Aria. It's a pleasure to meet you, Linda."

After some niceties, her mom excused herself to give them privacy.

"I can see where you got your looks. Your mom's beautiful."

"Why are you here?" Aubrey blurted, her voice cracking with worry. "Is something wrong? Is he okay?"

"I wouldn't go so far as to say he's *okay*. He's alive." When Aubrey's expression became overcast with worry, Aria reached out to hold her hand. "I'm here to chauffeur you to him. Even if it means I have to kidnap you."

"Why didn't Landon come himself?"

"He's been assigned other important tasks. And I couldn't trust him to drive safely with you in the car. He's already a nervous wreck." Aria raised an elegant brow at Aubrey. "Please don't turn me into a pregnant-woman snatcher. Come with me?"

"Right now?"

"If you would be so kind." She grasped Aubrey's hands tightly, her eyes beseeching. "I'll sing as many songs as you want on our drive."

Her friend's words drew a watery laugh from Aubrey even though she was shivering with nerves. Landon didn't want her. But what about his column? He'd said he loved her. He'd announced it to the world. She wasn't a secret anymore.

But why hadn't he told her himself? Maybe the article was a calculated ploy on his part to protect his precious reputation. He hadn't counted on her reading it.

Then why was Aria here to take her to him?

Okay, everyone shut up.

Aubrey blew out a long breath. It didn't matter. She couldn't go. He would know she was pregnant the moment he saw her. She couldn't risk trapping him, and herself, into a loveless relationship.

"I can't come with you. I don't want to see him."

"I know it's hard, but please listen to what he has to say." Aria pulled her into her arms again. "He loves you . . . and the baby."

"He knows?" Blood pounded in her ears. *He loves you.* If that were true, he had a fucked-up way of showing it.

"He found your message in a bottle."

Aubrey bit her lip and nodded for Aria to continue.

"He is so very happy, darling."

"Is that why he wants to see me? Because of the baby?"

"Oh, Aubrey, no. He'd been looking for a way back to you long before he found out about the baby. He loves *you.*"

"That's hard to believe."

Her mind's screen saver lit up with neon brightness. *I'm hopelessly in love with the pastry chef.* It was a stupid article he couldn't have known she would read. But she had to talk to him. The man had some explaining to do. Aubrey had a right to know why he'd broken her heart if he was *hopelessly in love* with her.

She might not like what he had to say, but at least she could stop wondering. Stop hoping. Because no matter how hard she tried to play dumb, his article had made her hope, damn it.

Even if he didn't want her—she would seriously deck him if he didn't want her after what he'd said in the article and sending Aria to kidnap her—she had her mom, Tara, and the baby. She wasn't whole without Landon, but she would never be alone again.

"This is crazy. I'm crazy." At the very least, she could give herself closure. "I need to pee and let my mom know I'm going with you."

Her mom gave her a hard hug as though she were pouring her own strength into her and putting a protective layer on her so Aubrey wouldn't get hurt. She hoped her mom's magic worked.

———

Aria drove up to a lovely two-story house near the Kern River and parked in the driveway. Aubrey had been prepared for a long drive to either Santa Monica or Bosque Verde and was surprised to find herself only twenty minutes from Weldon.

"Are you okay, sweetheart?" Aria asked, studying Aubrey's face in the fading light.

"Of course I'm not okay, you silly woman." Aria meant well, but she couldn't hope for a happy ending. "But I'm here, aren't I? I don't plan on plugging my ears to what he has to say."

"Good girl." Aria reached out and squeezed one of Aubrey's cold hands. "Okay, then. My work here's done. It's time for me to go home to my love."

After kissing Aria on the cheek, Aubrey stepped out of the car and watched the red Mercedes drive off. Although she'd put on a brave face, she had no idea what to expect from Landon. What if Aria was playing matchmaker? Maybe Landon had never asked her to bring her here. *Sure. That makes perfect sense.* Her friend would totally abandon her at a strange house close to sunset. With no car.

Aubrey growled and clamped down on her horror-prone imagination. Running away was a thing of the past for her. Straightening her shoulders and lifting her chin, Aubrey turned to face the house. It reminded her so much of the schoolhouse that her heart stuttered wildly. But there was no point in wondering or hoping. If he'd loved her, he wouldn't have broken her heart. He couldn't have. It would have hurt him too much. More than it had hurt her.

Confessing her love to him. Sharing her darkest insecurities with him. That had taken every last reserve of courage she'd had in her. Having her love slapped aside and her fears callously disregarded had caused her more pain than her mind had the capacity to grasp. Even then, walking away from Landon was the hardest thing she'd ever done. Witnessing his anguish as she'd left him had broken her tattered heart even more. Aubrey refused to be his secret—she was worth more than that, she deserved so much more—but she'd prayed with everything she had that he would stop hurting. Because she loved him. That was love.

And if he regretted what happened that night in Bosque Verde, he would have owned his mistake and come for her far before this. She was here for closure. She marched two steps toward the house when her hands flew to her mouth to cover a gasp. He was standing at the top of the steps like a statue.

Even in the fading light of the setting sun, her body recognized his tall, broad silhouette framed against the softly lit doorway. Anguish and longing shot through her. The force of her emotions made her hunch into herself, her arms instinctively coming around to cradle her stomach to shield the baby from harm when it was really the pain of Aubrey's heart breaking all over again.

Although her eyes were scrunched shut as she breathed through the pain, the sound of falling footsteps rang in her ear. Landon was running at breakneck speed to reach her.

"Aubrey." Warm, strong hands wrapped around her arms. "Aubrey, are you okay? What's happening? What do I need to do?"

"You need to," she said in between breaths, "calm down."

Fucking Braxton Hicks. The so-called practice contractions had been coming more often lately, and they hurt like hell. This one was likely triggered by the shock of seeing Landon again. But as always, the contractions faded quickly, and Aubrey straightened to her full height, belatedly jerking her arms out of his hands.

"We need to get you to a hospital. Let me grab my keys." Unfortunately, the panicking man in front of her hadn't calmed down like she'd instructed. "Fucking hell. I shouldn't have brought you here so suddenly. I thought I would die if I didn't see you again. I couldn't wait any longer. Goddamn it. I'm so sorry."

"Look at me." She kept her voice steady even though the words coming out of his mouth kicked her pulse up to an alarming rate. Only after she'd repeated herself a couple times did Landon raise his gaze to hers. "You see? I'm fine, so calm down."

"Are you sure you're okay?" His eyes darted over her face and body as though she might crumple to the ground any minute.

No, she wasn't okay. Why was everyone asking her that? Couldn't they see she was far from okay? Seeing Landon made her so fucking happy, mad, and terrified at the same time. She wanted to curl up into a ball and cry herself unconscious.

"Yes, I'm fine. But unless you're planning to stand out here to talk, I'd rather go inside and have a seat."

"Of course. I don't know what I was thinking."

He stepped to her side and moved as though he were about to wrap his arm around her. She stiffened and pulled away.

"Don't," she said with a burst of fury. "You do not get to touch me."

Landon cringed at her vehement words, but he dropped his arms and took a step away with sorrow swimming in his dark eyes. "After you."

The warmth of the house welcomed them as they stepped

inside, and she allowed Landon to take her coat. He was so careful not to touch her that she hurt a little for him.

"Thank you."

"You're welcome."

He wouldn't quite meet her eyes as he led her to a cozy living room with a fire gently burning in the fireplace. In the brightness of the room, Aubrey finally noticed how thin and gaunt Landon had become. He still appeared strong and broad, but his clothes hung loosely, his jawline was too sharp, and his cheeks had a sunken look to them. She could tell he'd shaved recently, but his overgrown hair curled at his collar, and there were dark shadows under his weary eyes. Landon looked sad and starkly beautiful as though he'd walked through hell to stand in front of her.

He offered her a deep, upholstered armchair, and she shook her head and chose a firm love seat instead. A deep, relieved sigh escaped her as she settled her tired body into it. Landon's gaze sharpened at the sound, but he didn't hover or fuss. He took an armchair close by her and sat forward, resting his elbows on his thighs.

"You found out about the baby," Aubrey said when Landon sat silently.

"Yes," he said huskily.

"Is that why I'm here?"

"Yes and no."

"Are we playing twenty questions? If I recall, you were the one who wanted to see me."

"And you didn't? Want to see me?" His softly spoken words twisted like a dagger in her heart, and his desperate, searching eyes clogged her throat with pain and resentment.

What could he possibly expect me to say? Fuck him. *Fuck him for breaking my heart. Fuck him for putting me through this.*

"I'm not going to apologize for not telling you about the

baby. If you'd let me explain what was in the bottle, you would've known months ago. But you made it clear that I was nothing more than a passing fling to you. There was no way I was letting you treat my baby like you treated me. You will not hide her in the shadows. She will never be your shameful secret. She is my heart, my blood, and she will be loved, cherished, and raised up high for the world to see."

"Please, Aubrey. I never meant . . . God, I'm so sorry. Please listen."

"I don't want your excuses or apologies." Suddenly, she felt depleted, and exhaustion rose in a wave to drown her. "I want closure. I need to move on. Whatever was between us is in the past."

"Nothing," he said brokenly. "*Nothing* is in the *past* for me, because I know in my heart we aren't finished. This is all about now and the future. Our future. That's why I asked you to come."

"Our future?" Aubrey blinked, her heart pounding in her ears. She shook her head. "Landon, there is no future for us. I'm not going to be your mistress."

He seemed to fall apart before her eyes. He dragged his hands down the sides of his face, his mouth gaping. She saw his bleeding, tortured soul. His eyes glistened with unshed tears, and desperation contorted every inch of his face.

"I love you, Aubrey. Being with you means more than my fucking reputation or my career. I love you, and I want forever with you."

"No, you don't." It felt as though her blood drained from the tips of her fingers, and her body became a heavy, hollow shell. "You don't love me. You can't. A part of me died that day."

"I know I hurt you, and I have to live with that for the rest of my life."

"No, you don't understand. It killed me to leave you even

after everything you'd said. I loved you so much, I died a little watching you hurt. Do you understand? You couldn't have done what you did to me if you'd loved me even a little."

"I was afraid. I was so afraid." Landon stumbled out of his chair and knelt at her feet. "I was a coward. I ran from everything that mattered to me when my dad abandoned us. Loving you meant I could disappoint and fail you like my father failed his family. I thought I was so much like him. I was terrified of fucking up and losing you."

What? A spark of hope lit and flickered in her soul. But how can I trust him?

"Then how?" she asked despite herself. "Why?"

"I thought if I pushed you away, then I would still be able to salvage what pathetic life I had left and protect you and your career. But it was already too late for me. I love you, Aubrey. I'm nothing without you. I can't . . . Please. God knows I don't deserve you, but please forgive me."

The truth of his words—the truth of his love—was painted on his pleading face. Woven into his imploring words.

Aubrey had thought she'd wanted to stop hoping. She'd thought she'd wanted closure. But she was wrong. She wasn't strong enough. She, too, was a coward in the face of what he was offering. His vulnerability. Her power. It was too much. If she opened her heart to him and he broke it again, she wouldn't be able to survive. Not this time.

Sorry, baby girl. Mommy's too afraid. I'm too afraid to fight anymore.

The light seemed to go out of Aubrey, and Landon's heart fell like a rock sinking to the bottom of the riverbed. *No. God, no.*

There was no hate. No anger. There was nothing. He would rather have her contempt and disgust. God knew he deserved that. But her empty eyes shot icy fear through him. He was too late. She was done with him.

"I'm sorry. I'm so sorry, Aubrey." He gripped her hands in desperation. *Get angry. Slap me if you'd like. Just don't leave me.*

"I can't. I'm sorry. I can't." Her voice was small and far away. Like she'd already left him.

"Everything went to hell when I let you go. I can't live without you." He blinked rapidly to ward off the moisture gathering in the corners of his eyes. He couldn't lose her again. "Please give us a chance."

"I can't. I tried, but I ended up losing you."

Landon clawed at his chest. It hurt so much. But he wasn't giving up. If this was what it took to win her back, then he'd suffer this and more.

"If you'll have me, you will never lose me. You'll never be rid of me." He huffed with nervous laughter. "I love you, and I'm going to fight for our love. I won't give up."

"I'm scared, Landon. I can't fight for us again."

"Then don't. I'll do the fighting for both of us. It took me so long to find my way back to you. This is it for me. You are my life. I would crawl through hell for you. I'll fight for us even if it means I have to carry you to do it. Trust me. I won't drop you. Losing you means losing myself. I will never give up on us. Please, Aubrey."

A sob wrenched from her, and she cried. Her agony and grief poured out of her and gutted him. He'd done this to her. He didn't deserve her forgiveness or love. He deserved to burn in hell. But he could never go because he had to stay with Aubrey and their baby to love, cherish, and protect them. To shout from the rooftops he was theirs. If only they'd have him.

"I'm here." He sat beside her and gathered her into his lap. "I'll always be here. I'll never let you go."

After a long while, her sobs quieted, and she stayed in his arms. His breath caught in his throat with a rush of hope.

"I'll spend the rest of my life cherishing you. If you'll have me, I'm forever yours—body, heart, and soul."

She sighed softly, warming his neck with her breath. He shivered and sat still, afraid she would disappear from his arms if he moved. Finally, she lifted her head and searched his face.

"Landon, what have you been doing to yourself?"

"Trying to survive, I guess. Trying not to feel, not to remember, not to hurt." He released his breath in a shuddering sigh, relieved that she was talking to him again. His reflection in the mirror that morning had been gaunt and pale. Eating and sleeping hadn't been on the top of his to-do list. "Mostly trying to keep myself away from you."

"Why? Why didn't you come for me sooner?"

"I couldn't even let myself hope that there was a chance you'd take me back. I'd hurt you so badly. I was too ashamed and too scared to go to you. But the more time has passed, the clearer it has become that I can't live without you."

"I read your article in *California Coast Monthly*," she said in a hushed tone.

"You did?" he said dumbly. He didn't know what else to say. Did she know, then? Did she understand how much he loved her? Landon rubbed a hand down his face.

"You said you were hopelessly in love with the pastry chef. I'm assuming you meant me."

"You. Only you. Always you."

"Landon?"

"Hmm?" He was staring at her like the lovesick man he was. He shook his head to clear it. "Sorry. What is it?"

"You've been saying *sorry* a lot."

"Because I am. I truly am."

"No, I mean, you never say the actual word *sorry*. You always own your mistakes and do everything in your power to make things right, but I've never heard you say *sorry* before."

"I never realized that." Landon cocked his head to the side and wondered what she meant. Did he really never use that word? He believed mere lip service was meaningless without action. "An apology feels pointless when it doesn't change anything. I guess I prefer to right my wrongs with actions rather than words."

"Then why now?"

"I don't know. I want you to know how miserable I am for hurting you. I wish my words, even if they don't fix anything, could soothe your wounds. I can't undo what I've done, but I want you to know I am sorry, and I want a chance to make up for it."

"Hmm." She nodded thoughtfully and glanced down at the hand she had pressed against his heart.

He followed her gaze, and his eyes fell on her rounded belly. Guilt twisted like a knife in his chest. "God, Aubrey. I had no idea. I should've been there for you. I didn't know until I opened the bottle."

"Even if you knew, I wouldn't have wanted you to stay with me because of the baby."

"No. It's you I want. I'll always want you. I'm ecstatic about our baby, but *you* are my life." Unable to hold back, he cupped her smooth cheek in his hand. "Having a baby with you is icing on the cake. When I found out you were pregnant, I realized I'd been dreaming of having a family with you."

Her shoulders rose and fell as she breathed deeply through her nose, and then she reached for his shaking hand and placed it on her stomach. For a moment, he felt nothing but the heat of her, and then a rounded edge nudged against his palm. Landon snatched his hand away, worried he'd startled the baby.

"Are you okay? Is the baby okay?"

"We're both fine. I think she wants to say hello," Aubrey said, some softness entering her voice.

"She?" His heart expanded with love he didn't know he was capable of.

"Yes, we're having a daughter. In just about three months."

How could I be so happy? He didn't deserve them, but he knew without a doubt that he couldn't live without them. Landon's neck and shoulders strained as though he were physically restraining the hope that was fighting to free itself within him. He couldn't let his desperation color what her words meant.

"Are you still afraid, Landon?"

"No, because I won't fail you."

"But that's not possible." He sucked in a breath to protest strongly, but Aubrey placed the tips of her fingers on his parted lips. Even at a time like this, his body jumped in response. "Life isn't perfect, but that's okay. If you falter, I'll catch you, and you'll do the same for me."

Landon froze and stopped breathing until air whooshed out from his lungs in a rush. "Does that mean . . . Does that mean you'll have me?"

"Oh, I'll have you, all right." Aubrey's voice was strong and bold as though nothing held her back.

Landon stared at her in awe. If he spoke, she might disappear. But a bright, wonderous smile lit her face.

"You're right. We are worth fighting for. No matter what."

"You're amazing." He gazed at her with wide-eyed wonder. "I don't deserve you."

"Landon Kim, I'm forever yours—heart, body, and soul,"

Aubrey said. "I'll hold and cherish your heart in mine, as I trust you to hold my heart in yours."

Relief, love, and joy rushed through him, and he began trembling.

"Oh, Landon." She tightened her arms around him. "Hush, love. We're together. Everything is all right now."

"Now that you're mine, I'm never letting you go." He spoke when his teeth finally stopped chattering.

"I'm counting on it." She leaned in to kiss him, but he rose from the couch, pulling her to her feet. *Not yet. We have time now.*

"Close your eyes and come with me." He led her down the hallway, tightly gripping her hand. "Now open them."

They were in the nursery. He hadn't known the sex of the baby, so Aria had suggested he paint the room a soft cream with a matching baby mobile and plush nursing chair. He hadn't known half the stuff in the room even existed, but he'd done his research to create a nursery that Aubrey would love. A place she would want to raise their baby in.

"Do you like it?" When she remained silent and still, Landon rubbed the back of his neck and rushed to explain himself. "You could change anything you don't like. I didn't know we were having a daughter."

"Is this your house? You bought a house by Weldon?"

"*Our* house. Your life, your friends, and your dream. It's all in Weldon. I would never take you away from that. I know you have a cottage, but with the baby coming, I thought we would need more room. Especially when we have more children." Heat rose from his neck, and he shrugged sheepishly. "I mean, if you want more children, that is."

"Landon, I love it. This nursery is perfect for her. And this wonderful house, we'll make it our home. For us and the rest of the munchkins to come."

He nodded again and again, the lump in his throat preventing him from speaking. Landon didn't know what he'd done to deserve Aubrey, but he would live the rest of his life becoming worthy of her.

Aubrey's gaze shifted from his face, and a strained silence fell. She walked around the room, running her hands over the furniture. "When did you do all this? The house? The nursery?"

"As soon as I found your message in a bottle. Aria and Lucien were a huge help. Annoying as hell, but helpful nonetheless." His words tripped over each other. "Will you and the baby live here with me?"

"*Of course.*" Aubrey cocked her head and gave Landon a mischievous look. "Where else would we stay? You'd better not be trying to get out of diaper duty."

With a burst of nervous laughter, Landon rushed to her side and grasped her hands, falling into the depths of her warm, brown eyes. Hardly believing she was real, he leaned down and kissed her until they were both breathless.

"Aubrey Choi, I love you with everything I am."

"And I love you more than words."

"Are you really mine?" he said, running his thumb across her rosy cheek.

"Yes. I'm yours forever and ever." She turned her head and placed a kiss in the palm of his hand.

"What did I do to deserve you?"

"Some guys just have all the luck."

25

Landon stepped out of the kitchen, drying his hands on a dish towel. He had some time before he needed to grill the meat, so he joined his younger brother on the porch.

"Lucky bastard," Seth mumbled, taking another bite out of the brownie cookie. Another Aubrey Choi masterpiece—a perfect amalgam of rich, dark chocolate and chewy cookie. "You get to eat this stuff whenever you want?"

He chuckled at his brother's envy, his eyes traveling to Aubrey at the other side of the backyard. She was laughing at something his mom said, her nose crinkled in the way he adored. His heart stopped for a split second before it kicked up double time. God, he loved her so much. As though she'd heard his thoughts, Aubrey's gaze sought his. When their eyes met across the way, time slowed and sound faded, and it was just the two of them. A soft blush spread across her cheeks, and love glowed on her face. He really did have all the luck.

"Close your mouth."

Seth's wry words brought him back to earth, and Landon

turned toward him, failing miserably to wipe the bliss off his face.

"I think you drooled a little, too. Here, let me wipe it off," his brother said, reaching out with his thumb.

"Watch it, kid. I'm your *hyung*. Show me some respect." Landon pushed away his hand with a huff of laughter. "Or I'm confiscating the cookies."

"Not cool, man." He managed to look injured before he stuffed a whole cookie in his mouth. "Not. Cool."

"I asked you to put those on the picnic table, not hoard them for yourself." Aubrey stood across from Seth, eight months' pregnant, with her fists placed firmly on her hips. "Besides, you have to save room for Landon's tri-tips and *gal-bi*."

"I'll take them there right now." His hotshot photographer brother rose to his feet, smiling sheepishly. He apparently would do anything for Aubrey, even give up his precious cookies.

"Thanks for putting up with my bossiness."

"You? Bossy?" Seth widened his eyes, shaking his head vehemently. "I have no idea what you're talking about."

"Enough," Landon said, laughing at Seth hamming it up for Aubrey. "Go put the cookies where they belong."

Seth swaggered off with a wide grin, heading toward the far table where Tara stood. Landon had caught his brother watching her with his mouth gaping and had felt a brief pang of concern. Seth had a reputation as a player, but Tara was in a league of her own. He shook his head. It was none of his business.

"Take a break, sweetheart." Landon tugged Aubrey down onto his lap and cradled her in his arms.

"Not you, too," she groaned. "Everyone keeps telling me to sit down. All I've done is take breaks. Now let me up before your mom sees us."

"My mom isn't that old-fashioned." He kissed her forehead and settled her more comfortably on his legs.

"You're right." She sighed and finally relaxed against him, her head falling to his shoulder. "I love how she sees beauty in the most mundane objects. Maybe that's why her paintings are so stunning."

"It's great to have our family and friends over, but please don't tire yourself out. The baby's coming in a few weeks."

"That's precisely why we're having this barbecue today. Besides, our moms won't let me lift a finger." She tilted her head to smile up at him and cupped his cheek with a warm hand. "You know I wanted to share our home with everyone before it's turned upside down by a tiny baby and two clueless parents."

"I know."

Aubrey was mostly teasing, but Landon's stomach dropped a little. She was going to be a wonderful mom, but he had no idea how to be a father. One thing was certain. He would always be there for his little girl and love her unconditionally.

"I guess I'm just jealous of sharing you," he said.

She blushed, smiling shyly, and Landon couldn't help but lean down and kiss her. It was meant to be soft and chaste, but she whimpered and pressed against him when he tried to pull back. *Well, then.* He parted her lips with his tongue and drank his fill until he was ready to carry her to their room.

"Ahem." He heard the sound from a distance. "Kids, please."

Aubrey pulled back with a gasp, and Landon glared at Tara, who just rolled her eyes at him.

"I'd tell you guys to get a room, but we need you to provide us with more delicious food. In the meantime, cool it just a bit. My parents have been staring at that fence since your lips touched. They're not as with the times as your moms."

"Would you please keep her company while I start the grill?" Aubrey had her face buried in her hands, and Landon carefully placed her on his seat as he stood. He grinned at Tara, unable to regret the kiss. "And just as a heads-up, she's been climbing up the kitchen counter and every other slippery high surface in the house. She's nesting and wants to clean *everything*."

"Stop crazy pregnant woman from going splat on the floor. Got it." Tara gave him a thumbs-up and took the seat next to Aubrey, who had finally come out of hiding to glare at the two of them.

"Ladies." With a slight nod, Landon left Aubrey in Tara's capable hands to cook for the most important people in his life.

———

Their guests had cleared out after erasing all traces of the backyard barbecue despite Aubrey's and Landon's protests. With no dishes and cleaning left for them, Aubrey let him pull her down onto the sofa for a foot massage. She had a ticklish spot he was tempted to press, but her swollen feet needed some serious ministrations.

"Mmm. That feels so good." She sighed softly as her eyes fluttered closed. "Thank you."

"It's what I'm here for," he said, wishing he could do more to ease her pregnancy aches and pains. It wasn't fair she had to do all the work to bring their child into the world. He felt pretty useless.

"You have other uses." She opened one eye, and a naughty grin spread across her face.

He laughed till his sides hurt even as he grew hard remembering his other uses. As his mirth receded, he was certain it was the right time.

"How tired are you?" he asked, scanning her face for signs of fatigue.

"Normal preggers tired. Why?"

"Do you want to take a drive?" His heart throbbed in his throat.

"Sure." She arched an eyebrow. "What are you up to?"

"Nothing. Why should I be up to anything?" *Oh, I'm up to something, all right.*

After making sure she was bundled up and toasty, he eased his car out of their driveway with one hand on the wheel at ten o'clock and the other on two o'clock. His breath threatened to grow shallow, and blood pounded in his ears.

"Is everything okay? You're acting strange."

"Of course. Why wouldn't everything be okay?" *Perfect. I'll just keep answering her questions with questions of my own. Because that isn't suspicious at all.* "We'll be there in ten minutes. Just hang on, okay?"

"Hmm."

Aubrey still looked puzzled when he parked outside the un-lit building. Landon felt light-headed and slightly nauseous, so she was in better shape than he was.

"Where are we?" she whispered as they walked into the building, and he turned on every light switch he passed.

He dragged in a shuddering breath. "Well, I'm hoping we're at my future restaurant."

"Your restaurant?" She gasped beside him, placing a hand on her belly. "When? How?"

"When I decided to bring you home, or die trying, I knew I had to stop running away from what matters most to me. I've been looking for a restaurant space since then."

"Why didn't you tell me? I thought you needed more time to take the leap, and I didn't want to pressure you by asking about your plans."

"I didn't tell you because I wasn't sure I could really do this. But when I saw this space, everything fell into place. I am doing this." He grasped both her hands in his own. "What do you think? Do you like it?"

She spun in a slow circle, taking in the spacious open kitchen and the intimate but not-too-crowded seating area. "Is that a garden out back?"

"Yeah, and I'm going to section off a part of it for an outdoor dining area." Eager to show her, he tugged her toward the garden, turning on the outdoor lights. "Remember the restaurant in Cambria? It won't be elaborate as that, but I loved the feeling of being surrounded by nature while we ate."

"Of course I remember. That sounds wonderful." Aubrey paused, and he waited for the *but*, unable to breathe. "But are you sure you don't want to start off somewhere hipper? Like Santa Monica or Venice? That crowd would line up around the block to try *the* Landon Kim's cooking."

"I don't want to cater to that sort of crowd. They would treat the restaurant like a reality TV show. Can the food critic actually cook? Or will he eat his words?" He cringed with distaste. "I want to run a restaurant here for the locals. But most importantly, I want to be close to you and the baby. Close to home."

"Oh, Landon." Aubrey held his face between her hands and rose on her toes to kiss him. "This is perfect. I'm so proud of you."

He pulled her into his arms, grateful for her love and support, but he needed one more important answer from her. Holding her gaze for strength, he knelt down on one knee.

"You've already given me so much happiness, but I can't help but want more. Will you make me the luckiest man in the world and be my wife?" She stared open-mouthed at the engagement ring he held out to her. Panic ran across his heart at her silence. "It doesn't have to be right away. We could wait as long as you need. I could hold on to the ring until you're ready."

"You have much to learn, Grasshopper," Aubrey said, her smile tremulous and radiant. "We're having the wedding next week if I have my way. Your bachelor days are so over."

He stayed kneeling, holding the ring in front of him like an idiot. *Is that a yes?*

"Landon Kim, I love you. Yes and yes, a thousand times over. I'll marry you." She guided his hand to place the ring on her finger and tugged impatiently at his hands. "Now, please stand up and kiss me."

———

They decided to wait four months to have their wedding. The moms didn't want a hurried, slapped-together wedding, and Landon was already hers in every sense of the word. Aubrey wasn't in a rush.

Morgan, on the other hand, wasn't quite as patient. Their dark-haired, wide-eyed daughter arrived two weeks before her due date. And she was perfect. She stole their hearts and sleep, and the first three months of her life passed in a blur of exhaustion and joy.

Now, a week after her hundredth-day celebration, it was time for Mommy and Daddy to declare their love and dedication to each other in front of their beloved family and friends. And Aubrey was having a hard time adjusting to being the center of attention after so long.

"Do you think he'll like the dress?" Aubrey asked, twisting around in front of the mirror.

Aria and Tara had convinced her to wear a shape-hugging wedding dress that emphasized her fuller figure. She had to admit it was good advice. Her new curves totally rocked the dress. Copious amounts of exquisite lace and appliqué covered the spaghetti-strap dress that dipped to the small of her back and a skirt that fell in a slim tapered line to her toes. The only things demure about the dress were the square neckline that housed her full breasts and the long fishtail train that swooshed behind her. It was a daring and stunning wedding dress, and she was nervous as hell.

"If you're fishing for a compliment, I'll humor you." Tara circled her slowly and then came to a stop in front of her. "The dress is incredible, and you're the loveliest bride in the whole wide world."

Aubrey grinned at her maid of honor. "I think you overshot it a bit, but it did the trick."

"I meant every word," she said without a trace of teasing. "You're so beautiful and I'm so happy for you, Bree."

"Thank you. I don't know what I'd do without you."

"Don't you dare cry. You'll make both of us ruin our makeup," Tara warned huskily. "Are you ready?"

Aubrey beamed at her. "Hell yes."

Tara helped her out of the pantry they'd been using as a bridal suite, and Aubrey stood ready at the top of the stairs to walk down the aisle. The restaurant's beautiful outdoor garden overlooked the Kern River, and the changing colors of spring made it all even lovelier.

When Landon had gotten down on his knee and proposed to her, she'd known his restaurant would be the perfect place for their wedding. The interior needed some finishing touches before it opened next month, but Aria had done an amazing job transforming it into a breathtaking venue for their intimate wedding.

Arrangements of lavender hydrangeas, white calla lilies, and champagne-colored peonies filled the rustic ceramic vases lining the aisles. The circular wedding arch was overflowing with the colors of spring, covered with glossy green leaves and rich vibrant blossoms. It glowed with the promise of a union and of steadfast devotion. Its beauty and meaning stole Aubrey's breath. The circular arch brought home how this day—their wedding—was a symbol of their forever.

"All right, babe." Her best friend winked at her. "See you on the other side."

As her maid of honor, Tara also had the honor of carrying the flower girl down the aisle. Morgan, in her cream satin dress dotted with pink bows, looked like an angel in the arms of Auntie Tara, who looked stunning in her crimson, mermaid dress. Happy tears stung Aubrey's eyes at the breathtaking sight of her favorite girls gliding toward the altar.

Aubrey jumped a little when the bridal processional began. She took her first hesitant steps down the stairway, nerves zapping through her body, but the mesmerized expression on Landon's face made her unafraid. His mouth remained parted, and his gaze—possessive and fierce—didn't stray from her for a second. Her heart thundered at how handsome he looked in his black tuxedo.

As she walked down the aisle strewn with white and pale green rose petals, Landon smiled. And Aubrey felt more certain of his love every step she took toward him—the keeper of her heart, the father of her child, and her soon-to-be husband.

When Aubrey met him at the altar, Landon pulled her close and drew back her veil, oblivious to everything but her. In that moment, she was only Aubrey—not a new mom, a daughter, or a baker. Just his Aubrey. She was seen and loved by this incredible man.

"You're beautiful, Aubrey Choi," he whispered in her ear, sending chills down her spine.

"I guess that'll be the last time I hear that from you." Confusion clouded her groom's face until she smiled at him with all the love inside her. "Because I'll be Aubrey Kim in a few minutes."

"You bet you will." His lips spread into a blinding smile, his dimple winking at her. The Smile still turned her into pink goo. "You'll be *my* Aubrey Kim."

"As you'll be mine," she whispered. "From now till forever."

BULGOGI RECIPE

Bulgogi (paper-thin rib eye in soy sauce marinade) is probably the best-known Korean dish in the U.S., and a staple in Korean-American households.

It's also my favorite deadline preparedness recipe because you can marinate and freeze it in perfect portions.

INGREDIENTS

3 tablespoons brown sugar (or granulated sugar)

⅓ cup soy sauce

1 tablespoon plum extract (or cooking wine, like Mirin)

1 tablespoon toasted sesame seed oil

1 tablespoon finely minced garlic

¼ cup grated onion

½ teaspoon toasted sesame seeds

Black pepper to taste

1 ½ lbs thinly sliced rib eye

DIRECTIONS

1. Mix all ingredients except the rib eye in a non-plastic mixing bowl until the sugar is dissolved.
2. Add the rib eye and mix gently until the marinade is evenly distributed.
3. Let marinate in fridge overnight.
4. Heat pan over medium-high heat and add a drizzle of oil. When the pan is hot but not smoking, add the meat and sauté until it is cooked through.
5. Plate the bulgogi and sprinkle some toasted sesame seeds on top, and serve immediately with rice (or noodles or salad).

JAYCI'S TIPS

I always add half a sliced onion to sauté with the bulgogi. If I feel fancy, I add a couple of scallions (sliced to about 3-inch pieces), and sliced button mushrooms, too.

PECAN CRANBERRY SHORTBREAD COOKIES RECIPE

INGREDIENTS

Cookies:

½ cup unsalted butter

¾ cup powdered sugar

1 teaspoon vanilla extract

¼ teaspoon salt

1 egg

1¼ cups all-purpose flour

½ cup cranberries, dried and sweetened

½ cup pecans, roasted and salted

White Chocolate Ganache:

1 cup white chocolate

½ cup heavy cream

DIRECTIONS

1. In the bowl of a mixer, combine the butter and powdered sugar and mix until light and fluffy.
2. Add the vanilla and salt and mix to combine.
3. Add in the egg and mix until just combined.
4. Slowly add the flour and mix until just blended in. Do not over mix.
5. Chop the cranberries and pecans and stir into the dough.
6. Bring the dough together on a piece of parchment paper and shape into a log, measuring about 12 inches long and 1½ inches in diameter. While wrapped in the parchment paper, roll to create a smooth log shape.
7. Refrigerate until firm.
8. Preheat the oven to 350°.
9. Line two baking sheets with parchment paper. Remove the dough log from the refrigerator and slice into ½-inch rounds, trying to maintain the shape as best you can. Lay rounds flat on the baking sheets and bake 15–18 minutes until lightly browned around the bottom edges.

While the cookies cool, prepare the ganache:

1. Chop white chocolate and place in a heatproof bowl.
2. Heat heavy cream until scalding and pour over the chocolate. Allow to stand for a few minutes, and then stir until completely smooth.
3. Once the cookies and ganache have cooled, dip cookies in ganache so that one half is covered and one half is bare. Allow ganache to set before serving.

ACKNOWLEDGMENTS

This book saved me. My world was crashing down around me, and I was being erased from my reality. It was this book that built me back up. Every time I sat down to write *A Sweet Mess*, I saw myself in it—and it was my best self. Not who I was or the shell of myself that wandered vacantly through life, but my very best self—the person I was meant to be. And through the publication of this dear book, I *am* who I'm meant to be.

I found my courage to live life to the fullest by writing this · book, and I hope that reading it gives my dear readers laughter, hope, and courage to thrive.

To my spectacular agent, Sarah Younger, thank you for believing in me, and for busting your ass to help make this book the best that it could be. My dream wouldn't have come true without your faith, frankness, support, and hard work. You are truly a blessing in my life.

To my editor, Tiffany Shelton, and your wonderful team at St. Martin's Griffin. Your passion and excitement for this book inspired me, and made me work harder than I thought possible. I hope our hard work enriches the lives of our readers, the way it enriched ours.

And to the very first people who read this book for me—my best friend, Lulu Lin, Eleanor Welke, Traci Critton, and author Jennifer Hoopes. Thank you for your loving support and for helping me believe in myself as a writer. Without you, I would not have finished this book.

To Judi Lauren, my freelance editor, who did my very first professional editorial letter. Thank you for convincing me not to shelve this book, and also for introducing me to Sonya Weiss, my straight-shooting mentor. Sonya, you taught me so much about writing and about life. You are an inspiration.

To my baker friend, Allison Holcher, thank you for coming into my life at the perfect moment—literally not a day too late or early—to create a delicious, A *Sweet Mess*-inspired cookie recipe for my readers. You are too sweet. And to Simone Dole, thank you for teaching me everything about the ins and outs of running a bakery. Aubrey sounds realistic and knowledgeable about running a bakery because of your help. Also, to the lovely duo of Shaida Kafe-ee and Luis Armando Gomez, thank you for patiently teaching me about the intricacies of commercial real estate and the work that goes into leasing a new location for a bakery.

And to my dearest family, thank you so very much for always being there for me. Especially to my dad, a poet, for giving me the writing gene, and my mom for teaching me the tenacity to persevere against all odds. I know your hearts broke to watch me struggle, but I hope you will be healed as I have been through the publication of this book, and the hope it carries with it. Now, I want your hearts to soar not sink when you watch me, because my struggles have made me stronger and made me the truest version of myself. Thank you for loving me without faltering through every stage of my journey. Your constant, unconditional faith in me is everything.